Acclaim for Kelly Irvin

"The second entry in Irvin's Amish Blessings series (after *Love's Dwelling*) delivers an elegant portrait of a young Amish woman caught between two worlds . . . Irvin skillfully conveys Abigail's internal conflict ('How could Abigail put into words the longing that thrummed in her chest? The sense of loss, of missing out, of missing it all,' she reminisces about Amish life). Fans of Amish romance will want to check this out."

—*Publishers Weekly*

"Just like the title, *Warmth of Sunshine* is a lovely and cozy story that will keep you reading until the very last page."

—Kathleen Fuller, *USA Today* bestselling author of The Mail-Order Amish Brides series

"This is a sweet story of rom [illegible] at heartstrings. It is another great st [illegible]

—*The Pa* [illegible] *ve's Dwelling*

"*Peace in the Valley* is a [illegible] ching exploration of faith, loyalty, and the ties tha [illegible] a family and a community together. Kelly Irvin's masterful storytelling pulled me breathlessly into Nora's world, her deep desire to do good, and her struggle to be true to herself and to the man she loves. Full of both sweet and stark details of Amish life, *Peace in the Valley* is realistic and poignant, profound and heartfelt. I highly recommend it!"

—Jennifer Beckstrand, author of *Andrew*

"With a lovely setting, this is a story of hope in the face of trouble and has an endearing heroine and other relatable characters that readers will empathize with."

—*The Parkersburg News and Sentinel* on *Mountains of Grace*

"Irvin (*Beneath the Summer Sun*) puts a new spin on the age-old problem of bad things happening to good people in this excellent Amish inspirational . . . Fans of both Amish and inspirational Christian fiction will enjoy this heart-pounding tale of the pain of loss and the joys of love."

—*Publishers Weekly* on *Mountains of Grace*

"Kelly Irvin's *Mountains of Grace* offers a beautiful and emotional journey into the Amish community. Readers will be captivated by a heartwarming tale of forgiveness and finding a renewed faith in God. The story will capture the hearts of those who love the Plain culture and an endearing romance. Once you open this book, you'll be hooked until the last page."

—Amy Clipston, bestselling author of *The Farm Stand*

"Irvin's fun story is simple (like Mary Katherine, who finds 'every day is a blessing and an adventure') but very satisfying."

—*Publishers Weekly* on *Through the Autumn Air*

"Kelly Irvin's *Through the Autumn Air* is a poignant journey of friendship and second chances that will illustrate for readers that God blesses us with a true love for all seasons."

—Amy Clipston, bestselling author of *Room on the Porch Swing*

"This second entry (after *Upon a Spring Breeze*) in Irvin's seasonal series diverges from the typical Amish coming-of-age tale with its focus on more mature protagonists who acutely feel their sense of loss. Fans of the genre seeking a broader variety of stories may find this new offering from [Irvin] more relatable than the usual fare."

—*Library Journal* on *Beneath the Summer Sun*

"Jennie's story will speak to any woman who has dealt with the horror of abuse and the emotional aftermath it carries, as well as readers who have questioned how God can allow such terrible things to happen. The choice Jennie makes to take a chance on love again and to open her heart to God after all she has suffered is brave and hopeful, leaving readers on an uplifting note."

—*RT Book Reviews*, 4-star review of *Beneath the Summer Sun*

"A moving and compelling tale about the power of grace and forgiveness that reminds us how we become strongest in our most broken moments."

—*Library Journal* on *Upon a Spring Breeze*

"Irvin's novel is an engaging story about despair, postnatal depression, God's grace, and second chances."

—*CBA Christian Market* on *Upon a Spring Breeze*

"A warm-hearted novel that is more than a romance, with lovable characters, including two innocent children caught in the red tape of government, and two people willing to risk breaking both the *Englisch* and Amish laws to help in whatever way they can. There are subplots that focus on the struggles of undocumented immigrants."

—*RT Book Reviews*, 4-star review of *The Saddle Maker's Son*

"Irvin has given her audience a continuation of *The Beekeeper's Son* with complicated young characters who must define themselves."

—*RT Book Reviews*, 4-star review of *The Bishop's Son*

"Once I started reading *The Bishop's Son*, it was difficult for me to put it down! This story of struggle, faith, and hope will draw you in to the final page . . . I have read countless stories of Amish men or women doubting their faith. I have never read a storyline quite like this one though. It was narrated with such heart. I was fully invested in Jesse's struggle. No doubt, what Jesse felt is often what modern-day Amish men and women must feel when they are at a crossroads in their faith. The story was brilliantly told and the struggle felt very real."

—Destination Amish

"Something new and delightful in the Amish fiction genre, this story is set in the barren, dusty landscape of Bee County, TX . . . Irvin writes with great insight into the range and depth of human emotion. Her characters are believable and well developed, and her storytelling skills are superb. Recommend to readers who are looking for something a little different in Amish fiction."

—*CBA Retailers + Resources* on *The Beekeeper's Son*

"*The Beekeeper's Son* is so well crafted. Each character is richly layered. I found myself deeply invested in the lives of both the King and Lantz families. I struggled as they struggled, laughed as they laughed—and even cried as they cried . . . This is one of the best novels I have read in the last six months. It's a refreshing read and worth every penny. *The Beekeeper's Son* is a keeper for your bookshelf!"

—Destination Amish

"Kelly Irvin's *The Beekeeper's Son* is a beautiful story of faith, hope, and second chances. Her characters are so real that they feel like old friends. Once you open the book, you won't put it down until you've reached the last page."

—Amy Clipston, bestselling author of *A Gift of Grace*

"*The Beekeeper's Son* is a perfect depiction of how God makes all things beautiful in His way. Rich with vivid descriptions and characters you can immediately relate to, Kelly Irvin's book is a must-read for Amish fans."

—Ruth Reid, bestselling author of *A Miracle of Hope*

"Kelly Irvin writes a moving tale that is sure to delight all fans of Amish fiction. Highly recommended."

—Kathleen Fuller, author of the Hearts of Middlefield and Middlefield Family novels

The Warmth *of* Sunshine

Also by Kelly Irvin

AMISH BLESSINGS NOVELS

Love's Dwelling

The Warmth of Sunshine

AMISH OF BIG SKY COUNTRY NOVELS

Mountains of Grace

A Long Bridge Home

Peace in the Valley

EVERY AMISH SEASON NOVELS

Upon a Spring Breeze

Beneath the Summer Sun

Through the Autumn Air

With Winter's First Frost

THE AMISH OF BEE COUNTY NOVELS

The Beekeeper's Son

The Bishop's Son

The Saddle Maker's Son

ROMANTIC SUSPENSE

Tell Her No Lies

Over the Line

Closer Than She Knows

Her Every Move

Trust Me

NOVELLAS

To Raise a Home included in *An Amish Barn Raising*

Holiday of Hope included in *An Amish Christmas Wedding*

Cakes and Kisses included in *An Amish Christmas Bakery*

Mended Hearts included in *An Amish Reunion*

A Christmas Visitor included in *An Amish Christmas Gift*

Sweeter than Honey included in *An Amish Market*
One Sweet Kiss included in *An Amish Summer*
Snow Angels included in *An Amish Christmas Love*
The Midwife's Dream included in *An Amish Heirloom*

The Warmth *of* Sunshine

AMISH BLESSINGS

KELLY IRVIN

ZONDERVAN®

ZONDERVAN

The Warmth of Sunshine

This title is also available as a Zondervan e-book.

Requests for information should be addressed to:

Zondervan, *3900 Sparks Dr. SE, Grand Rapids, Michigan 49546*

Library of Congress Cataloging-in-Publication Data

Names: Irvin, Kelly, author.
Title: The warmth of sunshine : Amish Blessings / Kelly Irvin.
Description: Grand Rapids, Michigan : Zondervan, [2022] | Series: Amish blessings ; 2 | Summary: "When a young Amish woman discovers that she was adopted and that her birth parents are English, she will have to determine what she believes and where her future lies"-- Provided by publisher.
Identifiers: LCCN 2022000978 (print) | LCCN 2022000979 (ebook) | ISBN 9780310364528 (paperback) | ISBN 9780310364535 (epub) | ISBN 9780310364542
Subjects: LCGFT: Novels.
Classification: LCC PS3609.R82 W37 2022 (print) | LCC PS3609.R82 (ebook) | DDC 813/.6--dc23
LC record available at https://lccn.loc.gov/2022000978
LC ebook record available at https://lccn.loc.gov/2022000979

Publisher's Note: This novel is a work of fiction. Names, characters, places, and incidents are either products of the author's imagination or used fictitiously. All characters are fictional, and any similarity to people living or dead is purely coincidental.

Printed in the United States of America

22 23 24 25 LSC 10 9 8 7 6 5 4 3 2 1

To my Kansas family,
love always.

Do not conform to the pattern of this world, but be transformed by the renewing of your mind. Then you will be able to test and approve what God's will is—his good, pleasing and perfect will.

Romans 12:2

Glossary of Deutsch*

aenti, aentis: aunt, aunts
beheef dich: behave yourself
bobblemoul: blabbermouth
bopli, boplin: baby, babies
bruder, brieder: brother, brothers
bruderkind, bruderkinner: niece or nephew, nieces or nephews
bu, buwe: boy, boys
bussi, bussis: cat, cats
daadi: grandfather
daed: father
danki: thank you
dawdy haus: attached home for grandparents when they retire
dochder, dechder: daughter, daughters
dummkopp, dummkepp: dummy, blockhead, dummies, blockheads
eck: the corner table where the bride and groom sit at the wedding reception
eldre: parents
Englisch, Englischer: English or non-Amish
eppies: cookies
Es dutt mer leed: I am sorry
faeriwell: good-bye
fehla: sin

fraa: wife
gaul, geil: horse, horses
geil un weggel: horse and buggy
Gelassenheit: submission to the will of God; attitude of tranquil humility
gern gschehme: you're welcome
Gmay: church district
Gott: God
groosmammi: grandmother
guder mariye: good morning
gut: good
gut nacht: good night
heess: hot
hund, hunde: dog, dogs
jah: yes
kaffi: coffee
kapp: prayer cap or head covering worn by Amish women
kind, kinner: child, children
kinnskind, kinnskinner: grandchild, grandchildren
kuss, boss: kiss (singular noun)
maed, maede: girl, girls
mammi: grandma, affectionate form
mann: husband
meidung: shunning, excommunication from the Amish church
mudder: mother
narrisch: foolish, silly
nee: no
onkel: uncle
Ordnung: written and unwritten rules in an Amish district
rumspringa: period of "running around" for Amish youth before

they decide whether they want to be baptized into the Amish faith

schtinkich faul: awfully (or stinking) lazy

schweschder, schwesdchdre: sister, sisters

sei so gut: please (be so kind)

suh: son

un: and

vun: of, from

Wer iss sei?: Who is she?

Wie bischt du?: How are you?

wunderbarr: wonderful

*The German dialect commonly referred to as Pennsylvania Dutch is not a written language and varies depending on the location and origin of the Amish settlement. These spellings are approximations. Most Amish children learn English after they start school. They also learn High German, which is used in their Sunday services.

Featured Families

Freeman and Lorene Bontrager

Abigail Jane Benny Nate Hope Eddie Rose Joel

Chester Kurtz (widower)

Owen Kayla Lee Claire Eli Micah

Mary Wagner (widow)

Tobias Lorie Jonas Lucy Matthew

Bryan (bishop) and Esther Miller

Nadine Serena Michael Micah

Samuel (deacon) and Anita Schrock

Adam Jana Seth

Delbert (minister) and Loretta Beachy

Emily Carrie Nicholas Chrissie John Robert Celia

John and Rachel Christner

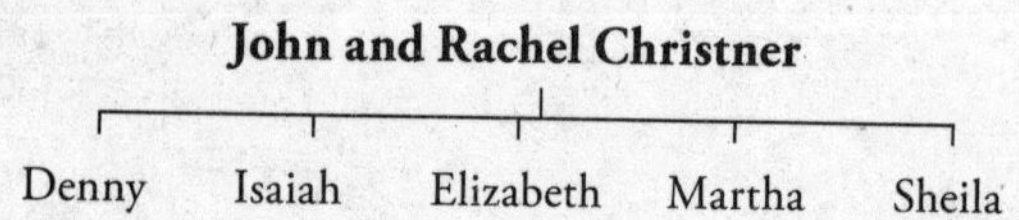

Denny Isaiah Elizabeth Martha Sheila

Joshua and Molly Hershberger

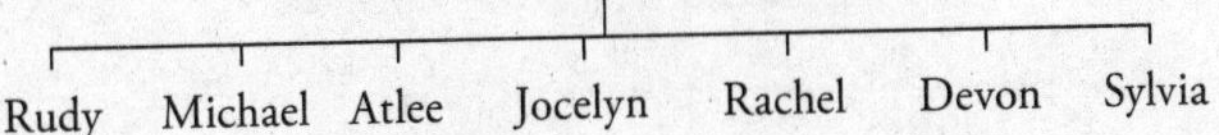

Job Keim (widower) and Dinah (deceased)

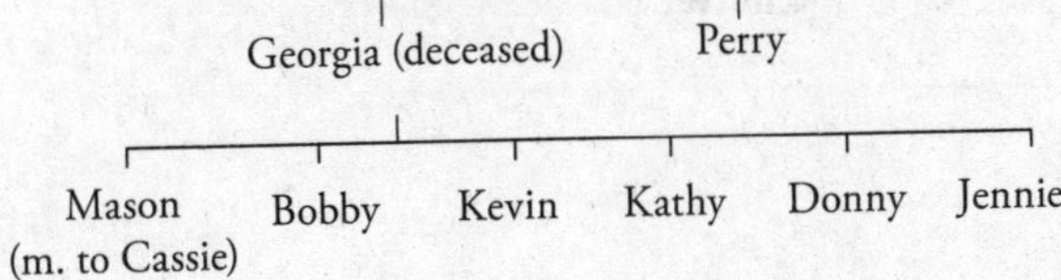

Wayne and Nelda Graber

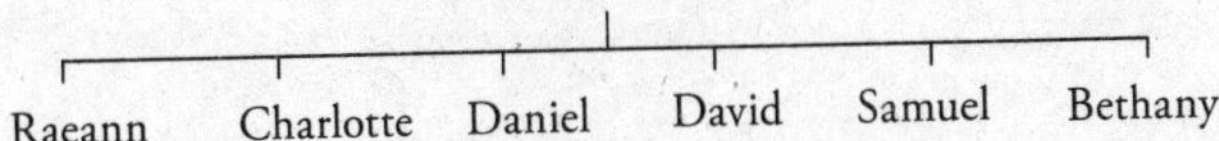

Heather and Dan Hanson (divorced)

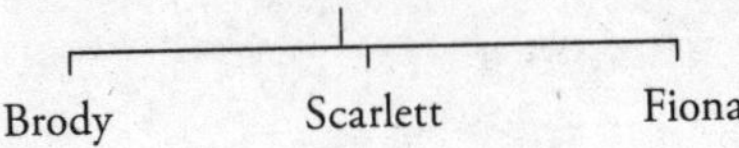

Eric and Susie Waters (divorced)

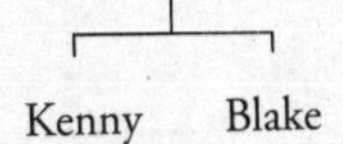

Helen and Miles Elliott (deceased) (grandparents)

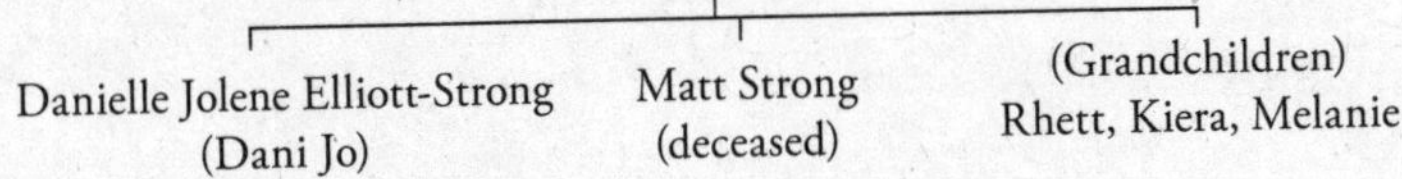

Chapter 1

Tractor engines made music. Even if only Abigail Bontrager could hear it. The deep-throated rumble of Grandpa's old tractor accompanied Abigail on Highway 96, the quickest route from the Yoder restaurant where she waitressed to her parents' farm outside Haven, six miles away. Others might fuss at the noise, but the sound served as a cheerful song to her ears after eight hours of dishes clattering, silverware clinking, and the steady buzz of mostly tourists talking at the Buggies and Bonnets restaurant.

Diesel fumes carried on black smoke perfumed the air in stark contrast to the mingled aromas of fresh bread, pot roast, fried chicken, and chocolate cream pie baked to perfection. Yep. The smell was Plain perfume. Plus it reminded her of family. When Grandpa and Grandma moved into the *dawdy haus*, Grandpa no longer needed the tractor.

Reveling in the sameness of it all, Abigail sang "Bringing in the Sheaves" at the top of her lungs to keep herself awake. The old John Deere's vibrations loosened the aching muscles in her shoulders, arms, and legs. The thirty-two dollars in tips tucked into her canvas bag—along with the satisfaction of a job well done—more than made up for it. Other than dumping a piece of lemon meringue pie into a customer's lap, today had been a good day. The money would help with expenses at home, and she would set aside a small portion in her nest egg for that day when she would set up housekeeping with her future husband.

Not too distant future, God willing. *Sei so gut, Gott.*

The image of towheaded Owen Kurtz with the bluest eyes in all of Haven floated in her mind. Stocky body, deep tan, calloused hands. Heat that had nothing to do with the Kansas late spring sun on her face warmed her. They'd taken a few buggy rides together. He hadn't even held her hand yet, but something about him kept her awake at night, imagining the day he would.

A horn blared. Abigail smiled and waved at the impatient truck driver as he passed. Amazingly, he waved back. Mother said the high road had the best view. Mother was always right.

Abigail turned onto the gravel road that led to the farm. The winter wheat was heading in the field on her right. On her left the shorn plants indicated Father and the boys had put up the first cutting of alfalfa. Early May's sunny days had been kind to their crops. *Danki, Gott.*

A dark-blue SUV sat at a precarious angle on the curve of the driveway in front of the sprawling house she'd grown up in. Someone had parked as if unsure of the proper etiquette. Or poised for a quick getaway. English guests for dinner? Mealtimes tended to be rowdy at the Bontrager homestead. Abigail's three younger sisters would have it under control, but the oldest sibling should do her fair share. She rushed to park the tractor in the barn, where Doolittle greeted her with his usual tail-wagging enthusiasm.

"I'm glad to see you too." She brushed back the long black bangs that hung in his eyes. "Did you defend the fortress from grizzly bears and four-eyed monsters while I was gone? *Gut hund, gut hund.*"

"Woof, woof."

It was a family joke. Doolittle mostly lived up to his name. "Indeed! You're the best do-little dog around."

Bobbing left and right to avoid tripping over the furry mountain of a dog as he ran circles around her, Abigail traipsed up the steps and through the back door into the kitchen. "*Mudder*, I'm here."

The aroma of chicken and onions simmering greeted her. But not her mother. An enormous pot of chicken soup bubbled on the stove. It bubbled so hard it had splattered the stove top. Hard, burned spots marred its surface. Chopped raw potatoes, carrots, and celery covered the cutting board next to the stove. Mother had stopped in the middle of making one-pot chicken stew. She called it her favorite—because it made a ton and it was filling—a must with four growing boys to feed. A pan of fresh-baked soda biscuits cooled on the trivet next to the board. Two peach pies shared the open window's sill. "Mudder? Jane? Rose? Hope?"

Doolittle meandered toward the pies.

"Don't you dare." Abigail shook her finger at him. He ducked his graying head and whined deep in his throat. She turned down the stove's flame and headed for the great room that served as both dining and living room. Doolittle followed, of course. The murmur of voices reached her. "Mudder?"

The murmuring ceased.

Mother sat in the pine rocker next to the empty limestone fireplace. She'd chosen the chair farthest from where an auburn-haired English woman perched on the sofa. Abigail's sisters were nowhere to be seen. Why weren't they in the kitchen?

The woman rose. She held out both hands. "You must be Abigail."

Mother moaned an awful, guttural sound. "Please, don't. Let me."

Doolittle rushed to her side. He whined again. He nosed her hands in her lap. She patted him without seeming to notice.

"Hello, I'm back." Silly thing to say. Of course they could see that.

How did this stranger know her name? "The chicken was boiling. I turned down the flame."

"I forgot . . . I forgot about it." Mudder continued to smooth Doolittle's thick fur. "This is Heather Holcomb, now Heather Hanson. She's the daughter of the Holcombs who were neighbors to *Mammi* and *Daadi* way back before they moved into your *onkel* Warren's dawdy haus."

The Holcombs were nice. Grandma and Grandpa used to take them gingerbread men at Christmas and check on them after storms. They returned the favor by supplying cranberry-nut bread and offers of rides when the roads were bad during the winter. "Why aren't the girls taking care of supper?"

"I sent them upstairs."

That made no sense. Abigail opened her mouth.

"You look just like me." The woman took two faltering steps toward Abigail. "I always imagined you would."

Abigail looked nothing like her. Her hair was bobbed below her ears, while Abigail's waist-length hair—neatly coiled in a bun under her *kapp*—was more blonde than strawberry. Sure, the woman had blue eyes, too, but lots of people had them. Mother and Father did. So did Jane. People always thought her younger sister and Abigail were twins even though they were born exactly eleven months apart.

Abigail peeked at her mother. Tears rolled down her plump face. Mother never cried. She found silver linings in every situation. When Grandma Evie died, Mother said she'd been whisked away to a better world. When lightning struck the barn and burned it to the ground, it was old and ramshackle and an eyesore. Besides, barn raisings were fun—the women laughing, talking, and working side by side to feed the men.

"What's this about, Mudder? What does she mean, I look like her?"

"I'm sorry. We should've told you. Your *daed* and I meant to tell you, but we could never find the right time." Mother's voice cracked on the word *father*. Her nose was running. She swiped at her face with her sleeve. Another thing Mother would never do. "The older you grew, the less it seemed to matter. You're ours. All ours."

Of course she was. Who else's would she be? "Tell me what?"

Mrs. Hanson stumbled forward, grabbed Abigail's hands, and pulled her against her body, all bony angles and sharp points. Not anything like Mother's round cushion of a body. "You're my daughter," she whispered into Abigail's ear. Her breath tickled. "I'm your mother."

Chapter 2

The English language ceased to make sense. Abigail ripped herself from Mrs. Hanson's grip. "Mudder, *wer iss sei?*"

"Mudder—that's me." The woman reached for Abigail again, caught herself, and ran her hands through her hair instead. "It's been twenty years since I've lived in Haven, but I still remember some of the words. I'm your mudder."

"That's the right word, but no, you're not." Mother shook her head so hard her kapp shifted. "You're not her mother, Heather. We have an agreement. You gave her to Freeman and me. You left."

"My parents made me do it." Heather spoke to Mother, but her beseeching gaze enveloped Abigail. "They forced me to break up with my boyfriend and sent me to live with my aunt in Abilene. I was sixteen. They didn't give me a choice."

The room shrank to a narrow funnel shape that spun wildly. Abigail put her hands to her ears. Her heartbeat cranked up to a hundred miles an hour. The chicken salad sandwich she'd eaten for lunch rose in her throat. "*Nee, nee. Mei naame iss* Abigail Bontrager. *Dochder vun* Freeman *un* Lorene Bontrager."

"Of course you're Abigail. Of course you're our daughter. Nothing will change that. Not ever." Mother hopped from the rocker and sped across the room. Doolittle, growling low in his throat, followed. Mother slid an arm around Abigail. Her fingers were cold. "You need to go, Heather. We had an agreement."

Heather ignored her and Doolittle, even though the dog eyed her like fresh meat.

Gut hund.

Murmuring to herself, Heather dug a billfold from an enormous leather bag. From the billfold she produced a laminated photo yellowed with age. "I bet this is the only baby photo of you that exists. Me and you. Together." She held it out. "I begged the nurse to take it before Freeman and Lorene showed up at the hospital."

Her hands were shaking. Abigail closed her eyes and opened them. Heather's offering still hung in the air between them. She blinked away unbelieving tears and took it. Heather had changed in twenty years. At the time of Abigail's birth, if the woman was to be believed, Heather had long, curly red hair. Despite being a new mother, her arms and face were thin. She wasn't smiling. The baby wasn't much more than a fluff of reddish-blonde hair wrapped in a pink receiving blanket.

"You were small. Five pounds, four ounces. That's because you came three weeks early." Heather spoke fast, her voice filled with a fierce desire to get the words out, as if she'd been saving them up for a long time. "I sang 'You Are My Sunshine' to you as soon as they laid you on my chest. You stopped crying and stared at me wide-eyed. Like 'I know you. You're my mommy.'"

Abigail turned over the photo. On the back someone had scrawled the words *Me and my baby, born at 3:34 a.m. on February 14.*

Abigail's birthday. Valentine's Day. Lots of people had that birthday.

Her fingers let go of the photo. It plummeted through time to the pine floor. Heather swooped down and retrieved it. "I can see why you'd be upset. I'd hoped Lorene and Freeman had told you about me." She slipped the photo back into the billfold. The billfold went back into the purse as if this action somehow assured her it would be safe. "I wrote letters. I told them I was coming."

"And I wrote and asked you *not* to come." Mother edged between Abigail and Heather. Doolittle growled and did the same. "I reminded you of our agreement. Abigail is our daughter. The adoption papers are in order."

"That doesn't mean I can't know my—can't know Abigail."

"What purpose would that serve?"

At the sound of Father's voice thundering from behind her, Abigail turned. He had that look. The one she always tried to avoid. Red cheeks. Wrinkled forehead. Woolly black eyebrows drawn up. His full lips parted so his slightly crooked teeth showed above his John the Baptist beard.

His woodshed-whipping look.

"Abigail has a right to know who she really is."

"I know who I am." At least she had until a few minutes earlier. Now her world twirled airborne like a tree ripped from the ground, roots and all, by a tornado. "I left my bag in the tractor. I'll be back."

Abigail broke free of her mother's grasp, dodged Heather, and darted toward the door. Doolittle tried to follow. "Nee, stay, hund."

She needed to be away from these people—strangers, all of them.

She needed to be with people she could trust.

Chapter 3

"Are you even listening to me?"

The whine in his younger brother's voice forced Owen Kurtz to shift his attention from the mare. Her restlessness suggested she would deliver her foal in the next few hours, if not minutes. "I'm listening. I'm also trying to make sure Daisy gets situated. She's all over the place."

Lee snorted. He sounded like barnyard livestock himself when he did that. "She's a mare. This is her second foal. She knows what she's doing. She doesn't need your help. What's going on? Why do you have that goofy grin on your face? You usually come home from work dragging like someone spit a big loogie in your *kaffi*."

"Do not." The smell of horse manure, dirty hay, and musty air calmed Owen's spirit. The barn—or any place on his family's farm—did that. Farming soothed his soul. Not building prefab structures with his father's crew. "It just takes me a minute to throw off the day when I get home, that's all."

"But not today." Lee pulled his straw hat back on his crazy wild hair and leaned against the stall gate as if to settle in for a long conversation. That was Lee. He could stretch a single thought into a daylong discussion. He would make a good bishop someday, if God decided to choose him. "What happened today?"

Nothing happened. Not yet. But there was still time. If Daisy would get busy, Owen would be done here in time to slip over to Abigail's house and take her for a buggy ride. He'd only driven her home from the singings a few times, but they'd had fun. She was a sweet girl—nervous and awkward—but sweet. Why he made her nervous, he couldn't imagine. Kayla insisted they were right for each other, but Abigail was like another sister—until recently.

Abigail had been a fixture in his life forever. His sister's friend. His friend, if Plain girls and boys could be friends. His feelings had been like a fine mist that grew into a sweet, steady rain until suddenly they became a deluge. When his fingers brushed hers or their knees accidently touched in the buggy, a sudden, fierce thunderstorm ensued.

All of which had to be guarded behind the locked, thick doors of his heart until he could be sure she felt the same.

God's plan for Abigail and for Owen surely meant for this meandering path to lead somewhere. On the other hand, a man who thought he knew God's plan was surely in for a headfirst dive into an abyss that appeared in his path. If anybody knew that, Owen and his family did.

Still, a man had to swing for the fence and be prepared to accept the curveballs life threw at him. Baseball was the best sport bar none.

"There it is again. That loopy, goofy grin." Lee chortled. He pointed his skinny index finger with the bruised, black nail from a misfire with a hammer at Owen. "This has something to do with Abigail, doesn't it? Come on, courting her must be like kissing your *schweschder*."

"There's been no kissing." *Not yet.*

"Why not?"

"Lee!"

"Well?"

"Well, nothing. A man doesn't kiss and tell. Even if he's not." Especially a Plain man. "How are things with Jocelyn?"

Turnabout was fair play. Lee had been courting Jocelyn Hershberger since he turned sixteen six months earlier. They had a complicated relationship according to Lee's long-winded descriptions. Owen kept his courtship stories—of which there were few—to himself.

"Don't try to change the subject."

"I'm not. You want to talk courting. How are things coming between you and Jocelyn?"

"That's between Jocelyn and me."

"Which is exactly what I'm saying about Abigail and me. Nothing to tell, anyway."

"But there's a spark, right?"

Owen turned at the sound of Kayla's voice. His sister loped through the barn doors. Kayla never walked anywhere. She raced, she rushed, she ran. Just watching her made Owen tired. "That's none of your business."

"Help me saddle a horse real quick." Kayla pulled the hood of her rain slicker over her head and buttoned the top button. "Daed says Abigail is out on the road in a buggy. He was turning in the drive and saw her. He stopped to ask what she was doing. She said she was driving by. But when he turned back, she was still sitting there in the rain and thunder and lightning."

"She comes here all the time. Why wouldn't she come on in?"

"I have no idea." Kayla grabbed a saddle from the saddle horse and thrust it at Owen. "Knowing Abigail, she doesn't want to bother anyone, or she's afraid Daed will think she came to see you this time."

"Why would Daed think that?" Owen placed the saddle back on its resting place. "It'll be faster to walk up there. I'll go with you. Daed doesn't know about Abigail and me."

"Sure he does. He knows everything that goes on with us." Kayla spun around and headed for the door. "Let's go."

"I'll keep Daisy company." Lee straightened. "If the Bontragers need anything, let us know."

That went without saying. Owen grabbed a raincoat from a peg on the wall and followed Kayla at an easy jog. Her legs were almost as long as his. She was built like their mother, tall for a woman and slender. He slid carefully past that image. Thoughts of his mother didn't hurt like they once had.

"And where was Daed? Why was he out in this weather?"

"Where do you think?" Kayla threw the question back at him without slowing down. "He wasn't at work this late."

Which meant in all likelihood he'd stopped at the Wagner house on his way home from work. Mary Wagner had been widowed less than a year. She had five young kids. She needed help. No one begrudged her that. Least of all Owen.

His dad had been father and mother to his six children for six years now. Seeing Mary surely gave Dad relief from the loneliness he undoubtedly faced day in and day out. *Danki, Gott, for that.*

A wild wind filled with a fine mist of cold rain slapped Owen's face. Kansas weather could turn on a man in a matter of minutes. He picked up speed. The mist turned to fat, heavy drops that splatted against his straw hat. Wind whipped his skin. He shoved the hat down hard to keep it from blowing away.

There she was. Shoulders slumped, head down, Abigail clung to the reins on the seat of her father's buggy at the corner where Haven Road met East Cable Road. Kayla beat him to the buggy by a few steps. "Abigail? Abigail!"

Her head came up. “Kayla. I’m sorry. You’re all wet. Owen, you didn’t have to come. I was just leaving.”

“No, you’re not. You’re coming up to the house, you silly goose.” Kayla hauled herself into the buggy. “Why are you sitting out here in the rain? You’ve been up to our house a thousand times.”

“I needed to talk to you.” Abigail swiped sodden strands of loose hair the wind had coaxed from under her kapp from her face. “But then I couldn’t. I couldn’t talk to anyone. I can’t make heads or tails out of anything.”

“Out of what?” Owen moved around to the other side of the buggy. “Scoot over. I’ll drive.”

Abigail did as she was told. Kayla put her arm around her friend while Owen picked up the reins. Lightning crackled across the black sky. A few seconds later thunder rumbled. Both girls jumped. “It’s okay. It wasn’t that close. We’ll get you up to the house, and Kayla will make you some tea. Abigail, are your folks okay? Your *brieder* and *schwesdchdre*?”

“They’re not my *eldre*. They’re not my brieder and schwesdchdre.”

She was talking nonsense. Owen snapped the reins. The horse picked up speed. “I don’t understand.”

“I can’t talk in front of your daed. He’ll think it was wrong of me to have come. It’s a family matter. My family.”

“We’ll find another dry, quiet place then.”

The farrowing building was empty at the moment.

Abigail didn’t protest. In fact, she didn’t say anything more. *Gott, please help her. Help me help her. Whatever it is, let us help her overcome it together.*

Because that’s what friends did. With time, they could be more than friends, but for now this was about Abigail, a family friend.

Once in the farrowing building, he lit two lanterns while Kayla helped Abigail down from the buggy and tucked a blanket around her shoulders. The two women settled onto a stack of feed bags.

Owen set a lantern on a workbench near the stalls where the sows gave birth to their litters. Abigail's expression was unfathomable. She didn't speak. The howling wind shook the rafters. Bits of hay and dust flitted in light cast by the kerosene lantern. Rain pounded against the roof. A sound like rocks beating the wood added to the rain's staccato. Hail. There went the strawberries and tomatoes the girls had planted only a few days earlier. And their flower garden.

He glanced at Kayla. Her thin eyebrows rose and she shrugged. She had no idea what to do next either. "Would it help if Owen left? Would you rather just tell me?"

"Nee. He can stay. It affects him too. At least I think it does. I'm just trying to puzzle it all out." Abigail took a long, shuddering breath. "I'm adopted."

Of all the statements Owen had anticipated, this had not been one that came to mind. "Nee, you're not."

Kayla scowled at him. She patted Abigail's shoulder. "How do you know? What happened?"

Abigail tugged the blanket tighter. She looked like a half-drowned kitten. Even so, nothing could make her any less pretty. It would be so nice to have the right to pat her face dry and brush her strawberry-blonde hair back under her kapp.

Owen jerked his gaze to the lantern in his hand. He set it on the shelf and settled on a stool across from where the girls sat.

"My *real* mother came to see me. Her name is Heather Hanson. She drove down from Abilene to meet me."

"Lorene raised you. Your whole life. She's your real mother." If only he could hold her hand. Hug her. Owen had daydreamed about doing both, but not under these circumstances. "You're the spitting image of your mudder. You and Jane are practically twins. Everyone says so. Your parents have never said anything about adoption, have they?"

"Nee. Not a word." Abigail patted her face dry with the blanket. "Nothing about us is the same. She has red hair. She wore flowered leggings, a purple blouse, and sandals. Her toenails were painted pink. She's *Englisch*."

English. Everything Owen knew about Abigail turned into a mess of squiggles he couldn't decipher. The story they'd just begun to write ebbed from the pages, the ink dark and smeared. "It doesn't matter. You're not Englisch. You're Plain. You've been baptized. You chose the faith. She can't just show up and change that."

"Can't she?" Abigail straightened and pulled away from Kayla. "She showed up today because she regrets giving me up for adoption. She wants to get to know me. She wants me to get to know her."

"Twenty years later? Just because she wants it, doesn't mean you have to have anything to do with her." Kayla stood and paced the hard-packed dirt floor that separated Owen and Abigail. "You have a choice. She can't force you to do anything. After all, she gave you up."

Abigail flinched. Kayla's words might be true, but they hurt. She didn't know how to soften her thoughts, only to fling them about like arrows from a bow. They'd never had to pick their words carefully around Abigail. Navigating such a painful revelation changed that.

Owen breathed in the odor of swine, dirt, and hay. "I'm sorry. That must hurt. Knowing she gave you up before she even knew you."

"I can't have it both ways, can I?" Abigail studied her hands as if they belonged to a stranger. "I can't be angry at her for giving me away at the same time I'm angry at her for wanting to know me."

"However you feel, you feel." Owen floundered for words. He was a farmer and a reluctant builder of engineered structures. What did he know about feelings? Other than how hard they were to keep locked up in cages. He'd been doing it since he was sixteen and his mother passed away suddenly, inexplicably, in the middle of the night. "Feelings just are."

His father would call that an unfortunate truth. Everyone wanted to obey Scripture that said, *Don't worry, obey, be humble, be kind, be joyful, be loving.* But sometimes feelings got in the way because humans were born with them.

"We are supposed to accept what happens to us as *Gott*'s plan." Abigail's thoughts seemed to be following the same path Owen's traversed. "Even if we don't understand—and I surely don't understand why this is happening to me."

"What exactly happened? Did she say how you ended up with your parents—with Freeman and Lorene?"

Abigail shared the bare facts she'd learned before she rushed from her parents' house. "I couldn't stay one more minute. I needed to think. I needed to figure out how to feel. It was like waking up and discovering I'd changed into a different person overnight. It's like the world has gone dark. I'm having trouble seeing. I'm afraid to move for fear I'll run into something."

"I'm sorry. I can imagine how hard this must be." Could he really? He hadn't suddenly acquired a new parent. Or two parents. "Did she say who the boyfriend was? Your biological father?"

"No. We didn't get that far. I ran. I shouldn't have." Abigail shrugged the blanket from her shoulders and folded it with precise movements. She handed it to Kayla. "It was wrong of me to run away from my parents—from Lorene and Freeman. I should go back. I just needed a moment to breathe. With people who won't think of me differently. You won't think of me differently, will you?"

Her gaze sideswiped Owen, bounced to the wall, and back to the floor.

"Of course not." Kayla laid the blanket aside. She grabbed Abigail's hand. "Don't be silly. You're my best friend. Owen is your . . . I don't know what, but he's my *bruder* and he's smart. He would never be mean to you. I wouldn't let him."

"You're adopted, not a leper. Lots of people are adopted." Owen's stomach dropped in a sickening lurch so like the one that signaled a terrible thing was about to happen and there was nothing anyone could do about it. Abigail's life had changed from one moment to the next. He of all people understood how that felt. "It'll take time, but you'll figure out how to handle it and go on being you."

Whoever that turned out to be. Whether that was Plain or English. Would she consider leaving her Plain life? Owen's heart squeezed painfully at the thought. His fledgling feelings for Abigail couldn't be allowed to matter. Not now.

"We'll help." Kayla tugged Abigail to her feet. "Come on. Let's go into the house for some hot tea. We're in this together, right, Owen?"

"Definitely."

Abigail's eyes were huge and dark in the lantern light. Cornflower blue turned to indigo. "I appreciate that, but I need to figure out who I am. No one can do that for me."

No matter how new it was, the looming loss of hope, the loss of sweet anticipation, the loss of possibilities turned his world from the lush green of Kansas's landscape to a dry wasteland, a desert thirsty for rain that wasn't coming. "Understood. Just know we're—I'm—here if you need help."

Owen doused the lanterns and led the women out into the howling wind and driving rain. They bent double in the struggle to make progress against its fierce power. Rain pelted Owen's face so hard he could barely see. He ducked to avoid tree branches turned into flying arrows. If either woman spoke, he couldn't hear them. The pain in Abigail's voice as she had told her story filled his ears. The hurt and confusion on her face accompanied him on the road to the house.

Not even a raging storm could inflict the kind of damage a woman named Heather Hanson had wrought in a few scant minutes. Buildings could be repaired and replaced. A young woman's world was much harder to fix.

Chapter 4

Which was scarier? The storm or Father's hulking body standing on Chester Kurtz's porch in the pouring rain? At first glance he could have been an enormous bear in the black slicker that covered his frame from shoulders to the ground. His growl added to the illusion. Abigail brushed past Owen and Kayla and trudged up the steps. "I'm here, Daed."

He whirled. His hat was missing. His thick, black curls and long, unruly beard flailed in the wind. "I came to get you home, but then I saw a funnel cloud touch down on the road. We need to take cover."

Lightning crackled overhead. A clap of thunder rent the air. The horse hitched to his buggy whinnied, a high, nervous sound.

"I'm sorry I ran away."

"We'll talk about it at home." He turned back and pounded on the door. "Chester, open up."

The front door flew open. Chester Kurtz loomed. "No need to break the door down."

"A tornado touched down west of the road."

Chester opened the door wider. "We'd better get to the basement then."

"Don't worry about your horse and buggy." Owen dashed back into the rain. "I'll stable them and meet you in the basement."

"What about Mudder and the *kinner*?" Fear burned a trail down Abigail's spine. She'd run away, and now Mother and the kids were alone in the path of a tornado. *Your fault. Your fault.* "We have to go home."

"It's too late for that." Father tugged her into the Kurtzes' living room. Their raincoats dripped steadily onto the welcome rug. He didn't seem to notice. "Your mudder knows what to do. They'll be safe in our basement."

Please, Gott.

The Kurtzes had their emergency plan well in hand. A few scant minutes later, Abigail followed Kayla and her siblings down the stairs into their cavernous basement filled with canned goods, extra firewood, and furniture odds and ends. The atmosphere was more like an impromptu frolic than an emergency sheltering. Kayla and her sister, Claire, lit half a dozen kerosene lanterns and a handful of homemade apple-cinnamon-scented candles, giving the room a cheery air. Lee snatched a pack of Uno cards from the shelf and settled at a card table with Eli and Micah, the youngest siblings. The family's two dogs sniffed the corners, then sprawled at his feet.

"Why are you here? What were you and Kayla whispering about? Is it about Owen?" Claire employed a stage whisper that echoed against the four walls. "Lee says Owen was in a dither because he—"

"Hush, Claire!" Lee aimed and let a card fly like a Frisbee at his sister's forehead. "Everyone can hear you."

Owen grabbed old towels from a stack on a shelf next to rows of canned peaches, cherries, green beans, pickles, tomatoes, and a bounty of other produce. He passed them around to Kayla, Abigail's father, and finally Abigail.

Trying to telegraph her feelings with her eyes, she accepted his offering. He nodded, his expression encouraging. She wiped her face and neck. The cool, dry basement didn't help. Shivers assailed her body. She removed her raincoat and hung it on a peg next to several others.

"*Danki* for sharing your basement with us." Father directed his words to Chester, who sprawled in one of several lawn chairs placed in a horseshoe beyond the card table. "Much as I'd like to get home, it didn't seem smart to try to outrun a tornado."

"The more the merrier." Chester waved to the empty chairs. "Pull up a seat. My dochder brought thermoses of hot chocolate. They can make a party from just about any occasion."

Father's gaze traveled to Abigail. Nothing could be said in front of the entire Kurtz family. That was certain. "Don't mind if I do."

His bleak stare did nothing to assuage the ache that filled up the spot that had once held Abigail's heart. He should have told her. Mother should have told her. Yet he was still the man who had been her North Star since she was old enough to remember sharing his lap with Jane while he read Scripture by a roaring fire before bedtime.

Sometimes he sang hymns in low, tuneless Pennsylvania German, his voice lulling her to sleep. Sometimes he told stories from the *Martyrs Mirror* or stories of his childhood in Ohio. Sometimes he said nothing at all, letting his girls rest against his chest, the beating of his heart soothing them.

Now, shoulders sloped as if suddenly old, he turned and strode over to Chester, who immediately launched into a replay of the weather and speculation regarding what repairs would be needed in the morning.

"Your daed has his exploding face on." Claire wrinkled her nose, blew up her cheeks, and drew her eyebrows together in an effort to demonstrate Father's infamous you're-in-trouble face. "What's he mad about?"

"Just you never mind." Kayla elbowed her sister, younger by two years but taller by two inches. "Give Abby a chance to breathe."

Only her friends called her Abby. Father didn't like the nickname. He thought Abigail was much nicer—so did Mother—and it was her given name. What would Heather have named her? Or maybe Heather picked the name Abigail. With a sidewise glance at the menfolk, Abigail drew farther into the farthest corner of the basement. A spiderweb brushed her face, sending a shiver scurrying across her neck. "What did Lee mean that Owen was in a dither?"

"Lee is full of hot air." Kayla rolled her blue eyes. "He thinks he knows way more than he does, and it makes him feel important. Owen wanted to take you for a ride tonight, that's all."

Abigail bit her lower lip to keep from groaning. She'd been too busy caterwauling about her problems to even think about what all this would mean to Owen. In a few short hours, everything had changed. He might not want to take a ride with her anymore. The future was full of shadowy ifs, shifting maybes, and uncertain probabilities. What man wanted to tangle with that? It'd be like trying to hug fog. "I'm sure he's having second thoughts about that now."

"Not Owen. He's crazy about you. Are you having second thoughts?"

"About him?"

"About anything." Kayla held up both hands, fingers wide, as if encompassing the whole world. "Owen, your vows, being Plain."

"I don't know. Maybe. No." She'd had her legs knocked out from under her. She might have to learn how to walk and think and talk all over again. "I don't know. It just happened."

It happened to someone else. No, she was someone else. An imposter in her own body. An English girl masquerading as a Plain one.

Another thought careened into the first one. Maybe this being

English explained everything. Maybe it explained her awkwardness. Her lack of interest in baking and sewing. The tough piecrusts and bread that didn't rise. The uneven hems and scraggly embroidery stitches. The accident-prone Abigail was never supposed to be Plain. Maybe it explained why she never quite fit in.

So why did she fit in fine with Owen? *Ach, Owen.* The one place where she could be herself happened to be on that buggy seat next to him.

Abigail peered over Kayla's shoulder to where he sat with his back to them. His blond hair hung in wet clumps under his straw hat. As usual he needed a haircut. His right steel-toed boot tapped on the floor in a steady rhythm. Her father likely made him nervous. He probably was chewing on the inside of his cheek and nodding. An endearing picture of a man who needed a wife to take care of him.

I'm so sorry, Owen.

Why was she sorry? She didn't do this to him. It was done to her.

Because the imposter Abigail had sold him a bill of goods. *What you see is not what you get. All sales final.*

Darkness cloaked the damage done by the storm by the time Abigail and the others emerged from the basement an hour later into the rain-cooled, humid night air. Tree limbs littered the front yard. A thick layer of leaves and twigs carpeted the porch and steps. The Kurtz house was intact and the barn still stood. A closer inspection would have to wait until morning light.

Father hustled Abigail out the door with a quick thanks to Chester for letting them ride out the storm here. They had to get home to make sure Mother and the others had weathered the storm safely. Owen again fetched the horse and buggy.

"I'll swing back by tomorrow with one of my *buwe* to pick up the other *geil un weggel*."

"I can drive it home." It would save him a trip the next day and provide Abigail with an excuse for postponing the conversation they were bound to have on the ride home. "I'll follow you."

"Nee." Father stalked out to meet Owen.

Her stomach tied in knots, Abigail accepted a quick hug from Kayla and followed. Owen handed over the reins to Father. He turned, his back to her father, smiled, and nodded at Abigail.

He had such a sweet, encouraging smile. The dark clouds didn't seem as dark. Abigail climbed into the buggy and looked down at him. "Danki."

He raised his hand in a quick salute. "Take care."

"Take care." His way of saying he cared?

Abigail faced forward and settled back on her seat. Maybe Father would save his lecture for when they arrived at the house. Then he and Mother could join forces.

Abigail should say she was sorry for running out on them. She was sorry. But she hadn't committed a lie of omission. She hadn't concealed a critical piece of information from people she professed to love. She hadn't allowed a stranger to deliver this news in their living room.

"Your mudder was worried."

He'd made it all the way to the main road before he spoke. Abigail swallowed a thousand recriminations pushing and shoving, furious, determined to be first in line. Mother was worried? Did she not feel sorry for what she'd done to Abigail? Did she not wish to apologize? "Worry is a sin."

"Don't be smart with me." Father snapped the reins. Jocko picked up speed. "I'm still your daed, and I have the piece of paper to prove it."

"I'm sorry." Trying to be sorry. There was a difference. "I don't understand."

"I know you don't." His voice tightened like a frayed rope about to break in two. "We should've told you."

One of those no-kidding statements. "Why didn't you?"

"You're our dochder. As much our flesh and blood as our other kinner." He paused as if searching his store of vocabulary from three languages for words that could somehow explain the unexplainable. "We waited at first, thinking it best to tell you when you were old enough to understand. Then time passed . . ."

Time passed until they lived in that warm, simple place past the point of no return. "My parents are Englisch. I can't fathom that."

"Your mudder and I are your eldre."

"Why are you angry?"

"I'm not. I am not angry. Not at you." He snapped the reins as if he wanted to make the horse go faster, to get home sooner, to end this uncomfortable conversation. "I'm angry with myself."

"Don't be mad. I'm not mad." Confused, hurt, addled, distressed, floundering, drowning.

Fine. Mad. Angry. Furious. Irate. These words couldn't scratch the surface of the boiling cauldron of emotion inside her. "Nee, I am a little mad, but it's because it was so unexpected."

"No daed wants to hurt his dochder."

"I know." *But you did.*

They drove the rest of the way in silence, the only sounds the creak of the buggy's wheels and the wind whistling through the trees that lined the road. Abigail closed her eyes and let the night air cool her warm face. This morning she had woken up an average, everyday Plain woman who did all the things Plain women did. In the space of a few minutes, a redheaded woman stripped that identity from her. Now she had to make herself from scratch. Starting tomorrow. Tonight she needed to mourn the old Abigail.

At the house Father pulled up at the front porch and halted. "I'll be in as soon as I stable the geil un weggel and check on the livestock. You check to make sure everyone is okay."

"If this Heather Holcomb hadn't shown up here, would you ever have told me who I really am?"

Father's shoulders hunched. "You know who you really are."

"And you know what I mean."

He clucked softly. Jocko tossed his head and whinnied. "I don't know."

An honest answer but not a satisfactory one.

Abigail found her mother sitting on the couch in the living room, a basket of sewing in her lap. Doolittle curled up on a rug at her feet. Her eyes were red. She didn't acknowledge Abigail's presence. Instead she kept darning the hole in the sock in her hand. Doolittle hopped up and dashed across the floor. His greeting dance nearly knocked Abigail from her feet. Her gaze still on her mother, she knelt to pet him. "Is everyone safe? Any damage from the storm?"

"It passed over us quickly. We were snug in the basement. The kinner played checkers and Connect 4. Your breider are out checking for damage now." Mother pushed the reading glasses she used for sewing up her nose and peered at the sock. "Where did you go?"

"The Kurtzes. Daed showed up, and we all hunkered down in their basement." Abigail backed away from Doolittle, who trailed after her and settled next to the hickory rocker by the dark fireplace. "I'm sorry I ran."

The words had to be said first. She owed her mother that much.

Mother tossed the sock into the basket and set it aside. "You didn't give me a chance to explain."

"I couldn't think."

"Abigail, you're here. You're home." Jane flew down the stairs. "Where were you? We were so worried! Did you see the funnel cloud? Benny—"

"Jane, go back upstairs. Make sure Hope and Rose are in bed."

"They're already—"

"Go."

"But—"

"Go, Dochder."

Jane shot a worried frown in Abigail's direction. *Later*, Abigail telegraphed back. Jane nodded and tromped up the stairs, every leaden footfall shouting her thoughts on this turn of events.

Mother stared at her hands, now splayed in her lap. "Heather isn't a bad person. She made a mistake a long time ago. She's had to live with it ever since."

"So I'm a mistake?"

"Nee. Giving you up was her mistake. Like she said, her parents insisted. I never understood that. I felt bad for her. When we went to the hospital in Wichita to fetch you, I was sure she would change her mind and refuse." Mother's face went still. Then a perplexed frown flitted across her face. "Her mudder stood next to the bed the entire time. She kept telling Heather it was for the best, that she would see it was for the best. It's not something I can imagine doing, even in those circumstances."

She spoke as if to herself. As if she had been trying to puzzle this out for many years. Abigail could see why. To give up a baby *was* unfathomable. Babies were gifts from God under all circumstances. They should not be punished for their parents' mistakes. "Why you and Daed? Why give her *bopli* to you?"

Mother rose. "I'm thirsty. Do you want some cold tea? Or lemonade? You didn't get supper. Are you hungry?"

"Nee. Nor thirsty."

Mother sat back down.

"Just tell me what happened. *Sei so gut.*"

"Like she said, her parents had been neighbors with Mammi and

Daadi. We knew them well enough to wave and say hi and ask about their health. Heather was younger, but we chatted when our visits coincided. She asked me a lot of questions about being Plain." Mother smoothed her wrinkled apron. Her restless fingers plucked at some thread or stain Abigail couldn't see. "Time passed. Your daed and I married, but no bopli came along. We were beginning to wonder if Gott had decided against kinner for us.

"One afternoon Heather showed up at our door. She was in a family way. She was sixteen years old. We had been married almost two years, and we had no bopli. Heather's parents wanted her to put the bopli up for adoption. They wanted her to go to college and get a good job before she got married and started a family. Her mudder kept saying Amish are gut people. They're gut parents. That I was a gut person.

"Your daed and I saw a young *maed* in need. We weren't sure if or when we would have our own. It was in Gott's hands. We knew that. We prayed. We talked late into the night. We went to see the bishop. He said to pray the will of Gott be done, so we did.

"The minute Heather's mudder handed you to me and I saw your wrinkled red face and crooked nose, I knew."

"Knew what?"

She stood and came to stand in front of Abigail. Her eyes, a shade of blue not so different from Abigail's, were wet with tears. "That we'd made the right decision. You were mine, and I would never give you up. Ever."

"People say Jane and I could be twins."

"When you were born we knew we'd have another baby. Jane came along eleven months later, but we never regretted our decision. Not for a second."

"Until now."

"We're not the ones regretting it now." Mother wrapped her in a quick, hard hug. "Not ever."

She whispered those last two words in Abigail's ear, let go, and headed toward the stairs. "It's bedtime. Tomorrow's another day."

Chapter 5

A whoop greeted Owen when he strode through the door of Miller & Kurtz Engineered Structures. Rob Miller, Owen's father, Lee, Denny Christner, and Alma Knapp, the receptionist, all grinned at him from their spots around the spartan office like a bunch of goobers caught loafing. Since Rob and Father owned the place, they really couldn't be accused of loafing. They only came into the company's building—which consisted of their two offices, a storage room, and the front lobby—for meetings.

Lunch pail in one hand, Owen bowed with a flourish. "If I had known gracing you folks with my presence would please you so much, I'd have knocked off for lunch earlier."

"I just hung up from talking with the guy from St. John who called last week wanting a quote on a horse barn." Father pushed away from the faux-granite countertop and mimicked Owen's bow. "He was calling to say he'll be up this afternoon to sign the paperwork. He wants us to start by the end of the week—or sooner."

"Gut news, indeed." Depending on the size and model the customer chose, this could be a forty-thousand-dollar job. The company built post-frame commercial buildings with metal roofs and siding, as well as traditional frame residences. This spring they had more work than they could handle—which was good because winter meant slim pickings. "I stopped by the Cotters' property. There were some downed limbs but no serious damage from the storm. I think we can still finish by Thursday, Friday at the latest."

"The other crew should finish the barn in Lyons about the same time. It didn't even rain there. It'll take both crews to do this job on the timeline he's wanting." Rob spun around in the office chair on wheels usually occupied by clients waiting to see him. The chair squeaked under his girth. He hoisted himself to his feet. "In the meantime I'm headed home for lunch. I'll be back before Mr. Nelson gets here. Alma, after you take your lunch break, please start the paperwork."

"Yes, sir." Alma tapped the monitor on the desk in front of her. "Already on it."

Owen waited for Rob to close the door behind him before he high-fived Denny, his best friend since their school days, and then Lee. "We'll be mighty busy for the next couple of months."

"That's gut. A steady paycheck is a gut thing." Father threw his two cents in before Denny could answer. "Especially for a man who's about to tie the knot."

"Tie the knot?" It took a second for his father's words to line up with Denny's sheepish grin and red face. Owen pointed at him. "You did it? You asked Emily to be your *fraa*?"

"I did. We talked to Bishop Bryan night before last." Denny plucked a white card from a pile on the counter. "Our banns will be published on Sunday. Here's a save-the-date card. Emily couldn't wait to get started."

"I already have one," Father objected. "Save those for your family in Jamesport and Garnett."

"True, but I want Owen to see it with his own two eyes. Otherwise he might not believe it." Denny waved it in Owen's face. "You'll be the last one of our bunch still single. Time for you to get busy, my friend."

"*Jah*, time to get busy, Bruder," Lee chimed in. He leaned closer to a box fan sitting on top of the counter. Sweat made a ring around his shirt's collar and stained his underarms, and the hottest part of the day hadn't even arrived yet. "You're running out of options."

Two weeks. Owen accepted Denny's offering and studied Emily's neat penmanship. She was the same age as Abigail. They'd all been in school together. Her voice had been the high, sweet one at the singings. Denny had been courting her for more than a year. "I'm happy for you. I'm sure my time will come, Gott willing, and in His time."

"You'd better pick up your feet. There aren't many choices left." Lee liked to spout off. "You-know-who is clumsy and not much of a cook, but she could still grow out of it."

Lee's halfhearted attempt to honor Owen's privacy didn't earn him any points. "It takes more than cooking to make a marriage work."

Father didn't seem to be paying attention to Lee's chiding. He moved toward the door to the back room that served double duty as storage and a break room. "I'll be in the back, Alma, if anyone needs me."

She murmured acknowledgment but kept on working.

"We're going to eat at the picnic table outside." Denny held up his black metal lunch box. "Are you coming?"

"I want to talk to Daed first. I'll catch up."

Talking and joshing the way young guys do, the two sped out the door. Owen paused by Alma's desk. "Alma, do you need anything? Have you had lunch?"

She shook her head and lifted her hand to shake her index finger, then went back to typing.

In the break room his father had both hands around a monster-size tuna salad sandwich. He looked up midbite. His eyebrows rose. He chewed and swallowed. "I figured you would go outside and eat with the boys. I prefer a few minutes of quiet."

His way of letting Owen know he wasn't in the mood for conversation. He rarely was, but opportunities to find him alone at home were nonexistent. "I wanted to pick your brain about something. I promise to make it quick."

Father eyed his sandwich. "Is it going to give me indigestion?"

"Nee. I was talking to Marty at the feedstore the other day—"

"There's your first mistake."

Marty was a big talker, but he always knew a little bit about a lot of things. He talked to all the farmers in the area. "Marty says sunflower seed prices are rising again this year. Growers in this part of the state are going to increase their acreage by sixty-two percent. They had a lot of snow in the Dakotas, so supply is down and prices are up."

"I think I know where you're going with this, *Suh*, and I don't see it." Father balled up the wax paper Claire had wrapped his pickles in and tossed it in the trash can near the table. "We've always planted milo, alfalfa, and corn. Prices are dropping now, but they'll come up. We don't have enough acreage for a big cash crop. Besides, the sunflowers grown in this region are for birdseed and oil. They don't bring the price that the confectionary varieties do."

Owen tugged a pamphlet from his lunch box. "Marty went to a meeting the Kansas Sunflower Commission had in Salina. The representative said they're a good rotation crop and they're drought tolerant. They have deep roots. He gave me a copy of the pamphlet they handed out."

"What's this really about?" Father ignored the papers. Instead he took a long swallow from a can of lemonade, set it down, and went back to his sandwich. "Your onkel Wayne has already planted the corn and cut the first round of hay."

"You've talked about selling the acreage to Onkel Wayne. I'd like to see us keep it." The pamphlet called sunflowers a high-value crop. A company in Hutchinson cleaned and packaged several million tons of Kansas-grown sunflower seeds each year. Mostly for birdseed, more when it snowed. "Sunflowers can be a cash crop for us."

"That doesn't make any sense." Daed hid a burp behind his big hand. How could he and Owen be so alike on the outside and so different on the inside? "We need to focus on our business here. It's enough work to keep us all busy and keep food on the table. Farming doesn't pay anymore—not for small farms."

"Four hundred acres isn't small."

"Compared to two thousand acres, it is. I thought you liked working with your bruder and me and Denny. It's honest, decent work. A job you can start a family on."

"I've been saving my money. I want to have my own house and my own plot of land to reap and sow on."

"That's a gut, honorable goal."

"What I'm trying to say is that at a certain point, I might not continue to work for you."

"As your younger brieder finish school, they'll join the business. You need only be patient."

Daed worked hard and took care of the whole family. He didn't need a naysayer making life more difficult. "Or we could keep the farm and I could farm it while you, Lee, Eli, and Micah can eventually work here. If one of them is interested in farming, he could help me out. Then we'd continue to have two sources of income."

"You've given this a lot of thought." Father patted his mouth with a paper napkin. The lines around his blue eyes deepened. "We're spread too thin. Farming takes every ounce of determination and energy to turn a profit. Building engineered structures is a more stable way to earn a living these days."

Still, he pulled the pamphlet toward him. "I don't have my head in the sand, Suh. I've heard talk about these so-called green crops. They draw butterflies and birds. They take toxins out of the air—"

"They do. Plus they don't need a lot of rain—"

"A lot of weeds grow in the fields, and they draw insects in addition to those butterflies. Both affect the yield. Plus there's a risk for combine fires during harvests. I read about three of them during last year's harvest because of the high oil content."

"If we know that going in, we can adjust for it."

"I'm not inclined in that direction. I'll allow that sunflowers are right pretty. There's a reason they're the state flower. That's why the sunflower farmers have all those Englisch people showing up to take pictures of themselves in the fields. We don't need that either." The finality in his tone was unmistakable. Father snapped his lunch box closed, flipped down the latches, and stood. "Wayne will want to stick to what he knows. We'll see how the milo does this fall. If yields and prices are down again, I'll likely sell. Wayne's been more than patient. Time to give him the acreage he needs to grow winter wheat."

"It still won't be enough."

"You need to think about getting yourself a fraa and starting a family in that house and plot of land you're talking about." Father tucked the box on the shelf in the refrigerator squeezed in next to a soda machine. "You know as well as I do that working here is a better option for a man with a family."

"Sometimes things don't work out like we plan. As you know."

Father paused at the table, a curiously diffident look on his face. He put both hands on the back of the chair and leaned in. "It's not my place to ask, so I won't. All I'm saying is don't wait too long."

"I won't." Owen bit the inside of his cheek to keep from saying more. The time had to be right for a man and a woman to join in marriage. Forever vows demanded that. It wasn't his place to ask about his father's visits to the Wagner farm either. Were Dad and Mary approaching that moment? "You shouldn't either."

"What's that supposed to mean?"

"Nothing."

His father's face turned a peculiar shade of red. "I've always done the best I can for you kinner. A man without a fraa does that."

"I didn't say anything different." This conversation had gone off the rails. Father had given them everything they needed in food and clothing on their backs. Some things only a mother could provide. They both knew that. "I miss Mudder, though. We never even talk about her anymore."

"There's nothing to talk about. Your mudder's days were numbered different from mine or yours. You know that."

He did. Owen had been told this fact enough times.

"And we have to keep living. We have to do what's best for us."

Did Mary Wagner figure into that equation? "I know that too."

"That includes working here, earning a keep, and helping the family." His father let go of the chair and moved toward the door. "Both our own and our *Gmay*."

Faith, family, community—in that order. Bowing to the greater good. Owen rose and followed his father into the reception area. "Understood."

"Do you dislike working here so much?"

He didn't dislike it. The smell of dirt and rain, the sound of the tractor, the sight of green plants sprouting, the taste of homegrown corn on the cob—those were the sensations that called to him every day. "Nee. I just like farming more."

"When you finish eating, get back to the Cotters' place. You should be ready to finish the roof later today. We need to wrap up that project."

"Will do. We will." Conversation over.

Owen left his father in the reception area, peering over Alma's shoulder as she proofread the horse barn contract. He slipped out the front door. Lee and Denny were tossing bits of bologna to a stray dog who'd taken up residence on the property. Owen slid onto the picnic table bench and opened his lunch box.

"So what'd he say?" Lee tried to steal Owen's cookies. He brushed his brother's hand away. Lee pretended to fuss. "Is he open to suggestions?"

"How did you know what I wanted to talk to him about?"

"I just knew it wasn't your health, Bruder."

"As it happens, he's not open to suggestions." Disappointment sat heavy on Owen's shoulders. He shrugged, trying to loosen up his muscles. "He'll wait to see how our crops do, but he's determined to sell to Onkel Wayne."

"It's not surprising." Denny tossed another chunk of bologna to the dog he'd named Hairy. For obvious reasons. "He likes building things. He has a family to feed."

His family might get bigger. Mary had five children, the oldest fifteen or thereabouts, the youngest two. "I know. It's his farm and this is his business—his and Rob's. It's his call." Owen opened his lunch box and pulled out a sandwich of thick homemade bread slathered with peanut butter and homemade strawberry preserves. All this jawing had given him a powerful hunger. "What I want or need is secondary."

"You could work for Onkel Wayne." Lee snitched a potato chip from Owen's bag. "He can always use help."

"Hey." Owen popped his brother's hand. "You had your lunch."

"I'm a growing boy."

"Right now Daed needs us. He'd have to pay other workers more if he hired outside the family—that includes you, Denny."

Denny inclined his head as if in appreciation.

Owen pulled out his thermos. Kayla's homemade root beer to wet his whistle might wash the disappointment out of his mouth. "I'll get over it."

"Start by counting your blessings that you have a place to work and a paycheck." Denny tossed a fat green grape at Owen, who caught it with one hand while sipping his drink. "Turn your thoughts to finding a fraa."

Good advice but unneeded.

"I think Daed has." Lee never bothered to censure his thoughts. They seemed to simply fly out of his mouth. "Did you see him talking to Mary after church last Sunday?"

So did the rest of the Gmay. "Hush up, *bobblemoul.* That's how rumors get started. She was just serving him sandwiches."

Lee made googly eyes at Owen. "Made with love?"

"So what do you think of the idea?"

"I've eaten Mary's strawberry-rhubarb pie." Lee closed his eyes and pretended to swoon. "She's a way better cook than Kayla and Claire. No one can replace Mudder, but Daed needs a fraa. It's expected."

Indeed it was. Families with both mothers and fathers did better.

"So do you." Denny pointed at Owen and smirked. "Time's a-wastin'."

They seemed to think Owen didn't want to find a wife. He did. He had his heart set on a particular woman. But now that woman had a difficult road to travel before she could think about love and marriage. He had to give her the room to do that. "Just because you're ready to tie the knot doesn't mean I am."

"Speaking of which, I'd like you to be one of my witnesses." His tone suddenly sober, Denny tipped his straw hat in Owen's direction. "If you're willing."

"I would be honored." To stand up with his best friend on the second most important day of his life was indeed an honor. "I'm happy for you."

"It's settled then." His lunch box in one hand, Denny dumped his trash into the trash can a few feet from the table. "Me and Lee better get back to work. Are you coming our way after you finish the Cotter house?"

"Jah."

After they took off in Denny's buggy, Owen patted the open spot on the wooden bench. "Come on, Hairy, I reckon it's just you and me."

Hairy hopped up on the bench and nudged Owen's arm with his nose. Owen shared every other bite of his sandwich with the dog. After a while he went inside, found an old plastic bowl, filled it with water, and set it on the ground next to the table. "If you're like me, you find peanut butter tends to stick in your throat."

Hairy was too busy lapping up the water to respond. Water and slobber dripped from his jowls.

"Hunds are gut company." Owen washed down the last of the sandwich with a slug of the root beer. "I could do worse."

If Abigail's English mother held sway over her daughter, Owen might be in need of company. He ate his cookies, threw away his trash, and strode to his buggy. Hairy followed in his wake. Owen studied the dog's graying jowls. Who did he belong to? He didn't have a collar. His ribs stuck out. "Come on, you might as well get on board."

Hairy didn't hesitate. He barked twice and jumped into the buggy.

Owen's father would think he was a crazy for bringing home another dog. But then, Father already thought he was foolish for wanting to farm sunflowers. What would he think if he knew Owen's heart was set on a clumsy girl who once spilled a whole platter of sandwiches in Father's lap at a school picnic?

Foolish or not, he wasn't giving up on the girl or his dream. Patience was a virtue, and he would need a wagon full of it.

Chapter 6

A picture of the baby's face belonged on a baby food jar. She had the biggest blue eyes, dumpling cheeks, and a cherubic smile. Trying not to stare at her, Abigail settled the enormous tray filled with the English family's order onto a portable table next to booth 7 at the Buggies and Bonnets restaurant.

What kind of mother gives away her own flesh and blood?

The little girl, seated on her mother's lap, was one of three boisterous children under the age of five. The other two were just as adorable.

The little boy, up on his knees so he could fiddle with salt and pepper shakers, was so starving he could eat three hamburgers. Could he have seconds? Could the stuffed animal dinosaur on the tan padded seat next to him have a burger too? The older girl, who already had an orange mustache, wanted to know if she could have seconds of the orange pop. It was *sooo* good and she was *sooo* thirsty. And could they have pie for dessert? With ice cream. Vanilla ice cream, not chocolate. "No, chocolate," the boy argued. The mother, who had the glazed, stoic look of a woman who hadn't had a full night's sleep in years, patiently wiped faces and answered questions while the father studied his phone as if his life depended on it.

Who gives up babies? It had been a week since her biological mother—what a cold turn of phrase for the one who gave birth to her—had shown up at her parents' door. With each passing day it became more of a surreal dream. Except for Mother's worried glances and Father's gruff attempts at conversation at the supper table. They didn't know what to say. Neither did she.

What would happen next? When the other shoe dropped, would it smack Abigail in the head?

"Could you move a little faster?" The English father finally glanced up from his phone with a sour expression. "The food's getting cold. Plus I have work calls to make."

"Yes, sir. Of course."

Focus. Abigail grabbed the dad's heavy plate of a steak sandwich, fries, and a side salad. In her haste to place it in front of him on the burgundy vinyl tablecloth, she knocked over the Mom's tall glass of water—extra ice. Time did that stupid, icky, slow-motion slide as she teetered, trying not to drop the plate but to stop the spill at the same time.

The mother's eyes widened. Her mouth opened. Water soaked the baby, splashed the mother, and trickled onto the linoleum floor below. The children giggled. Dad growled like a wounded bear. Baby shrieked and cried.

"I'm so, so sorry." Abigail landed the steak sandwich safely. She grabbed the children's cloth napkins, abandoned on the table, and tried to sop up the water on the howling baby. "I'm sorry."

"Don't touch my baby." The mother waved her away. "Back away. Please."

"I'll get paper towels."

"Just serve the food. Seriously. There's nothing worse than cold fries." The father's cold glare *was* worse. "And don't expect a tip."

Dana Miller, sister to the owner of the restaurant, materialized with a tube of paper towels. She offered them like the best thing since the discovery of penicillin. "Here, use these, Christie. We're sorry for the inconvenience, Jack. Your meals will be comped. How's that?"

The mother beamed and stuck a pacifier in the baby's mouth. Five free meals. That was a huge savings. The father offered a begrudging nod. The kids crowed. Sweat trickling between her shoulder blades, cheeks burning, Abigail finished serving their meal, shouldered the tray, and trudged toward the kitchen.

As expected Dana followed so closely her presence felt like a too-tight dress. Once safely inside the swinging doors, Abigail turned to face her.

"What is your problem today, Abby?" Dana managed a kind tone, but her frustration blazed across her face in big letters that read YOU'RE DANGEROUSLY CLOSE TO BEING FIRED. Her pudgy face was red. Her fingers punctuated each word, making the bat wings under her arms flap. "That's your third mishap today, and you're only half-way through your shift."

"I don't know. I'm trying, I really am." Abigail blotted her damp face with her apron. The kitchen heat and the competing odors of frying onions, grilled beef, chicken, and fish rolled over her. Her stomach rebelled at the smells. She swallowed back her breakfast of peanut butter toast and coffee. "I promise. I'm sorry, I really am."

"I know you're trying, honey. But we can't afford to keep comping meals to customers you've dumped food or water or whatever on. Or mixed up their orders or forgotten to take them their desserts. Surely you can see that."

"Yes, ma'am, I can. I promise I'll do better."

Kayla slipped through the swinging doors. She stopped behind Dana and waved wildly. Abigail forced her gaze back to her boss.

"I'm sure you'll try. Maybe you try too hard. Maybe that's the problem. I wonder if you'd be better off working in the kitchen or the bakery." Dana made a clicking sound of tongue against teeth. Her round cheeks reddened under the large ovals of her tortoise-shell glasses. "Or even the gift shop. Maybe I should talk to Michael about moving you."

Kayla pointed at the door and pantomimed something, who knew what, her face contorted in an almost-comical frown and lots of head jerks. She might be having a medical episode of some kind. Abigail scowled and shook her head.

"I know you don't want to switch, but maybe it's for the best." Dana had to raise her high voice to be heard over the banging of pots and shouting of orders. "Are you even paying attention to me now? Are you on some kind of medication? Is there something I need to know?"

No. Nothing earth-shattering. Just a monumental shift in the very foundation of Abigail's world. The kitchen wouldn't be so bad. She could make salads or chop vegetables. The bakery staff wouldn't want Abigail back there. Baking wasn't her strong suit. Tough piecrusts, cratered loaves of bread, burned cookies. Practice had not made perfect for this Plain girl. "No, there's nothing you need to know. Yes, I'm listening. No medication. Don't switch me, please. I promise to do better. I'll try harder."

"That's what I'm saying. You're trying too hard. Relax and try to enjoy the work." Dana peered through her glasses at Abigail with such keen intent that she surely saw into the dark void where Abigail's wounded heart struggled to find its rhythm. "If you have boy problems, you'll see. They'll get better. I dated three different boys before I found the love of my life. Got my heart broken three times and I survived. You will too. I promise."

"Thank you." Better she believe puppy love was at the root of Abigail's problems. "I promise. No more spills."

Tut, tut, tutting, Dana stuck both hands on her wide hips. "I hope so. Now skedaddle. You have new customers in booth 8, and you'd better check on the Jacksons. Keep them happy."

"Yes, ma'am."

Dana waddled toward the grills and began critiquing the gravy one of the cooks made. "Not enough salt, too watery . . ." Abigail wiped a trickle of sweat from her forehead and scurried over to Kayla, who danced around like a kid who needed to potty and had been instructed to hold it. "What are you doing? Trying to get me fired?"

"I think you're doing a pretty good job yourself on that front." If Kayla's grin was intended to take the sting from her words, it didn't. She pulled a folded piece of pink paper from the restaurant apron's pocket and held it out. "An Englisch woman stopped me by the register. She asked me if you were working. I said jah, and she asked me to give this to you."

Abigail stuck up both hands, palms up, and backed up a step. "What did she look like?"

"Like the woman you said showed up at your house." Eyes shining, Kayla turned the note over and over in her long fingers. She stuck it to her freckled nose. "It smells like roses. Want me to open it? Shall I read it?"

"Jah. Nee. Nee." Abigail snatched the note from her friend and stuck it in her apron pocket. "Is she still out there?"

"I don't know. You could ask Mariel if she seated her." Kayla pranced like a high-stepping horse. Mariel was the hostess. She didn't have time to ride herd on Abigail's long-lost relatives. "I would've known her anywhere. She does look like you in the face. She has your smile. I mean you have her smile."

"Nee, she doesn't. Nee, I don't." Abigail fingered the note. Curiosity fought with fear. Opening the note was a step in this woman's direction, a step toward a life Abigail never had, a step toward people she wasn't meant to know. Was this what Scripture called temptation? Or was it a door Gott had placed in front of her, expecting her to open it?

How did a country girl like her answer a question like that?

"Don't you want to know what she wants?" Kayla wiggled like an excited puppy. "You need to find out and then send her on her way. She's obviously not going to leave you alone until you do."

"What are you two doing still standing there?" Dana marched toward them. She waved both hands and stomped her feet. "Get to work, wait on people. You're not getting paid to stand around with your jaws flapping."

"Yes, ma'am," they chanted in unison.

Shooting Abigail a meaningful glare, Kayla whipped through the swinging doors. They came at Abigail. She shoved through them and waded into the crowded dining room. Heather Hanson could be anywhere. Abigail swerved toward the drink station, where she grabbed a pitcher of water and headed toward her section. No redhead seated at her three booths or four tables. Heaving a sigh of relief, she replenished water and handed out checks to folks who'd finished their meals.

A couple with a toddler took the booth next to the Jacksons, who mercifully seemed occupied with their food. She turned, intent on picking up a menu and silverware for the newcomers. Heather blocked her path. "There you are. Your friend Kayla said you were working today."

She could've been a teenager in her purple capris and white T-shirt covered with enormous sunflowers. YOU ARE MY SUNSHINE, it read in shiny blue letters. Like the song she'd sung to Abigail moments after her birth. She had to be about thirty-six or thirty-seven. Abigail shook off the thought.

"I *am* working. I can't talk to you right now." *Or ever.*

"Did you read my note?"

"I'm very busy. It's lunchtime."

"I'll take your section." Kayla materialized with a stack of menus in one hand and an order pad in the other. She squeezed closer to Abigail and whispered, "If Dana asks, I'll tell her you had a bathroom emergency."

Heat burned Abigail's cheeks. If she could melt through the floor, she would. "Don't say that," she whispered back.

"Just go." Kayla nudged Abigail with her shoulder. "You're due for a lunch break."

Not during the busiest time of the day. Heather didn't budge. Neither did Kayla. The busybody. Well-meaning busybody.

Abigail dodged Heather and went to the drink station, where she deposited the empty pitcher. Heather hovered nearby.

"I could buy you lunch."

"No." Mother's voice clamored in Abigail's head. There was never an excuse for being rude. "But thank you. We get a free lunch with each shift."

"We could talk in my car."

The idea of getting into a car with this stranger made Abigail's stomach rock. *She's not a serial killer. She's your mother.*

Biological mother.

She meandered toward the gift shop. Too crowded. "Let's just take a walk around the block."

"Perfect." Heather stretched out the first syllable so long she sounded like a cat purring. She smiled.

Abigail had seen that smile before. In the mirror in the Walmart dressing room that time she and Kayla tried on black skinny jeans and tank tops during their *rumspringa*. They had been dumbfounded by the difference clothes could make. Strangers gawked at them in the mirror. On the outside. Their insides never changed.

"A short walk."

Abigail ducked through the double doors into a warm, humid day. Heather stayed close. The chances were good someone Abigail knew would see them. She trotted across the street to Yoder's tiny, so-called plaza that held three picnic tables and a trash can arranged around a massive elm tree. The town elders had installed a white picket fence to make it homier.

"This is perfect." Heather breathed a funny little sigh. "Just you and me. We can talk."

"Talk about what?"

Heather squeezed onto the bench at the first table and patted the seat next to her. Abigail sat on the other side. Heather pulled a small photo album from her purse. She slid it across the table. Abigail slid it back.

"Please, just look at the photos." Heather held it out. "I made it especially for you. See, I bought it at the gift shop a few days ago." She cocked her head toward the restaurant. "There are so many cute things in there. I bought rooster salt and pepper shakers—"

"How long have you been hanging around the restaurant?"

"Just a couple of days. I went back to Abilene the day I came to your house." She fingered a heart-shaped pendant that hung from a gold chain around her neck. "But after having seen you, I couldn't just walk away."

"You did before."

"I know. I know I did." She opened the photo album to the first page, which held four six-by-four color photos. The first one was a boy with carroty orange hair and a swath of freckles across his nose and cheeks. He wore braces and a Garth Brooks concert T-shirt. "This is your brother Brody. He's fourteen."

"So you married my father . . . the man . . . after all."

"I didn't. He came to Abilene after me, but my aunt and uncle kept him from seeing me. I married a man named Dan Hanson a few years later, after I finished high school and earned my nursing degree at Kansas Wesleyan in Salina." She twisted a gold band studded with garnets on her right ring finger. "We're divorced now."

"Then Brody is my half brother."

"Technically, but I don't think of it that way. Brody likes skateboarding, swimming, soccer, and playing video games like *Minecraft*. He can't wait to meet you."

"He knows about me?"

"They all do. I told them a few weeks ago."

Everyone knew before she did. It wasn't right. All these people walking around with this important knowledge—except her—the one who should know. Were they happy to know they had a half sister they'd never even met? It had to be hard for them too.

Abigail pointed at the photo below Brody. Two girls in shorts, tank tops, and flip-flops, poised on their bicycles. "Who are they?"

"Scarlett and Fiona. Your sisters . . . half sisters. Scarlett is the one on the left. She's twelve. Fiona is nine."

Red hair in pigtails, sunburned faces, all skinny arms and legs. They were a little older than Rose and Hope but much skinnier. Not to mention the shorts, tank tops, and painted toenails. "They're cute."

"They're heck on wheels. Both of them. Stubborn as all get-out." Heather laughed. She had a laugh like a teenage girl on her first date, high and silly. "But they're good kids. They're practically raising themselves. I work so much. But they know it's because I have to put food on the table and clothes on their backs."

Idle questions floated from the abyss of emotions turned upside down and inside out. "How long have you been divorced?"

"Four years. Dan is an EMT in Salina. He gets the kids every other weekend and two weeks in the summer. He and his fiancée like it that way. That's where they are now."

She spoke matter-of-factly. Abigail studied the three faces. They had their mother's hair and coloring. Abigail saw nothing of herself in them. Did she look like the man who fathered her? "You wouldn't even know we're related."

"They take after their father. You take after yours. He lives in Abilene. His name is Eric Waters. We never got back together. He stayed with his grandparents and finished high school." Heather flipped through the album to the last page. "Dan never knew I kept these photos. Thank goodness. He would've had a steer."

The first photo revealed a tall, long-legged teenager in blue jeans held up by a belt with a huge silver buckle, a plaid western-style shirt, cowboy boots, and a tan cowboy hat that obscured much of his face. In the second photo, a young Heather sat with the cowboy on the tailgate of an old pickup truck. They mugged for the camera. Heather hoisted a red plastic cup in a toast while Eric stuck two fingers in a *V* behind her head. He had a big, toothy smile.

Abigail touched the hat. "What color are his eyes?"

As if that mattered. Heather patted her hand. Abigail snatched it back.

"His eyes are blue like ours. His hair is blond, but he tans real good. Not like me. His parents farm south of Yoder. He played basketball, did 4-H and FFA. He rodeoed some back in the day, won some big buckles, but cars were his thing more than horses. Now he teaches car repair and such at the technical college in Salina and restores classic cars on the side."

An English father who liked cars so much he made a job out of them. "He didn't want to farm like his dad?"

"No. He goes home now and again to get his horse fix. He keeps the cowboy thing going because women swoon over it." Heather's snort held amusement. "He knows what the ladies like. He always did. He could sell sand to the Saudis. He sure charmed me."

They'd gone through something hard and terrible as teenagers, the same age as Abigail's brother Benny. Benny worked hard, apprenticing with the only blacksmith in the area. He had a trade, and he helped Father on the farm. He also went to singings on Sunday night, hoping to meet his future wife. Could he swerve onto a path that led to this outcome? It seemed unlikely. *But not impossible*, the devil's advocate perched on her shoulder argued. "So you kept in touch with him?"

"Not when I was married, of course. But since my divorce and his divorce, we have a drink sometimes, get a pizza and pitcher of beer at Pizza Hut. We've gone bowling a few times. It took us all these years to put the past behind us. It took him that long to forgive me for giving you away. He used to threaten to come get you, but he didn't have legal standing. His name isn't on your birth certificate. He would've had to prove paternity."

It sounded like her biological parents were dating, picking up that high school romance where it left off. Maybe that's what spurred Heather to seek out the daughter she gave away. "Does he know you're here?"

"He offered to come with me, but I thought it would be too much. He's chomping at the bit to meet you."

Too much. As if showing up like a lightning bolt from the sky on a sunny day wasn't too much. "Doesn't he have his own kids?"

"You are his own kid, but yes, he has two boys, twelve and ten. Kenny and Blake, named for his two favorite singers." Heather tugged a tissue from her purse. She dabbed at her eyes, then her nose. "I know this is hard for you to understand, but we were sixteen, too young to be allowed to make our own decisions. We tried to move on, to get on with our lives after that."

Why dig up the past now? That's what Abigail was. Their past. She closed the album with a definitive snap. She stood. "I need to get back to work."

"Amish folks are known for their forgiveness." Heather held out the album a second time. "Please consider forgiving me. I'd so appreciate it if you would. Take the album. I made it for you."

Heather's words pricked like a big needle, deflating the hurt Abigail was working so hard to sustain. It would be better for everyone involved if she could nurture it, grow it, until she was unable to look this woman in the eye, let alone consider getting to know her and the rest of her family.

Heather's family, not Abigail's family.

She had no choice. Heather had found Abigail's Achilles' heel. She couldn't claim to be Plain and not act like it. Abigail accepted the album. "You're right about the forgiveness. It's wrong for me to hang on to my anger. You're forgiven."

Bishop Bryan Miller said people sometimes had to say the words and then work on meaning them. The process might take time. Better to start right away.

Heather let out a big breath as if she'd been holding it. "Thank you. Does that mean you'll come for a visit?"

"No." Abigail tucked the album close to her chest. "I'm sorry, but I really have to go. Thank you for the gift."

Thank you for creating a rift between the life I had before you rode roughshod on it and the one I'll have now.

She didn't fit in Heather's world. But, truth be told, she didn't fit in this world either.

Abigail trudged back toward the restaurant, Heather's gaze burrowing between her shoulders. At the door Abigail gave in to the impulse and looked back. Heather still sat at the table. She waved.

"Be kind." Mother's voice echoed in Abigail's head. *"Be kind and*

gracious." How could Abigail hear her voice at a time like this? Because real mothers stuck it out, no matter the situation.

She waved and went inside, where she stowed the album in her tiny cubby in the break room and went back to work. By God's grace the rest of the day passed without another mishap and no visits from long-lost relatives. By the time her shift ended, all she could think about was her comfy bed shared with Jane.

Back in the break room Abigail removed her restaurant apron. Something crinkled in the vicinity of the pocket.

The note. Kayla was right. It did smell like roses. With shaking fingers Abigail unfolded it. Heather had neat cursive writing that slanted the way a left-handed writer's often did.

> Dear Abigail,
>
> Ever since I saw you that day at your house, I haven't been able to stop thinking about you. I want you to know I have always loved you. I never stopped loving you. There can't be too much love in the world, can there? This world has enough room for both Lorene and me to love you. You hit the jackpot. Two mothers. I hope you'll learn to see it that way. I'd love to talk to you some more.
>
> Heather aka Mom

She'd added a sentence below it and then scratched it out. It might've been a telephone number. Below it was an address in Abilene—in case Abigail wanted to write her a letter.

Abigail slipped the note into the album.

"Are you crying?" Kayla emerged from a bathroom stall and tossed her apron into the laundry bag next to the row of hooks that held their personal aprons. "Your eyes are red."

Abigail shook her head. "Tired. My feet hurt. My elbows hurt. I can't wait to get home. See you tomorrow."

"Whoa, wait. What did Heather say? What did she want?"

"Not now." The lump in Abigail's throat swelled. "Just not now."

She shoved the album into her canvas bag and lurched out the door before her best friend could protest.

Chapter 7

The blaring of the tractor's horn announced Kayla's imminent arrival. As if Owen wouldn't have heard the tractor's rumble. Hairy popped up from his spot in front of the corral gate and barked. He would make a good guard dog. "Hush. I hear her."

Hairy instantly quieted. He obeyed better than Owen's younger brothers and sisters. Owen waved at Kayla, then resumed watching the mare and her foal frolic in the early evening breeze warmed by a sun sinking toward its nightly rest. The foal's long, spindly legs still wanted to go in all directions. Still she cavorted. She reminded Owen of Abigail. Some folks took longer to grow into their skins than others. The sound of the tractor died. A few seconds later Kayla joined him at the fence.

"You stopped short. Don't you want to drive the tractor into the barn?" He leaned forward and stretched both arms and his shoulders. Finishing the siding on the Cotter house had left his muscles tired and sore, but it was a good tired, bolstered by the satisfaction of knowing Father and Rob were pleased with the big job contract signed earlier in the week. "Daed won't be happy if you leave it outside overnight. We might get a sprinkle or two after dark."

Kayla bent to pat Hairy, whose tongue hung out as he huffed in obvious delight. "Who's this?"

"Hairy. He's new around here."

"Daed won't be happy about him either." Kayla scratched behind Hairy's ears. The dog plopped on the ground, rolled over, and offered his skinny belly for a rub. "Another mouth to feed, he'll say."

"Then he'll feed him ham or pieces of chicken under the table during supper." One thing that never changed in their world was their father's kindness toward those in need—two- or four-legged. "Lee and Denny were already feeding him at the shop. I figured, what's one more mouth? The more the merrier."

"You won't fill up that hole in your heart with animals." Kayla straightened. She nudged Owen with her sharp elbow. "I know you love animals, but *hunde* aren't substitutes for kinner or a fraa."

Sometimes Kayla came up with these nuggets of wisdom others would have to search far and wide for years to find. For a girl who'd been without a mother for a good portion of her growing-up years, she seemed to understand the world in ways that others didn't—certainly not Owen. "I'm not trying to fill up anything. I love animals. I don't like to see them suffer."

"I don't like to see you suffer."

"What makes you think I'm suffering?"

"You think you hide it well, but you don't. Tell Daed you want to farm. He'll understand."

"I did. He doesn't. And he's right. What I want isn't important. You sound like an *Englischer*, spouting if it feels gut, do it. Self-gratification." Owen smacked his fists on the railing. He loosened his fingers and spread them wide. *Easy.* Kayla was simply trying to help. "Have you forgotten the pillars of our faith so soon? Obedience. Humility. Dying to self. *Gelassenheit.* This isn't about what I want but what's best for us all."

"Obedience to a daed is different from obedience to Gott."

"Gott first, family second, community third."

This conversation sounded more like a baptism class than two siblings chatting at the end of a long day of hard but satisfying work. Kayla didn't respond. Owen squatted, grabbed a stick left over from the storm debris, stood, and tossed it toward the open field next to the corral. With a joyous bark Hairy took off after it.

With an exaggerated sigh Kayla put her hands in the air like twin stop signs. "You're right. I don't mean to make it harder for you. The will of Gott be done."

Another creed drilled into Plain children from birth. God had a plan. They only had to wait for it to unfold. *Forgive me for my impatience. For my hubris of thinking I know what I need better than You do. Thank You for Daed, the shop, the kinner, for all You have given me.*

"How was your day?" Owen strove for a lighter tone as he took the stick from a jubilant Hairy. The dog's tail wagged so hard it made a *whap, whap* sound. "Gut hund, gut hund. Another go at it? Go get it." He tossed the stick.

Hairy's mad dash across the field lacked grace but made up for it with a puppy's exuberance. "Anything interesting happen at Buggies and Bonnets?"

Kayla's nose wrinkled like she smelled something bad. "I'd better get inside and help the *maede* get supper on the table." Usually Kayla regaled anyone who would listen with stories about her day at work. Not today.

"I'll stow the tractor for you."

"Danki." She raised her hand to shelter her eyes from the sun. "I think Daed is coming up the drive. You should talk to him again."

"Nee. Not at the end of a long day. He'll be tired." And short of patience, although he never raised his voice or spoke sharply. "He deserves a gut supper and a quiet evening with his newspapers."

"I'm thinking he'll be stepping out later, after we go to bed."

Like teenagers on their rumspringa. Only Mary had children. She couldn't gallivant across the countryside. Maybe they sat on the front porch, drinking lemonade and holding hands.

A painful tremor ran through Owen. Mudder used to say he had far too great an imagination. Monsters under the bed, ghosts in the rafters, imaginary friends at the breakfast table. Fortunately, he'd outgrown that. No one wanted to imagine his father with a woman other than his mother. Or even his mother.

Kayla skipped—literally, something no other girl her age would do—toward the house. She twirled as if dancing around a May pole. Also something Plain girls didn't do. "You asked what happened at the restaurant today. Abigail's birth mother happened. She showed up."

"What did she want?" One foot on the tractor's step, Owen stopped, his other foot dangled over the edge. "Surely Abigail sent her packing."

Again.

Kayla's breathless response floated above the sound of Father's buggy approaching. "Nee. She gave Abigail a photo album of her other family. She invited her to go to Abilene to meet them."

"So is she going?"

"I don't think she's decided, but she left the restaurant like her dress was on fire. You should go find out. Before it's too late."

"Too late for what?"

"Don't be a *dummkopp*." Kayla stopped twirling. She planted her feet and stuck her hands on her hips. "Or a coward."

"Hey!"

"I'm just saying. Maybe she knows you like her. Maybe she knows you want to help her through this hard time. Maybe she knows you'll wait for her to figure it out." Kayla shook her head and rolled her eyes.

"Or maybe she doesn't know any of that because you haven't talked to her since the storm."

His sister was a pest, a busybody, and way too big for her apron. "What makes you think Abigail wants me to wait around for her?"

Kayla whirled and waltzed toward the house.

"Kayla?"

She disappeared through the door.

Meddler. Nosy. Matchmaker.

All the words that came to mind didn't encompass Owen's irritation—at himself. Kayla was right. Not that he would ever tell her that. "Fine," he muttered as he fired up the tractor. "I'll go."

After supper he would go to the Bontrager house. All he had to lose was his pride, and that would be no loss.

Chapter 8

Privacy simply couldn't be had in a house filled with ten people. Which was why Abigail had chosen to make a pit stop after she left the restaurant. In fact, finding a place to be alone in small towns like Yoder and Haven presented a challenge. Finally she pulled the tractor off the road near the only pond on her father's property. The early evening sun, still working its way down to its resting place, shone in her eyes, but a nice breeze made up for its heat.

Abigail stared at the album on the dashboard. It had been a foreboding presence the entire drive from Yoder, through Haven, to the farm. "Don't be *narrisch*," she scolded herself.

A startled blue jay answered with a shriek from a nearby sycamore tree. Leaves rustled in the breeze. Crickets chattered. Even here she had an audience.

She sighed and picked up the album and, without further ado, opened it. More photos of her half siblings. Scarlett played softball. Fiona danced. One picture showed her in a ballerina outfit, her arms overhead in a half circle. In the other one she wore black tights, a leotard, and bright red lipstick. What kind of dance was that? They both posed for the pictures as if they were used to being the center of attention. Sometimes they stuck out their tongues; other times they had their arms up in the air in a celebratory high five.

Brody liked his skateboard, but most of the photos showed him in the house in front of a huge TV screen. He usually appeared peeved, as if he'd been interrupted.

None of them looked like her with their curly carrottops, freckles, and fair complexions. Abigail held the photos up close, one by one, as if she could discern the children's essences from a still photo. She'd never had her own photo taken. Would she be sullen like Brody or perpetually happy-go-lucky like his sisters?

The later pages were reserved for pictures of Heather. None included the man who had fathered her other three children. Brightly colored clothes, sporty cars, skimpy swimsuits. Pink polish on fingernails and toes that matched her lipstick. She was all bright and light.

So different from Mother in her simple dark blues, greens, and browns. Dresses that covered everything. By choice, of course. Plain people chose not to draw attention to themselves. Always turned away from the adulation of others. Turned toward Jesus. How would Mother have appeared in English clothes? Had she ever tried them on the way Abigail and Kayla had during their rumspringa? Abigail never asked.

Finally she used the tip of her index finger to turn to that last page. The last photo, displayed alone. She slipped it from its plastic holder and held it close. "So you're my father."

Not her daed. No *Deutsch* words described this man in his cowboy hat and mammoth silver buckle. He could have modeled for covers of the western romances Jane liked to read. His smile seemed vaguely familiar. His eyes were hidden by his hat, as was his hair. He had a long nose, high cheekbones, and a strong jaw.

None of which told her who he was. He and Heather crossed paths for a brief time in those wonderful, terrible teenage years when feelings that started as a trickle turned into a hurricane at the lightest touch, the softest breath on tender skin, the chance crossing of glances. Now, older, the world shrunk and easier to wear, they had reconnected. Edges were smoother, more worn, but life was no easier.

Abigail stuck the photo back into its slot. She smoothed her fingers over the plastic. "I don't know you. I can't know you from a piece of film developed and printed years ago."

Did she want to know him? She knew everything about Father. He liked his eggs scrambled in bacon grease, three pieces of bacon on the side, two pieces of toast for breakfast. His coffee strong, black, and scalding hot. He believed in Jesus, his Lord and Savior. He didn't cotton to folks who didn't, but he let them go their own way. He didn't allow back talk or rudeness to others.

He played softball better than men half his age. He was the best tickler this side of the Mississippi. Until a few weeks ago, Abigail had thought him the most honest man alive.

Were there other secrets? What else weren't Mother and Father telling Abigail or the rest of their children?

What were her biological parents truly like? Or her adoptive parents? So strange to think of them like that. It seemed no more probable than the revelation that the world was indeed flat. The pictures only led to more questions. Heather likely knew this would be the case. She offered Abigail a tantalizing glimpse of could-have-beens. The real question was whether Abigail wanted to know more.

The answer couldn't be found in this album.

Abigail laid it back on the dash and headed home. She had two choices. Edge her way around this enormous crater in the road and dedicate herself to moving on as if the hole had been filled or never happened at all. Or explore the world of might-have-been in Abilene with Heather and her other family. The one Heather would argue was Abigail's "real" family.

Which would it be? Abigail needed time to figure that out.

The dirt road curved and opened up. Bishop Bryan Miller stood on the front porch with Samuel Shrock, the deacon, talking to Father.

All three looked up. Father waved. Abigail pulled in next to Bryan's buggy. No one could miss the distinctly relieved expression on her father's face.

Time, apparently, was in short supply.

Chapter 9

Mealtime was no time for deep discussions. Glad for her father's oft-stated rule, Abigail placed a saucer bearing a generous wedge of chocolate cream pie in front of Bryan while Jane did the same for Samuel. Mother had already disappeared into the kitchen with the younger girls. The conversation over fried chicken, mashed potatoes, gravy, green beans, and homemade sliced sourdough bread had wound its way through the storm damage, alfalfa cutting, prospects for a good crop of milo, to the summer events, such as the Fourth of July celebration and Yoder's Heritage Day. No one had asked about her day. Grown men didn't tend to think much about what a waitress did all day. Or women who laundered clothes, baked, cleaned, gardened, and put supper on the table. The girls were out of school now, so Mother had plenty of help taking care of the homestead.

Not that she needed much help.

"Abigail, sit down." Father motioned toward the chair across from the bishop. "Bryan and Samuel want to talk with us for a few minutes."

"I was just going to help with the dishes."

The muscle in Father's jaw twitched. Abigail slid into the chair. Bread crumbs dotted the pine table. She itched to wipe it down.

Bryan took a big bite of pie, closed his eyes for a second, chewing, swallowed, then smiled. "Your fraa does make a fine pie, Freeman."

"Jah. No complaints here." Father leaned back and patted his paunch. "I may partake a little too much."

How could they talk about pie while her life hung in the balance? Abigail swept the crumbs to the edge of the table. She would dispose of them later.

"Your daed spoke to Samuel and me about this situation with the Englisch woman."

Now Abigail was a "situation." She bit the inside of her lip to keep from retorting, *"You mean my birth mother?"* Her job here was to listen unless asked a direct question. She peeked at Father. His gaze was fastened on Bryan, as if he could somehow fix her "situation."

"I wasn't the bishop, obviously, when this decision was made." Bryan used his fist to tap his chest and belched. He seemed unaware of the crumbs nestled in his dark-brown beard. "So I didn't know about it until your daed came to me today."

No matter. Many people knew. Old Bishop Harold. Everyone who saw Lorene and Freeman with a baby when she'd never been in a family way. One day a baby simply appeared in her arms at church and had to be explained.

Samuel pushed his plate of half-eaten pie aside and put his elbows on the table so he could clasp his hands together. He had the same gentle countenance he had during baptism lessons. He'd always been so kind, so earnest in his explanations of the Articles of Confession. "I vaguely remember my parents talking about it. They thought it was a kind thing for your eldre to do. It was a blessing for them and for you."

"Being Plain isn't a matter of birth." Bryan jumped back in. "You know that a person chooses his Plain faith when he's baptized. You are Plain by your upbringing and by the vows you took when you chose baptism. This woman has no hold on you."

"Heather doesn't agree with that way of thinking." Abigail cringed inwardly. *Don't dig yourself a hole.* "She just wants me to know I have another family."

"*We* are your family." Father gritted his teeth. The cords in his neck bulged. He massaged them with both hands. "For twenty years we have loved you and raised you as our dochder. Not as a choice or an adopted *kind*, but as ours. That woman chose to give you to us. She can't take you back."

"I know." Seeing the hurt suffuse in his red face and neck made Abigail's heart contract in painful commiseration. "*Es dutt mer*, Daed."

Being sorry wasn't enough. He lifted his empty coffee cup to his lips, then lowered it.

Mother trotted into the great room carrying a pot of coffee. "*Mann*, all is well?" She poured more into Father's mug. Her gaze strayed to Abigail. It read, *Tread carefully.* "More pie?"

"Nee." Father drew the mug close and blew on the liquid. His blue eyes seemed to swallow her up. "We're fine. Sit with us."

Mother poured more coffee for the other men. Then she slipped onto the bench so close to Abigail she could smell her mother's scent of dish soap and hard work. Now there were four of them and one of Abigail. They wanted what was best for her. No doubt whatsoever. Still, their words drained away into oblivion. A blathering in her ears that made no sense. She curled her fingers around her apron's hem and waited until she could escape.

After a minute words registered. "We believe it is best if you don't see this Heather Hanson again."

Abigail focused on Bryan's lips. What was he saying? "Your father will write her a letter, telling her to stay away. If she comes around, simply tell her you don't want to see her. This is a case of being too close to the ways of the world."

Ways of the world. Having a child out of wedlock. Giving her up.

Marrying another man. Divorcing. Yes, that was apparent. But how could they cast the first stone? Everyone was a sinner and fell short of the glory of God. Wasn't that what Scripture told them?

"Abigail?" Mother touched her hand. "Do you understand what Bryan is saying?"

"What would happen if I did want to see her or spend time with her family?"

Mother's face blanched. Her hand tightened on Abigail's.

"It depends." Bryan's lips thinned. "If you decided to live among them or adopt their way of dressing or marry an Englischer, that would result in *meidung*. I'm sure you realize that."

Shunning. No longer able to worship, sit down to a meal, or play games with her brothers and sisters. Her true parents. Abigail swallowed hard against the growing lump in her throat. Her chest hurt. Her whole body ached.

"You wouldn't do that, Dochder, would you?" Mother let go of Abigail's hand. Instead she slid her arm around Abigail's shoulders and squeezed. "You're an obedient believer, aren't you?"

She always had been. But she'd never been confronted by a new, alien identity either.

"I need to think." Abigail leaned closer to Mother. Her heat warmed Abigail's cold heart. "I would never deny my vows. But I can't imagine having this door open only to close it again before I know what's on the other side. What harm does it do to know where I came from?"

No one spoke for a few moments.

Sparrows chirped outside the open windows. The girls sang "This Little Light of Mine" while they washed dishes. His legs moving as if he chased rabbits through a meadow, Doolittle woofed in his sleep on the rug by the empty fireplace.

Her posture rigid, Mother rose and collected the pie plates. She left the room as if she'd said all she could say. Heard all she needed to hear.

"Gott knows what's on the other side of that door." At last Samuel offered his opinion. His voice was gruff but kind. "Pray that His will be done, not yours, not ours. His. I don't believe He brought you this far as a Plain child to have you stumble from the path now. Everything He does is for our gut. Prayer is what we need now."

"Prayer and a load of common sense." Bryan tapped on the table with his index finger, a sharp *rat-ta-tat-tat*. "Ask yourself what purpose it will serve to upset a blessed, gut way of life because a selfish woman can't live with a decision she made twenty years ago."

None. It would serve none. But this wasn't about common sense. This was a matter of the heart.

Abigail studied the grooves in the pine table made thirty years earlier by her grandpa. She couldn't risk peeking at Father. They would see what was in her heart and be hurt by it. "In fairness to my . . . to Heather, it wasn't a decision she willingly made. I don't want to upset anything. I just want to talk to her, to know her a little more."

"If you go down that path, you may find it much harder than you think to find your way back. Weigh the consequences before you decide to ignore your elders' recommendation. Now, you must have chores to do before you turn in for the night." Bryan jerked his head toward the door. "I hear your schwesdchdre in the kitchen working. It sounds like they enjoy their work very much."

Whether intended or not, it sounded like a criticism. *"Gut nacht."* Abigail raised her head high and marched into the kitchen.

Jane, Rose, and Hope spun around and chorused, "What did they say? What did they want?"

"Where's Mudder?"

"She put the coffeepot on the counter and went outside without saying a word." Her eyes wide, Rose spread her hands in the air. "I asked her what happened, but she didn't answer."

"They came to tell me what to do." Or not do. "They have gut intentions. Rose, Hope, can you finish on your own?"

Disappointment acute in their faces, one round, the other thin, they nodded. They did everything as a unit.

"Jane, I need to show you something."

Outside Abigail surveyed the yard. No sign of Mother. She led her sister to the tractor. Jane climbed in and took a seat while Abigail balanced on the steps. She handed the album to her sister and then turned on the flashlight in the gathering dusk.

Jane turned the pages slowly, pausing to stare at each photo. "The English woman gave this to you?"

"Jah. I don't know what to think. Bryan and Samuel and Mudder and Daed want me to forget I ever met her. To not see her." Abigail bit the inside of her lip, concentrating on the small pain to keep from sobbing. "I don't think I can."

"I can see why." Jane sounded almost wistful. Her forehead wrinkled. "I don't see how you can either. You have a bruder and schwesdchdre you don't even know. How strange is that?"

"Bryan's afraid they'll lead me astray. Is my faith so small that I would allow that to happen? Maybe this is Gott's way of testing it?"

"And this man?" Jane pointed to Eric Waters.

"My biological daed."

"You have a cowboy daed." She slid her finger across Eric's oversized cowboy hat. Jane loved cowboy stories. She read westerns and mail-order bride novels in her spare moments. "It's so strange to think there's this other family."

"It's strange and rare, but it's also painful for Mudder and Daed. I don't want to hurt them. I didn't create this situation, though. They did."

"By not telling you."

"By letting Heather tell me first."

Jane closed the album. She rubbed her fingers over the glossy flowered cover. "You're my big schweschder. Promise me you always will be."

"I promise."

"Go meet these people, if you must. Tell Mudder and Daed that you are only going for a visit. You have no plan to adopt the Englisch ways. Promise you'll come back."

"I'm not sure I'm ready to go there. Maybe it's enough just to talk to Heather."

Jane laid the album on the tractor's dash and brushed her hands together. "I hope it's enough, but if it's not, go. You're the Plainest person I know. Mudder and Daed know that."

Jane was right, but nothing had ever happened in Abigail's life to shake her faith. Until now. "I hope they do. The elders spoke of meidung."

"They are afraid for you. They care for you."

The reminder helped.

Lights shone in the distance, moving toward them. Abigail back-stepped from the tractor so Jane could get down. "Someone's coming."

Jane chuckled. "I think it's for you. You're popular, Schweschder." She hugged Abigail's neck and left her standing in the drive.

Indeed it was. Owen approached. A friendly face, a man after her own heart. Just the medicine she needed after the meeting with Bryan and the others. He was a good listener. He'd had his own cross to bear in life. He would understand.

She had to find her way on her own, but it helped to know Owen would be there for her.

Chapter 10

Darkness had fallen. Which made it hard for Owen to gauge Abigail's demeanor. He hazarded a glance at her. His plan to take her for a ride and help her forget the English woman who turned her quiet, peaceful world inside out didn't seem to be working. She held herself tight on the buggy seat, her hands clasped in her lap, her gaze pinned to something in the murky dusk beyond the buggy's headlights.

Bryan Miller's horse and buggy had been parked in front of the house. Maybe she was worn out from talking to him. Maybe Owen had waited too long, given her too much time to adjust to her new world. Kayla said yes. Lee said no. Kayla knew more about this stuff than their little brother. 'Course that didn't keep him from having an opinion.

Owen had tried small talk, the new foal's progress, the new house they'd finished, the replanting of the tomatoes and strawberries after the storm wrecked the vegetable garden, all the work the girls had put in replacing the flower garden. Her responses came quickly, softly, but she contributed nothing of her own to the conversation. Owen wasn't the best talker. One of the reasons he was still a single man at twenty-two and living at home.

That and Father needed Owen's help raising the children. He

needed another adult with whom he could make conversation at the end of the day.

Maybe it was best to get the elephant in the buggy out in the open. "Kayla says your biological mother showed up at the restaurant today." Owen tugged on the reins. Cupcake wanted to forge ahead this evening. Maybe she sensed the uneasiness that hung between the two humans who sat behind her. "Kayla says she seems to be stalking you."

"That's an exaggeration. Did Kayla tell you she gave me a picture of my father—my biological father?" Abigail drew out the two syllables *fa-ther*, as if tasting them for the first time. "His name is Eric Waters. He's a cowboy, but he restores classic cars. He loves cars more than horses."

"That must've been almost as hard as learning you have an English mother." The words bounced around in his head before he said them. Finding just the right ones might be the difference between a budding courtship and a courtship shut down before it even started. "Does he want to know you too?"

"She says he was mad about her giving me away. They both married other people." Abigail's voice still had that peculiar monotone so different from her normal cheery chatter. "Now they're both divorced, so they drink beer and eat pizza together. And go bowling."

This revelation didn't come as a big surprise. The English lived in a different world. Plain folks like Owen and Abigail weren't to judge, but there was a reason they adhered to Romans 12:2. "And be not conformed to this world: but be ye transformed by the renewing of your mind, that ye may prove what is that good, and acceptable, and perfect, will of God."

He'd heard that verse in sermons on Sunday from the time he was old enough to sit on his mother's lap and eat the crackers she pulled from her canvas bag.

"She gave me pictures of my half brother and two half sisters. She says they like the idea of having a big schweschder."

Abigail had experience in that department with her seven younger siblings, but the English world was a far different place. Owen directed Cupcake to turn left onto the dirt road that would take them to the one small pond on the Bontragers' property. This time of day the bullfrogs sang duets while the crickets played backup music. Maybe it would soothe Abigail and help her to relax. "You have plenty of brieder and schwesdchdre here."

Abigail slumped against the seat as if the air had suddenly gone out of her. "That's what I told her. But I can't stop thinking about them. About her. She wants to know me. She wants them to know me. Bryan and my eldre don't want me to see her anymore. They're afraid she'll lead me away from my faith."

Bryan's job was to guide them on the path of faithfulness. His concern was understandable. "She's narrisch. She can't just turn up here and expect you to be her dochder after all these years."

"I know." Abigail chewed a fingernail for a few seconds, then drew her arms around her middle, her hands hidden under them. "But then I had a thought. What if that's the reason I'm so clumsy and awkward? Maybe this is why I find baking so hard. And why I really don't like to sew. I'd rather go hunting or fishing or hiking any day." The words rushed out in a huge swoosh as if she'd been holding them in until the dam broke and she could no longer control them.

"Whoa, whoa." Owen halted the buggy at the pond's edge with an abrupt tug on the reins that made Cupcake toss her head and whinny. "Sorry, girl. Abigail, you're not clumsy and awkward, and your apple pie is . . . pretty gut."

"Lying is a sin."

Point well taken. Tripping over her own feet on the way to the blackboard at school had resulted in two black eyes when she hit her face on a desk. Falling out of a tree led to a broken wrist. Dumping a cup of hot coffee in the bishop's lap had sent him scrambling, which caused Abigail to drop the mug and break it. The first time Owen tried one of her peanut butter cookies, he almost broke a tooth. But she'd taken down the first deer during hunting season more than one year. Folks laughed about Abigail's trials and tribulations. Not in a mean way. More in awe and wonder that she survived unmaimed.

That didn't make her English.

The buggy's headlights illuminated weeds and cattails blowing in a humid night breeze. Mosquitoes buzzed Owen's face. Cupcake's tail slapped away flies. Owen chose his words like a man edging along a narrow cliff with a deep canyon below. "What I mean is, those were growing pains. Some people have more than others. Kayla says you're a gut waitress now. You almost never spill anything. You're a cheerful, hard worker. You do your best with baking and sewing. You embraced your baptismal vows. You are Plain."

"Who are you trying to convince? Yourself or me?"

Her tart tone stung. The muscles in Owen's shoulders tightened. *It's not her fault. She's upset.* "No one. I've known you forever. I'm telling you what I see from my spot in the world."

"I'm sorry." She laughed a high, nervous laugh. "I'm so mixed up I don't know which direction is north. Up is down."

"You are who you are. That hasn't changed." This was the truth. His heart said so. Owen wasn't a scientist or a fancy psychologist with degrees in how children were changed by who their parents were and where they lived, but he knew what he saw. "Gott has a plan for you. You grew up with Plain parents. Don't you think that's what He intended for you to be? Otherwise, why let it happen?"

"Gott can bring gut from all things." She murmured the words as if talking to herself. "All things."

"That's right. That's what Scripture tells us."

"Jane says I'm as Plain as anybody she knows. That my faith is as strong. She doesn't see how it's been shaken by this secret. It must not have been so very strong after all."

A sea of platitudes threatened to drown Owen. "These trials hone our faith. A faith not tested would be a weak faith."

Abigail's hand slid across the buggy seat until it reached the halfway point. Owen stared at it, then at her. If only the darkness didn't obscure her expression. She wanted something from him. She needed something from him. The realization sent a strange but nice warmth bubbling up in him.

He slid his hand over hers. She didn't withdraw. He rubbed his hands over hers to warm them. The heat wound its way through him instead. She was warm, as warm as sunshine, her skin soft. He didn't move, didn't breathe. Let this moment last.

If only a touch could say the words he couldn't seem to utter. *I'm sorry. I care. I wish this wasn't happening to you.*

Abigail sighed, a sound replete with a deep sadness.

Whatever he offered, it wasn't enough. *Give me the words, Gott. Please give me the words.* "I'm sorry this is happening to you."

"It's not your fault. There's really nothing you can do to help. No one can."

What could he say to that? They'd known each other forever—but hardly knew each other at all. Plain men and women were like that. "Your eldre must be hurting something awful."

"They're sorry they didn't tell me sooner." Her voice trembled. "They're scared. That's why they don't want me to see her. They're afraid she's right. That I belong more to her than them."

"I think they're right to be afraid."

Abigail snatched her hand from his, hopped from the buggy, and left Owen sitting by himself.

Okay, so that wasn't the right thing to say.

"I reckon that's easy for you and them to tell me to ignore something so big it fills up all the space around me." She threw the observation over her shoulder like a parting shot. "You can't imagine what it's like to have your world jerked out from under you from one moment to the next."

Not true. Not fair. But then this was about her pain, not his.

Owen hauled himself from the buggy. He tromped through the weeds, his boots squelching in the mud. Grasshoppers and bugs flew out in every direction. Mosquitoes buzzed his face in an angry cavalcade. A toad hurled itself into the hinterlands.

Owen stopped within arm's reach of Abigail at the pond's edge. The storm earlier in the week had left it swollen. A breeze rippled the murky surface. Owen breathed in the night smells of mud, water, and summer just on the horizon. "I think I understand a little of what you're going through. But from a different perspective. Being able to talk to your mudder—in your case to both of them—is a gift not everyone receives."

This time her hand came all the way across the big divide first. Her fingers found his and squeezed. "I'm sorry," she whispered. "I'm wallowing in my own self-pity with no thought of how it must seem to you."

To be awakened by his father in the dark predawn of a hot August day to find himself motherless had turned Owen's world into a gray, grim place for a long spell. Gradually light and color returned. His father's steady voice and warm hand on Owen's shoulder helped. His grandparents, his aunts and uncles, his mother's friends—everyone embraced the Kurtz children in a perpetual hug.

Still, Owen's world no longer included his mother. "You don't owe me an apology. My daed would say to pray for the will of Gott and wait for His plan to unfold."

"If you had a chance to talk to your mudder again, you would take it, wouldn't you?"

"That's a fanciful question." But one he had entertained on those first awful nights when he contemplated how much darker the world was knowing his mother no longer slumbered in the room down the hallway. The sound of Lee's sobs muffled in his pillow broke the eerie silence. Micah's nightmares. Claire's sleepwalking. They all stumbled around in a darkness that had nothing to do with the night.

Yes, Owen desperately wanted to talk to her one more time. To tell her not to go. To ask her why she went. In the days that followed, the doctors could not pinpoint definitively why she died. Not knowing made it worse. Father said it was the will of God, pure and simple. Not so simple, from the vantage point of a sixteen-year-old boy who missed his mother. "It makes no sense to consider it. She died. It was the will of Gott. Her days were done."

"I have that chance. It seems wrong to ignore it." Abigail faced Owen. The buggy headlights silhouetted her body. Shadows hid her expression. "I'm an Englisch girl adopted by Plain people. Who does that make me?"

Did bloodline trump the Plain world that had embraced Abigail since birth? It did not. Haven had another family in its midst that proved this truth. "Maybe you should talk to Cassie and Mason Keim."

"Their situation is different. It's reversed. Those kinner were brought up Englisch and then sent to live with the Keims."

Not so different. Mason and his five brothers and sisters were brought up English by their mother, who left the faith after she became in a family way with Mason. When she died she left a will that said she wanted her parents, Job and Dinah Keim, to raise them. Eventually Mason was baptized in the Plain faith and married Cassie.

"They didn't know they were Plain. They didn't know their Plain family. Now they're growing up in the faith." Some of them. Bobby

Keim had chosen to finish high school so he could go to college. He wanted to be a police officer. God's plan? "Cassie adopted those children as her own. Knowing what they went through might help you with what you're going through."

"Those kinner experienced both lives, and they're deciding for themselves which one they'll choose."

The quiver in her voice reverberated in Owen's heart. How could he help her? He squeezed her hand again. "If you think it will help, go to Abilene, experience your Englisch roots."

"Bryan says I risk meidung if I stay too long, adopt their ways, or even decide to marry an Englischer."

Had that thought crossed her mind? The darkness was a welcome friend, masking Owen's embarrassment at how his mind raced ahead of him—of them. "Going to Abilene doesn't mean you're giving up on your Plain life." He wrangled his voice into a gentle tone. "It's better for you to understand what all this means now. Otherwise it will always be there in the back of your mind. You'll always wonder."

Abigail inched closer. Her scent of soap and fresh mint enveloped him. "I know this isn't how you wanted this evening to go."

"I want you to be happy." Owen touched her cheek for one brief second. The newly sprouted, tender plant they'd been nurturing between them stretched and reached for the sky, new leaves unfurling. "You need time to figure this out. I'm still figuring out some things in my own life. We have time."

"If I decide to go, I can't ask you to wait for me to come back. It wouldn't be fair."

"I know what's between us is new." Owen picked his words with great care. "But I was looking forward to helping it grow. I'm not giving up on that or you, but we both need to be sure of who we are and what we want in order to make things work. Okay?"

"Okay."

"You don't have to make any promises. If you decide to go off in search of the real you, don't let my feelings stand in your way."

Abigail nodded. "No promises. And you don't have to wait for me. You shouldn't have to wait."

It wasn't about waiting so much as searching and finding and ending up in the same place someday. Someday soon.

Their farewell in front of the Bontragers' house was quick and wordless. Everything had been said. Owen took his time driving home. That hole Kayla claimed he was trying to fill with Hairy and a gangly foal gaped, dark and empty. He'd done the right thing, said the right things, but the lonely night still stretched before him.

He pulled up on the reins and halted the buggy in the middle of the road.

The expanse of night sky with glittering stars unobscured by city lights served as one of the great pleasures of living in the Kansas countryside. Owen traced the Big Dipper and searched for the North Star. The celestial skies were so big and so unending. He was small and alone. And far from God.

"What are you doing, Suh?"

He jumped and swiveled. He'd been so intent on his soul searching, Owen hadn't heard the approach of another buggy. His father halted his buggy even with Owen's. The darkness hid his expression but not the fact that he wasn't alone. Mary sat on the seat next to him.

"I was just . . . thinking."

"You shouldn't do that in the middle of the road. We thought something was wrong."

"Jah, we wanted to offer help." Mary had a soft, high voice that floated on the breeze in the dark. "I'm glad you're okay."

Okay didn't best describe Owen's acute discomfort. The last people on earth he wanted to see on the road tonight were his father and the woman he was courting. "I was studying the stars."

Could he sound any lamer?

"I like to study the stars too. Tom had a book of the constellations." Mary seemed oblivious to the awkward nature of the encounter. Or she was better at hiding it? "He used to point them out to me."

Mary had always been nice to them but especially after Mother died. She brought casseroles to the house and helped the other women with the laundry and the housecleaning those first days and weeks. Her husband helped with chores. Tom Wagner had been a tall, skinny man with a belly laugh and the biggest Adam's apple ever. He died in a tractor-truck accident on the highway last year after cutting a load of alfalfa. Then it had been Father and Owen's turn to help Mary's family with chores. Kayla and Claire minded the little ones during the viewing and the funeral.

Parallel experiences threw two grieving adults together not once but twice. Could a new life be built on similar losses? Mary was younger than Father by a decade. Did that matter? Who was with the children now?

Not Owen's business. He was the son, not the father. "Well, it's late. Dawn comes early. I'd better be getting back to the house."

"Be careful." Father clucked and snapped the reins. He turned the buggy around so they headed in the opposite direction. "See you in a bit."

"See you in a bit."

This night had not gone according to plan. At this rate his father would marry before Owen did. How had their lives become so topsy-turvy?

Chapter 11

Two more days. Two excruciating days with no Heather sightings—as Kayla had taken to calling them. Finally Abigail's day off arrived. She rushed to mow the yard and weeded the vegetable garden. Outdoor chores done, she told Mother she wanted to run over for a visit with Cassie Keim—if it was all right with Mother. Her glance worried—as it seemed to be all the time now—she nodded and pumped the treadle machine harder, making new pants for the growing boys in the family. Whatever was going on in her head, she didn't share.

Abigail's conversation with Owen replayed in her head a dozen times a day. He insisted he would wait for her. Asking him to do that was unfair. Was she throwing away her future to reclaim a past she didn't even know? Could a person build a solid future on a shaky foundation of an unknown, unexplored past? She had to be certain who Abigail Bontrager was before she could become a wife and mother. Maybe taking Owen's advice would help somehow.

Abigail pulled the buggy into the driveway in front of Job Keim's house. Immediately a flock of children surrounded her. "Abigail, you're here, you're here." Jennie, brown as a bun fresh from the oven, her brown curls spilling from her kapp, whirled around on bare feet in a spirited dance. "Mudder didn't say you were coming."

Almost two years had passed since Jennie and her four siblings came to live with the Keims, her grandparents. Mason and Cassie had married a year ago. Already Jennie called her Mommy. But she was young, only six.

"I didn't even know I was coming until this morning." Abigail hopped from the buggy and turned to pull out a basket. "I brought some of my mudder's Triple Threat *eppies*. How does that sound?"

"Why are they called triple threat?" Jennie sang her question. "Because they're the yummiest?"

"They're peanut butter cookies with M&M's, chocolate chips, and butterscotch chips. They're definitely the yummiest."

"*Wunderbarr*!" Donny, at eight, a taller, skinnier version of Jennie, threw his straw hat in the air and caught it one-handed. That he managed to do it without dropping the kitten in his other arm was a minor miracle. "Can I give one to my friend Lucas? We're going fishing with Grandpa this afternoon."

"Of course you can." Abigail waved at their older sister Kathy, who sat on the porch steps reading while scratching at mosquito bites on her ankles. Kathy smiled, waved, and went back to reading. "Where's your mudder?"

"Here I am." Cassie pushed through the screen door with a basket of laundry in her arms. A short woman, her enormous swollen belly preceded her. "Kathy, hang these up for me, sei so gut."

Kathy immediately tucked a bookmark in her paperback and set it aside. "You should've called me sooner. I would've carried it out for you. Jennie, help me hang the laundry."

"I want eppies."

"As soon as we finish hanging the laundry."

The two girls took off, Donny trailing after them, the kitten snuggled in the crook of his arm and a dog trotting at his side.

They looked as if they'd always lived there. Always been Plain.

Cassie took Abigail's offering of cookies. Her face glowed with a fine sheen of perspiration and her cheeks were pink from exertion, but she smiled. "It's gut to see you. It's been a while."

They'd been in the same grade in school. Nadine had been Cassie's best friend, but they made room for Abigail at singings and frolics. "There's been so much going on. Too much."

"So I've heard. Word does get around this little town." Cassie led the way to the kitchen. "I'll pour us some tea, and you can tell me all about it."

The grapevine was a well-tended, overwatered and overfed plant that meandered through the district. Abigail settled into a chair at the prep table while Cassie poured cold tea and placed cookies on a plate. "It smells so gut in here."

"I just took a rhubarb crumble out of the oven." Cassie cocked her head toward the counter where the dish sat. "And I have a spicy sausage-and-potato casserole baking now. You should stay for lunch. The kinner love company. They love to talk."

Lunch with the Keims would be nice. To avoid lunch with her own parents? No, of course not.

"Are you having trouble knowing where to start?" Cassie set the tea in front of Abigail. "You know you'll get no judgment from me. I've been the subject of plenty of gossip myself. It doesn't feel gut."

Abigail told her story in fits and starts between sips. "So you see, I'm between that stupid big rock and the hardest place they're always talking about. I love my eldre, but they lied."

"A well-meaning lie of omission, but even so."

"Your kinner. They were Englisch. Then they came here. They're

Plain or becoming Plain. That's not a simple thing, is it? But they're kinner. They're younger. They have more time."

"You're right. It's not a simple thing. It doesn't just happen from one day to the next. Mason and I talk about it a lot. We pray for Gott's will every day." Cassie winced. She rubbed her belly with both hands. "Ach. This little one. He's playing kickball in there."

"I can't imagine." A wave of longing washed over Abigail. What would it feel like to give birth to a child, to hold that child in her arms and call him son or daughter? "You must be so excited for the birth of a bopli that is a blessing of this union you have with Mason."

"We are equally blessed by the kinner we already have." Cassie's words held a gentle but unmistakable rebuke. "I will love this bopli no more and no less than I love Jennie or Donny, Kathy, or the older boys. They are my *boplin* too. Heart and soul. Mind and body. I love them with every fiber of my being."

Cassie's warm brown eyes filled with tears. "Sorry, it must be hormones. I'm so weepy these days."

"Don't apologize. I'm trying to understand, that's all. I feel torn in two. Plain is all I've ever known, but now there's this niggling, constant thought in the back of my head. What if you weren't? What if you were meant for another life? What if this was a mistake?"

"You're right, in some ways. The younger kinner have it easier. They're more adaptable. They're happy in the moment. They don't seem to miss TV or movies or wearing Englisch clothes. And Kathy is happy as long as she has her books. Kevin is eleven now. I think he misses his old life more than the others. He remembers more, but he likes hunting, fishing, and riding, so he doesn't complain. Bobby finished high school. He's headed to community college in the fall. Once he gets his associate's degree in criminal justice, he wants to attend the police academy." She bit into a cookie, chewed, and rolled her eyes. "This bopli has such a sweet tooth. Tell your mudder danki for me."

"Is Mason okay with Bobby choosing that path?"

"It's hard to let him go, but we agreed we wouldn't pressure any of the kinner. Theirs has been a difficult enough row to hoe. Bobby's staying with his onkel Perry in Wichita this summer, and he'll start school there in the fall. Perry will keep an eye on him, make sure he doesn't get into trouble."

Indeed, a very hard row to hoe. To lose their parents so young. To be transported to another world so different from their own. Abigail had little room to complain.

"Your position isn't easy, either, I reckon." Cassie rose, went to the stove, and opened the oven door. The mouthwatering aroma of spicy venison sausage rolled through the kitchen. She grabbed hot pads and moved the casserole to the counter. "It seems as though the question is whether you believe your mudder and daed were following Gott's plan for you when they adopted you."

"I'm sure they thought so." Abigail's headed pounded. She rubbed her temples. Her broken sleep of the last few weeks was catching up with her. "They had a chance to give a bopli a life dedicated to our faith. I took vows. How can I step back now?"

"I'm sure everyone wants to tell you what you should do." Cassie returned to her seat at the table. She spread her swollen, dishwater-red hands on the table between them. "But could I offer a small observation?"

"Sei so gut."

"Spending time with your birth mother and meeting the family she's made isn't a rejection of your Plain life. Maybe it will add richness." The sound of children's laughter floated through the open windows. "I don't think we can have too much family. However we come by them."

"My eldre and the bishop, they seem to fear I will be lured away by Heather and her worldly ways."

"Dinah used to say a faith untested is a weak muscle. Is yours so weak it can't withstand time spent out there in the world?" Sadness flickered in Cassie's face, but she smiled and shook her head. "I don't believe that for a second."

"It's hard to believe Dinah's been gone for two years already." Job's wife had died from a diabetes-related ailment not long after the children came to live with her and Job. "You were blessed to know her well. You soaked up a lot of her wisdom."

"I'm just a person whose faith muscle has gotten a workout in the last few years. There's no going around the trials in our lives. There's no avoiding them. You have to dig in your heels and embrace them. That's the only way to learn from them. The only way to grow. You'll do what's right, I know you will."

"That's the problem. I don't know what's right."

"You'll figure it out."

Abigail took a cookie and settled back in her chair. She would need fortification. Her workout had just begun.

A detour between the Cotter construction site and the office wouldn't take too long. Owen entertained that thought for the tenth time as he squatted next to Mason Keim's tractor. The other man was positioned under it, preparing to change the oil. No one would have guessed that only two years ago Mason had driven an SUV, warmed his carryout food in a microwave, and hadn't been to church in years. He wore a faded blue cotton shirt. His homemade black denim pants had patched knees and his black boots were scuffed and caked with mud. He was the picture of a man who liked to work hard and get dirty.

"Hand me that seventeen-millimeter socket wrench, will you?"

Mason held up one work-gloved hand from his spot flat on his back. "It's gut to see you. It's been a while."

Owen obliged. "A lot going on."

"So I've heard. Take this and hand me one of those rags piled up on the seat." Mason returned the wrench and lifted his hand up for the rag. "I need to clean off the plug and the gasket."

Owen gladly followed instructions. It might be easier to have this conversation with Mason half hidden under a tractor and unable to see Owen's face.

"So what brings you out here now?"

Nice of Mason to get the ball rolling for him. Owen let the humid morning breeze cool his warm face as he sought the words. *I'm lost. I don't want her to go. This is stupid. This is about her, not me. She'll be back. She's the one.* Round and round. "I thought I'd pick your brain."

"About?"

"Are you happy working on Obie's crew rehabbing houses?" He would start there and work his way over to adoption . . . and Abigail. "Is that what you pictured yourself doing?"

"Sort of. My big plan before my mudder died was to own my own business buying houses, rehabbing them, and flipping them. This is close enough, though. I like working with my hands. It's what I'm gut at."

"Now that you're living on a farm, you don't think of farming for a living?"

"I honestly don't know much about farming. That's why I leave it to Job for now. He's teaching Kevin, in case he decides he wants to stay around. Why?"

A perfect opportunity to broach the subject of Kevin's English-to-Plain journey and Abigail's adoption. Owen opened his mouth. "I want to grow sunflowers as a cash crop."

Mason pulled himself out from under the tractor. He stared up at Owen. "Sunflowers?"

"Haven't you seen the articles? Sunflowers are doing really well in Kansas. In this area it's for the oil and birdseed. Out in western Kansas, they grow the seeds for eating."

"Why sunflowers?"

"It doesn't take huge acreage, there's a big market, and they're good for the land."

"Huh." Mason disappeared back under the tractor. "What does your daed say?"

"He's happy with his engineered-structures business. He's thinking of selling our acreage to my onkel."

"You could work with your onkel."

"I could, but my daed really needs me to work for him so he doesn't have to hire paid workers. I live at home. I don't have the expenses those workers would have."

"I'm not really the person to ask about farming sunflowers. And besides, I have a feeling that's not what you came out here to ask me about."

Owen used the toe of his boot to dig at a rock stuck in the soil. The rock turned over, revealing roly-poly bugs underneath. "You and Cassie are raising the kinner like they're your own."

"They are our own. Bruder, schweschder, dochder, suh. Family."

"Abigail Bontrager is adopted."

"I heard."

Of course he'd heard. Small towns, big mouths. "Where?"

"They were talking about it at the hardware store last week. Flapping jaws being what they are."

"We have the benefit of hindsight, I know, but it would've been so much easier if Freeman and Lorene had told her about the adoption."

"Easier for who?"

"It wouldn't have come as such a shock. She would've been prepared when this Heather woman showed up in her parents' living room." Owen picked up the new oil filter. He turned it round and round in his hands, like it was a foreign object he'd never seen before. "I imagine it was something similar to what you felt when you found out after your mudder died that her family was Plain and she wanted her Plain parents to finish raising you."

Mason pulled himself out from under the tractor again and sat up. He tugged the container filled with dirty black oil out on a piece of cardboard. His face and hands were dirty, but he smiled. "You've been thinking on this, haven't you?"

Mason hopped to his feet and wiped his face on another rag. "It was a shock, no doubt about it. I did wonder why she never mentioned it in all those years. I still wonder why she didn't bring us to see our grandparents and know them. We could've used family. Why didn't she tell us about them? We'll never know. Why did we have to go through learning how to be Plain, deciding to be Plain—or not, like Bobby? But we're here now, and we're better for it. I have Cassie and a bopli on the way. This was Gott's plan—there's no doubt in my mind."

He pointed to the filter in Owen's hands. "Write the date and mileage on that for me, will you, while I get the old one off?"

Owen did as directed. It gave him time to digest Mason's words. He grabbed a Sharpie pen from the tractor's seat and wrote the information on the filter while Mason removed the old one and let the excess oil drip into the bucket below.

Kathy and Jennie skipped toward the house, swinging an empty laundry basket between them. Their laughter carried like a song. Donny trotted behind them, a kitten in one arm, his hand on the collar of a big dog who walked with him. All three were barefoot. Their faces glowed with the sun's warmth.

The picture of life for Plain children on a fine May day.

"Now you and Cassie are parents to five kinner with another on the way. They call Cassie Mudder. They're growing up Plain. What if one day they decide it was a mistake and they want to be English again?"

"They'll have that choice when they go through rumspringa, just like every other Plain teenager." Mason took the new filter and turned back to the tractor. "What's really eating at you?"

"Abigail is Plain through and through."

"Only now she knows she could've been something different, someone different."

"Jah."

"Better she finds out now than later, don't you think?"

Owen did think that. He just didn't like it. "It's none of my business what she decides, I reckon."

"It must be. You're here talking to me about it." Mason wiped his hands on a rag and stepped back from the tractor. "Done. I've worked up a powerful thirst, and my stomach is rumbling. I tell you what. Come up to the house and have lunch with us. Cassie loves company, and so do the kinner. I happen to know she made a sausage-and-potato casserole that hits the spot every time."

Maybe Cassie would have some words of wisdom. No, he couldn't ask a woman what she thought about the situation. It wouldn't be seemly. Would it? "I could eat."

Mason grinned and slapped Owen on the back. "I can always eat. So can those kinner. Lord have mercy, can they eat. Watch out or you'll lose a hand trying to serve yourself a piece of bread."

Together they walked around the house to the back porch and into the kitchen. "Fraa, look who is joining us for lunch."

Cassie sat at the table. Across from her sat none other than Abigail. Her mouth dropped open. Her cheeks turned red. "Owen."

Owen was fairly certain his did the same. "Abigail."

Chapter 12

WHAT WAS OWEN DOING HERE AT THE KEIMS' HOUSE? ABIGAIL SET A basket of hot biscuits on the table in front of him. He'd been the one who suggested she talk to Cassie and Mason. But why would he talk to them himself?

Abigail grabbed a pitcher of water and filled Job's glass, then Mason's. When she arrived at Owen's place, he held up his glass. She took it. Her fingers brushed against his. Sudden heat toasted her cheeks. She thrust the glass back at him. "Here you go." Water sloshed over the side of the pitcher. It splashed on Owen's shirt and lap. Clumsy, as usual. "Ach, I'm sorry."

"No worries. It's a hot day. It'll cool me off." His gaze locked on hers. "Besides, it's only water."

That wasn't the point. Abigail eased the pitcher onto the table before she spilled any more. She slid into a chair across from him and stared at her plate.

"Abigail, is your daed still making house calls?" Job helped himself to a heaping helping of steaming-hot casserole. The spicy aroma made Abigail's stomach gurgle. "Daisy threw a shoe yesterday."

Many years ago Father had apprenticed to a blacksmith and taken up shoeing horses as a sideline to supplement their income. He said it was important to be nimble when it came to earning a living. "He is. When I see him tonight I'll tell him to come by when he can."

"Missy had a litter of kittens in the barn again." Donny announced this bit of news with a big whoop as punctuation. "Do you want to see them, Abigail?"

"I do."

Donny slid from the bench.

"After lunch, Donny," Cassie gently admonished. "Eat your sausage."

"I like pizza better." Jennie pushed the sausage around on her plate with her biscuit. "Can we have pepperoni pizza for supper?"

"Maybe another day." Cassie handed her a napkin. "Wipe your face, kind."

Abigail wiggled her shoulders and tried to relax. She stabbed a piece of sausage and lifted it to her mouth. Her throat closed. She laid her fork on the table. Maybe a drink of water first.

She peeked at Owen. He was busy toying with his fork. The heap of potatoes and sausage on his plate didn't seem to have shrunk. His head came up. He offered her that smile. That and his kind heart. *We'll figure it out. We have time.*

She forced a return smile. *I don't know how long it will take. Or where it will take me.*

"So what brings you out here today, Abigail?" Mason picked up the biscuit Donny dropped on the floor and laid it aside without missing a beat. "You didn't have to work at Buggies and Bonnets?"

"My day off." Abigail sipped her water. "I just felt like a visit."

Mason chuckled. "There seems to be a lot of that going around."

For a while everyone focused on eating. The children did all the talking. His expression puzzled, Job simply frowned.

"How are your parents?" Owen offered the basket of biscuits. Abigail waved it away. He took another and laid it on his plate, even though he still had an untouched one on it. "Is your daed overrun with work?"

"He keeps busy. They both do." Was he talking about her adoptive parents or her biological parents? "The kinner are out of school so they help out."

"Kayla was saying you've been busy at work."

Busy with customers or busy with visits from Heather? Everything he said now seemed fraught with hidden meaning. "Tourist season is upon us."

"Indeed. The kinner have been helping me by manning the produce stand." Cassie's gaze traveled from Abigail to Owen and back. "I've been baking bread and cookies, and Kathy's embroidered hot pads are big sellers. Plus I have canned goods from last year that are popular."

"I'm carving bugs." Donny volunteered this tidbit through a full mouth. "And toads."

"That you are. Job is showing him how." Cassie's face glowed with pride. "Everyone pitches in."

The way family should. Abigail forced herself to eat the casserole. It would be shameful to waste Cassie's good cooking. No excuse existed for rudeness. "This is really gut. I need the recipe."

"I'll write it down for you."

The small talk petered out.

The second Owen took the last bite of casserole and laid down his fork, Abigail hopped up and grabbed his plate. "I'll help the girls clear, Cassie. You rest. You look tuckered out."

"I'm fine." One hand on the table, the other on the chair's back, she hauled herself to her feet. "You don't have to do that."

"I want to. And then I have to get back. I need to help Mudder with the sewing. The buwe are growing like weeds. And the maede need new dresses." As if they needed to know this. Babble. Babble. "We're planting more vegetables too."

"I'd better skedaddle too." Owen pushed back his chair. "Daed hired a driver to take us out to the job we're starting in Lyons. He doesn't like to wait."

"You two can't go without having rhubarb crumble." Cassie patted Kathy's head. "Kathy, you and Jennie can help me serve it, little one."

"Maybe Owen better take his to go." Abigail grabbed his tea glass and set it on top of the stack of plates. "We don't want to keep Chester waiting. He has work to do."

Everyone moved at once. While the girls served the rest of the family their dessert, Cassie packaged up some for her guests. Owen thanked her three times, then rushed out the door.

Even so, when Abigail trotted down the back porch steps after helping the girls with the dishes and accepting Cassie's recipe, Owen was waiting next to her buggy. She walked around him and climbed in. "Did Mason have any words of wisdom about my situation?"

"I think I was asking more for myself than for you, truth be told." He climbed into the buggy next to her, close but not too close. "He said everything worked out as it should, as Gott planned. That doesn't mean it wasn't a hard patch to get through. If anyone knows how it feels, it's Mason. Maybe you should've talked to him and I should've talked to Cassie." His chuckle was rueful.

"They're so happy now."

"You'd never know he was raised Englisch."

"His roots are Plain."

"Maybe in the end none of that matters." Owen leaned closer still. How could heat make a person shiver? His scent of soap, mint toothpaste, and man sweat enveloped Abigail. Man smells were so different, so earthy. "What matters is your heart."

Her heart had decided to race ahead of this conversation. Abigail clutched the reins in both hands. "My heart wants to be in two places at once. It suddenly doesn't know where it belongs."

"What did Cassie say?"

"She said I have to figure it out for myself." She looked up at Owen with his inquisitive eyes and that smile. She had so much to gain by spending time with Heather. She also had much to lose. "But I already knew that."

Owen brushed a wisp of hair back toward her prayer covering. "Jah, you did. So did I. As hard as it will be, I'm stepping back. Don't let me or my feelings stand in the way of finding out who you are. Promise me that."

"I'm sorry—"

"Don't be. Do what you need to do." He gripped her hand for one scant second, then let go. "Promise."

"Owen—"

"Promise."

"I promise." Abigail's heart didn't slow. It sped up. "*Faeriwell*, Owen," she whispered.

Chapter 13

"She's here."

Abigail looked up from collecting her five-dollar tip from a table just vacated by a family of six. Her shoulders, back, and elbows ached, and she was only halfway through her shift. "Heather?"

"Of course Heather." Kayla's tone turned tart. "You want me to tell her to get lost?"

"You think I should tell my mudder to get lost?"

"She's not your real mother. Lorene is." Kayla's usual perky smile disappeared. She pocketed her order pad in her apron and grabbed a pitcher of iced tea from the drink station. "You're my best friend. My bruder likes you. I don't want you to stop being Plain. Or to go away. Not to mention your salvation. I won't even go there—"

"I'm not going to stop being Plain." Even if she might never have been Plain to start with if Heather Hanson hadn't decided to give her away. Abigail couldn't see table 16 from her vantage point. She'd been waiting for days for this moment. Now it was here. Curiosity vied with uncertainty and confusion. They would battle to the death, and she still wouldn't know what to do. "Can you cover my tables for me?"

"Sure, if you really want to do this."

"I really need to do this."

"Fine. I'll bring you some lunch. Get this over with so we can go back to planning our weddings."

Their imaginary weddings. Kayla was no closer to marriage than Abigail, even though she had plenty of opportunities. The boys liked her happy-go-lucky personality and pert smile. She was picky. That was her problem. Abigail wasn't picky, just caught in a quandary not of her making. "I'm not hungry."

"You have to eat."

"Maybe next week or next month." Or next year. When this nightmare receded. "I promise."

Abigail took a deep breath and let it out. *Gott, help me.* Shoulders back, head up, she marched between tables and dodged waitstaff and customers until she reached table 16. Heather picked at a turkey-bacon salad with her fork and stared at her cell phone. Abigail cleared her throat. "You're here."

Heather's head came up.

"I'm here. Your friend Kayla said you have an hour coming for lunch." She smiled bigger. Her eyes crinkled at the corners. Her teeth were so straight and so white. She had the same pointy chin as Abigail. "Can you spare a few of those minutes to talk with me?"

Abigail sat. "I looked at the photo album."

"What went through your head when you saw those pictures?"

Heather had something green stuck between those white front teeth. Abigail stared at it. Should she say something? She tore her gaze from Heather's mouth, which continued to move with words Abigail couldn't seem to understand, to her hands on the table. Heather's fingernails were painted bubblegum pink.

Abigail laid her own hands on the table in a similar fashion. She spread out her fingers and studied her dry skin. She needed to use some lotion. Her fingernails were bitten to the quick. A bad habit getting worse by the minute. The sound of people chattering at nearby tables ballooned in her ears.

"Did you take the car for an oil change yesterday?"

"Bryson got a D in math. You need to talk to him. He's headed for summer school."

"This fried chicken is finger-lickin' good. Ask the waitress for more napkins."

"I love that show *The Bachelor*. Don't you love it?"

"The bill is $28.53. How much do I tip?"

Silverware clinked against dishes. A baby cried. A man sneezed, then coughed.

The aroma of fried catfish, homemade bread, and grilled chicken mingled in the air. Abigail's stomach roiled. She put her hand to her mouth. *Nee, Gott, nee.*

"Abigail? Abby? Do you go by Abby? Are you all right, honey?" Heather reached across the table and touched Abigail's other hand. Her fingers were warm. "You look peaked, sweetheart."

Abigail withdrew her hands and stuck them in her lap. "Abigail. It's Abigail." Not honey. Definitely not sweetheart. "I'm just tired. I haven't been sleeping well."

Something that had never been a problem before.

"I wanted to give you your name. I thought of naming you Opal or India, you know, from the book *Because of Winn-Dixie*."

Abigail didn't know. Her reading was limited to historical romances and cozy mysteries. "But you couldn't because you gave me away."

"I keep telling you, I had no choice. Surely you know what that's like. You're a woman in an Amish district run by men. You live at home. Your dad makes all your decisions. Then you get married and your husband makes all the decisions. Surely you get it."

Her view of the Plain world was skewed. Women voted on *Ordnung* rule changes. Wives and husbands discussed issues before decisions were made at home. Ultimately Father's decision stood, but he listened to Mother first. Especially when it came to their children. "What do you expect to gain by spending time with me?"

Heather stood and slipped to Abigail's side of the table. She settled into the chair next to her, scooching it closer. Their arms touched. She pushed something on the phone. It began to ring. Two faces appeared on the screen. "Mom? Mom! What's up?"

"I want you to meet your half sister Abigail." Heather moved the phone screen. Abigail's face appeared in a square in the top-right corner. "Abigail, we're FaceTiming with your sisters Scarlett and Fiona. Girls, say hello."

The two carrottopped girls from the photos squealed and waved. "Hey, Abigail, we can't wait to meet you in person."

"Yeah, we even cleaned up the guest room so it's ready for you to sleep in." The shorter girl, Fiona, grinned. "I washed the sheets."

"I washed the sheets. She mostly watched." Scarlett rolled her eyes. "We have an extra bike. You can go biking with us to Eisenhower Park. We can go swimming if you want."

"That's enough, girls, don't overwhelm her."

"When are you coming?"

They were cute and sweet and trying so hard. The image of Hope and Rose playing checkers on a card table next to the fireplace on a cold winter night surfaced. *Gott, what do I do?* "Soon."

"Come in time for my dance recital next week." Fiona twirled around and came back toward the phone camera. "And Scarlett's softball game. It'll be fun. I promise."

"It sounds like fun. It was nice to meet you."

"Talk to you soon. Bye, Abigail. Bye, Mommy."

And then they were gone.

Kayla sashayed up to the table and set a tray on it. "I brought your lunch—a cheeseburger and sweet potato fries. You have to keep your strength up." She slid the plate in front of Abigail and added a glass of iced tea. "You're the hardest worker here, after all."

What was she up to? Abigail shot her friend a meaningful glance. "I told you I wasn't hungry."

"Everyone here loves Abigail. She works hard and takes shifts for other waitresses. She has a nest egg for when she gets married. She and my brother are courting—"

"Kayla, I see a customer in my section looking for a server. You're supposed to be taking care of them."

"Oh, I am, I am." Kayla picked up Heather's dirty dishes. She smiled sweetly. "Mrs. Hanson, did you need anything else?"

"A piece of that apple pie would be nice, and call me Heather." She returned the smile. The green stuff still held its position between her two front teeth. "You're a good friend. It's so nice to meet a friend of my daughter's. Put her lunch on my bill, will you?"

"We get one free meal with each shift." Abigail scowled at Heather. "There's no need."

She didn't need Heather to pay her way. Like a mother might.

Kayla swiped at the table with a washrag and stepped back. "If you need anything else, just wave at me and I'll come running."

She was trying to help. She didn't want to lose a friend. Abigail marshaled a smile for her friend. "I'll be back to work in a few minutes."

"No worries." Kayla scooted away to take care of Abigail's customer.

Abigail pushed the plate of food toward the middle of the table. The aroma, normally so enticing, turned her stomach. She stood. "I really do have to get back to work. It's not fair to Kayla to make her cover my section too."

"Understood, understood. But you'll come to Abilene? To meet the girls and Brody in person?"

"Can I ask you a question?"

"Of course. Anything."

"Why now? Why all of a sudden, after all these years, did you decide to find me and invite me into your life?"

Heather's eager smile faded, but she didn't look away. "I've always wanted to see you. But I seemed to go from one mess to the next." She sat up straight and smoothed her hair with both hands. "I never felt like I really had my act together. But now I do. I'm finally all grown up. That may sound ridiculous, considering I'm divorced and raising three kids practically on my own. But I woke up one day and realized I can handle this. I'm a good mother. I'm a nurse. I'm a homeowner. I'm not a scared sixteen-year-old anymore. I can be a good mother to you."

She took a deep breath and blew it out. "That's it. All of it."

It would be a wonderful thing to wake up one day and feel all grown up. To fit in. To be able to handle whatever life brought. To know who she was. "I'll come. This Saturday. For two weeks."

"Two weeks is a start." Grinning, Heather picked up her leather purse decorated with tooled flowers in a bouquet of colors. She dug around in it for a few seconds. Finally she produced a phone. "Here. I got this for you. That way we can keep in touch. Don't worry. It was cheap. It's disposable. I bought prepaid minutes for it."

Already the decisions had to be made. English and Plain and the spaces in between. The narrow cliffs and wide canyons navigated. Abigail slid from the booth and stood. "I can't, not yet. I'll not take a phone into my parents' house. It would disrespect them. Save it for when I come to Abilene."

"Sounds like a plan." Heather dropped the phone back into the cavernous purse. "I can't wait."

She produced a pen, wrote a telephone number on a napkin, and held it out. "Call me from one of the sanctioned phones, and I'll come down to talk to them if you want. Call me if you change your mind. But don't change your mind. Please. You won't regret this."

The sparkle in her eyes spoke of the scenes she was already imagining. Memories in the making. Abigail sitting at her supper table, gabbing with her other kids, laughing and acting like they'd known each other their whole lives. Dreams that eclipsed the lost years filled with memories made with another family.

Not many people had the chance to change their life stories so completely. To be someone different. Abigail took the napkin. "I won't change my mind. See you Saturday."

Chapter 14

"Don't go, Schweschder. Don't go."

Abigail started and opened her eyes. She squinted in the dusky predawn light. Rose leaned over the bed, her face was so close to Abigail's, she could see the tiny scar on her nose where she fell from her high chair and smell her childish scent of milk and peanut butter. Someone had helped herself to a cookie before breakfast. Abigail scooched toward the middle of the bed and held out her arms. "Get in."

Still clad in her faded cotton nightgown, Rose climbed onto the mattress and curled around Abigail's body. "You can't go."

"It's only for a while. I'll be back."

"Mudder cried."

Abigail's arms tightened around her sister's chunky, warm body. "When?"

"Last night. I got up to get a drink of water. I heard her. She was sad." Rose's dimples, always on display, were missing in action. Her forehead crinkled. She shook her head. "It made me sad."

"I know. Me too. But this is something I need to do. Mudder understands that. Sometimes at night things seem worse. After a gut night's sleep, the sun shines again." Mother and Father hadn't argued when she told them of her decision. Father simply stood and left the kitchen. Mother turned her back and busied herself with making a taco casserole for supper. Abigail's favorite. No one knew more casserole recipes than her mother. "It's only for two weeks. Before you all know it, I'll be back and everything will be the same as before."

It would never be the same. A second family couldn't be taken back.

"You already have me and Hope and Benny and Nate and Jane and Eddie." Rose ticked their siblings' names off on her chubby fingers. "And Joel, I suppose. He's a pest, but he's still your bruder."

At five Joel could be a pest, but a sweet, silly one.

"That's seven brieder and schwesdchdre." Rose served up a severe frown of the kind only a thwarted seven-year-old could produce. "Isn't that enough? Why do you need three more?"

Abigail had gathered her younger siblings around the previous evening and explained to them where she was going and why. Hope turned up her nose and marched away, while Eddie suggested she should forget the whole thing. Who needed English relatives, after all? Who indeed? Joel climbed into her lap and refused to get down. "It's not a question of needing more. They just are. This isn't a situation of my making, but I'm trying to make the best of it."

"Look at you two. *Schtinkich faul.*" Jane stood in the doorway. She folded her arms and shook her head in mock disgust. "Still in bed at this hour. So lazy. You'd better get up. Mudder is down there making breakfast for the entire district, it seems. Pancakes, eggs, bacon, toast, grits, biscuits."

"I'm being driven to Abilene. Not hiking the whole way." Abigail tickled Rose, who giggled and slid from the bed at a run toward the safety of Jane's solid figure. Plus Abigail's stomach had tied itself up in knots overnight. "I'm not really hungry."

"Don't tell her that." Jane took Rose's hand. "Get dressed, Rose.

We need to get down there and help Mudder. And you'd better hurry, Abigail. I think your Englisch mudder is sitting in her car outside."

"Ach. Nee. Already?" Abigail struggled to disentangle herself from the sheets. She shoved them aside and went to the tall window that faced the east. Sure enough. A dark-blue SUV was parked at the *V* where the road split toward the house on one side and the barn on the other. "She must've left Abilene in the middle of the night."

"Or spent the night in her car." Jane chuckled. "It's nice to know she's that excited about your visit."

Jane took Rose's hand and left Abigail to dress, do her hair, and finish packing. This was silly. Really. Mother and Father would want Heather to come in and eat breakfast with them. That would be the neighborly thing to do. Abigail grabbed her ancient suitcase, a hand-me-down from her grandparents, and sped down the stairs. She'd never had to use a suitcase for anything. She'd never gone on a trip on her own in her entire life.

Anticipation, all shiny and bright, made it hard to see the stair-steps. She pounded down them and out to the kitchen. "Mudder, Heather is out—"

"I know." Mother held up a brown paper sack and a large thermos. "I packed your breakfast—enough for both of you. You'll want to get on the road. No point in delaying."

"But I thought . . ." Abigail had thought wrong. "Where's Daed?"

"He had to go into Yoder."

"This early?" The stores weren't even open yet. "He didn't want to say faeriwell?"

"I reckon he said that last night." Mother thrust the sack and the thermos at Abigail. "You can bring the thermos back when you return." Her voice broke.

A whine deep in his throat, Doolittle rose from his spot in front of the propane stove and trotted over to stand next to her. His grizzled face puzzled, he woofed at Mother, then Abigail.

"It's okay, hund. We're just talking." Abigail accepted her mother's offerings. She set them on the table. Mother tried to turn away, but Abigail tugged at her arm. "I will be back in two weeks."

Mudder wiped at her face with her free hand. "See that you do."

"I have my job at the restaurant. Dana gave me two weeks off. After that she won't hold my slot. This is the busiest time of year for the restaurant."

And many young girls in the area waited in line for local jobs.

"For the job, you'd come back." Faint bitterness marred Mother's words. She whirled and trotted to the counter. "On your way out, tell Jane and Rose to set the table. Breakfast is getting cold. Go on. Heather's waiting."

"Mudder."

She didn't respond.

"Faeriwell."

Nothing.

Juggling the suitcase, sack, and thermos while attempting not to get tangled up with Doolittle, who insisted on accompanying her through the house, wasn't easy. The great room was empty. The boys were already outside doing their morning chores.

"Rose, Hope, Jane?"

No response. The suitcase thumping on the pine floor, Abigail shoved through the front door, across the porch, and down the steps.

Heather's car shot into the yard. The driver's side window lowered with a hum. "Hop in. Let's get this show on the road."

"Why are you here so early, and why didn't you come to the door?"

Heather slid from the car and raced around to the back hatch, which seemed to magically open without her touching it. "Put your suitcase back here. I couldn't sleep last night. I finally got up and started driving. But I didn't want to disturb your family so early."

"We get up early."

"I know. I know." Heather held out her hand to Doolittle. He sniffed it, huffed, and backed away. "That's a big dog. Is he coming with us?"

"No. He belongs here."

Abigail handed the breakfast to Heather and turned to Doolittle. At least he wanted to say good-bye to her. He nudged Abigail's hand with his wet nose. "Jah, jah." She knelt and smoothed his unruly fur with both hands. "You stay here. Your job is to keep an eye on the kinner for me. Keep everyone safe while I'm gone."

If only he could carry a message to Owen for her. What would that message say? *Don't give up on me? I'm sorry? I need to do this?* If she couldn't understand her feelings, how could she expect Owen to understand?

Doolittle's rough, warm tongue scraped her cheek and nose. *Woof.*

"Danki for der *boss*, hund." Dog kisses were almost as sweet as toddler kisses. And as wet. "I have to go."

She rose and got into the car. Her body felt light, like she might float away in the unreality of this moment. She was no longer simply Abigail Bontrager, Plain woman. She was Abigail Bontrager, daughter of an English couple. A woman's high voice crooned a song about a lover who left too soon. Heather's citrusy scent wafted on the air that blasted from the vents.

Abigail shivered and hugged her canvas bag to her chest. A string of purple beads hung from the rearview mirror. The center console held a Starbucks coffee cup, a cell phone, napkins, and tissues. The second cupholder was filled with quarters.

Heather plopped onto the seat next to her. She slid the car around in a wide arc and gunned the engine. "Here we go. Are you ready for a new adventure?"

Abigail worked to stick the seat belt into its latch. It fought back. Finally it clicked. She grabbed the door handle. "I'm ready. Let's go."

No looking back.

Chapter 15

The welcoming committee at Heather's house in Abilene consisted of Scarlett, Fiona, Heather's two sisters, a cousin, and a neighbor lady, whom Heather promptly told to scram. She claimed they were just hanging around because they were nosy. Abigail didn't try to remember their names as they hugged her, pumped her hand, and promised to return later. Her hands and feet were frozen from the car's AC, and her head hurt from the high-pitched music Heather described as "pop" that had accompanied the ninety-minute drive from Haven to Abilene.

"I'll take your suitcase to your room." Scarlett tugged the handle from Abigail. "Your hands are frozen. What did you do to her, Mom? She's always hot, Abigail. You just have to demand that she turn the AC down. Otherwise we all freeze."

Abigail managed a nod. The girls surely must be cold. Scarlett wore a purple tank top that didn't quite reach the waist of her jean shorts. Her long, skinny legs were bare. Fiona's shirt looked more like a swimming suit top, and her shorts barely covered her behind. Neither wore shoes.

Shivering, Abigail followed them through a living room filled with western-style décor. A painting of a cowboy on a bucking horse hung on one wall. A huge flat-screen TV hung across from it. A bunch of kids ran around on the screen, but the sound was muted. The air was almost as cold as it had been in Heather's SUV.

"You're in the guest room." Fiona did a cartwheel across the room and landed on her feet directly in front of Abigail. "That's where Grandma and Grandpa stay when they come to visit. But they're not coming while you're here."

"Grandma doesn't think it's a good idea for you to be here," Scarlett added. "She says—"

"That's enough, girls." Heather's face turned pink. "Where's your brother?"

So not everyone on Heather's side of the issue thought bringing Abigail into her family's life was a good idea either. Good to know. Or maybe it was bad. She stuck out like a turtle in a school of goldfish that darted around her, never stopping.

"He went to Max's house to play video games." Fiona's words had the distinct tone of a tattletale. She wrinkled her nose. "He said he didn't need no stinkin' half sister. He has too many sisters already."

Abigail followed them down a carpeted hallway to the second door on the left. It stood open. The room was twice the size of the one she shared with Jane. It held a double bed, a matching dresser, a desk and chair, and several bookcases filled with paperbacks and framed photographs. Prints of flowers in vases and one portrait of Heather with her children and an elderly couple who must be the grandparents adorned the walls.

The walk-in closet was bigger than the room Rose and Hope shared.

At least Brody was honest. "My brothers would probably agree with him. They have four sisters."

"Wow. Four sisters." Fiona's mouth formed a large *O*. "How many brothers are there in your family?"

"Three. Benny, Eddie, and Joel."

"I don't know how you stand it." Fiona pretended to stick her finger in her throat and gag. "Brody is ridiculous. Seriously."

"He's not so bad." Scarlett bounced on the bed. She threw herself back and sprawled across a floral comforter. "Daddy says he just needs a firm hand. I don't know what that means, but it sounds good to me."

"Get your dirty feet off the comforter. It means your daddy would like to use his hand on Brody's backside. Call him and tell him to get his behind home." Heather tickled Scarlett's foot. The girl shrieked and rolled off the bed. "Take your time unpacking, Abigail. Girls, give Abigail some breathing room. Do you need a nap? Are you hungry? Or would you like a tour of the house?"

They'd eaten the egg and bacon on toast sandwiches on the road and washed them down with coffee. The contents of Abigail's stomach burbled. "No thank you. I'm still full from breakfast. I really don't have much to unpack."

Scarlett tucked a pink cell phone into the back pocket of her shorts. "Brody says he'll be home in a while—as soon as they finish this game."

"Which could be hours. That kid has no sense of time." Heather moved to the dresser and opened the middle drawer. "It's okay that you didn't bring a lot of stuff. I bought you a few things. I thought you might like to try something a little different. Nothing too drastic, I promise, but maybe not so warm. It gets awfully hot in June."

Not any hotter than in Haven. And how could a person tell with the cold air rushing from the overhead vents? Abigail took the pile of clothes. Several pairs of tan, white, and brown cotton capris. Short-sleeved knit tops in solid blues, greens, and purples. Heather kept the clothes simple and plain. A pair of brown leather sandals finished out the gift. Such kind generosity. Such thoughtfulness. "Thank you. These are nice."

Better choices than she and Kayla had made in that dressing room during their rumspringa. A picture formed in Abigail's mind as she ran her fingers across the soft cloth of a short-sleeve lilac polo shirt. Abigail English Girl. What if she'd grown up in this house, big sister to these girls? Would she spin around the room, somersault, and stop to check her text messages? Abigail English Girl might decide she liked hot pink shorts and a tank top on this summer day. She might even cut her hair short and wear mascara.

"I thought these would be perfect if you decided to ride a bike. You could ride mine. Or if you wanted to hang out at the park. Or maybe Brody will show you how to skateboard." Heather took one of the shirts and held it up in front of Abigail. "I had to guess what size, but we're so close in height and size—you probably even wear the same size I do."

Abigail had come here to find out if she was meant to be English. The experiment started now. "I'll try them on after I finish unpacking."

"Perfect." Heather clapped as if applauding a performance. "Not that there's anything wrong with dresses. I wish the girls would wear them more often, but there's nothing wrong with being comfortable either."

"I think your dress is pretty. It's different. It makes you stand out. It's like the clothes you get in used clothing stores, you know, like vintage." Scarlett wrinkled her nose. Her head tilted, she stared at Abigail with a critical air. "I'm going to be a fashion designer when I grow up. I'm going to make clothes girls can wear that aren't itchy or too tight or show your boobs when you bend over. The lilac color is nice. Pastels work for some people. Purple is my power color, though."

All those attributes fit the clothes Abigail wore. Scarlett had the right idea.

"'Course I would make it shorter 'cuz you would get tangled

up in that skirt. It would be hard to ride a horse, run, dance, and play softball in a dress like that. My clothes will let girls move like boys."

Why would girls want to move like boys? Wasn't the whole idea for girls to be girls and boys to be boys? Mulling over a response that wouldn't seem like arguing, Abigail opened her suitcase, full of dresses just like the one she wore. "Amish folks don't dance. Amish women play softball and volleyball in dresses just fine. They wear pants under their dresses when they ride horses."

Amish women, not her. For the next two weeks Abigail wasn't Amish Abigail.

"No dancing?" Fiona yelled. She threw herself into a series of twirls on her tippy-toes and then segued into some impossible forward and back dips at the waist all the while shimmying her skinny hips. "How do you stand it?"

She wasn't even out of breath. Could she fathom that a person didn't miss what she never had or did?

"To each their own." Heather caught her daughter by the shoulders and slid her arms around her. "Don't judge."

"I hafta dance. I would die if I couldn't dance."

"Don't mind her. She's my drama queen." Heather kissed the top of Fiona's head. "I invited a few folks over for a barbecue this evening to celebrate your visit. I need to get the brisket going and make the hamburger patties. I made the potato salad and coleslaw yesterday. Your aunt Nydia is bringing seven-layer dip. Your aunt DeeDee is bringing her famous sausage dip and chips. We call it crack dip because it's addictive. We'll make homemade ice cream. I have all the fixin's. It'll be fun."

Fun. A social gathering with a bunch of people Abigail had never met. Who wanted to see Heather's Plain daughter for themselves. "Will my . . . Will Eric Waters come?"

"Who's Eric Waters?" Scarlett perked up from her spot on the bed. "Is he the guy you—"

"Just never you mind." Heather's smile disappeared. "You girls are way too nosy."

"I love, love, love ice cream." Fiona pulled away from Heather. "Me and Scarlett decorated the deck with sparkly lights and tiki torches."

"Scarlett and I. Don't talk like an ignorant hick, child." Heather pulled a dress from the suitcase and stuck it on a hanger. She shook her head and clucked. "How you must swelter in this thing." She disappeared into the closet and reappeared a second later without the offending dress. "Anyway, let the girls give you a tour of the place while I ice down the beer."

The beer? Did Abigail English Girl drink alcohol? The room spun as if she'd already taken a swig.

"We'll have pop too. No worries." Heather must've caught Abigail's expression. "It's all good, or gut, as you would say."

"Come on, I want to show you my room." Scarlett grabbed Abigail's hand and tugged. "And the game room."

"She means our room." Fiona grabbed Abigail's other hand. "We have to share 'cuz Mom wants a guest room for the grandmas and grandpas. It's not fair that Brody gets his own room just because he's a boy."

"It's not because he's a boy. He's the oldest. It's not like it would make sense for one of you girls to share a room with him." Heather ran the words together like an often-recited prayer. "I'm not one of those sexist people, and you know it."

Her expression suddenly tentative, Heather paused next to the dresser. "There's one more thing. One more present." She picked up a small rectangular box with a pink bow around it. "I know you said you couldn't use one in Haven. But while you're here in Abilene, it sure would make life easier if I can keep in touch with you. If you get lost or separated from us, you'll be able to call us. It's about safety."

The contents of the box came as no surprise. Abigail let the phone sit in her hand, light, cool to the touch. It didn't feel like a viper. It didn't bite or sting. Yet it was seen as an umbilical cord to all the festering worldliness Plain people chose to avoid by staying off the electrical grid. Such a small piece of electronics for such a destructive path.

At least that's what Samuel said when he taught the baptism classes. "And be not conformed to this world: but be ye transformed by the renewing of your mind, that ye may prove what is that good, and acceptable, and perfect, will of God."

Plenty of youngies got cell phones during their rumspringas. Abigail couldn't afford one.

Dive in. This is where you find out who you are. The voice in her left ear sounded euphoric, full of joy at being set free. *Did she have to do it all at once? One step at a time.* The voice in her right ear sounded like Mother's.

"Thank you. It's very nice of you." Abigail turned the phone over in her palm. It had a sparkly purple case on it. Very pretty. It didn't look like an instrument of evil. "I imagine the girls would be happy to show me how to use it."

"You betcha!" Fiona chortled. "We can add Insta so you can do some reels about your new life. I bet they would go viral in a snap—"

"One thing at a time, child." Heather retrieved the phone from Abigail. "I already set it up for you." She pushed a button on the side. Eventually the screen lit up with a photo of Heather and the kids. "All our numbers are in here. Let's start with that and worry about all that social media garbage later. In the meantime I'll let the girls take it from here."

She handed the phone back and strolled from the room.

She was trying so hard. "Heather."

Heather looked back and Abigail smiled. "Thank you for coming to look for me."

Her face lit up. "You're welcome, daughter of mine."

Daughter of mine. The words rang in Abigail's ears as she followed the girls down the hallway to their bedroom. It likely was bigger than the guest bedroom, but it seemed smaller because it was so stuffed with . . . stuff. The girls had bunk beds, matching dressers and desks, stuffed animals, a flat-screen TV, computers, and shelves that contained plastic buckets filled with toys. Large dolls sat on the top shelf, Barbies on a middle shelf next to an enormous three-story dollhouse. The walls were purple, the comforters purple and neon green, and the curtains a lighter shade of the same color. It looked like a paint can had exploded. Posters of unicorns, horses, and boys with musical instruments covered what little free wall space remained.

Sleeping in this room must lead to nightmares or, at the very least, indigestion.

"Isn't it pretty?" Fiona scooped up the closest doll, a redhead dressed in a ballerina outfit. She held her out to Abigail. "This is Emmaline, my American Girl doll. She's a dancer too."

Some dolls were foreigners? "Pleased to meet you, Emmaline."

Fiona giggled. "And this is—"

"She doesn't want to meet all your stupid dolls, silly." Scarlett fiddled with buttons on an electronic thingamajig. Music with a pulsating beat and the sound of a man's voice chanting barely understandable words poured into the room. "Do you like rap?"

"I don't know."

"I love it," Fiona yelled as she gyrated around the room. "I have a recital coming up. You gotta come."

Abigail pressed her hands to her ears. The headache that bloomed on the ride to Abilene grew. "It's too loud."

"Sorry." Scarlett fiddled some more. The music subsided. "We like to feel the beat." She spun around and held up her phone. Clicking noises ensued.

"What are you doing?"

"Taking your picture."

"Why? Don't—"

"It's for Insta. My followers will love you." Scarlett slid her arm around Abigail's waist and held the phone up in the air. "Look at the camera and smile big."

"Why—?"

"I'm posting selfies on all my social media apps. I want to be an influencer."

The last thing a Plain woman wanted to do was influence others. Abigail English Girl would have to get used to this new world. She backed away. "One thing at a time, okay?"

Fiona grabbed Abigail's hand. "I know you said you don't dance—"

"I said Amish folks don't dance."

"What if I teach you a few dance steps? I want to post a new video on TikTok. That's where I post all my dance videos. It would be cool to show me teaching you your first dance."

"Yeah, it'll be fun. Dancing is the best." Scarlett turned the music back up. "The dancing Amish girl. I bet it goes viral."

What was viral? It sounded like a disease. When the children were sick, the doctor said they had a virus. Even antibiotics didn't help with a virus. "I'm not sure I'm ready just yet. It's my first day here. Please turn the music down."

"Do it." Brody stomped into the room, past Scarlett, straight to the electronic thing. A second later the music disappeared. "Are you trying to make her run home?"

"Just because you like that corny country music doesn't mean we have to." Scarlett grabbed a brush and held it up like a microphone.

"My wife left me, I drank forty beers, and my dog died so I jumped in my truck and ran it into a ditch. Oh me, oh my, I wanna die," she warbled. "Oh me, oh my, I wanna die."

"Whatever." Brody turned to Abigail with a pained smile that revealed braces. He was taller than his pictures and looked older than fourteen. He wore a Keith Urban T-shirt, basketball shorts, and flip-flops. "What's up, Big Sis? What's the deal with the getup? Are you studying to be a nun or what?"

"A nun?"

"She's Amish. Which Mom already explained to you." Fiona shoved past her brother and planted herself between Abigail and him. "Go away. We're having girl time."

"Mom made me come home. Here I am."

"Go clean your room. Mom says we all have to clean house."

"Do you play video games?" That question was directed to Abigail. Brody cocked his head. "Or are you more into hide-and-seek under that white thing on your head, maybe?"

Was he trying to be funny or making fun? "It's called a kapp. It's a prayer covering. The only things under it are my hair and my head."

"You should pray for someone to get you out of here." His thin shoulders shook, he laughed so hard at his own joke. "This is a crazy bunch of people. They put the *d* in dysfunctional, if you know what I mean."

She didn't, but Brody didn't bother to stop talking long enough for her to say so.

"If you were smart, you'd run like crazy back to that one-stoplight town you came from. The people who come to Abilene come here to die a slow, painful death of boredom."

"Don't listen to him." Fiona pushed Brody toward the door, but his feet were planted and she weighed half of what he did—if that.

"Get out. Your room is off-limits to us. You don't get to come into our room."

"Who wants to come in here? Someone threw up grape Kool-Aid all over the room." He swatted at Fiona like she was an annoying mosquito. "I just wanted to see what the long-lost daughter was like."

Sudden anger pulsed through Abigail. She hadn't asked to come here. She'd been invited. The nerves, lack of sleep, and thrumming headache combined to overcome her. "I wasn't lost. I've always known where I was. So did your mother. She's the one who gave me away, not the other way around."

"True. That's Mom, a one-woman wrecking machine." He sketched a half salute. "Good luck, Sis. I'm going back to my game."

"Mom says no video games until tomorrow. We have to clean up the house for the party tonight." Scarlett smiled sweetly at her older brother. "No candy bar wrappers in the game room or Flamin' Cheeto crumbs all over the carpet. She wants you to clean up your mess for a change."

Eye rolls and frowns were followed by a one-fingered salute. Abigail averted her gaze. This family had all sorts of nonspoken ways of responding to one another. None of them good. "I can go back to my room. I don't want to be in the way."

"It's not your room." Brody brushed past her on his way to the door. "So don't get too comfortable."

Chapter 16

Work was the best medicine for a restless heart. Or so they said. Who was *they*? Owen pulled his buggy into the drive in front of his uncle Wayne's barn and hopped out. Hairy followed. In the weeks since his rescue, Hairy had become Owen's shadow. Where Owen went, Hairy went. Owen didn't mind. He'd wanted company. He now had it. He surveyed the barn and corral. No Uncle Wayne. A horn sounded. There he was. Headed up the drive in a tractor pulling a flatbed.

On this first week of June, the weather was mild—perfect for planting corn and soybeans. Or cutting the second round of alfalfa. The bigger farms were harvesting wheat. It was also a perfect time for planting sunflowers. Instead Owen had spent the day overseeing the final touches to a garage in Parsons. The twenty-six-gauge metal siding was complete. Time to move on to the horse barn in Lyons.

He waved and waited for Wayne to pull up and turn off the tractor. His uncle looked nothing like Father. Instead he was shaped like an oversized, hard-boiled egg on toothpick legs. He'd gone gray in his late twenties. His belly preceded him when he hopped from the tractor and headed Owen's direction. "Howdy, *Bruderkind*. If you came to help us plant corn, you're a day late and a dollar short."

"I'm sorry I missed it."

"If anybody else said that, I'd laugh, but you I know. You love sowing and reaping. It's in your blood. I wish my boys were more inclined in that direction."

"Where are my cousins?"

"Daniel is breaking a horse for the Hoyts in Pretty Prairie. Samuel came back early. He's been feeling poorly the last few days. David is in the barn, repairing tack."

Samuel was one of the unfortunate folks whose symptoms from Lyme disease, contracted after hunting deer the previous season, hadn't abated with a course of antibiotics. "So Samuel's not any better?"

"Nee. The doctors gave him a stronger round of antibiotics. They say to give them time to work, but in the meantime he's a mess and trying not to show it. Today he overdid it."

"I'm sorry."

"Nothing to be sorry about. If it is the will of Gott, this too shall pass."

Uncle Wayne took off his straw hat and wiped down the fringe of gray hair that ringed his bald pate with a bandanna that had been wrapped around his neck. Every bit of exposed skin was a deep bronze, making his blue eyes startling in contrast. Sun wrinkles decorated his pudgy face.

Together they walked toward the weather-beaten house Uncle Wayne shared with his wife, Nelda, and their six kids. "I wanted to talk to you about something."

"About the sunflowers, I reckon."

"Daed told you?"

"He might have mentioned it."

"What do you think?"

"I think it's worth considering, given what I'm seeing in the markets. We'll not break even on our crops this year."

Excitement revved through Owen. "So you'll plant sunflowers this year?"

"Next year. If we can afford it." Uncle Wayne slapped the hat back on his head. His shoulders drooped. "If your daed doesn't sell to the McCormacks."

"The McCormacks," Owen sputtered. The English family already owned half of Reno County, it seemed. "How do they figure in?"

Uncle Wayne knocked his boots against the porch step, sending dust and dead straw flying. "Bill McCormack approached your daed yesterday about buying his acreage."

"But you were all set to buy it."

"He's offering a bucketload of money—I don't have it. In fact, I would have to make payments. I'm not holding your daed to our deal when it's not nearly as gut. It wouldn't be right."

Owen had been putting away most of his earnings since he started working at fourteen to fund his dream of owning his own farm. "I have some money in savings—"

"Not that kind of money, and your daed won't take money from his own suh. He feels bad enough about selling it out from under you." Uncle Wayne held the screen door open, allowing Owen to enter the kitchen first. The tantalizing scent of homemade barbecue sauce wafted in the air. "At least with me we could still work together."

A welcoming smile on her face, Aunt Nelda stopped in the middle of the kitchen. She held a basket of rolls. "Hey, Bruderkind. I didn't know you were here. I'm glad I made an extra-big batch of barbecued baked pork chops." She cocked her head toward his cousin Bethany. "Dochder, set another place at the table."

Bethany shot a gap-toothed grin at Owen as she gathered up a plate and silverware. "We're having macaroni-and-cheese casserole and pea salad and my favorite—rhubarb cream pie for dessert. I helped make them—we made two."

"I love rhubarb cream pie."

"Me too."

Aunt Nelda handed off the rolls to his cousin Raeann. She followed her sister Charlotte, who carried the mac-and-cheese casserole.

"You two get cleaned up. Food's getting cold." Aunt Nelda scooped up a water pitcher. She lingered in the doorway for a second. "And whatever you're talking about, finish up, because it doesn't look like it's pleasant."

Owen waited for her to leave the room. "What did Daed tell Bill?"

"That he wanted to think about it and talk to his family first. Bill's a gut man. He isn't pressuring. But he wants a decision in time to plan for next year's crops. The more acreage he has, the better his profit margin."

Big farms were taking over the state. Smaller farms had a hard time competing. Father had bought their property the year before he married Mother, with the intention of making farming his livelihood. Over the years that had become harder and harder until he couldn't support his growing family with the proceeds. The construction business was more profitable by far.

If only Father and some of the other Plain farmers could combine properties and forces instead of selling out to the big English farmers. It might be the only way to preserve their way of life. "Maybe we should talk to some of the others about creating a co-op—our own big farm."

"Big farms require more machinery and more mechanization to be efficient. Every aspect of such an operation would require Gmay meetings, discussions, and votes." The lines deepened around Uncle Wayne's mouth and eyes. His gaze on the window over the kitchen sink, he washed his hands longer than necessary. "You know as well as I do that *quick* isn't a word that applies to change for Plain folks.

Our way of life hasn't changed much in several hundred years for a reason."

"Yet my daed makes a living by building metal buildings." Owen's response sounded more critical than he had intended. Their work was honorable and supplemented the crops they raised to feed themselves and their livestock. "A necessary change supported by the district. I don't mean to knock it. Our people have stayed close to the earth for centuries. I'm trying to uphold our tradition and our way of life."

"I know it seems like we're talking out both sides of our mouths." Uncle Wayne dried his hands and dropped the towel on the counter. "But your daed has a lot on his plate right now. He's thinking ahead like a gut provider. Whatever he decides, I'm gut with it."

"What do you mean . . . a lot on his plate?"

"I don't want to speak out of turn."

"Are you talking about Mary?"

"It's best to let that sleeping dog lie. We'd better get in there and eat before my fraa comes back for us." The laugh lines around Uncle Wayne's eyes crinkled. "She doesn't like it when I let the food get cold."

Only a passing reference to his father's courting could be allowed. Life kept changing, but no one wanted to acknowledge those changes—just as they had pretended everything was fine in those weeks after Mother died. Once Owen had happened on his father in the barn sobbing, his face contorted with grief and wet with tears, feeding the horses. He hadn't said a word. He simply sidestepped Owen and strode from the barn.

Uncle Wayne led the way into the great room. He took the chair at the head of the table, grabbed a glass of water, and downed half of it. "Have you talked to your daed about this co-op idea?"

Moving right along. "Nee. I've been turning it over in my head, trying to find a solution to this problem."

"You're the only one who sees it as a problem."

"What will you do if Daed sells to Bill?"

"Bill has offered me work."

It wouldn't be that different from working with his dad. Except Bill was an Englisher with big equipment and many workers. "At least there's that."

Before Owen could answer, Aunt Nelda leaned between them and plopped down a huge pan of pork chops. "Food's ready."

Her meaningful glance said it all. Everyone settled down. Heads bowed. Eyes closed.

Gott, thank You for this food. Thank You for these folks. And sei so gut, heal Samuel's body. He is young and seeks to work hard, marry, and have a family—if it is Your will. And Gott, please watch over Abigail. If it is your will, bring her home quickly and with no lasting effects from her time with her Englisch family. And watch over Daed. And our family. And the farm.

"Amen."

From the emphatic sound, it might not have been the first amen. Sometimes a man had a lot to pray about. He might even get lost in his prayers. Owen opened his eyes, grabbed the tongs, and handed them to his uncle. "This looks gut."

It was. The pork chops fell off the bone and melted in his mouth. The tangy barbecue sauce woke up all the taste buds. Pea salad made with fresh peas from Aunt Nelda's garden were a perfect side to the creamy mac and cheese made with sharp cheddar. Chatter was sparse. Everyone was too busy stuffing their faces to talk.

Finally Uncle Wayne leaned back in his chair and patted his paunch. "You can see why my gut is expanding. My fraa is a gut cook."

Owen's sisters were good cooks, but they didn't have the years of experience Aunt Nelda did. Having a woman in the house made a difference. Mary's spinach lasagna was tasty. So was her tuna casserole.

A way to a man's heart was through his stomach, or so the saying went. Aunt Nelda's thoughts must have followed a similar path. Her forehead furrowed and she shook her head. "It's nothing special. Just plain, old food. How are the girls doing?"

"Everyone is doing gut."

"Really?" Charlotte giggled. Frowning, Raeann poked her with her elbow. "Ouch. I'm just saying there aren't that many girls left your age who aren't married."

It seemed everyone knew about Owen's situation with Abigail. He ignored Charlotte's jab.

"That's enough." Aunt Nelda scowled at Charlotte. "Go fetch the pie."

Charlotte pouted. Her day hadn't come yet. Someday, if she didn't guard her heart, she, too, would know how it felt to have her most prized possession hanging in the balance while the person she loved tried to make up his mind.

"I'm so full, I don't think I can eat another bite." Owen stood. "I should get back. They'll be wondering what happened to me."

"You said rhubarb cream pie was your favorite." Bethany joined her sister in pouting. "I helped make it."

Owen sat back down. He didn't like to disappoint.

Which led him right back to Abigail. Had he disappointed her by not trying to convince her to stay? And then there was his father. Had he disappointed him by not wanting to be in the construction business with him?

"I can't miss out on pie."

Bethany grinned. At least one person wasn't disappointed in him. Pie was easy.

Chapter 17

"Don't get too comfortable." Brody's words ricocheted around Abigail's head. No chance of that.

At least forty people crowded Heather's long, narrow three-quarter-acre backyard filled with oak, elm, and sycamore trees that provided much-needed shade from the early evening sun. Abigail's hand hurt from all the shaking. She'd lost track of names by the fifth or sixth person. The only ones she remembered for sure were Heather's sisters DeeDee and Nydia.

They looked nothing like Heather, but they talked just as fast and just as much. They were determined to make her feel at home, alternately shoving at her dip and chips and root beer over crushed ice. Finally DeeDee rushed away to reheat the "crack" dip while Nydia went to consult with the "DJ," a high school kid who favored what Nydia called "hip-hop" to the preferred "pop" music requested by Heather.

Abigail sank into a canvas camp chair positioned near the picnic tables alongside the wraparound back porch. From here she had a full view of the big gas grill Heather called her "baby," the two tables full of side dishes and all the "fixin's," as well as the dozens of lawn chairs that dotted the grass beyond the porch. The aroma of hamburgers, hot dogs, and brats grilling tantalized the taste buds. White Christmas lights strung across the porch twinkled, giving the scene a festive air.

She smoothed the worn cotton of the dress she'd decided to wear for this gathering—after much internal debate. She'd tried on the clothes Heather bought her, which fit perfectly, but it was just too much. Day one, she'd had her picture taken, danced with her half sisters, and accepted a phone, which currently lay on the dresser in her room. Baby steps, but steps. The clothes would be next—when she was ready.

Scarlett and her friends practiced cheerleader moves in the light cast by the tiki torches. Fiona presided over the ice cream maker, an electric gizmo that churned the mix on its own. In the creeping dusk the evening took on a dreamy quality. Maybe Abigail was dreaming. Maybe she was still at home. She would roll over and wake up to the sound of Jane's tiny snores.

"So they left the guest of honor all alone."

Abigail peered up at the owner of the inquiring voice. He seemed tall, but maybe that was because she was sitting. A chocolate-brown cowboy hat hid his eyes. He tipped it in her direction and took a seat in the camp chair next to her. He immediately leaned back and stretched out long jean-clad legs. His boots matched his hat. "That wasn't very nice of them. Heather throws a great shindig, like a big block party or a family reunion. Everyone knows everyone. Unless you're new in town. I'm Rhett Strong, grandson of your next-door neighbor to the right."

How could she tell him she was perfectly happy with the respite? Or that she shouldn't sit here in public talking to an English man? No, old rules didn't apply to her in this strange, new life that was hers for the choosing. "Nice to meet you."

"Abigail, right?"

She nodded.

"Well, Abigail, tell me. What's your first impression of these fine folks and the sprawling metropolis of Abilene, Kansas, one of the state's most enduring tourist destinations?"

He had a funny way of talking. Like a radio announcer.

"They seem very nice." Tourists came to Yoder to buy Amish quilts and furniture, take pictures of the Amish riding on tractors, and eat at Buggies and Bonnets. Abigail had lived her entire life one hundred miles from Abilene, but she knew little about the town. "I haven't seen much of it yet."

Rhett shoved his hat back on his curly walnut-brown hair. His eyes also matched his hat and boots. They were framed by matching crow's feet. Either he liked to laugh, or he spent a lot of time in the sun. His tan suggested the latter, but it could be both.

"You mean you haven't seen the world's biggest spur yet?" He chortled. He had a nice laugh. "It's certified by the *Guinness World Records* book. I'll have to take you for a look-see."

"What would you need a big spur for?"

He threw his head back and laughed even harder. "No reason. That's the whole point, my friend."

They'd just met and they were already friends? "I see." She really didn't, but Rhett seemed nice. "Tourists come to Abilene to see a big spur?"

"And to visit the Dwight D. Eisenhower Presidential Library and Museum, and the Greyhound Hall of Fame, the Jeffcoat Photo Studio Museum, the Seelye Mansion, and Old Abilene Town, a cow town replica where you can drink sarsaparilla in the saloon and watch can-can girls perform or go outside to watch the gunslingers shoot each other in the street."

Rhett reeled off the attractions rapid-fire, then heaved a big breath. "Who knew such a small town could have that many places to visit?

Oh, and I forgot the Abilene and Smoky Valley train rides, if you have a hankering to ride in a 1919 steam locomotive."

Indeed. Abigail had read about President Eisenhower as part of her history lessons in school. They'd planned a field trip to the presidential complex, but a bad storm had forced its cancellation. For some reason it hadn't been rescheduled before she graduated. The cow town replica was new to her. So was the train. "Why would anyone want to watch people shoot each other?"

"It's a reenactment. No one dies, I promise." He sipped from a Coke and settled the can into the cupholder. "Tell me about yourself, Abigail Bontrager."

"There's not much to tell."

That he didn't already know. He knew what everyone in the world seemed to know. The circumstances of her birth. Heather didn't care that everyone in her circle of friends and family knew she'd given birth to a child out of wedlock and given that baby to another couple to raise. In the English world that might not be unusual, but it didn't happen often in Abigail's world. If a Plain couple committed the sin of fornication and the girl found herself in a family way, they went to the bishop, confessed their sin, and married in a small, quiet wedding.

"You're not chatty, are you?" Rhett smiled. His bottom teeth were slightly crooked, but all of them were a startling white. "I don't mind. If you'd rather, we can just sit here and not talk."

"That would be nice." Heat toasted her neck and spread across her cheeks. "Is that rude? I don't mean to be rude."

"No, just honest. I prefer honest, don't you?"

Abigail nodded. She rested the root beer in its cupholder so she could shove a wisp of damp hair stuck on her forehead back under her kapp. After the frigid air in the house, the evening air hung thick and warm on her skin. Nydia had done her duty, and the music no longer pounded like a hammer on Abigail's head. The scent of grilling meat made her mouth water. Her stomach rumbled. She hadn't eaten since breakfast. No wonder her head hurt.

"Can I get you a plate?"

Had he heard her stomach? The heat on her cheeks intensified. "That's all right. You don't have to do that."

"I don't mind."

"Men don't get food for women."

More laughter. "Maybe not in your neck of the woods, but around here chivalry is not dead, my dear."

"It's just that I wouldn't feel right, your waiting on me."

"Why don't we go together, then?"

He was trying so hard. Abigail surveyed the yard. No one else seemed to be paying any attention. "That would be nice."

It was. His presence seemed to keep the others at bay, at least for the time being. Abigail made a hamburger with strips of bacon, cheddar cheese, and all the fixings, then added potato salad, coleslaw, and chips, along with a scoop of whipped cream fruit salad. None of the "crack" dip for her.

"You're hungry." Grinning, Rhett nodded at her plate from the other side of the table. "I guess I am too."

His plate was even fuller than hers. He'd added a pile of brisket and a large puddle of barbecue sauce. They sat at a picnic table on the grass next to two older couples engaged in a fierce debate about something called economic recovery. Whatever that was, they weren't happy with the way it was going.

"I get the feeling you don't get out much." Rhett unrolled the paper napkin from around the plastic utensils and laid it aside. "This must be overwhelming."

"We have lots of frolics." Abigail searched for words to describe the difference. Frolics involved a work project of some kind. Plain families visited on Sundays or on holidays when no one worked, but these were quieter affairs. No music. A volleyball or a softball game. Table games. Spirited conversations, yes, but not at such decibels. "But I know everyone in Haven and everyone knows me. We grew up together. A lot of us are related. It's not so . . . noisy."

"Abilene isn't a big town. Maybe sixty-four hundred people. But it must seem big compared to Yoder. It has like twenty-eight people, doesn't it?"

"More than that combined with Haven—not much more. It's not that." Rhett hadn't sat next to her to talk about population and tourist attractions. Was he simply being nice? Or did he want something from her? "Everyone here is very nice. Heather is nice. The girls are nice. They just don't understand how different they live than we do. It'll take me a minute to get used to this."

"Do you want to get used to it?"

Technically she'd already had her chance during her rumspringa. She'd tried on English clothes and gone to a movie in Hutchinson and one truly awful keg party in a farmer's pasture. At the time it had been fun, but she hadn't longed for more. "We live the way we do, we dress the way we do, for a reason. A reason that is important to us. Our faith. I took vows. Changing that mindset from one day to the next is discombobulating."

"I've done some reading about the Amish." Rhett picked up a pickle and sniffed it. "Yum. I love my grandma's homemade bread-and-butter pickles. Anyway, I get that you want to avoid the pitfalls of a fallen world. It makes sense in the context of your history and cultural background."

"You're the first person to say that today." Relief eased the tension in Abigail's shoulders. For all his laughter, Rhett had a serious side. He'd bothered to learn about the Amish. "We're not sideshow freaks. Our traditions have meaning."

"Of course they do. That's why I want to write an article about you for the newspaper." Rhett picked up his hamburger with both hands, but he didn't take a bite. "I'm a reporter at the *Reflector-Chronicle* newspaper here in town. I think folks would be real interested in knowing more about what you believe and why you do the things you do."

A newspaper reporter. That was the last occupation she would've picked for the man in front of her. "But you look like a cowboy." She blurted the words without thinking how they would sound.

"I am. Sort of. My parents owned a ranch out by Dodge City. When I was sixteen my dad died, my mom sold the ranch, and we came here to live with Grandma. When I was in high school, my mom headed out west to Hays for a job and left us kids here." His smile never wavered. Whatever emotions these memories stirred up, he hid them well. "Anyway, I'm a cowboy without a horse, so to speak. What do you say? About the interview, I mean?"

He was being nice because he wanted something. Irritation burbled up in Abigail. Going through this upheaval in her life was hard enough without having a spotlight cast on her. Amish folks surely weren't the only people who didn't care to have their private trials made public spectacles. "No thank you."

"Are you sure? It's a chance to educate folks about the Amish way of life. To dispel the myths." Rhett shifted the burger to one hand and grabbed a napkin. He dabbed at his face, but he completely missed the glob of catsup on his upper lip. "Every family in town and most of the families in Dickinson County subscribe to the paper."

"It's not my job to educate people about the Amish way of life. That's not why I'm here. What I'm going through is private."

Rhett dropped the half-eaten burger. He planted both elbows on the table and thoroughly wiped his face. He tossed the napkin onto the table, still staring at Abigail. Finally he cleared his throat. "I can appreciate your reasons. Not everyone wants their five minutes of fame. But if you change your mind, let me know."

"I don't think I will, but if I do, I'll tell you." Abigail relaxed and concentrated on the potato salad. It tasted of Dijon mustard. Her mom would like it. Her mom Lorene. "I'm nothing special. I'm plain old boring. I've never been anywhere or done anything except clean house and work as a waitress."

"It's not about where you've been. You're different. Different is interesting." Rhett sighed. "It's hard to find different around here. I'm up to my eyeballs in 4-H and FFA projects. I'm tired of writing about hogs and pigs."

"Maybe you should write about how small family farms are being eaten up by bigger farms. A whole way of life is disappearing." Abigail's father frequently lamented this shift with other men over Sunday lunch after worship service. "Or about sunflowers being a cash crop. I know people who are thinking about growing sunflowers instead of wheat."

People like Owen. What was he doing right now?

"Wow. You're a fount of story ideas. I've considered the first one, but the second one I hadn't given much thought to." He burped quietly behind his hand. "My boss is more interested in people features, slice-of-life stories. People eat that stuff up. But no worries, you're off the hook. And to make it up to you for springing the story idea on you, I'm going to bring you some ice cream. How does that sound?"

"Good. It sounds good."

"What kind of toppings?"

"Chocolate syrup, nuts, cherries . . . the works."

"Aww, living dangerously. I like that. I'll be right back. Don't let anyone steal my seat."

Rhett returned a few minutes later with two astonishingly full Styrofoam bowls of ice cream. Even the other couples at the table stared, both dumbfounded and obviously jealous, when he set hers on the table with a flourish.

Instead of sitting across from her, he swung his long legs over the bench and squeezed in next to her. He had a small scar on his chin. "It'll be easier to talk. It's so loud I feel like I'm shouting."

"It is loud." Abigail didn't dare scoot any farther to her right. She'd fall off the bench. She hugged her elbows close to her body and leaned closer to the table for that first bite of ice cream. Chocolate syrup mixed with the sweet, milky flavor of soft-serve vanilla ice cream, chocolate chips, and chopped walnuts. Even Rhett's proximity couldn't spoil that first bite. "Mmmm."

"It's the best, right?" Rhett took a second bite, a low hum in his throat. He thrust his spoon in the air and circled it like a cowboy lassoing. "Woo-hoo. That's good stuff."

He reminded Abigail of Rose and Joel and their love of sweets. The thought evoked a wave of homesickness. She sighed and took another bite.

"Don't be sad, girl." His shoulder touched hers. His breath tickled her skin. "It'll be okay, I promise."

A shiver ran down Abigail's spine. Heat spiraled in her chest. She didn't dare move. She hunched her shoulders, trying to make herself small. "I'm not sad. Just tired."

"Eat your ice cream. A sugar infusion is just what the doctor ordered." Rhett held out his serving-size spoon—obviously stolen from the table—loaded with chocolate ice cream, nuts, a dollop of whipped cream, and a cherry. "Take your medicine, girl."

She had no choice, really. She opened her mouth, and the scrumptious sweetness slid onto her tongue. "Hmmm."

"Don't you feel a second wave of energy flowing through you?"

It flowed more from his nearness than the sugary concoction. "I do feel more awake."

"Good, because I think the fun is about to begin."

His concept of fun became apparent a few seconds later. Heather appeared on the deck's top step with a microphone in her hand. "I hope you folks are enjoying the party. Eat hearty. There's still a ton of food. Be prepared to take something home with you. I don't have room in my fridge for all of it. Not that it's time to think about going home. No sirree, Bob. You know what time it is?"

"Party time!" A kid who squatted in the grass next to Scarlett yelled it out. "It's always party time at your house, Mrs. Hanson."

A ripple of laughter and clapping spread across the yard.

"You got that right, Chris," Heather shouted. The microphone squeaked. "Sorry about that. It's karaoke time, folks. That's what time it is. And that means it's time to dance. Clear your chairs out of the grass, make room for the dance floor. Who wants to go first?"

"Me, me!" Fiona jumped up, turned a series of cartwheels, and landed in front of the steps. "Me and the girls."

"Let's let the grown-ups go first. You kids will get your turns. Just be patient." Heather waggled the mic. "Come on, ladies and gents. Who wants to give it a whirl? You know you do, Nate. Come on, Tiff. Get up here."

A couple, presumably Nate and Tiff, scooted from a nearby bench and trotted to the deck. They held hands and whooped like they'd just won a million dollars. After a loud whispering conversation, the music blared. A song with a heavy bass beat boomed over the big speakers that flanked the deck. The two had terrible voices, but no one seemed to mind. They were too busy gyrating around the yard to lyrics that spoke of the newfound freedom after a breakup.

"Come on, you want to, you know you do." Rhett slid his arm

around Abigail's shoulders and squeezed. His spicy aftershave tickled her nose. He leaned so close his breath warmed her ear as he spoke. "I know you've never danced before. Let me show you how."

"I couldn't . . ." Could she? Dancing in the girls' bedroom was one thing. In a crowd of people, another. Not to this wild music. To a ballad, maybe. If she closed her eyes so she could pretend no one could see her dancing. And she couldn't see them either. "Go ahead, dance with one of the other girls."

"I'd rather dance with you." His arm slackened. He had to raise his voice to be heard over the music's pounding rhythm. "I'm sorry if I'm being too forward."

"I'm not used to it."

"I don't mean to make you uncomfortable."

They were practically shouting at each other.

"You're not." In fact, she liked it a little too much. She liked him. "I just don't want you to get the wrong idea."

The song ended just as she blurted that last sentence. It got quiet. Then someone giggled. Someone else laughed.

"Rhett, get up here." A man in a huge white cowboy hat clomped up the steps and grabbed the microphone. "Come on, buddy, gotta give us your rendition of 'Sweet Home Alabama.' No one does it better than you do. Bring your little lady friend with you."

His hand on her elbow, Rhett rose and brought Abigail upright with him. Her heart catapulting in her chest, she tugged free. "I'm a terrible singer. I don't know the song."

Not true on either count. She had a passable voice and "Sweet Home Alabama" played on the oldies country music station in the restaurant kitchen. Everyone knew the words to it.

"You wanted to see just how English you could be." Rhett took a step back. "It's up to you, but this is a good opportunity to see how it feels."

Was this the "big chance" she'd envisioned? Abigail the English Girl said yes.

Her legs hadn't received the message yet. They shook and wobbled. "Let's do it."

Rhett linked arms with her, and together they mounted the steps onto the deck. He took the microphone. "Here we go!"

A yard full of smiling, expectant faces stared up at Abigail. Fiona waved and held up a thumb. "You go, girl," Scarlett yelled. "Whoop!"

An icy sweat formed on Abigail's face. Her stomach heaved. Her heart hammered against her rib cage. She opened her mouth. Nothing came out.

"Wait until I start the music." Rhett's hand no longer held her up. Abigail's body threatened to sink through the slats in the deck and ooze into the earth below. "Here we go."

The familiar guitar licks sounded. The drums followed. A roar went up. All the younger folks crowded the grassy makeshift dance floor. Rhett snapped his fingers and thrust the microphone between them. He had a deep, melodic voice. He pointed at the screen where the words flowed.

Abigail mumbled a few lines. Rhett shot a mock scowl at her. "Come on, girl, you can do better than that."

She could do better. *Come on, you're here. This is what you wanted. Get on with it.*

The voice was back on her left shoulder, loud and clear.

So she did. Miraculously, she did. Her voice climbed to match Rhett's. A grin split his face. His hand rubbed her back.

The people danced, clapped, and sang along, their voices rising to the dark Kansas sky. The white lights twinkled. A night breeze ruffled the welcome banner that hung over the railing.

In a few scant minutes, it was over. Lightning didn't strike Abigail. She didn't descend into hell. A lightness buoyed her steps as she slipped from the deck with Rhett right behind her. The crowd continued to clap and cheer.

"Way to go, Sis." Scarlett raised her hand in a high five. "You sounded good up there."

"I can't believe I did that."

"Believe it." Heather shimmied across the grass, her arms out wide. "I knew my daughter was in there somewhere."

Abigail stepped into her hug. Tomorrow she might feel differently, but tonight she was Heather's daughter, Abigail English Girl.

Chapter 18

Blessed silence reigned in the Hanson house. Abigail tiptoed barefoot through the dining room toward the kitchen. Early morning sunlight peeked through the windows that lined one wall. She'd stayed in bed as long as she could, waiting for sounds or signs that Heather was up. Nothing. Water followed by coffee could wait no longer.

After her impromptu performance with Rhett, she'd pleaded exhaustion, slipped into the house, stripped out of the dress, showered, and curled up under a blanket she'd found in the closet. Her nerves jangled, she couldn't stop shivering. She'd begun the day a Plain woman and ended it singing karaoke at a backyard party with a man she'd just met.

For her first foray into the world as a woman of English descent, the experience had been bigger than life, bigger than her puny imagination could've created. The question was, did she like it?

Did she want to follow this road no matter where it led?

Rhett Strong's scent of spicy aftershave teased her. It couldn't still linger in the air around her. Yet his presence pressed against her. His warm breath tickled her ear. His hand pulled her to her feet with ease. His fingers on her back. No one could think clearly under those circumstances. No one as untested, as unworldly as a young, simple Plain woman. Rhett was the opposite of Owen in most ways, but he had the same spark of kindness in him. And an eagerness to know her.

Owen of the blue eyes and earnest face. Owen who'd stepped back to give her room to find herself—not many Amish men would have done that. Amish women didn't need to find themselves.

Time to let Plain Abigail give herself a talking-to. *You've never been away from home before. You've never had this much freedom before. Slow down. Ease into it.*

Today was a new day. She would avoid Rhett Strong, be nice to Brody, spend time with Heather, and allow herself to experience life in an English world in small servings.

Newly resolute, Abigail paused in the doorway to the kitchen. Dirty serving dishes, utensils, pots, pans, skillets, spices, dirty towels, washrags, half-empty chip bags, spilled soda, and empty liquor bottles littered the counters, table, and floor. What tornado tore through here and didn't wake her?

Stepping over an empty sour cream container that had fallen to the floor, she went to the windows that faced the backyard. It didn't fare much better. Apparently the womenfolk didn't see a need to help with the cleanup after a gathering. Cleaning up immediately kept food from drying on the dishes, especially the pots and pans. It made them so much easier to clean.

This was something Abigail knew how to do. She pushed up her sleeves and turned back to the kitchen. "If I were a garbage bag, where would I be?"

A walk-in pantry provided the answer to her question. The cleaning supplies and plastic bags occupied their own shelves. She went to work. With a short break for orange juice discovered in the refrigerator behind two bottles of Sprite, she worked her way through the kitchen in the first round, simply throwing away trash and stacking dirty dishes on the kitchen counter. Heather had a dishwasher. Working at a restaurant made them old hat for this Plain woman. After she gathered all the dishes, she would load and run it.

Outside, wind chimes swaying from a sycamore tree made music on a soft breeze. A mourning dove cooed in response. The slick, dewy grass tickled her bare feet. Singing softly, Abigail made her way through the picnic tables, across the deck, and down the steps, filling a second garbage bag. This she knew how to do. Beer cans, beer bottles, pop cans, paper plates, plastic cups, Styrofoam plates, napkins, plastic utensils. Folks had deposited their trash in the cans Heather placed by the steps until they overflowed. Others didn't bother to pick up after themselves.

The party had gone on long after Abigail had gone inside. Even with a pillow over her head, she'd still been able to hear the music. The last time she peered at the bed-stand clock, the red numbers read eleven thirty. The neighbors didn't mind. They were all at the party.

"Well, at least they had a good time." Abigail smiled at the robin perched in an oak tree that shaded the deck. The bird chirped and took flight. "Me too."

"Talking to yourself?"

Abigail jumped, dropped the garbage bag, and whirled.

Rhett peered over the graying wooden fence that separated his grandmother's house from Heather's. Instead of the cowboy hat, he wore a red Kansas City Chiefs cap. Brown stubble darkened his chin and lower cheeks. "Sorry, didn't mean to startle you."

So much for keeping her distance. How did a person do that when the man lived next door? *"Keep your distance. Be polite, but firm."* Her mother's voice whispered in Abigail's ear. *"Be gut."* Abigail picked up her bag. "Yes, you did."

"I'm not mean, really I'm not." His grin faded. "I had fun last night. I hope you did, too, but I know it might have been a little too much a little too fast. It's just that you're not like any girl I've ever known. You're skittish as a new foal."

"Are you saying I'm a horse?"

"No, no. I'm saying you're temperamental."

"No, I'm not."

"Why don't you let me make it up to you? Let me help with the cleanup."

Too close. "Where I'm from, men don't clean house."

"You were the guest of honor. You shouldn't have to clean up after your own party. Also, Heather's kids should be doing it. They're spoiled rotten."

Technically Heather's kids included Abigail. "She gave the party for me. The least I can do is clean up."

"You're too nice. I'll be right there."

"That's really not—" He was already gone.

A few minutes later Rhett reappeared around the side of the house. Gone were the jeans and cowboy boots, replaced by basketball shorts, a shimmering white T-shirt, and dirty sneakers. Abigail pointed to the box of bags on the table. *Make the best of it.* "You do trash. I'll carry dirty dishes inside."

"Let's start over. Let's call this the getting-to-know-you phase of a friendship." Rhett picked up a stack of paper plates and dumped them into the bag. "Let's start with the fact that we're both early birds. I don't require a lot of sleep. I like being up before everyone else. And I don't drink, so I'm not nursing a hangover like most of the knuckleheads who stumbled home from here last night."

"Why don't you drink?"

"Never had a taste for it."

Something in his tone suggested there was more to it than that, but prying into his business wasn't a good idea. Abigail picked up an oversized spatula and two sets of tongs lying next to the grill. They were coated in congealed grease. "Doesn't anyone go to church on Sunday morning?"

"Heather doesn't go, as far as I know, but I don't know her that well. I went when I was in college, before I came home to live with Grandma. But I don't want to go to her church, which is kind of awkward. I keep putting off finding the right one for me."

Having choices for church would be an odd quandary indeed. "What's wrong with your grandmother's church?"

"Nothing. It's right for her, but they're mostly older folks. They like old hymns and lots of reciting of creeds and corporate prayers. The services put me to sleep. I'm more into faith music with a band and lots of energy. People really getting into it with amens and hallelujahs, even some dancing in the aisles. Worship with a capital *W*. When I find one, I'll take you."

He wouldn't like three-hour Plain services in which a single hymn could last ten minutes or more. How would she feel in an English church service, especially one like that? "I'm only here for two weeks."

"So you're already planning to cut and run?"

His tone stung. "I'm only here for a visit. I never said I was staying."

"Really? Heather told my grandmother you were coming to live with her."

So that was her plan all along. "I have a family who loves me back in Haven." And a man who might grow to love her if given the chance. "Heather knows that. She made it happen. It's hard to understand why she's trying to take it back now. It's awfully late to try to change me back to English."

"So why did you come?"

Good question. "To find out who I am."

Rhett loomed over her, his dark eyes piercing. "The Amish woman speaks truth. You thought maybe you'd like this life better."

"I thought maybe I would fit better here." Maybe this was where God always intended her to be. How would she know if she didn't give it a proper chance? How could she discern God's plan if she didn't force her heart to be open to new possibilities? "I've always been clumsy. Really clumsy and awkward. I'm not a good cook and I don't like to sew. I think maybe it's because I don't really fit in where I live. Maybe I was never intended to be Plain."

"No one cares if you're clumsy. Not here, anyway. It's endearing." Rhett stomped up the porch steps with a full garbage bag in one hand. He halted in Abigail's path. "It's cute. You're cute."

"There's nothing cute about a grown woman spilling tea on a customer or falling up the steps on the way to church." Abigail ducked around him. She dropped a dirty serving spoon in her tub and picked up the overflowing receptacle. "I can't seem to control my arms and legs."

For some unfathomable reason Abigail could admit her anguish over this flaw to an English man—a virtual stranger—standing in her English mother's backyard. Maybe it was because she would leave here in two weeks and never see Rhett again. "What kind of wife and mother will that make me? What if I drop the baby or spill hot coffee on the children or fall and break my neck and can't take care of them? How will I feed my family when I'm a terrible cook? Their clothes will look awful because I can't sew a straight seam if my life depended on it."

"Whoa, whoa, whoa!" Rhett dropped the garbage bag. He took the tub from her. "The more you worry, the more you tense up, the more you stress out, the more likely you are to have a problem. You need to relax."

How was she supposed to relax with this man so near? He filled up the space around her, sucking up the air. He didn't even seem to notice his effect on others. "Easy for you to say."

She zigzagged around him and fled to the kitchen. Rhett followed. He deposited the tub on the counter near the dishwasher. "You need to meet my sister."

"I'm sure she's very nice." Abigail opened the dishwasher and began to fill it with dishes. That way she didn't have to see his expression when she admitted her flaws and frailties. "But how will that help?"

Rhett rearranged the saucers she'd placed on the top shelf and started on the glasses. "Kiera's a personal coach."

A personal coach. That didn't sound like something a Plain woman could have.

"Don't worry." He took a plate from her hand and stashed it on the bottom shelf. "She'll love coaching you. You're so interesting, she'll do it for free. She's out of town at a spiritual retreat this week, but I'll introduce you the minute she gets back."

"I really don't think—"

"Wait until you try the mindfulness techniques. They really work."

"Aren't you two chummy so early in the morning. Or maybe it was a late night turned morning."

Abigail turned. Brody sauntered into the kitchen with a skateboard under one arm. He proceeded directly to the refrigerator, where he extracted a bottle of water. The meaning of his words sank in.

"No, there was no late night. No anything." Abigail sidestepped away from the dishwasher—away from Rhett. "We were just cleaning up—"

"Something you should've done." Rhett's cool tone said he'd caught the implication as well. He leaned against the counter, the picture of a relaxed man. "You should shut up about things you know nothing about."

"Just making an observation." Brody's nose wrinkled. "Having a party wasn't my idea. No way I'm cleaning up. I'm out of here." He spun around and strolled from the room.

"Drop a bomb and head for the hills. The kid is predictable." Rhett's full lips curled in disgust. "Somebody should put a muzzle on him."

"He's a kid. A child." Growing up with divorced parents, including a mother who one day brought home an older sister he was supposed to welcome with open arms, was difficult. "You should go. I can finish up here."

"Why should I let a punk kid get under my skin? Don't you either."

"He's my half brother."

"All the more reason he should learn some manners."

"Your brothers never needle you?"

"I only have sisters. I'm the oldest. Then Kiera, the personal coach, and Melanie, a freshman at K-State. She wants to be a kindergarten teacher." Rhett ticked them off on his fingers. He said their names with obvious affection. "And you. Besides bigmouth, Fiona, and Scarlett. Who else do you have?"

"You should really go. I can finish up."

He groaned. "You care too much what other people think."

"It's not a matter of what people think or what Brody thinks. It's what is right or wrong. I shouldn't spend time with a man—any man—alone."

"I respect your beliefs. I really do. I just don't agree." He walked around the island that separated them. That scent of spicy aftershave arrived at the same time.

Abigail stood stock-still like a deer hoping the trees would provide camouflage. He raised his hand.

His fingers traced a line along her jaw, then her chin. "But for now, I'll go. I'll give you the space to learn these things a little bit at a time."

And he was gone.

Space? A little bit at a time? A truck full of sensations dumped its contents on her all at once. An avalanche of emotions, thoughts, and feelings pinned her body to the island. So much for taking it slow.

Stay or go? Do something simple like start the dishwasher. The buttons flummoxed her. Her brain refused to cooperate. Go or stay?

"Good, you're up."

Abigail jumped. She slapped both hands on the island to catch herself. *You're not falling. It just feels that way.*

Heather shuffled into the room. Her eyes were red, her hair stuck in a messy ponytail, and she had catsup stains on her blouse. She yawned so wide her back teeth showed. "Your dad called. He wants to take us out to breakfast."

Chapter 19

Us didn't include Brody and the girls. Abigail got out of Heather's SUV in front of Joe Snuffy's Old Fashioned Grill. The building with its metal siding painted blue was typical of the type of structures the Kurtz family built. Which reminded Abigail of Owen. Was he still waiting for her?

Gritting her teeth, she closed the car door and waited for Heather to lead the way. Her mother paused and pointed. "He's here. There's his car. Isn't it beautiful? It's a '69 Chevy Chevelle SS. I'm surprised he brought it out. He lives in fear someone will bump it with a door and scratch that snazzy paint job."

The car, a sparkly green with a black vinyl top, simply looked old, but her biological father seemed to keep his cars pristine. That was a good quality, wasn't it? "It's pretty."

If cars could be considered pretty.

Inside, she paused on the welcome rug and surveyed the restaurant. Snuffy's had two seating areas, one with dark, rectangular wooden chairs. The second had round tables covered with blue vinyl tablecloths. Both were full. The buzz of people talking grew even as they waited for the hostess to seat them.

The aroma of bacon, fried onions, and toasted bread mingled in the AC-refrigerated air. Bacon smells were the best, whether in a Plain kitchen or an English restaurant. Even so, Abigail's stomach clenched. Despite the AC sweat dampened her palms.

The entire ride from the house had been filled with what-ifs. What if he was disappointed in her? What if he was disagreeable? What if they had nothing to talk about? What if he never wanted to see her again? What if she never wanted to see him again?

Eric Waters had wanted her. No, he had wanted the baby he fathered with Heather. Would he want the grown-up version?

Knowing was better than not knowing. Meeting her biological father was another step toward filling in the blanks in her past. Abigail squared her shoulders and lifted her chin. "Do you see him?"

"There he is." Heather pointed toward a table along the back red-brick wall. Waving wildly, she bolted past the hostess approaching with menus in hand. "We're with him."

Abigail gave the hostess, a round woman in a black Snuffy's T-shirt and jeans, an apologetic smile. "Is that okay?"

"Sure, sure. Heather's a regular here. Everyone knows how she is."

How exactly was she? Abigail didn't frame the question. The man at the table stood. He hadn't changed much from the young man in the photo. A few sprigs of silver accented his blond hair. His eyes were a faded blue that matched his western-style shirt and much-washed jeans. A short, pale beard covered his chin. He held out his hand. "You must be Abigail." He gripped her hand hard, but his palm was sweaty. "I've waited a long time to meet you."

What could she say to that? She hadn't even known of his existence until a month earlier. "Hi."

"Have a seat." He pulled out a chair for her. At Heather's grunt he did the same for her. "You have your mother's face."

"I can't see that."

"You have her mouth and her skin when she was younger." Eric eased back into his chair. Behind him hung a sign that read STRESSED SPELLED BACKWARD IS DESSERTS. A second sign said LIFE IS SHORT. EAT DESSERT FIRST. So like the fun items to be found in the gift shop at the Buggies and Bonnets Restaurant back home. "You also have her eyes. We call it cornflower blue. Pretty."

Abigail's throat went dry. He thought she was pretty. Her eyes were pretty. Like her mother's. Mother—Lorene—had blue eyes, too, but they were darker and bigger. Much prettier. "Thank you."

"I'm sorry. I didn't mean to embarrass you. You're even prettier than you were in the pictures."

"Pictures?"

Heather squirmed in her seat. "I may have taken some photos of you outside the restaurant."

"May have?"

"I was unobtrusive. Obviously." She toyed with the salt and pepper shakers. "I promised Eric I would get some pictures."

"You've both lived in Haven. You know how we feel about getting our pictures taken." Abigail studied the menu, but the words didn't make sense. Or they were written in a language she could no longer understand. "This was a bad idea. I should go home."

"Don't do that. Just give us a chance. Please." Eric tugged at his shirt collar, then fingered the shirt's pearl-covered snaps. His fingers were long. He had a scar on two of them, like a slash that overlapped. "We're just figuring this out too. We've made mistakes, twenty years ago and now, but we'd like a chance to make them up to you."

He sounded so sincere. His face was so kind. How could she not give him a chance? "Maybe we could just start with breakfast."

"Yeah, sure." He picked up his menu, then laid it down. "They have really good breakfast here. I always get the Joe Snuffy's Breakfast

Skillet. A big pile of hash browns with two eggs on top, however you like them, your choice of bacon, sausage, or ham, and onion and green pepper. Plus toast."

"That sounds like a lot of food." Abigail's throat threatened to close. She gulped a long swallow of water. "I'm not a big eater."

"I always have the french toast. It's to die for." Heather laid her hand across her forehead, palm out, and mimed a swoon. "Three pieces of Texas toast, dipped in egg, toasted on the griddle, and dusted with powdered sugar. Served with warm syrup on the side."

"Maybe scrambled eggs, bacon, and toast?"

After the waitress took their orders, Heather sipped her Diet Coke, set it on a coaster, and leaned both elbows on the table. "So what did you think of Rhett? He's nice, isn't he? Did he tell you he has a college degree? It's in journalism, but still. He's smart. He works at the *Abilene Reflector-Chronicle* because he wants to stay in Abilene to take care of his grandma. Isn't that sweet? That guy's going places. Did you like—?"

"Rhett Strong. When did she meet Rhett?" Eric ripped open a packet of sugar, sending granules flying. What remained he stirred into his coffee with such force it slopped over the sides of the thick white mug. "What's he doing hanging around her?"

"He was at the party. The one you didn't come to."

"I just wanted to give her a chance to get acclimated. You know I thought the party was a bad idea. It was too soon, wasn't it, Abigail?"

Both stared at Abigail expectantly. She gulped her coffee, scalded her tongue, and gasped. "Ach, *heess.*"

"Slow down, girl." Eric grabbed her glass of water and held it out. "We'll try to do the same."

Abigail chugged water until the burning subsided. They were acting like parents—her parents. It gave the ordinary act of eating breakfast a strange, surreal quality. "Rhett is nice, but he doesn't really understand what it means to be Plain. He didn't grow up around Plain people the way you did."

You should understand. "He wants to interview me for the newspaper. I said no."

"Is he pressuring you?" Eric snatched his phone from the table. "I know his boss. I'll shut him down."

"No, he's not. He gave up gracefully." She shouldn't have mentioned it. "Besides, he means well." *Just like you do.*

All that talk about a personal coach to help her with her clumsiness. He thought he could fix her, just like Heather thought she could make her English with some clothes and a cell phone.

"Rhett's a good kid, but he needs to back off and give Abigail time to get her bearings." Eric scowled at Heather. "She's lived a sheltered life. You need to make sure he understands that."

"You don't know me. I can take care of myself." The words sounded foolish the moment they came out of Abigail's mouth. She'd never spoken that way to a man in her life. "I'm sorry. I don't know how to do this."

"No, I'm the one who's sorry. I didn't mean to offend you." Eric ran his hand through his already tangled mess of curls. "This isn't the way I imagined things going. I can't seem to say the right thing."

The crow's feet around his eyes deepened. He massaged his neck with one hand. "Did Heather tell you that I didn't agree with giving you away? I wanted to keep you, but our parents refused to allow it."

"Yes, she told me."

"Just so you know." He slumped in his chair. "I wanted to marry your mother. We could've been a family. Things could've been different."

"But they weren't, Eric. We were just kids." Heather scooted her chair around until she could reach him. She took his hand. "Say we did that. We don't know how that would've turned out. We could be divorced from each other instead of other people. We can't rewrite history."

His head down, Eric rubbed his fingers across Heather's. His were big and tanned, hers thin and white. They seemed to have forgotten Abigail sat across from them. These two Englishers tied together by a daughter neither of them really knew. "No, but we can write the next chapter. We're adults now. No one can tell us what we can or can't do."

"Maybe what happened was Gott's plan." Did they even believe in God? Abigail stumbled over the words but plowed ahead. "Maybe I was supposed to be brought up Amish, while you went on to have your own families."

God frowned on divorce, but it wasn't Abigail's place to judge or lecture.

"Maybe." Eric slid his arm around Heather. "Or maybe we had to go through trials in order to find our way back to each other. Did Heather tell you we've been hanging out some since our divorces?"

Fortunately, the waitress arrived with their food at that precise moment. Eric and Heather separated. The next several minutes were spent digging into the food. They were right. The scrambled eggs were light and fluffy, the bacon crisp, and the toast hot and buttery. Heather insisted Abigail have a small portion of her french toast. It melted in her mouth, sweet with a touch of cinnamon.

"Oh my, I might need a wheelbarrow to cart me out to the car." It was nice to talk about something simple and good. "I'm stuffed."

"Me too." Heather popped the last piece of toast into her mouth and chewed with gusto. "Eric, can you carry us out on your back?"

He wiped his mouth with the paper napkin and laid it on top of the scant remains of his skillet breakfast. "Who'll carry me?"

Heather tapped her phone's screen. "Poop. It's after twelve. I told the girls we could go to the movies in Salina this afternoon. We'd better get moving."

"Seriously? We just started talking." Eric's smile disappeared. "You've had a bunch of chances to talk to Abigail. I haven't."

"I don't go to movies—"

"There you go." Eric signaled to the waitress for the bill. "Why don't you come with me, Abigail? I can show you around Abilene."

"I don't know—"

"Fine. I'll take the girls to the movies." Her nose wrinkling, Heather rummaged through her purse, produced a lip gloss tube, and occupied herself reapplying it to puckered lips. "You have Abigail back at my house by suppertime."

"What if she wants to eat supper with me and the boys?"

"Have you even told them about her?"

Eric picked at bread crumbs on the table. Heather closed the lip gloss with a flourish and stuck it back in her purse. "That's what I thought. Have her home by supper. Talk to your boys. Then you can talk about having a sleepover."

A sleepover? Abigail was twenty years old. Her biological parents were planning her life for her like she was a seven-year-old. "Why haven't you told your sons about me?"

One cowboy boot bouncing in a steady *tap-tap* on the wood floor, Eric dug his billfold from his back pocket. He laid a credit card on the table. "They're kids. Explaining a daughter I had when I was sixteen isn't easy. I had the talk with them, of course, but I told them it wasn't something you do until you love someone enough to marry her. It makes me seem like a big, fat hypocrite."

Or a man trying to be a good father. His sons were twelve and ten. He couldn't simply show up at the house with a daughter in tow and expect his sons to be thrilled. "Were you ashamed to tell them?"

Eric picked up his phone and studied its screen. He rolled his shoulder and cranked his head side to side. "No, not ashamed. Just not sure how they'd take it, what they'd do with it. What do I tell them? Do as I say and not as I do? Learn from my mistakes? It was wrong, but I'm not sorry. Plus there's the fallout with their mother. She loves finding new ways to twist the knife in my back. A love child from my wild teenage years? She'd eat that up."

He surely sounded ashamed. And more concerned about his ex-wife's reaction than Abigail's feelings. He might be her biological father, but he was no Freeman Bontrager either. "I'm not a love child. I'm not a mistake. Babies are gifts from God."

"I know that now." Eric stopped fiddling with his phone and looked her in the eye. "I wish I'd known it then. I was just a kid. You folks believe in forgiveness. Forgive me and we can start fresh."

He sounded just like Heather. Sometimes it seemed that the only true fact English people knew about Plain folks was that they believed in forgiveness. What was so strange and wondrous about that? Scripture called all believers to forgive. Everyone knew that. "I'm really worn out. I'd like to go back to the house."

"Abigail, please—"

"After you figure out how to tell your sons about me, maybe you can introduce us."

"That settles it then." Heather tossed her napkin on the table. "Thanks for breakfast, Eric. I feel a nap coming on before we go to the movies. It's a family tradition, Abigail. A nice Sunday brunch followed by a nap."

Where did church and faith fit into her Sunday traditions? Soon they were in the SUV headed back to the house. "Does your church meet every other Sunday too?"

"What do you mean, too? What church are you talking about, hon?"

"We meet for church every other Sunday. I thought maybe this was your off Sunday."

"It's been years of Sundays off." Heather waved at a woman weeding a flower bed in her front yard. The woman waved back. "I know how important religion is to Plain folks. I grew up around them. My parents were big on it, too, but it never really stuck."

"What does that mean, it didn't stick?"

"If you want to know the truth, I really soured on religion after I got pregnant with you." Heather stopped for a couple on a tandem bike in the crosswalk. She waved. They waved back. Abilene might be bigger than Haven, but it still had that small-town feel. "The people in my parents' church—the one I grew up in—were so judgmental about it. Whispering when I came into the sanctuary, talking about me at the potlucks, turning their noses up at me. Telling their daughters to stay away from me like being pregnant was contagious. I figured if that's what being a Christian meant, I wasn't much interested."

"When our folks do something sinful, they can make a freewill confession and everyone forgives them. It's forgiven and we move on. God is the one, true Judge."

"That's a nice sentiment. My parents ended up sending me to Abilene to live with my aunt so I could get a fresh start. I think they might have even changed churches, but in a tiny community like Haven, everyone knows everyone's business. Even in Abilene, that's true."

"Doesn't it bother you to think of Brody and Scarlett and Fiona growing up without Jesus? What if one of them dies—?"

"Bite your tongue, girl." Heather slammed on the brakes. Abigail's seat belt bit into her chest. The car screeched to a halt at a stop sign. "Why would you even say such a thing?"

"Because I believe heaven and hell are real. People who die without accepting Jesus as their Savior have no chance of going to heaven."

"Honey, I was only sixteen when I handed you over to Freeman and Lorene. I didn't really understand much about what they believed."

Heather started forward again. "Some people think there's some brainwashing involved. I wouldn't go that far, but I'm not scaring my kids into believing they'll go to hell if they aren't in church every Sunday."

"I'm not brainwashed."

"You haven't been taught to think for yourself. That's obvious, honey. You don't decide what clothes to wear, how to wear your hair, whether you want to have a cell phone, and you sure don't get to decide what you believe."

"I had a choice. I decided to be baptized."

"After eighteen years of being told what to think and a couple of years of running around to see what the world was really like and some classes where an old fart hammered home the same lessons you've been taught your whole life." Heather pulled into the driveway at her house, put the car in Park, and turned off the engine. She made no move to get out. "Did you have any classes on world religions? Did you attend other churches during your rumspringa? Did you get any more book learning beyond eighth grade?"

Her questions pummeled Abigail. The floodgates had opened. "You gave me to a Plain couple. You knew how I would be brought up. It's not surprising to you, is it?"

"My perspective has changed since back then. At the time I was relieved I didn't have to hand you off to strangers. Now I look back and I see a kid made to feel like a harlot by a bunch of narrow-minded, bigoted old ladies who claimed to be Christians." Heather ran her hands around the wheel. She stared out the windshield, but her expression said she was seeing something long ago and far away.

"I've had a lot of time to think about what happened. I'm an adult now with my own daughters. I would never expose them to that kind of thinking. I hope they're never in the position I was in, but if they are, I'll be the best grandma to that baby you'll ever see."

"Not all Christians are like that."

"I know, but I wish I could've had a hand in your beliefs, a voice in your upbringing. Now that you're here, I want you to know you have choices. That the Amish way isn't the only way to heaven. You can wear pants, drive a car, go to college, and marry a non-Amish guy and still get to heaven. It's not about your clothes or your education. It's about what you believe."

"What do you believe?"

"I believe God loves me with all my faults. He loves me even if I don't sit in a pew on Sunday morning."

"You never go?"

"Not once in the last twenty years."

A bleak sadness pervaded the SUV. Abigail swallowed back tears. People who claimed to be Christians had driven one of their own from the faith as surely as if they'd shoved her out the church doors and locked them behind her. "I'm so sorry."

"It's not your fault." Heather opened her door and grabbed her purse. "I need the nap. The girls will be chomping at the bit to go to the movies in an hour or two. You could probably use one too."

Napping was the last thing on Abigail's mind now. Plain folks didn't tell people what to believe—at least her Gmay didn't. They believed in showing their faith by example. Figuring out how to do that for her half siblings and her birth mother was a tall order—one that would keep her up at night.

Chapter 20

A PERSON SHOULDN'T WALK OUT OF A CHURCH SERVICE WITH A CHIP on his shoulder. Owen strode from the Keims' barn behind the first wave of kids in a hurry for after-church fun but ahead of the older men. At the corral fence, he stretched his arms over his head, then leaned against the wooden railing with his forearms. He raised his face to the sun and closed his eyes for a second. Plump robins vying for seeds in the Keims' bird feeder chattered. A dragonfly buzzed his ear. Kids giggled. *Gott is gut.*

Bryan often reminded his fellow believers of this fact during his sermons. *"In this world you will have trouble. But take heart! I have overcome the world."* Jesus told his followers this two thousand years ago. Nothing had changed. God was still on the throne, in charge, in control.

Not Owen.

Gott, I'm sorry for being so proud and full of myself. I want what I want—instead of what You want for me. Please forgive me.

"Are you planning to eat, or are you headed home in a snit?"

Owen opened his eyes and swiveled in time to see his father prop one boot on the lowest corral fence railing and shove his black hat back on his head.

"I'm not in a snit."

"You sat through church with a frown on your face. Like last night's chicken enchiladas gave you a powerful case of the runs." A faint grimace flittered across Father's face. "Sometimes Kayla's cooking can test even an iron stomach like mine, but I thought Friday's tater-tot casserole was tasty."

Owen's preoccupation had nothing to do with Kayla's cooking, and Father knew it. "I was concentrating on the service."

Father snorted. "What was it about?"

"Adam and Eve, the serpent, and how what happened to them can just as easily happen to us." It was a good guess, being one of Bryan's favorite topics. Owen pushed away from the railing. "I'm going to get a sandwich. You coming?"

"That was two weeks ago. Today's focused on the sin of pride."

Contrition blew through Owen. He was like a young boy who still needed to be chastised for not paying attention in church. "I admit, I've got a lot on my mind, but that's no excuse. I'll do better."

"About the other night—"

"We don't have to talk about that." Especially with Mary Wagner at the picnic table nearby dishing out fruit salad. "It was awkward, and your business is your business."

"It might become your business one day." Father craned his head from side to side and rubbed his neck with one hand. "I'm hoping it will be, leastways, for all you kinner."

"You'll do what you think is best."

"I know it's awkward to talk about." Father stomped dried, dead grass from his go-to-church boots. "I sure don't want to talk about it, but I can't go around pretending you didn't see what you saw."

"What did I see?"

"Your daed courting."

There. It was out in the open. "Gut for you."

"Do you mean that?"

Owen ducked his head and studied the weeds that surrounded his boots. "I reckon it's expected of you. The kinner could use someone to mother them."

"No one will take your mudder's place, but Mary's kinner need a daed too."

"I reckon I can understand that."

"I'm glad we got that out of the way." His sunburn couldn't completely account for the redness of Father's face. "Wayne told me he might have mentioned to you about Bill McCormack's offer to buy the farm. I was going to tell you after I had given it some more thought. I'm not sure yet what I want to do."

Out of the frying pan into the fire. "That's also your decision."

"That it is." Father clasped the railing so tightly his knuckles whitened. "It's not an easy decision. Especially knowing how you feel about it. I have to balance everyone's needs and wants with the needs weighing more than the wants. The entire family is affected by my decision."

Which he shouldn't have to justify to Owen. "Understood."

"Do you?" His father's voice grew hoarse. "We all do what we have to do. I would never have imagined I would be raising the kinner without your mudder, but Gott had a different plan. One that seems to involve Mary, I think. I'm doing the best I can to follow His lead."

"And I'm not making it any easier." Owen faced his father. "I'm sorry. Do what you have to do—not that you need my permission. I'll keep working at ES for as long as I'm needed."

"I appreciate that, Suh." Father rolled his shoulders. Rivulets of sweat trickled from his sideburns down his cheeks. "It's only the beginning of June, but it feels more like August. I've got a hankerin' for something cold. I saw some watermelon on the table. It'll hit the spot. You coming?"

"Sure."

Halfway across the yard Bryan joined them. The bishop had a tall glass of lemonade in one hand. "I've been thinking."

Which wasn't always a good thing when it came to Bryan's penchant for wading waist-deep into family concerns—with the best of intentions. Talking to him about Abigail was on Owen's list, but now that the opportunity presented itself, a clammy cold tickled his neck. He couldn't talk about his feelings for Abigail. It wasn't done. But he could ask for Bryan's thoughts on her sojourn into the English world. His advice. "Me too."

"Sit with me. Both of you." Bryan settled at the closest picnic table. He took a long drink of his lemonade and set the glass in front of him. "Giving the message always gives me a powerful hunger. Like I used up all the energy in my body just standing up there in front of family and friends, hoping the Lord will put the words in my mouth He would have the members of our Gmay hear."

"The Lord never fails." Father's steely gaze landed on Owen rather than Bryan. "His plan will reveal itself in due time."

Sometimes the plan was unfathomable. Like Mother's inexplicable death. Owen kept that thought to himself.

Raucous laughter filled the air. He swiveled. At the next table his sisters were laughing with their friends as they offered potato salad, coleslaw, macaroni salad, and whipped cream fruit salad to the men. They were so carefree. So sunny. Had they heard from Abigail? What did they know about when she might return? Owen tore his gaze from Jane's face damp with sweat and turned back to Bryan. *Go slow. Ease into it.* "You still get nervous?"

"I may have drawn the lot, but I'm no more equipped to speak for the Lord than any other member of our Gmay."

"God chose you, so He equips you, I reckon."

"Your suh is a smart young man, Chester." Bryan was only four or five years older than Owen, but something about wearing that mantle of responsibility had marked him. Silver glinted in his brown hair, lines carved themselves around his mouth, and his shoulders bowed prematurely. "Which is one of the reasons I wanted to have a sit-down with you."

Maybe Bryan would broach the subject then. Owen waited while Kayla planted a plate filled with a ham-and-cheese sandwich, potato salad, barbecue beans, and chips with dill dip in front of him while Carrie Beachy did the same for Father.

Jane delivered Bryan's plate with a flourish. "We're playing baseball after everyone is done eating." Grinning, she set down silverware wrapped in a napkin. Her blue eyes lit up with good humor. How could she be Abigail's twin and not be related to her by birth? "You should get the guys to join us, Owen."

"What about me and Chester?" Bryan used his fork, laden with potato salad, to point at Owen's father. "What are we, chopped liver?"

"Eww. Chopped liver. Yuck." Kayla put her hands on her hips and rolled her eyes. "We figured you older folks would rather sit in your lawn chairs and let your food digest while we play."

"Jah, and we wouldn't want you to break a hip or stub a toe," Carrie added. A mischievous smile stretched across her face. Her dimples deepened. "Come on, Owen, you were always the best baseball player at school."

"You were the best batter—for a maed—if memory serves." The give and take was nice after the tense conversation with his father. These girls didn't seem to have a care in the world. Carrie had been two years behind him in school. She'd been a string bean in those days, but her figure had filled out since then. Owen averted his eyes. "You had a pretty gut arm too."

"For a maed? Ha!" Kayla hooted. "Meet us on the field as soon as you finish. We'll see who plays gut for a maed."

The good-natured chatter continued as they trotted away to prepare and deliver more plates.

"They seem especially eager for you to play baseball with them." A sly smile on his face, Father raised one eyebrow and let it drop. How did he do that? "You should probably take them up on that."

"They're just being narrisch girls." Owen made a show of sipping his cold tea. "It's been a long while since I played baseball. My arm's rusty."

"Speaking of silly maede, I understand you might have had a word with Abigail before she left for Abilene." His expression suddenly somber, Bryan patted his mouth with his napkin. "I wonder if you could tell me what she said, what her thoughts were."

How did he know about their conversation? How much had Abigail told her parents? Courting was private. They wouldn't have pried. "About what?"

"About her intentions. Why did she feel the need to go? Does she really plan to come back in two weeks?"

"I'm sure she told her parents what her intentions are." Owen stabbed at a sweet pickle with his plastic fork. It skittered across his plate and landed on the picnic table. An escapee. He'd like to escape this conversation. "What did she tell her parents?"

"Freeman and Lorene know you and Abigail were courting. There's no need to be coy about it. They want to know what she told you, but they don't feel right about asking you themselves."

Coy? What Plain man had ever been accused of being coy? "She said she might fit in better there. She wondered if her clumsiness, her poor sewing skills, her bad cooking were all because she was meant to be Englisch. Not knowing was tearing her apart."

Owen stopped. He should've tried harder to convince her to stay. Maybe if he had been more certain of their relationship, she wouldn't have gone. "I told her she belonged here with her real family. I told her I would step back and let her figure this out. Better now than after she's married and has kinner." Owen broke a chip into pieces. He studied his plate. "It wasn't easy for me to say that, I admit, but this situation isn't about me. It's about Abigail."

"A little clumsiness is nothing when compared to eternal salvation." Bryan pushed barbecue beans into his potato salad and mixed them together. "I talked to her about this. So did her eldre. It's understandable if she's feeling at a loss or unsteady, but she needs to cling to her faith, not abandon it."

"She's not abandoning it. She's finding her way. It's like a fork in the road suddenly appeared in her life. She isn't sure which way to go, so she's exploring both."

Bryan took a big bite of his concoction. A look of pure satisfaction filled his face, and he chewed vigorously, then swallowed. Another long gulp of lemonade and he was ready to continue. "Her daed wants to go to Abilene and bring her home. He wants me to go with him."

"I've thought of doing that myself, but I told her I would take a step back. I'm trying to stick to my word."

"Regardless of what you told her, it's not your place." Father spoke for the first time. He tore his napkin into long strips and laid them across his plate. He'd barely touched his food. "You're not her mann. Her eldre should be the ones to intervene."

In the process of demolishing the rest of his sandwich, Bryan simply nodded while he chewed. The man liked his food. Finally he spoke again. "Your daed's right. I only asked you about her because you had spent time with her recently—since her biological mudder made her appearance. We don't want you drawn into her situation—especially if she should choose to stay."

"She won't."

Sei so gut, Gott.

"Let her family handle it, Suh." Father's expression darkened. "It is a family matter, after all."

"I've recommended to Freeman and his fraa that we wait the full two weeks. If she were to come home on her own, as promised, it would be so much better. Your daed is right. Let us handle it." Bryan inclined his head toward Father. "You should go play some baseball."

Two seconds later a smile replaced Father's scowl. Owen followed his gaze. Mary approached the bench with a lemon meringue pie in one hand and a pie server in the other. Despite being the mother of five, she was still a slim woman. Or maybe because of it. She had dark-blonde hair, hazel eyes, and a nut-brown complexion earned from plenty of time in the sun. "I'm handing out pie. Any takers?"

"Owen was just going to play some baseball," Bryan said. "Us old men will take some."

Owen scooted the bench back and hauled himself to his feet. "I do know one thing. Pressuring Abigail to return will likely push her further away. She needs time to see that she doesn't belong with her birth mudder. She's smart. She'll figure it out. She'll come back just as she promised."

Bryan was occupied with watching Mary cut and deposit a big wedge of pie on his plate. Was he even listening? He picked up his fork. "Danki, Mary." He waved the fork at Owen. "I hope you're right."

So did Owen. *Sei so gut, Gott, sei so gut.*

Chapter 21

THE SMACK OF THE BALL AGAINST THE ALUMINUM BAT SENT OWEN wheeling backward on the makeshift baseball field, glove lifted high, his free hand over his eyes to shield them from the sun. His spirit lifted with the sound. Nothing like a friendly game of baseball to make a guy feel better. At least for a moment. He staggered to his right. A little more. A little more. "Got it, got it."

The ball made a nice thud when it hit his mitt. *Boom.* At that moment his body collided with Carrie's. Down they went, sprawled on the imaginary line that ran between second and third base.

"Whoops! Are you okay?" Laughing, breathless, Carrie rolled away from him. She held one hand to her forehead. Sprigs of dried grass and dirt decorated her cheek and forehead. Her kapp sagged lopsided on her head. "I think your elbow got me in the head."

"Sorry about that. Did I hurt you?" Owen struggled upright. The ball was still in his mitt. He tapped Carrie on the arm. "You're out, by the way."

"Hey, no fair. You blocked the runner's path." She had a big belly laugh for a small girl. "You didn't have to knock me down to get me out."

"That part was an accident." He hopped to his feet and held out his hand. "But you're still out. And so is Kayla."

Carrie took his hand and allowed him to pull her to her feet. She was a tiny wren of a girl with blonde hair and blue eyes. She was always smiling. He'd never noticed her smile before.

Probably because he'd been busy looking at Abigail.

"You can let go now."

He still held her hand. He dropped it like a burning ember from the fireplace. "Sorry. Do you need an ice pack?"

"Nee. I'm gut." Her cheeks dimpled. "I'm used to playing with my big brieder."

"Gut. That's gut."

Kayla, who'd been behind the pop-up, trotted toward them. She had Carrie's glove in one hand. "You two have to stop meeting like that. Someone will end up with a black eye or a broken arm." She tossed Carrie her mitt. "That was three outs."

Kayla directed a frown at Owen. Like he'd run into Carrie on purpose? He dusted himself off and spun around to head to the sidelines. He was first up to bat for his side. Girls against boys wasn't fair. The boys always won, especially when the older guys like himself deigned to play. He grabbed a bat and went to the chalk-drawn batter's box. Claire was pitching. His little sister had quite an arm on her—better than most the boys her age. And she was fearless.

He shot her a ferocious scowl, waggled the bat, and pointed it toward the open field behind their makeshift diamond. "Show me what you've got, Little Schweschder. Be careful. I'll send it into outer space."

The chatter from the girls reached a crescendo. Even the folks sitting in lawn chairs alongside the field joined in the good-natured trash talk.

"Promises, promises!" Claire went into her exaggerated windup and let the pitch rip.

Owen swung and missed.

"Whoop! Whoop!" The girls cheered. A collective groan went up from his teammates.

"I let you have that one." He choked up and took a few practice swings. "Give me your best shot this time."

The next pitch came straight down the alley. He hit it hard and took off for first base. The line drive headed straight at Carrie, who held down the second baseman's slot. She stuck out her glove and captured it.

By that time Owen had rounded first base. Carrie danced around the chunk of old carpet that served as second base and whooped. "Turnabout is fair play!"

"Indeed it is." He doffed his hat at her and trotted back to the wooden benches that served as a "dugout" for his team.

"What was that?" A bat in one hand, Lee stood next to the bench. "You're so busy making goo-goo eyes at a girl that you can't get a decent hit."

"Goo-goo eyes. I don't make goo-goo eyes at anybody ever."

Lee edged closer to Owen. "You're doing the right thing—that's all I'm saying. Abigail's gone, and who knows if she's coming back? You need to move on."

"You have no idea what you're talking about. Abigail's coming back."

"Jocelyn told me Carrie's been sweet on you since forever. That's why she's still single."

"You need to hush up. This isn't the time or place."

"Touchy, touchy!"

A bitter taste in his mouth, Owen made a wide turn around Lee and headed for the Igloo cooler filled with water sitting on the far bench. He stayed there, watching as his team scored two runs fueled by Lee's triple. His brother did a decent job of hefting a bat. He should focus on playing instead of spouting nonsense about courting.

Could he be right about Carrie? She was a kind, decent girl with a pretty soprano voice that rose above the others at the singings. According to the grapevine she'd been courted by Michael Hershberger before he decided to marry a girl from Garnett. That was over a year ago.

"You'd better get out there." Kayla zipped over to the Igloo. She grabbed a plastic cup. "You're the best player in the infield."

"I'm going."

"Don't give up on Abigail."

He halted. Everyone thought he needed their advice. "I stepped back. What Abigail does is up to her, not me or you."

"I'm just saying. Carrie's nice and all, but you and Abigail fit together like peanut butter and jelly."

"Who's the peanut butter and who's the jelly?"

"I'm serious. She's coming back."

"I know."

"If she doesn't come back in two weeks, you should go after her."

"Bryan and Daed don't want me involved. Bryan says he and Freeman will handle it."

"They're old. They've forgotten what it's like."

"They're also our elders."

"You're right. You're right." Kayla poured a cup of water over her face and shook her head like a puppy after a bath. "But sometimes a girl needs a big gesture. Something that lets her know how much she's wanted."

That didn't sound like a Plain sentiment. "I'm not gut at big gestures."

"How do you know unless you try?"

Everyone had an opinion. Only one opinion counted.

Gott, what should I do?

No answer.

Carrie approached the Igloo with her red cup in hand. Despite the ugly red blotch on her forehead, she was smiling. "A person works up a powerful thirst getting knocked down like that."

"I am sorry. I could get some ice for you."

"Nee. I'll live." She pushed the spigot and began to fill her cup, but her gaze stayed on Owen. "I haven't seen you at a singing in a while. You used to come all the time."

"I'm getting old for singings."

"Me too." Water overflowed her cup and streamed onto the ground. She didn't seem to notice. "But they're fun, aren't they?"

She sounded so wistful. Singings were one of the few ways girls and guys could get together and mingle sanctioned by their families. "Your cup is full."

"What?" She looked down. "Ach, and me busy chatting. You'd better get out there."

"Jah, I'd better." Suddenly reluctant, he laid his cup on the bench and picked up his glove. "I might decide to drop in at a singing sometime."

Her face brightened. "I was thinking of doing that myself."

"Then I guess we might see each other there."

"We might."

Owen picked up his pace and headed out to his spot at shortstop. Lee's words sang in his head like the refrain of a sad song. *"Abigail's gone, and who knows if she's coming back? You need to move on."*

So why did he feel like he had just cheated on her?

Chapter 22

Time at Heather's house passed quickly—too quickly with a week gone—in a whirlwind of activity designed to introduce Abigail to every single person who lived in Abilene. Or so it seemed. Supper at Nydia's house, then DeeDee's. Fiona's dance recital. Brody's soccer game. Heather's clinic and all her coworkers. A steady stream of faces and names. Abigail kept a list in a notebook Heather had given her to "record her memories."

Not that her experiences weren't being recorded enough already. Between Heather's photos and Scarlett's and Fiona's posts on apps with names like Snapchat, Instagram, and TikTok, the whole world had an instant digital scrapbook of her visit.

The only people not to show their faces again so far were Eric and Rhett. Abigail contemplated her reflection in the bathroom mirror. Did she want her biological father to come rushing back into her life? What should she read into his apparent unwillingness to tell his sons about her? And this friendly English stranger with strong hands and a nice smile? What should she make of him?

The woman staring back at her offered no answers. The tan capris fit snugly around her long legs. The short-sleeved paisley blouse was modest by English standards, but Mother would be horrified to see her daughter "parading about" in it with her bare arms exposed.

"Well? Are you coming out or what?" Fiona coupled her impatient queries with two raps on the bathroom door. "Come on. We wanna see!"

Abigail smoothed the shirt's pleated hem with sweaty palms. It was one thing to wear English clothes around the house while bicycling and to Nydia's. What Fiona and Scarlett really wanted was for Abigail to wear a swimsuit. She shuddered. The gift from Heather was one piece and had a skirt around the bottom, but it still allowed more skin to show than was seemly. The capris were a better option. "Calm down. I'm coming out."

She opened the door. Squealing, Fiona grabbed her hand and tugged her into the bedroom. "I thought you were putting on the swimsuit."

"Sorry, I'm not there yet."

"At least take the kapp off." Fiona made a grab for the offending headpiece. "You don't go swimming with it on, do you?"

Abigail fended her off. "It helps keep my hair in place. Having my hair up is cooler."

When she and her girlfriends went swimming at the pond, they wore shorts and old cast-off boys' shirts under their dresses. They could pull off their dresses after they reached the pond. They covered their heads with scarves. They didn't invite the boys. They never went swimming at public pools. Their parents didn't want the boys hanging around scantily dressed girls either. Her half sisters wouldn't understand this.

"I suppose." Fiona wrinkled her nose. She wore her bushy red curls in a knot on top of her head. She'd already donned a skimpy bikini and wore short shorts over the bottom portion. Her freckles were partially obscured by a sunburn across her cheeks. "It's okay. Once you get in the water, you'll be cool as a Popsicle. Just bring a change of clothes. I already put our beach towels in the car."

The temperatures had climbed into the nineties this first week of June. Abigail had never really noticed the heat until she spent so many days in one air-conditioned building after another. She was acclimating far too quickly. In more ways than one.

"Let's go, girls. Time's a wastin'." Heather paused in the doorway. She had her purse strap over one shoulder and car keys in her hand. Like the girls, she already wore her swimsuit and shorts. Her top covered only slightly more than Fiona's. "I hear a margarita calling my name."

"Ma! Who will drive us home?" Fiona grabbed her glittery purple backpack and slid its straps around her arms. "You know what happens when you drink tequila."

"I don't care what the song says. My clothes do *not* fall off."

She and the girls guffawed.

"What's so funny?" Abigail picked up a hanger and stuck her dress on it. "Drinking and driving isn't funny."

"It's a country song. No worries. I'll stop at one drink."

Somehow little comfort came at those words. Abigail stuck her phone in her back pocket and followed the gaggle of girls out to the car.

Fifteen minutes later they pulled into a parking space outside the public swimming pool in Eisenhower Park, the town's biggest park. Fiona kept up a running commentary like a petite tour guide from her spot next to Abigail in the SUV's middle row.

The fresh, stringent smell of chlorine hit Abigail in the face the second she opened the car door. It mingled with the aroma of hot dogs barbecuing. Smoke rolled from a huge barbecue pit stationed inside the fence that secured the pool. According to Fiona, the Barton family had rented the pool for a hefty fee in order to celebrate their twin daughters' fourteenth birthdays. They were in Brody's eighth-grade class and would join him as freshmen at Abilene High School in the fall. Thus the invitation.

"Brody has a crush on Tammy. Or maybe it's Tanya." Scarlett rolled out from the back-row seat and reached her skinny arms over her head in an exaggerated stretch. "I can't tell them apart."

"Do not. Shut your big mouth." Brody threw a beach towel over his sister's head. "Don't listen to her. She's full of—"

"Stop the incessant bickering or we go home now." Heather handed a stack of towels to Abigail. "Take these. I'll carry the gifts. I'm sorry you have to listen to them talk like that. They're like alley cats."

Or brothers and sisters. No family was perfect.

Abigail took the towels and followed Heather to the front entrance. There the hallways split. Boys to the right, girls to the left. Into humid dressing rooms filled with lockers and showers. Girls in various states of undress wandered about, chattering nonstop. The fruity scent of sunscreen wafted through the air, competing with the smells of shampoo, soap, and sweat.

A rotund woman stood under a shower with a little girl who fussed because she didn't like the cold water. No one seemed to mind that they didn't have clothes on. Abigail averted her gaze to the wet cement floor. It seemed the only safe place. She stumbled into the row of benches in front of the first set of lockers, banging her knee. "Ouch."

"Watch where you're going." Scarlett giggled. "You walk like you've been drinking the tequila."

Not funny.

Heather and the girls shed their shorts and sandals, then stowed their change of clothes in lockers. "I brought your suit in case you changed your mind." Heather held up the black-and-gold suit. Abigail's cap took more material to make. "Last chance."

"No, but thanks." Abigail managed to meet Heather's gaze. Getting used to capris and short-sleeved shirts had taken time. A swimsuit might be the next step—but not today. "I'm fine."

"It'll be right here in my locker if you change your mind."

Finally they emerged into the brilliant sunshine that bounced off the water, blinding Abigail. The cement was rough under her bare feet. The water lapped against the side of the pool, inviting in its cool blueness. A boy cannonballed off the side into the deep end. Girls sprawled on towels nearby screeched. A lifeguard blew his whistle and yelled at some kids chasing each other on the other side.

They were having fun. Fun was good. Abigail took a deep breath and let it out. It was a social gathering like hundreds she'd attended growing up. Just people enjoying themselves and others. *They're just people.*

The girls dropped their towels and sailed in the pool feet first. "It's cold. It's cold," Fiona shrieked as she bobbed in the water. "Come in, Abigail. It's perfect."

"In a minute." Heather tucked her arm through Abigail's and propelled her toward the barbecue pit and concession stand. "Let's find the Bartons first. I want to introduce you and give the gifts to the girls. You, too, Brody. You're the reason we're here."

Brody, dressed in black trunks that bagged down to his knees and a white T-shirt, shuffled after them with a towel around his neck and his phone in one hand. His usual cocky grin was missing. "We don't have to make a big production out of it. Just put the presents on the pile, Ma."

"It's polite to say hello to your hosts and thank them for the invitation." Heather stopped at a picnic table piled high with gifts. She laid two boxes wrapped in shiny red paper on top of the closest pile.

"Besides, you haven't seen the girls since school let out. I'm sure you'll want to say hi."

Something about his expression tipped off Abigail. His gaze skipped to the row of teenage girls sprawled on their stomachs, backs bared to the sun. Heather seemed oblivious to his discomfort. Had he seen the Barton girls? Or was something else going on?

"Why would I want to say hi?" His fair skin reddened an even deeper ruddy hue. "I told you I didn't even want to come to the party."

"One minute you're chomping at the bit to go to a boy-girl party at some kid's house. The next I can't drag you to a party you've been invited to. I don't get it."

"If you don't know the difference, I'm not explaining it."

The difference was in how many adults were invited or present. Even Abigail knew that. It was the difference between a social gathering on a Sunday afternoon after church and a keg party in a farmer's cornfield on a Saturday night during her rumspringa. Every teenager knew that. Heather had known it once. Now she was the parent of a teenager and didn't remember—or didn't want to remember—what that heady freedom felt like.

"Brody! Dude, you came."

Two girls clad in the barest hint of bikinis called out in unison. They strolled toward Brody as if Heather and Abigail were invisible. Everything about them matched, from their curly blonde hair, caught back in ponytails that hung down to their waists, to their blue eyes, dimples, and rosebud lips. They had long legs, flat stomachs, and well-developed bosoms. All on display. Abigail concentrated on the girls' bare feet. They had painted their toenails candy-apple red to match their bikinis and their fingernails.

Brody's mouth dropped open. His jaw flapped. Abigail fought the urge to giggle. It wasn't funny. Not really.

Heather must've seen it too. "Tammy, Tanya, happy birthday!" She picked up one of the gifts and held it up. "I hope you like your presents. You've got quite a haul going on here. Thanks for inviting the whole family to your shindig."

"Mom said we had to." Both of the girls made pouty faces. "We wanted a party with just our classmates, you know, boy-girl, but Dad said no way. It was a family thing or nothing."

Not exactly a thanks-for-coming. Heather returned the box to the pile. Her expression didn't change. "I'm with your parents on that one."

"Who's this, Brody? Your date?" Both girls gave Abigail the once-over, their gazes traveling foot to face and back. It would be nice to know which girl was which. "Aren't you going to introduce us?"

"She's not my date." Brody's voice squeaked. His red face turned a molten shade of crimson. "She's my half sister."

"Girls, this is my daughter Abigail." Heather rescued her son. "She's visiting this summer. We're hoping she'll decide to stay permanently. Abigail, this is Tanya—raise your hand so we know which is which—and Tammy."

The girls obliged. Tanya was the one on the right. She might be a smidge taller than Tammy. Otherwise the two were identical. Abigail didn't take the time to examine them more closely. She was too busy dealing with Heather's statement. It was the first time her birth mother had voiced her hope aloud.

A door opened to a long hallway teeming with more what-ifs and why-nots and half-materialized wishes. This wasn't the time or place. "Heather—"

"Your daughter, Mrs. Hanson? Like you're adopting her?" Tanya's face screwed up in a puzzled frown. "Isn't she kind of old for that?"

They were talking about Abigail like she wasn't there. "I've already been adopted. By my parents."

The puzzled frown grew. "Huh?"

"It doesn't matter. She's not staying." Brody finally found his voice. He jerked his head toward the pool. "Are we gonna swim or what?"

"Yeah, let's swim." Tammy flung her ponytail over her shoulder. "Shawn and Bryson and the rest of the gang are down at the deep end."

Just like that. The novelty of Abigail's presence faded away. Tammy and Tanya swiveled as a unit. Their ponytails swayed in tandem as they strolled away, Brody two steps behind.

"Sorry about that. Brody's brain turns into cotton candy whenever he's around girls his age." Heather fussed with her sunglasses. They concealed her eyes and her real thoughts. "I worry about him, but that was no reason for them or him to be rude."

"It's okay. It is a hard thing to figure out." Abigail didn't understand it either. "What you said about me staying permanently—"

"Food for thought, honey, food for thought."

The sun's broiling heat turned the cement into a frying pan. Her head seemed to float on the humid air. Her stomach flopped. This food for thought didn't sit well. "I can't stay. I have family back home."

"Let's not worry about that right now. Let's just have fun."

One person's fun was another person's torture. Abigail hung close to Heather for the obligatory introductions to the Bartons, who looked as if they lived in the sun with their dark tans and sleek swimsuits. Finally there was no avoiding it. Time to get in the water.

"Just jump in," Fiona yelled from the middle of the pool, teeming with teenagers dunking one another, playing water volleyball, and screeching. "It's better to get it over all at once. You warm up fast."

"Whoa, hold on there." A girl in a T-shirt with LIFEGUARD emblazoned across the front and a whistle around her neck padded on bare feet toward Abigail. Her skin was tanned a deep bronze and her blonde hair bleached almost white. "It's against the rules to swim in your street clothes. Gotta wear a suit."

"I'm sorry. I didn't know." Embarrassment burned worse than the sun. Sweat trickled down Abigail's forehead and into her eyes. Her mouth was so dry her tongue stuck to the roof of her mouth. "I can't wear a suit."

"Then you can't swim here. I'm sorry." The lifeguard punctuated her words with a snap of her bubble gum. "The dyes in the clothes are bad for the water's chemistry. You'll have to sit out."

"Aww, don't be a such a stickler, Cathy." Scarlett bobbed on the pool's edge, her wet hair straggling across her face. "One time won't hurt."

"If I don't enforce the rules, I lose my job. It's not exactly my dream job, but it makes my car payment. No suit, no swim."

With that she pivoted and trotted back to her tall chair at the midway point. She blew her whistle and yelled, "No running, boys. You know better."

"Sorry, Sis." Scarlett let go of the edge and floated on her back. "Run in and put on the suit. It's no biggie. You'll fit right in."

Wasn't that what Abigail longed for? To fit in? To feel comfortable in her own skin? Her heart pounding so hard it might catapult from her chest, Abigail marched back to the changing room. The showers were deserted now. No audience. Could she really do this?

"You can do it. This is what you wanted," she muttered. *Come on, Abigail English Girl, get with the program.* "Don't be a chicken. If you were brought up by Heather and Eric, you'd do it without even thinking about it. You'd already be out there bobbing in the water."

Her words echoed against the stone walls. The humid air hung heavy on her skin. Sweat dripped from her chin. She snatched the suit from Heather's locker and held it up. Less than a yard of stretchy black material with gold trim. A piece of cloth that stretched until it became a narrow, treacherous, swaying bridge between her vows, her faith, her family, and the world before her.

With shaking fingers she unbuttoned her shirt and shed the capris. Despite the heavy heat, she shivered. Sweat made it hard to pull up the nylon. She hopped around on one foot and then sat hard on the wooden bench. The suit fit like a tight glove. Her angular hip bones protruded over her flat belly. The black blared against her skinny white legs.

Abigail glanced around and over her shoulder. No one to see. She shucked off the shirt and pulled up the suit in one quick motion. Done. No flames flickered around her feet. No bolt of lightning shattered the roof and found her floundering in her sin.

She smoothed the sparkly gold material that formed the skirt. It brushed the top of her thighs. It hid nothing. Nor did the scooped neck that revealed white skin that had never been kissed by the sun. She closed her eyes. *It's just a swimsuit, Gott.*

Why tell God anything? He knew. He saw. He would judge.

She heaved a breath and stood. She'd come this far. One step, two steps, three steps. She paused, then scurried back to the bench where she picked up an oversized orange-and-red beach towel. She draped it around her shoulders and clutched it to her chest.

Now she was ready. *World, here I come.*

Leaving the safe confines of the dressing room took years. Or not. The blinding sun made it impossible to see. If she couldn't see them, maybe they couldn't see her.

Wishful thinking.

"You did it, you did it!"

That sounded like Scarlett. Abigail blinked and squinted. She edged closer to the water.

A high, piercing wolf whistle carried over the noisy pool chatter. Abigail froze.

"Abigail, over here."

She unglued her feet from the cement and turned. Rhett had his fingers wound around the fence's lockwire. He wore aviator sunglasses that hid his eyes, but his wolfish grin stretched from ear to ear. "You look great!"

Abigail whirled and raced back to the building's dark cave of a dressing room like Beelzebub himself was chasing her.

Maybe he was.

Chapter 23

Getting the swimsuit off her sweaty body proved even harder than getting it on. Like grappling with an octopus that had a dozen arms with tentacles that latched on and refused to release her. Sweat dripping into her eyes, burning like tears, Abigail wiggled and gyrated until it fell at her feet. What was Rhett doing out there? How had he known where they were? Was he looking for them or for her specifically? Did it matter? He'd seen her half dressed. A quarter dressed. Or less.

Why did that matter? So had all the other people out there. They didn't care. They were underdressed too. Abigail collapsed on the bench, covered her face with her sweat-slickened hands, and practiced breathing. *You can't have it both ways, dummkopp.*

That voice on her shoulder had a snarky told-you-so tone reminiscent of busybody women hunched over a half-done quilt.

Pick a life and stay in it.

What kind of advice was that?

The kind you give to a Plain woman who's waffling.

She grabbed her clothes. As it turned out, putting on capris was almost as hard. They stuck on her toes, on her feet, on her calves. The shirt was easier. But not much.

"Sweet Home Alabama" wafted from Heather's cubby. Rhett. After the party Heather had changed his ringtone to "their" song.

Abigail tugged it from its spot between Heather's shorts and sandals. Rhett, his face half covered by his cowboy hat, filled the screen. She jabbed the green dot. "Hello."

"You answered. I wasn't sure you would." His disembodied, husky voice sent a tremor through Abigail. Kind, calm, a touch of humor. "I'm sorry, Abigail. I didn't mean to embarrass you. I was just so taken with how cute you were in that swimsuit, and it was so unexpected. I shouldn't've whistled. It was ungentlemanly."

"It's okay." Not really, but an English girl would've taken the whistle as a compliment. If Abigail wanted to be an English woman, she'd better start getting used to being treated like one. "I don't know what I was thinking. I'm just not ready."

"If you're not ready, you're not ready."

"How did you get this number?"

"Heather gave it to me. She suggested I call you." The music and pool noise receded. He must have gotten in his car. "I have her blessing to take you away from here. I imagine you don't want to go back out to the pool."

She certainly did not. On the other hand, did she want to go someplace alone with Rhett? The answer was a flat-out yes. Abigail English Girl gave the idea a big thumbs-up. The Plain part winced and shook her head. A definitive no-no. "Where would we go?"

"Let me worry about that. Just get dressed and come get in my car. It's an old beat-up Mustang. Midnight blue. I'll wave."

Abigail hung up and finished dressing. Five minutes later she trudged out the front door to find a blue car idling by the curb. Rhett lowered his window. "There you are. Shall we go for a ride?"

"That actually sounds good." She slid onto the soft leather seat. Immediately cool air and the scent of pine trees enveloped her. Acoustic guitar music wafted from the speakers. Tinted windows muted the sun. "Thank you."

"For what?" Rhett slid his cowboy hat back and looked her over. "You're doing me a favor. I'm bored senseless this Friday night. I stopped by your house and no one was there. Grandma said everyone was headed to the Bartons' birthday bash, so here I am, begging you for your company."

"Why me?" The question slipped out before Abigail could stop it. It reeked of requiring a compliment. "I mean, surely you have friends you can hang out with. A girlfriend."

"No girlfriend. There was one. In college. But she chose a big-city newspaper. I couldn't go there, and she couldn't come here, so we called it a draw, shook hands, and said, '*Vaya con Dios*,' like the George Strait song says."

Abigail wasn't familiar with that song or the Spanish words, but she got his drift. Like Owen and her. Sweet Owen. What would he think of her disastrous outing with the swimming suit? Or the sight of her sitting in an English man's car? A tremor of guilt ran through her. *Sorry, Owen. I'm just doing what I came to do.*

Excuses, excuses.

"I'm sorry it didn't work out."

"It's okay. If it was meant to be, it would've been."

Did that apply to Owen and her? *Stop it.* "Where are we going?"

"I thought I'd buy you some pizza and then decide where we go from there."

Surprisingly, pizza sounded good. In her capris and blouse, Abigail fit in like every other girl on a date on a Friday night in a small town where the Pizza Hut was the gathering place for singles her age. Rhett regaled her with stories from his childhood designed to make her laugh. He never seemed to run out of them. Or stories of oddities he'd covered as a reporter.

Full of Canadian bacon and pineapple pizza, she turned down the offer of ice cream. "I should probably head home."

"Seriously?" He glanced at his phone. "It's barely nine o'clock. Heather and the kids probably aren't home yet. It's Friday night. Let's cruise."

So he drove her by the Seelye Mansion, the Greyhound Hall of Fame, and Old Abilene Town. Dusk fell. Rhett didn't seem to mind that Abigail didn't fill the spaces with small talk. He tapped his fingers on the wheel to the beat of the music and hummed along. Abigail relaxed into the soft leather. Her heartbeat slowed. The pounding in her head ceased.

"The dresses suit you better."

Abigail jolted upright. "You don't think I should wear English clothes?"

"I'm just saying, don't let them pressure you into change. Be who you are."

I don't know who that is anymore. "If I'm not English, then I shouldn't be in this car with you."

"Now there's a dilemma. What you're asking me is if I'm selfish enough to want you to change so I can enjoy your company?" Despite the mocking humor infused in his words, Rhett didn't crack a smile. "Or am I selfless enough to want you to do what's best and right for you? That's a deep philosophical well you've fallen into. It's a good thing I'm not given to fits of introspection."

Sometimes Rhett's words didn't make much sense. "So which is it?"

"I'll let you know. In the meantime, all I can say is don't change for everyone else. You'll never be happy. I could stop wearing my western shirts, cowboy hats, and boots. I'm a reporter, not a wrangler. But I don't. Because this is me. What you see is what you get."

No one was that transparent. Least of all Rhett, who had drawn the line at a superficial glossing over of his father's death and the reasons he didn't drink. Plain folks became much closer simply because they didn't hide behind fancy clothes, makeup, jewelry, big houses, and expensive cars. Still, even people like Owen and Abigail hid behind cardboard cutouts of the people others expected them to be, wanted them to be, demanded that they be. "What about your sister, the personal coach? Wasn't the plan to have her fix me?"

"I'm sorry if that's how I made you feel." Remorse softened the words. He said them with such sincerity a person could feel guilty for confronting him in the first place. "You don't need fixing. You said you feel clumsy and like you don't fit in. Kiera can help with that. If you want. I told you, I think clumsy is cute."

He had said that. He couldn't be blamed for her prickliness. Only his view of the world in which women who tripped over their own feet were somehow cute. "I really should go home."

"One more stop."

Rhett pulled into the parking lot of a building that bore the sign RITTEL'S WESTERN WEAR. Underneath the sign the store advertised saddles, tack, boots, and clothing. The lot was virtually empty, the store closed for the evening. He shut off the engine and leaned back. "Spectacular, isn't it?"

An oversized spur sprang from the ground near the store's entrance. It could be described as solid and a reddish brown, but spectacular? "I guess so."

"Where's your sense of whimsy?" He shoved open his door. "Come on, let's take a closer gander."

What exactly was whimsy? Abigail followed Rhett to the base of the spur. He patted the steel footing like they were good friends. "It's twenty-eight feet tall and weighs a ton. A farrier from New Mexico named Larry Houston fabricated it. He had to cut it into three pieces to haul it to Abilene in 2003."

"Why?"

"Why not?" Rhett tugged Abigail toward the spur. He gently laid his cowboy hat on the spur's cement base and turned to her. He held up his phone over their heads. "Smile. Say cheese."

The girls had taken Abigail's photo so many times, she'd given up trying to convince them to stop. She did as Rhett directed. He lowered the phone, pivoted, and took another photo of her alone leaning on the spur. "I'd have to stand on the other side of Buckeye to get a picture with the spur in it."

Luckily he didn't seem inclined to jog across the busy road.

"The spur used to be in front of the rodeo arena at Eisenhower Park, but the owners decided they wanted it here and had it moved. It's been in the *Guinness World Records* book since 2011."

More than Abigail had ever wanted or needed to know about this piece of metal. "Why is it important enough for people to stop to take pictures of?"

"Novelty. People like novelties." Rhett patted her cheek as if she were a student who needed an extra bit of tutoring. "Why do you think they come to Yoder to visit your stores and eat in the Buggies and Bonnets restaurant?"

"We're not a novelty to be gawked at."

"Yet, you are." He leaned in and planted a kiss on her forehead. "A beautiful, interesting oddity. The more you folks try to make yourselves recede into the woodwork, to not be a part of the world, the more of an attraction you become to the rest of the world."

Heat spiraled through Abigail. As first kisses went, it had been unexpected and fleeting. His lips were warm, his touch light. Not even Owen had gone so far, and they'd known each other for years. "Th-th-th-at's not f-f-fair." Her tongue tied itself in knots. Her heart banged against its cage. "We j-j-just want to be left a-a-alone."

"I'm sorry. I didn't mean to shake you up." Rhett's uncontrite grin suggested otherwise. "How old are you? Eighteen, nineteen? Never been kissed? You're too cute."

"I'm twenty." Embarrassment mingled with anger and shame. "We don't know each other well enough for kissing."

"I think you're upset because you liked it." Rhett touched her chin, forcing her to tilt her head up. He brushed his lips against hers in a feathery-soft kiss that lingered a little longer this time. "See there, wasn't that nice?"

Abigail slid past him and marched toward the car. Rhett's lazy laughter followed her. "Come on, Abigail, don't be mad. It was just a kiss."

Where Abigail came from, kisses meant something. Rhett shouldn't have kissed her unless he meant it. Or even then. They hadn't known each other long. They weren't courting. He wasn't her beau. Things moved too fast in this English world.

Rhett was right about one thing. She had liked it. A lot. What did that say about her?

Chapter 24

The lights were off and the house dark when Abigail slipped from Rhett's car and ran up the sidewalk to the front porch. With any luck that meant everyone was asleep. She shucked off her sneakers and slipped them under her arm, then used the house key Heather had given her on her first day in her new home. The cool air hit her face the second she entered the dark foyer. On tiptoe she closed the door behind her and hustled down the tiled hallway past the arched entryway to the living room.

"Is that you, Abigail?"

Still on tippy-toe, cringing, she paused. "It's me."

"Come talk to me for a minute."

Not now. "I'm really tired. I'm headed to bed."

"Now, Abigail. This is your mother speaking." Heather had employed the mother voice she used with her kids—her other kids.

Abigail trudged into the living room. Her eyes adjusted to the dark enough to see her mother propped up on a pile of pillows on the couch. She held a half-full wine glass.

"I thought everyone was asleep."

"I couldn't sleep, not with my girl out there gallivanting about town."

In a small town like Abilene, there was little gallivanting to be done, but her point was well taken. "I'm sorry if you were worried."

"You're twenty years old, for goodness' sake, and brought up right by your parents, probably better than I would have done." Heather sat up and switched on the lamp on the table next to the couch. The sudden brightness made her wince. "But I'm new to parenting children of dating age. My other children aren't there yet."

Abigail hadn't intended to be on a date at all. She settled into the glider rocker across from the couch. "I don't think it'll be too long before you'll be in the midst of it with Brody."

"From the look on his face today, I think you're right." Heather took a sip of wine and grimaced. "Those Barton twins will use him, abuse him, and throw him away. It won't be any fun for him or the rest of us who have to live with him."

Abigail had no experience with the likes of the Barton twins, but Heather was surely right to worry about Brody's future at the hands of the two sisters.

"Which brings me to the topic most on my mind now. Rhett Strong." Heather swirled the pale liquid in her glass. "I don't even know how much experience you have with men. I can't imagine it's very much, given what I know about the Amish. Certainly not with a man like Rhett. Have you even dated before?"

Embarrassment cascaded over Abigail like a waterfall of boiling water. Despite the AC-cooled air, sweat welled on her forehead and under her arms. She'd never talked to her mother—to Lorene—about such matters. How could she speak of them to this woman she hardly knew? "I've been to some singings."

"That's right. That's how it starts with you all. Right, you go to singings and then afterward couple up. Do you have a boyfriend, someone you met at the singings?"

"I took a few buggy rides with a man I've known for years. He's my good friend's brother."

"No chemistry."

"I'm not sure what that means."

"Did he make you swoon when he kissed you? Did you lay in bed thinking about him at night? Did you wrap yourself in knots and wonder if he would come calling again? Did you get tongue-tied around him? Did you practice writing your first name with his last name?"

"He never kissed me." They'd come close, but one of them pulled away each time—both unsure of how the song went. Unsure of what came next, when, and how. "But I did think about it."

A lot.

"Chemistry. What happened?"

"You happened."

Heather set the glass on the coffee table. "Me? You mean me showing up? Me asking you to come here? Or you being adopted? Like that was a reason not to like you?"

"Owen doesn't care about me being adopted. I care. If I'm more English than Amish, I need to know now. It's not fair to him to go on courting if I'm not really Amish."

"Honey, from where I'm sitting, you seem awfully Amish. Putting on English clothes and carrying a cell phone hasn't changed who you are."

"I sang karaoke. I put on a swimming suit—"

"And immediately took it off."

I let Rhett kiss me the first time we went anywhere together. She couldn't say the words aloud, not even to this woman who wouldn't be shocked or dismayed. "I let Rhett drive me around in his car tonight like a date. Plain girls don't date English men."

"He didn't try to pressure you into more, did he?" Heather's frown deepened into a scowl. "If I have to have a word with him, I will. I'll talk to his grandmother. She'll set him straight, believe you me."

"Please don't do that. Rhett didn't force me into his car. I can take responsibility for my own actions." No blaming a man with great confidence in his ability to charm a woman with little experience in man-woman things. "That's one of the reasons I came here. To know whether I belong with someone like Rhett."

Maybe not Rhett specifically, but an English man, an English life.

"The thing you have to understand about Rhett is that he's confused about who he is and what he wants."

He didn't seem at all confused when he kissed her. "He's a newspaper reporter."

"He's a twenty-four-year-old man living with his grandmother, working at a small-town newspaper when he really wants to be anywhere but here."

"He loves his grandma. He's taking care of her. Isn't that a good thing? That's what Plain families do. They take care of their elders."

"Rhett grew up on a ranch. His father took some wrong turns. He knew he was going to lose his ranch. He started drinking. One night he had a few drinks too many, went out and drove his truck into a tree, and ended up dead. Rhett's mother sold the ranch and sent her kids to live with their grandmother here in Abilene, but I think there's plenty of times when Rhett's still out there on that ranch with his dad, wondering what he could've done to change the outcome."

This explained so much about Rhett, but it wasn't Heather's story to tell. If Rhett had wanted Abigail to know, he would have told her himself. "He was just a child."

"It doesn't matter. You know that. I wished I could go back and change lots of things, like giving in to my parents when they insisted I put you up for adoption." Heather rubbed her face with both hands.

Her eyes were bloodshot and red rimmed. Without makeup she looked older than her thirty-six years. "But life marches on. If I'd married Eric, I wouldn't have had Brody, Scarlett, and Fiona with Dan. He's a good man. We had some tolerable years. I love my children. Eric loves his boys. Maybe life has a way of working itself out, if we just get out of the way and let it unfold."

Life didn't work itself out. God took care of it. "We believe in bowing to God's will and waiting for His plan to become clear to us."

"I think if we wait on God, we'll be waiting a long time. Better to get on with it. If Rhett comes on too strong, you just let me know and I'll set him straight."

"If I'm going to be here and be something different than I was before, don't I have to learn to handle these things myself?"

"If my mom had been more willing to talk to me about dating and boy-girl stuff, I might not have gotten into such a pickle when I was sixteen. Everything I knew about boys I learned from other girls at sleepovers and *Cosmopolitan* magazine. You can believe I've already had the talk with Brody and the girls."

"The talk." Nobody came right out and said the words in Plain families. Farm life being what it was, kids figured it out. They knew from going to church their whole lives what was expected of them. That didn't make it easy. Doing the right thing wasn't always easy.

Heather's head came up. She frowned again. "It occurs to me. Do I need to have the talk with you? I'm betting your folks didn't spell it out for you."

"No, no, you don't have to spell it out. Please, don't spell it out." The mere thought propelled Abigail from her chair, ready to hightail it to her room. "It's late. I should go to bed."

"Wait. There is something else, daughter of mine." Heather's low laugh sounded like the feel of velvet. "I love saying that. I hope it's not too painful for you to hear."

"No, it's not." In fact, it was getting easier. Especially because Heather said it with such love. Such caring. How could a person reject such sweetness? Abigail returned to the chair. "What is it?"

"This isn't just about you getting to know us, your other family. I want you to think about your future. Not as a wife and mother, but as a woman who is smart and has options."

"I have options?"

"You do if you stay here with me. Giving you up for adoption was the hardest thing I've ever done, but because I did it, I finished high school and went to college. I became a nurse. I can support myself and my kids. If you stay here, Abigail, you have many choices. The question is, do you want them?"

She had no idea. Her aspirations sprang from a secure, tradition-filled, time-tested mold. No new thought required. No room for wild imagination. Wife. Mother. Her imagination was defined by the world she knew best. A Plain girl didn't come home from school one day and announce she planned to be an engineer when she grew up. Not and stay Plain. "I can't imagine—"

"Imagine. Please take just a little time to imagine yourself being anything you want to be. You could go to college. You could have a career. Doctor. Nurse like me. Teacher. Scientist. Engineer. Diplomat."

Abigail had an eighth-grade education. "All I've ever wanted to be is a wife and mother."

"Because that's the only future you were allowed to imagine."

Abigail's small world grew bigger. A straight road widened, then split into a multitude of directions. The horizon shrank into the distance.

"Just think about it, for me."

"Good night, Heather."

"Abigail."

Abigail swung back around. Heather stood and edged out from

between the couch and coffee table. "Do you think you might give your birth mom a good-night hug?"

How could anyone say no to that? Abigail met her halfway. Her mother's thin arms were surprisingly strong. Heather patted Abigail's back. The seconds ticked by. Her hold didn't lessen. She began to hum.

A faintly familiar melody. Abigail closed her eyes. Sleep beckoned. "What's that you're humming?" she whispered.

"'You Are My Sunshine.'" Heather swayed. Abigail swayed with her. "Have you ever listened to the lyrics?"

"They're sad, aren't they?"

"The writer is sad that the one she loves is gone. She begs them not to take her sunshine away." A quiver bloomed in her fading voice. Abigail had to strain to hear her. "She says her loved one will never know how much she loves him. I used to lay in bed at night and sing that song to myself over and over. That's why I had to see you, know you. I wanted you to know how much I love you. I couldn't let you go through life unaware of how much this person loves you."

Abigail rested her forehead on Heather's shoulder. Behind the silly laugh, the pink fingernail polish, the prattle, lived a woman with a deep well of love to offer. A woman couldn't have too many folks love her. "I'm glad you found me. No matter how hard this is, no matter what the consequences, secrets need to be told. Truth needs to win out."

Amazingly, the words rang true. They weren't simply to comfort or placate Heather. Abigail gently disengaged from her mother. "Thank you for finding me. The timing was God's. I needed to know before I married and had children. I need to sort this out so I can be who God wants me to be. Whoever that is."

"Good. Gut, as you would say." Her smile sheepish, Heather snatched up her glass and gulped down the remaining liquid. "I'm not drunk, I promise. I just needed to say my piece. Now get some sleep. Sleep tight, don't let the bedbugs bite. And no, I don't have bugs in my house."

She laughed. Abigail joined in. The semi-hysterical laugh of two people punchy from lack of sleep and emotional overload. Abigail scurried to her room. This experiment got harder by the day. Breaking the Ordnung rules was one thing. Learning to care for—even love—her birth family was quite another. How could she not? What happened if she did? The questions chased her down the hallway, nipping at her ankles.

Chapter 25

The movie theater wrapped Abigail in a cool, dark cocoon. Music boomed from the speakers. The larger-than-life figures might pop off the screen any second and sit between her and her siblings. Fiona dug into the greasy popcorn without taking her gaze from the movie. Giggling, Scarlett ate a tortilla chip drenched in runny cheese and jalapeño slices. The two occasionally delivered the dialogue along with the movie's characters—a bunch of toys. According to Heather, it was a rerelease of a classic called *Toy Story*.

Brody had claimed to be too old for a kid movie. He was spending the night with a friend. The mouthwatering aromas in the lobby had made Abigail cave to Fiona's insistence that she have a hot dog and popcorn despite the exorbitant cost.

The hot dog was great. The movie was cute. The theater was cold. Shivering, Abigail wrapped the hoodie Heather had loaned her tighter around her body. The icy root beer only made her colder. She slid down in her seat and tugged her phone from her pocket. No texts from Rhett. He'd kissed her and then disappeared from her life.

How did a woman put a kiss out of her mind? Her two weeks would be up tomorrow. Abigail the English Girl wanted to stay in Abilene. She couldn't leave without knowing what it meant. Plain

Abigail hadn't known what the English world had in store for her when she'd committed to returning home in only two weeks. She had no idea her biological father would have such a hard time figuring out their relationship. Eric still hadn't called. She'd spent no time with him. Instead her half siblings had insisted she learn to bowl, ride bicycles all over town, and go to movies. The more time she spent with them, the harder it became to contemplate leaving them. And then there was Rhett.

And what about Rhett? Only people who loved each other kissed, didn't they? She'd had the chance to ask Heather, and she'd been too chicken to do it. Heather's eagerness to impart her wisdom about men-women stuff notwithstanding, it was hard to imagine saying the words aloud to anyone. *Rhett kissed me. Then he dropped me off at your house, walked me to the door, and drove next door where his car disappeared into his grandma's garage. No fuss, no muss.*

In the mornings his car rumbled when he pulled out of the driveway. She would peek through the curtains in time to see him pull away. She wasn't pining for him. Just curious about how a man she hardly knew could be so annoyingly present in her thoughts. Who could kiss and walk away like it was nothing?

But what about Plain Abigail's family, her parents, Jane, even Doolittle, the do-nothing dog, her friend Kayla? And what about Owen? Owen who'd stepped back to give her the time to find her way home. Home where she would be a wife, a mother, and a faithful member of her community. Home to the vows she'd made when she was baptized.

Two families. Two lives. How long could she straddle the fence between English and Plain?

"Don't you like the movie?" Heather didn't bother to keep her voice down. They were the only ones sitting in the bottom section directly in front of the mammoth screen. She held out a bag of peanut

M&M's. "Woody the sheriff and Buzz Lightyear—who could ask for a better Friday night?"

Abigail took the bag. Who could turn down chocolate-covered peanuts? "It's very cute."

"So do I need to gas up the SUV after we get out of here?" Heather leaned closer to be heard over Buzz Lightyear's exclamation of "To infinity and beyond!" "You haven't said anything, but I know your two weeks are up."

Abigail popped two brown M&M's into her mouth. How could they have a conversation in the middle of a movie? "I honestly don't know what to do."

"Mom, stop talking." Scarlett shook her greasy finger at her mom. "You're missing the best part."

"The whole movie is the best part."

"Shhh!"

Heather sank onto her seat. "I have to go to the bathroom. Come with me?"

"The tickets were really expensive."

"We'll come back."

Abigail followed Heather out into the plush carpeted hallway. Even soundproofing didn't stop the distant *boom, boom* of the bass from filtering through the walls. Together they traipsed into the bathroom and took care of their business. Dozens of stalls and they all appeared to be empty.

"Don't keep me in suspense." Heather checked her makeup and patted her hair. "Tell me you're staying. Please."

"I told my parents and the bishop and Owen—my friend—that I would be home in two weeks."

"You had no idea what you were getting into when you made that promise."

True, but that couldn't be allowed to matter. "I don't want to hurt my parents—Freeman and Lorene—more than I already have." Abigail turned her back on the mirror. Seeing herself in English clothes still wasn't easy. "It's not fair to them."

"They've had you for twenty years, and I get two weeks?" Heather dug around in her purse and produced a lip balm. "I'm trying not to be whiny, but you haven't even spent time with your dad yet."

"That's not my fault."

"I know it's not. He's an idiot. But surely you understand that this is hard for him too. He's not as evolved as I am when it comes to parenting." Heather applied the lip balm and then held it out to Abigail. "Want some?"

Abigail declined. "I don't understand."

"He doesn't know how to talk to his boys about stuff like this. He's a caveman."

"How long should I wait around for him to figure it out?"

"I suppose that's a question only you can answer." Heather moved away from the counter to allow an elderly woman in a jogging suit to wash her hands. "I just know two weeks isn't enough time to figure out the rest of your life."

Abigail held the door so the woman could exit. She waited for the door to swing shut. "I don't have to figure it all out at once. Just because I go back to Haven doesn't mean we can't see each other again."

"I'm just asking for one summer. It's not a lifetime." Her expression grim, Heather slung her purse strap over her hunched shoulder. "Once you go back to Haven, you'll slip back into your Plain clothes. You won't take the phone. You'll go back to being the Abigail you were before."

"What's so wrong with that Abigail?"

"Nothing." Heather patted Abigail's cheek. "Nothing at all. I just want more for my daughter."

Here came the "you can be anything or anybody you want" speech.

Anybody but a Plain woman content to be a wife and mother.

"I'll stay a little longer, but no promises for how long."

"Whoop!"

A woman with a toddler on one hip and a small boy trailing behind her looked up, her eyebrows raised, expression curious.

Heather giggled. "Sorry!" She put her hand over her mouth and headed for the door. "Let's go back to the movie."

"Go ahead. I'm right behind you."

Abigail stepped into the hallway. She needed to call her parents. Tugging her phone from her pocket, she picked a spot in front of a poster for an upcoming science fiction movie involving spaceships and "frontiers where no man has gone before," and punched in the number.

It rang and rang. Finally an answering machine picked up. Her father's voice, slow and gruff, sounded in her ear. *Ach, Daed.* If only some way existed to explain to him why staying was a necessity. How to make him understand? To tell him all the experiences that had bombarded her in two short weeks? To wrap it all up in a quick nutshell that he could understand?

A person couldn't do that on the phone. He wouldn't hear the angst in her voice and see the pain in her eyes as she spoke. He wouldn't hear all the voices clamoring for attention in her head as she tried to take all those experiences and bind them together in a small, neatly folded package for him to open.

"Daed, it's me. Your dochder. Abigail." As if he wouldn't recognize her voice. "I know my two weeks are up tomorrow, but I can't come home yet. I will come home, just not yet."

She paused. The words were inadequate. "Tell Mudder—"

The machine shut off. The line went dead.

Chapter 26

The two-week mark came and went. No Abigail at church the following day. No Abigail waitressing at the restaurant. No letter. Jane teared up and walked away when Owen asked about her. He'd gone about his business—working, researching sunflowers, mending a fence on the back pasture, determined not to dwell on it. Bryan and Freeman still hadn't gone to Abilene. They didn't say why. Dad said they didn't owe him an explanation.

Another week passed. Nothing. Abigail had made her choice, it seemed. Stepping back had been hard but the right thing to do. Now he could or should move on.

If only it were that simple.

Kayla was determined to help. She followed him from the kitchen to the living room after supper like a pesky mosquito buzzing around his head. "Instead of sitting around with a long face, come to the singing with me. It'll be fun."

Abigail might have made her choice, but it would take Owen a little longer than Kayla to accept it. A person didn't bounce back from having his heart rejected that fast—at least Owen didn't. "Nee."

"Jah."

"Nee." He grabbed a horticulture magazine from his dad's desk, plopped down on the glider rocker, and opened it up. "Go away. I'm reading."

"Do you want to grow old and die alone?"

"I thought Abigail was your friend."

"She is, but you're my bruder. If she's decided to go have another life, you should do the same."

"We don't know what she's decided."

"Has she written you a letter? Has she written anyone?"

"Nee."

"Has she called?"

"Jane said she left a message for Freeman. She said she wasn't coming home yet, but she would. Eventually."

"So you're just going to wait indefinitely? It could be two months or two years." Kayla grabbed his arm and tugged. Like a Chihuahua trying to herd a Labrador. "Life goes on. You're getting old. You don't have time to waste."

"I'm not that old."

Kayla dug in with both feet. She put all her weight into dragging him from the chair. "Let's go."

"Okay, okay." Make that a bulldog. Owen tugged free. Kayla staggered back, giving him room to stand. "At least let me put on a clean shirt."

An hour and a half later he found himself sitting on a bench in the Christners' barn, his throat scratchy, sweat soaking the back of his neck, singing an English hymn called "Blessed Assurance."

Singings had been fun once upon a time. Now they reminded Owen of his singleness at age twenty-two. Sure, lots of men were still single at this age. A man didn't rush into marriage. Marriage was permanent, till-death-do-us-part stuff. But most of the guys his age had chosen their wives and started families. Kayla and Jane sat across from him, Carrie Beachy between them.

Her gaze met his. Her dimples deepened. She opened her mouth wider and sang out. She had a nice soprano, while Owen's baritone had a squeaky, needs-oil rust to it.

Finally the song ended. Isaiah Christner stood. He grabbed a pitcher of water and poured himself a plastic cup full. That served as a signal that the time for refueling on snacks and mingling had arrived.

Owen edged toward the picnic table covered with plates of cookies, crackers, and assorted candy. Carrie had a napkin in one hand and a brownie in the other. She held both out to Owen. "You came."

He could barely hear her over the mess of noise made by two dozen excited, nervous, pretending-to-be-neither people all talking at once. Some of them crowded the table, loading up on snacks. Not a place for conversation. He inclined his head toward the open barn doors. She nodded.

Outside the night air, heavy with mist, cooled his face. Owen raised his head to the sky. Dark clouds hid the moon and stars. Wind whipped at his skin. He grabbed his hat.

"Are you contemplating running away?"

He turned. Carrie pulled even with him. He shook his head. "I just needed a breath of air. It's kind of hard to carry on a conversation with all that racket. I'd forgotten how loud the singings get."

"You didn't come last time."

"I chickened out." He kept thinking—hoping—that Abigail would return home. "This feels like a step back. I thought I was past all this."

Her expression matter-of-fact, she shrugged. "Me, too, but things don't always go the way we think they should or hope they will."

"But that doesn't mean we should give up, does it?"

"It's not about giving up; it's about accepting Gott's will for us, His plan." She patted the mist from her face with her apron. "It's about being open to new, better possibilities."

Was Carrie his new, better possibility? She was smart in school, pleasing to the eye, and faithful. So why didn't his heart fire up like a jackhammer when she came near? "I'm trying."

She smiled. "Gut. So am I."

She had a nice smile. Owen heaved a breath. Her smile disappeared. "You shouldn't have to try so hard. If it is, it's too soon."

"It's not about you." Owen took a tentative step toward her. How did a man bridge the gap between a dream turned to ashes and a shiny, hopeful new one? "How much do you know about my situation?"

"Probably as much as you know about mine." Her tone turned tart. "The grapevine being what it is."

"I'm—"

Atlee Hershberger, Lee, and Michael Schrock tumbled through the barn doors, laughing and shoving. Atlee held a cell phone up high as if trying to keep it from his friend's grabby hands. "Stop it, you dummkopp, stop it."

"Come on, let us see, let us see." Lee swiped at the phone, missed, and stumbled into Carrie. "Ach, sorry, sorry."

His words petered out. All three boys stopped talking. They stopped moving. Guilt plastered their faces.

It wasn't unusual for Plain teenagers to have cell phones during their rumspringas. They kept them hidden from view so as not to rub their parents' noses in it. Why look so guilty?

"What do you have there?" Owen took a step toward Atlee. The teenager edged backward and stuck the phone behind his back like a child about to be punished. "What's so funny about the phone?"

"Nothing." Atlee took another step back. His gaze, which bounced to Lee, held a plea for help. "We were just being narrisch."

"From the way you're carrying on, it was more than that."

"Show him, Atlee." Lee shoved his buddy toward Owen. "He deserves to see. He should know what she's doing."

"What who's doing?" Owen's gut clenched. This couldn't be about Abigail. How could she possibly leave a message on Atlee's phone? How would she get his number? If she made a phone call, it would be to the phone shack on her parents' property, not to a kid's rumspringa cell phone. "Why would I care who left you a message?"

"It's not a message." Lee swiped Atlee's phone from his hand. He scooted closer to Owen. "It's pictures. Atlee's friends with some Englisch people on social media apps. Some of them have friends in Abilene. They got tagged in some photos and they liked them, so they showed up in Atlee's newsfeed."

Lee had stopped speaking *Deutsch*. Owen didn't live under a rock. Social media was everywhere. But he'd never had the desire to partake himself. He never even bought a cell phone during his rumspringa. His stomach bucked. Nausea rolled through him. "What are you talking about? Show me."

"Are you sure you want to see them?" Lee shook his head. "You might be better off to let it go."

"Show me."

Lee held out the phone. Abigail's smiling face stared back at Owen on the small screen. She stood nestled close to a man with curly brown hair and a goofy smile on his face. Above the photo the man had written "Showing my Amish friend Abigail the sights in Abilene. She's bowled over by the world's biggest spur. I'm bowled over by how cute she is."

Abigail wasn't wearing a dress. That was obvious. She had on a sleeveless blouse. Her arms were bare. She could be wearing a skirt or pants. It was impossible to tell. Her kapp was crooked. Her strawberry-blonde hair peeked out. Some would argue it was only clothes, but Plain folks knew better. "When was this made?"

"It was posted a week ago."

Two weeks and Abigail had abandoned the Ordnung.

"There's more." Lee did some swiping and touching on the screen. "Here, her sisters—half sisters—posted some videos."

Videos. Owen gritted his teeth against the vomit in the back of his throat. "How do I make them play?"

Lee fiddled with the phone some more. The first video featured Abigail singing a country-western song with the same man. The girl named Scarlett who posted it said his name was Rhett. No last name. They called it karaoke. It was a party celebrating Abigail's arrival. On her first day in Abilene, she'd sung for a crowd with a man she'd just met and let them record it. At least she still wore her dress and her prayer covering.

When she said she needed to find out if she was English, she'd meant it. That was a fact, but how could she throw off her Plain learning, faith, and vows like shedding an old coat so quickly?

"There's one more." Apology seeped into Lee's words. "There's a bunch more photos, but only one more video."

Only one more. A young girl with carrot hair danced around a room holding on to Abigail's arm. They were dancing to loud, ugly hip-hop music. To her credit Abigail looked pained, but she hadn't stopped it. She danced, knowing she was being recorded, knowing most likely it would be posted for all the world to see—or at least all the English world to see. She probably never thought her Plain friends would see her.

If only that were true. If only he could unsee it. Owen thrust the phone at Atlee. "Is there some way to get those off the screen, off the app or whatever it is?"

"Nee. I mean, we can hide them from our newsfeed so we don't have to see them, but everyone who's friends with that guy and her sisters will still see them. They're out there forever."

"I have to go."

"Bruder—"

"Don't go around showing these to your friends. You shouldn't be on those social media places at all, let alone looking at these videos."

"We were just—"

"I know what you were doing. It's your rumspringa, so it's your choice, but remember that you can never unsee some things. They do damage to you and to others. Like Bryan says, trash in, trash out. It's not right to act like it's no big deal because it's your rumspringa. It is a big deal."

"I know. It seemed like you should know, though."

"Now I know. Go back to the singing. Go back to the clean fun we can really enjoy instead of being voyeurs in other people's lives."

"We will," Lee spoke gently, like he would to a skittish horse. "You should let it go too. Stay for the singing." His gaze strayed toward Carrie. "Have that gut, clean fun."

"I have to go."

Carrie stepped into his path. "Owen—"

"I have to go." He zigzagged around her and raced to his buggy. He couldn't outrun the images. They breathed down his neck, crowded him on the seat, whispered in his ear. Bryan and Freeman were wrong.

They'd waited too long.

Chapter 27

A HALF HOUR LATER OWEN FOUND HIMSELF PARKED IN FRONT OF Bryan's house. No lights shone in the windows of the bishop's two-story, wooden A-frame. The heavy mist had turned into the patter of large raindrops. Owen hunched under the buggy's roof and contemplated his options. He should sleep on it. As if he could sleep. His horse nickered. A dog barked. The wind chimes hanging from Bryan's porch roof replied with sweet high notes.

A light went on in a front window. Seconds later the front door opened. Bryan stuck out his head. "Is that you, Owen?"

"It is."

"Well, get in here before you wake up my whole family."

Owen ducked his head against the rain and made a run for it.

Inside, Bryan padded barefoot into the kitchen, carrying a kerosene lantern. He still wore his work shirt and pants, but his suspenders hung down around his hips. He plopped the lantern on the counter and picked up the teakettle. "Have a seat. I'd offer you coffee, but you're obviously having enough problems sleeping. My fraa keeps a canister of chamomile tea bags on hand for my sleepless nights."

"Do you have a lot of those?"

"Since I became bishop, jah." He lit the gas under the kettle and adjusted the flame. "I shouldn't let worry interrupt my sleep. If I were a more devout man, I would sleep like a log, knowing Gott is in charge, not me."

It was quite an admission. Bryan seemed like such a pious man. "No one is perfect."

"You don't have to be perfect, just willing to give up control."

As if that were easy. "I have never felt in control of anything. Not in a long time, leastways."

Bryan picked up a canister and a honey bear. He brought both to the table. He set them in front of Owen. "So, my friend, what brings you out here past my bedtime?"

Now that he had Bryan's ear, Owen hesitated. What he was about to tell the bishop would threaten Abigail's good standing with the Gmay. *Tattletale. Tattletale.* This wasn't like ratting out his sister for stealing a cookie. Abigail's life as a Plain woman hung in the balance. Her eternal salvation. He had to separate his feelings for her as a man from his duty as a brother in Christ, a member of this Plain district. When he'd told her he would step back while she explored her English side, he'd meant it. Hadn't he? Should he intervene? Would she forgive him if he did? *Gott?*

Ultimately it would be up to Bryan and Freeman to decide what to do with this information. They were older and wiser than Owen. For the sake of Abigail, the Plain woman with whom he'd grown up, Owen would tell Bryan.

Still there was the issue of Atlee and the phone. This would require finesse.

"When you're ready." Bryan sounded amazingly patient for a man with perpetual weariness etched on his face. "But it is past my bedtime and yours."

"It's about . . . Abigail."

"That much I figured." Bryan tapped his fingers on the counter as if that would make the water boil faster. "If you'd spit it out before the sun comes up, I'd sure appreciate it. So would my fraa. She says I'm cranky when I don't get enough shut-eye."

"Can I ask why you and Freeman didn't go for her when she didn't come back after two weeks? I thought that was the plan."

"Abigail left a message for Freeman. She said she needed to stay a little longer but that she would be back." Bryan stretched his hands out wide and shrugged. "Freeman and I agreed she needs to come back of her own accord. Two weeks wasn't enough. We're not leaving it open-ended, however. She has to make a decision—and soon—or meidung will be our only recourse."

"I think she has made her choice." Owen let the story pour out.

Bryan didn't say anything at first. The teakettle sang. He poured water over the tea bags and brought out spoons to stir in the honey. Finally he slid onto a chair across from Owen. Still, he didn't speak.

"Well?"

He poured a generous dollop of honey into his tea and stirred. "How did you come to see these videos and photos?"

"I'd rather not say."

"Ah."

"It doesn't really matter, does it? The facts are the facts."

"You came here from the singing, I assume, so it had to be a cell phone belonging to one of our youngies on his rumspringa."

"That's neither here nor there."

"I suppose you're right. Rumspringa and all." Bryan sipped his tea. He contemplated the contents of his mug as if he might find an answer there. "I can see why you're concerned."

"I'd like to talk to her again, to tell her how everyone is concerned for her and misses her. Surely she misses her family and her friends." Did she miss him? *It's not about you.* "Maybe something's going on with her biological parents that's keeping her there."

"Like she's being held against her will?" Bryan grimaced and chuckled. "Or brainwashed?"

"This isn't funny."

"I agree, it's not funny. But it's not your place to try to influence her decision. You're not her daed or her bruder. Or an onkel. Or her bishop."

Just someone who cares for her. "So you talk to her."

The words hung out there in the air, quivering with impatience and frustration. Owen's pulse pounded in his ears. He'd stepped over the line. How dare he tell the bishop what to do, what's more, demand he do it?

Bryan laid both hands on the table and spread his stubby fingers wide. His expression remained serene. The pause stretched.

"Sorry. I'm sorry."

"You're worried." Bryan's gaze bore into Owen—right between the eyes. "I understand that. But you're not relying on Gott's provision. Have you prayed for Gott to intervene in her situation? Have you accepted that He is in control? That He will decide what happens, not you or me or Freeman?"

Owen wiggled on the hard oak chair. He shouldn't have come here. "So you won't go?"

"I didn't say that. I will speak with Freeman in the morning. I'll talk with Samuel and Delbert. We'll make a plan. That's our responsibility, not yours. But you understand we won't force her to return. She must come of her own free will."

"I just want her to know that I'm here for her. I may have stepped back, but that doesn't mean I stopped caring. Sometimes I wish I could, but I can't."

"You told her you would give her room to figure out who she is. That means you made room for the possibility that she might decide she's more Englisch than Plain."

"If I stood in her way, those questions would always haunt her. If she was unhappy in her life as a Plain woman, she might perceive it as my fault. That wouldn't be fertile ground for a marriage."

"See, you're wise beyond your years, Owen. Stick to what you know is true." Bryan tugged absently at his beard. "Will you be able to accept that she has chosen a different road? That Gott has something different in store for you?"

Owen wouldn't have a choice. "I don't know."

"Gott is the one who will work in her life, not you."

"I'm working on accepting that and bowing to His will."

"That's a start, but you need to work harder. You wouldn't be here if you weren't struggling with it." Bryan helped himself to a chocolate chip cookie and slid the plate in Owen's direction. "I reckon that's something else you need to figure out. I get the feeling this situation with Abigail isn't the only one keeping you up at night."

He wasn't hungry, but Owen grabbed a cookie anyway. It gave him something to do with his hands. "Everything's a mess. I'm a mess. I'm not proud. I don't mind admitting it to you."

"You do mind, but I'll let that small fib go." Bryan brushed cookie crumbs from his beard. "Is this about your daed and Mary Wagner?"

"Jah and nee. I respect my daed's wishes. I want him to be happy. If Mary makes him happy, so be it. If working in construction makes him happy, that's gut too. I'm trying to find a way to be happy in it as well."

"But you're not happy—that is easy to see. You want easy answers, and I don't have any of those."

"I know there are no easy answers. I've known that since my mudder died." Her days were numbered. So were his. So were Bryan's. Figuring out how to use those days best was the crux of the matter. "I want to do the right thing. I'm just not sure what that is."

"You're proud. You want what you want. Both a product of your human sin nature." Bryan's tone was mild, but his forehead furled about his raised eyebrows. "You say your daed is in charge, and you'll do whatever is best for your family. You say all the right things. Yet here you are, creating a blanket of humility to throw over what's really flat-out complaining because you're not getting your way."

The words stung with the ferocity of a dozen wasp stings. As they were intended to. Disagreeing with a bishop would only make Bryan's point for him. "If I decide that the best way to contribute to my family and my community is to pursue sunflower farming so that we have a gut future income that will support my fraa and kinner, is that pride, or is it fulfilling my duty as a member of the Gmay, a mann, and a daed?"

"A question you will have to answer for yourself, my friend." Grinning, Bryan clapped softly. "But you're moving in the right direction by asking the right questions. Listen for the will of Gott. Be a gut suh. Help others who need it. Seek a fraa. Wait for Gott's timing with patience and goodwill. You can do all those things and still realize your dream of being a farmer. We often ask questions, and we keep asking them, hoping we'll get different answers. In this case I don't think you will, my friend."

God knew what He was doing when He made Bryan the bishop.

"Daed?"

Bryan glanced past Owen. He swiveled to follow the bishop's gaze. Little Micah stood at the bottom of the stairs. With his tousled brown hair and huge eyes, he was the spitting image of his father, even at age two.

"What are you doing up, little one?"

"Hungry."

Bryan laughed. He pushed back his chair and went to pick up his son. "It's the middle of the night, Suh. You should've eaten the hamburger-corn casserole your mudder put on your plate for supper."

"Nee." The boy snuggled against his father's chest. "Eppie. Micah wants eppie."

"Tomorrow—but not for breakfast. Your mudder wouldn't like that."

"Now." Micah rubbed his eyes and yawned widely. "Daed up. Micah up."

"Daed is a grown-up." Bryan rubbed his son's back. He cocked his head toward the door. "Go home, Owen. Get some sleep. It will be tomorrow before we know it. We'll all be cranky."

Owen would go home, but he wouldn't sleep. His future awaited him. He couldn't afford an entire farm, but he could use his savings toward a house for the family he would one day have. God willing. With or without Abigail. *Sei so gut, Gott, let it be with her.*

He could seek a job with a sunflower grower to learn the business from the ground floor up. His younger brothers would step into the family business in his place.

He had a plan. To be a good son and, someday, a good husband and father.

Now to see what God's plan was.

Chapter 28

Kisses. The first thought that came to Abigail when she woke every morning involved kisses. What did they mean? Anything? Nothing? Did they mean something different for Abigail English Girl than they did for Plain Abigail?

Still no word from Rhett. Not even a phone call. Which was a good thing. So why couldn't she stop thinking about it?

Abigail smoothed the comforter on her bed and fluffed the pillows. Breakfast at the Hanson house was every person for herself—a bowl of cereal, peanut butter and toast, or Pop-Tarts. She'd eaten her bagel and cream cheese and escaped back to her bedroom to ponder her dilemma. She should go home. Her parents would be hurting. Owen. Kayla. Jane. Her younger brothers and sisters.

Two families. Two lives. How long could she straddle the fence between English and Plain?

She went to the mirror over her dresser and redid her bun. All those years of doing it without a mirror, and now she needed one. She studied her face. Her cheeks were pink just thinking about kisses. Kisses were something, not nothing. At least they should be. She'd daydreamed about kissing Owen. The thought that Rhett would kiss her had never crossed her mind until he did it. Now the thought crowded out everything else.

Her phone rang. Despite the fact that it was now a regular occurrence, she jumped. If it wasn't Heather calling from work just to check up on her or Scarlett wanting to know what she was fixing for supper, it was someone trying to sell her something. Or extend the warranty on her nonexistent car.

Eric Waters's name appeared on the screen along with a photo of him in full cowboy regalia. Her fingers hovered over the green button. After three weeks he'd finally decided to call. Heather had been in touch with him. Sometimes she hung up abruptly from a call when Abigail entered the kitchen. She always had guilty written all over her face.

Get it over with. "Hello."

Eric's deep voice boomed in her ear. "It's your . . . it's me . . . it's Eric."

"I know."

"I know it's been a while."

How did he define "a while"?

"It was harder than I thought it would be . . . meeting you after all this time." His tone softened, his voice turned hoarse. "Telling my boys wasn't the problem, really. I had to figure some things out first."

What did he want her to say to that? Did he want her to apologize? She stared at the painting of a cowboy riding a horse down a hill into a deep valley where a farmhouse sat in the distance. Rhett had described himself as a cowboy without a horse. He sounded sad. Every cowboy should have a horse.

"Abigail, are you there?"

She switched the phone to her other ear. "I'm still here."

"I told the boys about you. I should've done it sooner."

"Good for you."

"Turns out they didn't think twice about it. They thought it was cool. Kenny and Blake want to meet their big sister."

Half sister. Two more half siblings to add to the three Abigail already had.

She smoothed the blue knit shirt. It was short sleeved and had a scoop neck. With each passing day it became a little easier to slip into her English clothes. Her English father would be pleased when he saw her. What would her half brothers think of her? "I would like to meet them too."

"I thought maybe you could go to Kenny's baseball game with us. It starts at eleven. We could go out for lunch afterward."

Abigail studied the lilac bushes that filled the space between the house and the fence that separated Heather's property from Rhett's grandmother's. They were so pretty. She could almost smell them from here.

"Abigail?"

"I'm here."

"So what do you think?"

I think this is hard. But then it was hard for Eric too. The boys wanted to meet her. None of this was their fault. The girls were camping with their scout troop. Brody spent his Saturdays playing video games or skateboarding with his friends. It was good timing. "I'll have to ask Heather. She said something about taking me to the zoo in Salina."

"I already did. She said it was too hot for the zoo, and you have drawn the line at going to the pool again. She didn't say what that was all about."

Because Heather had repeatedly said she didn't understand what the big deal was about a suit and a "complimentary" wolf whistle from a nice guy like Rhett. "You asked her before you asked me?"

"She'd be mad if I didn't ask her first."

He was right about that. "Okay."

"It'll be fun."

"I know."

"Be sure to wear sunscreen. We'll be by in an hour."

After slathering sunscreen on her face, neck, and hands, she went in search of Heather. She found her in the living room, lying on the couch, an open *Prevention* magazine propped up on her chest. Her eyes were closed.

Abigail started to tiptoe away.

"Did Eric call?"

"He did."

"So you're going?"

"I am."

"Good. You'll like his boys. They're not as crazy as my kids." Heather opened her eyes and sat up. "I know he disappointed you. Give him a chance. He'll make it up to you."

"I said yes."

"That's a start. He's a nice man. He's a good dad."

To the boys he'd raised. "I'm going to wait on the front porch."

Heather lay back and put the magazine over her chest. "Godspeed, my child."

What an odd thing for a woman who didn't go to church to say.

Abigail wandered out to the porch and sat on the swing. It creaked under her weight. The June heat hugged her tight, dampening her skin. Back home on a Saturday morning, Jane, Hope, and Rose were probably working in the garden, pulling weeds. They might be canning. Mother was probably sewing pants for the boys. They outgrew them as fast as she made them. Father could be mending tack or cutting another round of alfalfa.

They worked. They chatted or sang or daydreamed while they worked in peaceful silence. That's what they did.

She pushed against the porch's wooden floor with her sneaker. Swinging made a small breeze that did little to cool her face. She closed her eyes. An engine rumbled. She opened them and stood.

A white van pulled up in front of the curb and stopped. It wasn't Eric's fancy classic car. The front passenger-side door opened at the same time as the side sliding door. Out hopped Bryan followed by her father. Her real father.

They'd come for her.

Chapter 29

ABIGAIL STOOD AND WAVED ONE OF THOSE AWKWARD PARADE waves. What else could she do? Bryan smiled and waved back, but Father's grim expression didn't change. Nor did he acknowledge the wave. He simply followed Bryan's brisk walk up the sidewalk to the porch. The van drove away, underlining the fact that this was not intended to be a quick visit. Abigail met the men at the top of the steps.

"I'm so surprised to see you. Happy to see you." Abigail fumbled the words. She would never lie to the bishop or her father. Surprise, no doubt. Happy? A wave of homesickness rolled over her. Just seeing her father's bulky frame and thick black beard already highlighted with silver strands sent an aching arrow through her heart. His broad shoulders, the hulking way he walked, his favorite sweat-stained straw hat—everything about him spoke of home. "What brings you to Abilene?"

Like she didn't know. But why now?

"We're concerned." Bryan halted with one boot on the bottom step. Father moved to stand next to him, his meaty hand on the railing. The bishop's smile cooled to a scowl that matched her father's. "With reason, I see."

Heat seared Abigail's face, curled around her neck, and burned all the way to her toes. She stuck her hands behind her back as if that would hide her bare arms. Her clothes were modest ones by the world's standards, but she was practically naked by Plain standards. The scoop neck, the bare arms, pants that ended just below her knees. By the grace of God she still wore her prayer covering. "Wearing Englisch clothes was part of the experience of being here."

Her words sounded so wooden, so stilted.

Bryan went on as if he hadn't heard her. "We felt a need to speak with you personally. Some news of your . . . activities came to us."

Which activities? The acute burn worse than touching a candle's flame spread across Abigail's shoulders. How? Who? Why?

"Hello, hello!" The screen door slammed. Heather charged onto the porch. Her arm came around Abigail's shoulders and squeezed. "I thought I heard voices out here. I thought it was . . . well, never mind who I thought it was. It's good to see you again, Freeman. Who's your friend?"

Father introduced Bryan, who allowed Heather to pump his hand like he was a visiting dignitary. "Come inside, come inside. I'll pour us some iced tea, or would you rather have bottled water? I might be able to rustle up some lemonade—not fresh, but still a thirst quencher. What brings you to our neck of the woods?"

She hustled them inside before they could begin to answer her questions fired at them willy-nilly. Before Abigail could gather her wits, they were seated in the living room, Bryan and her father on the couch, Abigail on an upright recliner, and Heather poised in front of them like a waitress eager to take their orders. "What can I get you to drink? How about a late breakfast? I can whip up some omelets."

"I'm fine. We're fine." Bryan waved her off with a kindly smile. "No need to wait on us hand and foot. We came to talk to Abigail."

"I figured as much. As her mother, though, I really feel like I should be in the room, you know, to give her moral support." Heather made her point by plopping down on the arm of the recliner. "We've become very close in the last few weeks. We've bonded. Isn't that right, Abigail?"

That late-night chat about men, courting, and love had been good. The hug good, but it didn't compare with twenty years of teaching a girl about life, faith, family, and love. Her parents might not hand out hugs with abandon, but they gave a girl everything she needed to live in this world as a good, kind, faithful person who would become a good wife and mother.

Maybe Heather would have done the same, given the chance, but she'd given up the chance. "We've gotten to know each other better. A month isn't a long time, but we've made a good start."

"A good start?" Father's jaw jutted out in a hard line. "What kind of mother lets her children dance around half naked and lets them put videos of it on their phones for the whole world to see?"

That Abigail's father understood the concept of social media—even a little—boggled the mind. The hot flush that encased Abigail's body intensified. Had he seen the videos of her dancing with the girls? Singing with Rhett?

"They weren't half naked." Pink spots spread on Heather's creamy white cheeks. "They were dressed in perfectly acceptable shorts and tank tops. Abigail was wearing her dress."

"And you." Father's penetrating gaze shifted to Abigail. "You sang a song in public with an English man using a microphone on your first night here. How quickly you forgot your vows, forgot the Ordnung, forgot respect for your parents and your community."

The hurt and bewilderment in his face wounded far more than the words alone. Now wasn't the time to remind him of her reason for coming to Abilene. "Es dutt mer leed, Daed."

"It's not enough to be sorry." Bryan tilted his head and paused. His tone hadn't changed. "Before you left, we discussed the consequences of embracing English customs after having taken your vows of baptism. You chose to jump in with both feet, it seems."

How quickly they had forgotten the other part of their conversation—her reason for coming here. She had to defend herself. "I had to try on this way of life to know my place."

"Your place is in Haven with your family—your *real* family." Bryan rubbed both hands against the rough black denim of his pants. He leaned forward, his keen gaze drilling into Abigail from across the room. "You tried it out. You don't belong here. Purpose accomplished. It's time to come home before you slide farther down this slippery slope to the point of no return."

"She is home. This is her home." Heather wiggled so she could grab Abigail's hand. Her fingers were cold and clammy. "She's just getting to know her brother and sisters—"

"Half brother and sisters." Father growled the words. His face contorted into that whipping-shed expression. Heather had no way of knowing she was playing with fire. "She has brothers and sisters at home who miss her. Her mother misses her. I miss her."

For him to say these words aloud was monumental. Plain men in general weren't likely to speak of their feelings, and her father in particular never did. Ever. At least not in front of his children. The urge to run to him, to hug him, infused Abigail's body right down to the marrow in her bones. "I miss you too. All of you."

Heather stiffened. She drew away from Abigail. "You agreed to stay for the Fourth of July celebration. My parents are coming. We made plans."

So they had. Fireworks, hot dogs, a parade, homemade ice cream, the entire Holcomb-Hanson tribe. Two great forces pulled at Abigail, threatening to tear her in two. Four weeks and she still didn't know where she belonged. She had one foot in this world of Instagram, swimsuits, and karaoke and another foot in a world of vegetable gardens, fry pies, and church every other Sunday. *Gott, help me.*

"Change your clothes, Abigail. Pack your things. It's time to go." Father gripped his hands together in his lap, his knuckles white. "Your mother is waiting at home for you."

Heather rose. She slapped her hands on her hips, legs akimbo. "*I'm* her mother."

"Only by an accident of birth."

The urge to scream enveloped Abigail. They were fighting over her. Tearing her limb by limb. *Please stop. Please stop.*

"Abigail, you must decide where you belong. We can't make this decision for you." Bryan intervened, his tone calm, steady. Heather couldn't know how unusual it was for Plain people to openly disagree with an English person. "We are concerned for your salvation, above all else. Consider your vows when you make this decision."

Abigail reached for Heather's hand. Her birth mother grabbed her hand and held on. "I have to go, Heather. It doesn't mean we won't see each other again. This isn't the end."

"We need more time."

"There'll be more time." Abigail stood and squeezed past Heather. "I'll get my things."

"I'll help you." Heather followed close on Abigail's heels. "We'll be right back."

Abigail dragged her ancient suitcase from the closet and hauled it up on the bed while Heather paced and chewed at a fingernail. "You don't have to go, you know. You're an adult. They can't tell you what to do."

"It doesn't work that way in Plain families." Abigail slipped into the walk-in closet. She quickly shed the offending clothes and donned her favorite lilac dress. On her way out she grabbed her other dresses. "I think you know that. I don't want to go, but that's my father out there. And my bishop. I took vows. I've broken rules here. They're worried about me."

"You took those vows under false pretenses. You thought you were born Amish." Heather took a dress from the suitcase and put it back on the hanger. "They should've told you the truth first so you could make your decision knowing all the facts."

"Maybe. I don't know." That was the truth. Had she known who she really was, would she have chosen baptism? It couldn't be undone now. Abigail tugged the dress from Heather's hands and removed the hanger. "But that's not what happened. I was trying to come to terms with who I was as a Plain woman who didn't quite fit in."

"You can't go without saying good-bye to Brody and the girls."

"Maybe they'll understand now what they did when they posted those videos and photos of me on the internet. I told them not to take my picture, but they did it anyway. They didn't respect my wishes."

"Because they weren't really your wishes. They are the wishes of those men out there." Heather returned to her pacing. She jerked her thumb in the general direction of the living room. "You have a mind of your own. I know you do. You're my flesh and blood."

Flesh and blood was such a small part of what made a person who she was. The other part—the big part—was the people around the person, the lessons taught through words and deeds, the examples set. Abigail might be Heather's flesh and blood, but she couldn't learn all those lessons in a few weeks. "That's my bishop out there. If I don't go now, I may not be able to go back later."

"You don't belong with them. Would that be so terrible?"

"I don't know. I honestly don't know." Abigail plopped onto the bed and inhaled a big breath. Let it out. She closed her eyes. She needed Heather simply not to talk for a minute. "I need to think. I need time. I don't have enough time."

The squeak of the mattress signaled Heather's presence next to her. She rubbed Abigail's back in a soothing circular motion. "It's okay. Take the time. Those men out there can just wait."

A melodic *ding, ding, ding* floated in the air.

Sudden horror on her face, Heather bolted for the door. "Doorbell. Your dad. Your other dad."

The words floated over Heather's shoulder. It took a second for them to sink in.

Eric Waters had arrived.

Abigail was all out of time.

Chapter 30

Plain folks didn't believe in Murphy's Law. This might have been a contest to see which development was more horrifying. Abigail's legs wanted no part of entering the living room. Her stomach rebelled too. In fact, her whole body begged to flee.

A belligerent scowl on his face, Eric stood in the living room's arched doorway. But that wasn't all. Owen had joined the crowd invading Heather's house. His face a stunning, ripe tomato red, he perched on the edge of the glider rocker. He'd removed his straw hat and proceeded to turn it round and round in his hands.

The scene defied reality. Her father, her birth father, her bishop, her birth mother. And Owen. The only person missing was her adoptive mother. No one spoke. Her father—Freeman—studied his clasped hands. Bryan sat ramrod straight. No one moved.

No running away. The only open seat was the recliner. Abigail sat.

"Well. Has everyone met?" Head held high, Heather planted herself in the middle of the room. "No?"

She proceeded to make the introductions until she arrived at Owen. "I don't know you."

"That's Owen," Eric piped up. "We met in the driveway. He's our daughter's boyfriend."

"He is?"

"I didn't say that."

Abigail's and Owen's words walked on each other's. Owen ducked his head and stared at the floor. Even if it were true, they shouldn't be talking about it in front of all these people. Especially her father—Freeman—and their bishop.

"That's clear as mud. If you're not Abigail's boyfriend, what are you doing here?"

"I saw the videos. I was concerned for her . . . faith."

A rush of heat turned to a cascade of boiling water. Abigail's fingernails bit into the palm of her hand. The tiny pain anchored her in reality. She breathed and tried to calm the gymnastics roiling in her stomach. He'd seen her singing with Rhett. How was that possible?

Another fact hit Abigail like a storm-fraught wind that took her breath away. Owen had seen the videos. He'd been the one to tell Bryan and her father about them.

He cares, the voice on her right shoulder whispered. *He betrayed you, he tattled*, whispered the voice on her left shoulder.

Shut up, both of you.

"Because you like her." Heather nodded knowingly. "I can see why. My daughter is a catch."

"She's a Plain woman. Her family misses her. They're concerned for her. We all are." Owen's voice turned hoarse. "Her parents spent the last twenty years teaching her about faith, family, and community. We're just asking you to honor them for doing what you asked them to do—raise your daughter."

"Owen's right. We understand that you have regrets about a decision you made as a teenager, but trying to undo the past just isn't possible." Bryan's tone was soft, respectful. "That doesn't mean you can't be a part of her life—her Plain life in Haven."

Owen missed her. He was concerned for her. Despite her rejection and her decision to come to Abilene, he hadn't given up on her. Abigail tucked that thought away for later when she could turn it over in the light, so she could figure out how she felt about it and what it meant.

Heather giggled, that silly, high school–girl giggle. No one else joined in. "Oh, come on, you guys. Can't you see a little humor in this? Even a little?" She turned around in a circle, eyeing each of the men. No one spoke. "Fine. Be that way. Eric, these gentlemen have come to take your daughter back to Haven."

"They can't." Eric shifted from one foot to the other. "We had plans for today. My boys are waiting in the car to meet Abigail. I haven't had my turn yet."

"She's been here a month, my friend." Heather shrugged. "You have no one to blame but yourself on that score."

"You said she was staying all summer. You said she might stay permanently."

Father opened his mouth. Heather held up both hands. "I said I hoped she would stay. I hoped she would want to stay. There's a difference. You dithered around too long."

"I had to think about my boys—"

"Just like years ago you had to think about your future instead of me and your baby?"

"That's not fair—"

"Let's not rehash the rehash." Heather moved until she stood next to Eric. "We're Abigail's birth parents. We're just asking for visitation rights. For now. We want Abigail to see that she has a choice about how she lives her life from here on out. Or maybe it's a blend of the two."

"I do see that, Heather, but I'm not a child. You don't get visitation rights to a grown woman. It's something I have to decide for myself." How little Heather understood the Amish way of life had never been clearer than in her handling of this situation. Abigail stood. "I'll get my suitcase."

"Don't you want to meet your half brothers?" Eric stepped into her path. "They're sitting out there in the SUV, waiting. They're excited."

Abigail glanced back at the bishop. His eyebrows rose. His lips thinned in a narrow frown. He didn't understand. None of them did. They weren't stuck halfway between two worlds. "I do. I truly do, but don't you see, I can't? They're here to take me back to my life."

"Your life there is limited to having babies and being a wife." Eric bounced on the balls of his feet. His words picked up speed. "Not that there's anything wrong with that. But you seem like a smart girl. You could do so much more with your life. Stay and we'll help you figure out what that is. You could get your GED and go to college. You could be anything you want to be. Think about that. This isn't just about who your family is. It's about what the rest of your life will be like. You haven't had enough time to consider your options and the repercussions of your choices."

He stopped, heaved a breath, and crossed his arms. Argument delivered.

The same speech Heather had given her in the dark that Saturday night not so long ago.

An argument she'd turned over and over in her head until the possibilities were a jumbled mess. Like a rope so knotted there was no straightening it out again.

"I guess I should've thought of that before I gave her to an Amish couple." Heather pointed out the obvious. "But I knew she'd be loved and well taken care of. She'd eat healthy foods and live a wholesome life. I didn't worry about the adult. I had to worry about the baby."

"You did the right thing." Bryan flapped his hands toward the doorway. "Get your suitcase, Abigail. The van driver will return shortly. We'll give you a minute to say good-bye."

Bryan and Father rose and headed for the doorway. Heather took Eric's hand and drew him out of their way.

Owen didn't move. He was a stubborn man. A good man but stubborn. Abigail caught his gaze. "You can go. I just want to say good-bye."

"Not good-bye." Heather draped her arm around Abigail and drew her into a circle with Eric. "We're not giving up that easy."

Nothing about this had been easy.

Owen wiped his sweaty palms on his pants and stood. Everything seemed to move in slow motion. Which was fine. It gave him time to rearrange his feelings. This wasn't about him. It was about Abigail and what was best for her. She still wore her dress and her kapp. She still had the same fair complexion and blue eyes. Outwardly she was Plain. But there were some differences. She was more outspoken, less soft. She'd learned something about herself here in Abilene. Wasn't that a good thing?

Owen edged past the tight circle made up of Abigail and her birth parents. Eric. His name was Eric. He had one arm around Heather and the other around Abigail. Like a circling of the wagons. Abigail was coming home, but somehow it seemed as if her birth parents had won.

This wasn't a game. No one won or lost.

"We'll wait outside for you, Abigail."

She nodded but didn't make eye contact.

Outside, Owen sucked in fresh air like a swimmer breaking the surface after a deep dive into dark waters. The blazing sun seared away the icy AC chill and the cold feeling he'd stuck his nose where it didn't belong. The scent of honeysuckle and pink roses planted in front of Heather's porch couldn't hide the stench of his own sweat.

He'd been the odd man out in that room. The one who had no business being there. He'd set out that morning with all the good intentions of a man who believed no one else was acting in Abigail's best interest.

Everyone knew the road to hell was paved with good intentions.

He hadn't known Bryan had finally decided it was time to come for her.

He hadn't asked, thinking he could beg forgiveness later.

Bryan and Freeman, deep in discussion, stood next to their van. Bryan glanced up and crooked his index finger in Owen's direction. An abiding sense of dread weighing down his steps, Owen trudged down the sidewalk.

"Hey, mister. Where's our dad? Is Abigail in there?"

Owen put his hand to his forehead, blocking the sun. The questions came from two blond boys with their heads sticking out the windows of an SUV parked behind the minivan that had carried Owen to Abilene. It was parked behind the white Econoline that had brought Bryan and Freeman here. Vehicles crowded the street in front of Heather's. People would think she was having another party—like the karaoke one. These boys must be the sons Eric had mentioned. Owen swerved in their direction. The tongue-lashing from Bryan could wait.

"Owen."

He held up one hand. Bryan frowned but didn't insist.

"You must be Eric's boys." Owen stopped within reach of the boy in the front seat. He had his father's blue eyes. "He'll be out in a minute. He's talking to Heather and Abigail."

"She's our half sister. She's going to go to my baseball game." The older boy swiped at his sweaty face. "Leastways she was. It's hot out here. We're tired of waiting. If we don't hurry up, I'm gonna be late, and the coach hates it when we're late. He won't let me start, and then I'll have to run laps."

"Sorry about that. I think there's been a kink in the plan." It wasn't Owen's place to tell these boys their half sister wouldn't be attending the baseball game. "Your dad will explain."

"Are you our half brother too?" The younger boy hung so far out his window he was in danger of falling on his head. "Dad didn't say anything about a half brother."

"No, I'm a . . . friend of Abigail's."

"What's she like? Is she nice? Dad says she's Amish. I never knew anyone Amish. Are you Amish? Is that why you wear those weird clothes?"

"Shut up, Blake, you ask too many questions."

"You shut up, Kenny. We're not supposed to say shut up."

A good rule. "Abigail is very nice. She's Amish. So am I."

"Why do you wear those weird clothes?" Blake was a fountain of questions. "What does Amish mean?"

"Those are good questions, but they're more than I can answer right now. Maybe you can ask the librarian at your library to give you some information about the Amish."

"Naw, I'll just google it for him." Kenny stuck a baseball mitt out the window and pounded his fist into it. "What I don't get is why people give away babies for adoption and then want them back. Like what good is that? Dad has us. What does he need another kid for? Especially one who's grown up."

More questions Owen couldn't answer. "I reckon your dad explained all this to you."

Kenny snorted. Blake followed suit.

"Stop copying me, Blake."

"Stop copying me, Kenny."

"I'm gonna pound your face into the ground—"

"I have to go." Owen backed away with a quick wave. "It was nice meeting you. Good luck with your baseball game."

"Could you tell my dad to hurry up? He told us to wait out here, so we can't go in."

"I can't go back inside either."

"You'll get in trouble too?" Blake sounded like that made them best friends. "I get it. My dad gets really mad if we don't do what he says."

Fortunately for all of them, at that moment the screen door squeaked. Eric emerged from the house with Abigail and Heather behind him. None of them carried a suitcase.

The three stopped at the porch steps. They arranged themselves in a row with Abigail in the middle. Like a united front. Where was the suitcase?

Owen beat a quick path to the sidewalk where Bryan and Freeman stood.

"Abigail has decided to stay." Heather spoke first. "For now."

"We hope you'll respect her wishes." Eric's arm went around Abigail in a protective—or was it possessive—gesture. "Please don't make it harder for her."

Without a word Freeman pivoted, jerked open the van door, and got in. The door slammed shut behind him.

"Surely Abigail can speak for herself." Bryan stood his ground. "Is this what you want?"

"It is." Her tone was firm, but she studied the ground as if searching for a lost penny. "I still haven't figured everything out."

"Don't you miss your family, your friends? Your life?" Owen tried to reel in his anger, his fear, his frustration. They milled around, pushing and shoving one another, making it hard to think, let alone speak. *Don't you miss me?* "Will you turn your back on your life, your vows—?"

"Owen." Bryan's sharp tone pierced to the bone. "This is Abigail's choice to make."

Ignoring the bishop's warning, Owen strode to the porch and stopped at the first step. "You are missed, Abigail, by everyone." *By me.* Speaking in their native language, he focused on Abigail alone, shutting out all the other people and their influences. For one moment he willed her to be alone on that porch with just him. "You came here to find yourself. To see if you're meant to be something other than Plain. I supported you in doing that. I just didn't know it would be so hard to let go. I guess I thought you would choose home and the life you've always known."

And me. That you would choose me.

"I haven't made a choice. Not yet." Her tone beseeched him to understand. "I just need more time."

"So there's still hope?"

"Jah, there's still hope. Don't give up on me."

A hand clamped down on Owen's shoulder. He glanced back. His face full of compassion, Bryan cocked his head toward the van. "Come, Owen. You've spoken your piece. We're done here." His somber gaze swiveled back to Abigail. He spoke in English. "Know this, Abigail. The choices you make have lasting consequences. We'll not be back. The next move is yours."

Owen tugged free. He stood his ground. "If you decide you want to come home, call my house anytime. I'll come for you."

"No need. If and when Abigail decides she wants to visit Haven, we can bring her." Heather's smile held triumph. "You don't need to worry about her."

Worry was a sin, but it didn't seem to matter. Owen would never stop feeling and caring for and worrying about Abigail. "See you soon."

"See you soon," Abigail whispered.

Owen forced himself to turn. Bryan had the van's sliding door open. "Tell your driver you're coming back with us. We can talk on the ride home."

It would've been nice to have those ninety minutes to figure out how to respond to Bryan's censure of his decision to come for Abigail despite being told to stay behind.

I meant well.

There were those good intentions again.

Chapter 31

They'd finally made it to the ball game. Kenny's coach wasn't happy, but he was short players, and apparently Kenny served as the Tigers' best hitter. Abigail joined the others in applauding his base hit in the bottom of the first. She clapped harder when he stretched the single into a double. The late-morning sun heated her face. The humid air, devoid of the slightest breeze, pressed on her. The other team's trash talk and the chatter among the parents ebbed and flowed around her, painfully ordinary after such a surreal scene earlier.

Don't think about it. Don't think about the incredulous bewilderment in Owen's deep-blue eyes. His willingness to ignore Bryan's commands. The hurt and the love, yes, the love, in his voice and his words and his deeds. He'd come for her and he'd do it again. He declared that in front of her father, their bishop, and her biological parents. For the whole word to know. *"See you soon."*

Don't think about it. Don't think about Father's crestfallen face when Heather announced Abigail would not be going home. Or the condemnation in Bryan's eyes and his tone. *"Know this, Abigail. The choices you make have lasting consequences. We'll not be back. The next move is yours."*

How had it happened? One minute she'd been packing her suitcase. The next minute she was unpacking it. One minute she was going. The next she was staying. In the moment it had felt right. Now the scene replayed in her head, each time more nauseating in the certainty of the pain she'd caused. Soon Father would be home. Mother would be waiting. She would hurry to the door. She would realize Abigail wasn't in the van. She would be so disappointed. Jane and the others would be disappointed.

They would think she had abandoned them. They would think she loved this new life more. She loved them. She was falling in love with her new family. And their way of life.

She hadn't been to church in a month. She couldn't be Abigail English Girl and run back to Haven for a church service—especially if it meant asking her English mother to drive her. Ninety minutes might as well be nine hundred minutes.

Gott, forgive me.

How could she stay with her new family when they didn't seem to have the slightest interest in God or faith? They weren't bad people. They didn't steal, cheat, murder, or covet. But did they believe in God? Did they believe Jesus was their Savior?

"Aren't you hot in that dress?" Blake, who sat next to her on the bleachers, held out a bottle of grape Gatorade dripping with condensation. His fair skin was already turning red from the sun. Sweat had soaked through his Kansas City Royals cap. "Want some of my drink? I'd rather have a Pepsi, but my dad says no. Pop's bad for our teeth, and he says he's the one who has to pay the dentist's bills."

"I'm used to wearing a dress." She hadn't taken the time to change back to the capris after Owen, Bryan, and her father left. Eric and his boys were already late to the game. Rushing kept her from thinking about the awful, forlorn look on Owen's face and the dark scowl on her father's face.

She forced herself to focus on the here and now, on the hard wooden bleacher underneath her, the baseball field, the electric-blue uniforms worn by Kenny's team, and the brightly colored umbrellas some parents were using for shade. She shook her head to the Gatorade.

Eric was behind Kenny's team's bench, talking to his coach. Probably apologizing again for being so late in hopes that Kenny wouldn't be punished with laps later. "I think your dad is probably right about the pop. Sugar is bad for your teeth."

"I never seen a girl wear a dress to a baseball game before."

He was a persistent kid. He reminded her of Eddie. Her little brother was like a dog with a bone when he wanted something. "I've played baseball in a dress. And volleyball and basketball. I've ridden a horse in a dress. With pants under the dress."

Blake's blue eyes got big. His mouth opened. "Why?"

"Why not?"

He cocked his head and chewed on his lower lip for a few seconds. Deep thought appeared to hurt. "I don't know. The girls around here wear pants or shorts. They hardly ever wear dresses."

"Each to their own."

Blake didn't seem convinced. He took a swig of Gatorade and stretched his skinny legs with their knobby knees out to the next rung of bleachers. Both knees sported Pokémon bandages. One dirty sneaker was untied. "How come you're Amish? If you're my dad's daughter, how can you be a different religion?"

Where to start? How much had Eric explained? Not enough, apparently. Abigail searched for an explanation a ten-year-old could understand. A different religion. "Do you and your dad go to church?"

"Naw. I go with my mom, though, sometimes, or Grandma. We go to VBS in the summer. Vacation Bible School. I like it 'cuz we get Hawaiian Punch and cookies and we do crafts and stuff." Blake scratched his forehead with his grubby fingers. "We go for Christmas and Easter, for sure. My mom says we're backsliding Baptists."

"Do you know who Jesus is?"

"Sure. He was the baby in the manger when the three kings of Or-E-Ant-R came bearing gifts they traveled afar." Blake grinned and sang the last part. "That's why we get presents on Christmas Day. It don't have nothing to do with Santa."

That was a start.

Eric had returned to the bleachers. He was working his way toward them. What role had he played in teaching his sons about Jesus?

"Yay, snow cones. Did you get me root beer flavored?" Blake's interest in religion disappeared. "Oh yay, oh yay."

"No, I got you sour pickle flavored. Of course I got you root beer." Eric laughed and handed the second one to Abigail. "I hope cherry is okay. It's my favorite."

"It's perfect." She took his offering. She held the paper cone to her warm cheek for a few seconds. "Thank you."

"What were you and Blake talking about? It looked awful serious."

"We were talking about Jesus," Blake volunteered. "And the wise men with the incense, myrrh, and Frankenstein."

"I think that's frankincense, Son."

"Whatever. Jesus got gifts, so I get gifts. That's all I care."

Eric settled on the bleacher next to Abigail. He wore a pained frown. Maybe the snow cone gave him a brain freeze. "Why were you asking Blake about Jesus?"

"He asked me about my religion. I haven't been to church since I came to Abilene. Heather says she hasn't been in twenty years."

The batter hit a long fly ball into center field. The fielder misjudged it. The ball dropped into the grass. Kenny took off from second. Eric jumped to his feet. "Go, go, go! Run, Kenny, run!"

Kenny rounded third and headed home. His coach jumped up

and down on the sidelines. The center fielder threw a hard strike at the catcher. Kenny slid in under the tag. Everyone—at least the families from Kenny's team—screamed, stomped on the bleachers, and clapped.

"Attaboy, Kenny, attaboy!" Eric pumped his free fist. He eased back on the bleacher and squinted at the scoreboard along the right field line. "Three to two. They take the lead."

"He did good." Abigail gathered up her enthusiasm. "He's a good player."

"What were we talking about?" Eric studied his snow cone. "Religion. My parents made me go when I was a kid. But it's been a while. Does it matter to you?"

Of course it mattered. "You don't worry about your sons' eternal salvation?"

"I'm teaching them to be law-abiding, hardworking citizens who treat women and children right. I figure that's a start."

Being good wouldn't get them into heaven. "I was brought up to believe it takes more."

"My ex makes sure the boys get some religion, so I figure that's enough." Eric sipped syrupy juice from the snow cone. His tongue was cherry red. "I don't believe in shoving religion down people's throats."

"Neither do I." His tone stung. "Neither do we. We show our faith by example."

"That's good. We're on the same page then."

Not even close. Abigail squirmed on the hard bench. Her behind hurt and her back longed for something to lean against, but not enough to take her mind from Eric's attitude toward faith. It wasn't her job to make sure her half brothers and sisters knew about Jesus. Or was it? What would Bryan say? Only God could do the work of salvation in their lives.

Couldn't she help? Shouldn't she help?

"What about this morning? Any second thoughts? Regrets?"

It took a minute to follow Eric's sudden shift in topic. Owen's woebegone face filled Abigail's mind. He came for her and she refused to go. What did that mean? She closed her eyes against the glaring sun. *I don't like hurting my father and mother. I don't like hurting my friends. Especially Owen. I miss my brothers and sisters. I could be with them right now.*

Would sharing those thoughts hurt her biological father? Could he expect her to have the same deep feelings for him that she had for the family she'd known her entire life? "I don't know how to feel, exactly. I thought I was going home, and then I didn't."

Eric crunched on snow cone ice. "You made the right decision."

Because it was the one he wanted her to make. In fact, begged her to make. "What does my staying mean to you?"

The pitcher threw a third strike for a third out. Kenny's team hustled to take the field. Eric seemed engrossed in watching them for a few seconds.

"I really need to know what it means."

He went back to his snow cone. "It means I get a chance to know my daughter a little better. But that doesn't mean I don't feel guilty about it."

"Why do you feel guilty?"

"I saw the pain on your dad's face. I'm not immune to the fact that he's your dad in ways that I will never be." Eric's shoulders hunched. He mussed Blake's blond hair with his free hand. The boy leaned back and grinned. "I keep telling myself blood is thicker than water, but I know how I'd feel if I thought someone was trying to steal my boys' affection from me. I feel that sometimes with my ex."

"Is that what you're trying to do? Steal my affection?"

Like he didn't have a right to it. Like it couldn't be shared. Like there wasn't a supply abundant enough for all of them.

"It must seem that way to your dad. Plus I want you to like me." Eric's voice turned gruff. "That probably sounds pathetic. I'm your dad, not some teenage punk wanting a girl to like me. I feel all out of whack about it. It's stupid."

"I don't think it's stupid."

"That's because Freeman and Lorene are good parents. They raised you to be kind. They raised you right."

The batter smacked a line drive between second and third. Kenny, who played shortstop, made a diving catch for the inning's first out.

Eric was on his feet with the crowd. "Yah, yah, that's my boy. Good catch, Kenny, good catch."

Abigail tossed the remnants of her snow cone in the rusted barrel parked just below her spot on the bleachers. She joined in the clapping. Everyone settled back down. Eric was a good dad who loved his sons. He wanted to love her too. Freeman and Lorene were good parents. They loved her.

Somehow there had to be room for all of them.

Chapter 32

Some conversations occur without a word being said aloud. Owen counted passing cars in his head. One, two, three, four, five, six . . . It wasn't his place to criticize the bishop's decision to leave without Abigail. What would he have done differently? Beg her? Demand she leave? Pick her up and throw her over his shoulder like a sack of potatoes? Plain folks didn't resort to pressure tactics or physical violence.

That didn't mean a man didn't have the urge. Not succumbing to baser instincts was part and parcel of their faith. Owen leaned his head against the van window's cool glass and surveyed his travel companions. Bryan scribbled notes in a leather journal. His writing was illegible. The pencil's tip broke under the pressure of his grip. Scowling, he muttered something, tossed the pencil into his leather satchel, and closed the journal.

Freeman glanced at Bryan for a scant second. The pain and hurt at his daughter's decision to stay in Abilene had etched new lines on his face, but he said nothing, letting the bluesy music piped through the van's speakers, the hum of the AC, and the rush of air outside the van fill the space.

In another twenty miles they would be in Haven. For seventy miles they'd let the subject of their trip lounge in that space as well.

With deliberate movements Bryan stowed his journal. He removed his reading glasses and stuck them in a cloth case. He leaned back against the seat. "Is there something you want to talk about, Owen?"

"I'm trying to figure out what more we can do to convince Abigail to come home. What more we should do."

"I told you before we wouldn't force her to come home. Abigail is an adult." Bryan clasped his hands over his flat stomach. "She knows what will happen if she doesn't come home. She's made her choice."

"I'm trying to put myself in her shoes, and I can't." Owen sought words to describe the great divide between what Bryan insisted they should do and what his heart said he should do. "Not one of us can imagine what it's like to suddenly discover you're not who you thought you were. It's not wrong to give her the leeway to figure out how she feels about that. At the same time we can't abandon her to a fallen world. We have to do our best to bring her back into the fold. Isn't that what Scripture says? That the shepherd will leave the flock to go rescue the one lost lamb?"

"Let it go, Owen."

Freeman spoke for the first time. His head remained turned toward the window, but his hands fisted in his lap.

"You would give up so easily?"

"The will of Gott be done."

"You think it is Gott's will that Abigail abandon her Plain faith and live with her Englisch family?"

"It's not for us to question." Freeman swiveled in his seat. He re-adjusted his seat belt. His eyes were red and his face lined with pain. His gruff voice was rougher than sixty-grit sandpaper. "My fraa and I did what we could. The rest is in Gott's hands. That doesn't mean I like it. It will break my fraa's heart when I come home without our dochder, but she will accept it as the will of Gott. He gives and He takes away."

"You think Gott is doing this? Is this some kind of test?" It made no sense. *I don't understand, Gott.* "Why give Abigail to you and Lorene and then take her away?"

"Abigail was never ours. Or Heather's." Freeman removed his straw hat and set it on his knees. His black hair streaked with a few strands of silver lay flat and damp with sweat. "She is a child of Gott. He will work in her life as He sees fit. My fraa and I need only stay out of his way."

"That doesn't mean we can't pray for the will of Gott to be done." Bryan offered Freeman an encouraging smile. "We can pray for discernment of His will and for the courage, patience, and endurance to run the race He has set before us."

"Can we pray Abigail comes to her senses and decides to come home?" Owen had heard all these words before—when his mother died. They gave him no more comfort now than they had then. "I feel like my character is plenty honed."

Freeman chuckled, a humorless sound. "I hate to break it to you, but you're just getting started."

"'I have told you these things, so that in me you may have peace. In this world you will have trouble.'" Bryan's voice took on that singsong quality he used when delivering the message during church. "'But take heart, I have overcome the world.' John 16:33."

Not one of Owen's favorite verses. Freeman and Lorene did a young unwed girl a special favor by taking her baby into their home and loving her for twenty years. That now-grown woman was intent on ripping that daughter away from them. What did God think of that? Did He approve? Was this a test of her or of Abigail, or Freeman and Lorene? A test of Owen?

Or all four? Owen stifled a groan.

"Go on, spit it out." Bryan leaned back and stretched his arms over his head. His fingers grazed the roof. "You're about to choke on your thoughts."

"Nee. So many people are touched by this situation. It's hard to know who is being tested or why."

"The why part is found in Scripture. We are honed by the fire. Our faith is strengthened."

"Mine should be as strong as iron by now. My daed's too. And Freeman and Lorene's."

"Compared to Job's?"

Okay. That wasn't fair. No one could compete with that kind of loss and suffering. Not that it was a competition. Owen pulled the seat belt from his chest and readjusted it. Nothing about this trip had turned out the way he'd hoped. "What's it like, Freeman?"

"What's what like?"

"Having someone give you a bopli to raise? Adopting a bopli?"

For the first time on this long ride, Freeman smiled. "It was an amazing gift. We'd done nothing to deserve such a beautiful gift. We went to the hospital and came home with this tiny mite of a bopli maed. She was small, but she had healthy lungs. She cried to eat every two hours at night. We took turns feeding her. We were new at it. Thanks to Gott we had my eldre and Lorene's to guide us. Lorene's schweschder came and stayed a spell with us."

"How was it different from having your own bopli?"

"It's different but the same. It's hard to explain. You've been given this bopli by someone who trusts you to do a better job than she could. It's a responsibility. You've been entrusted with the most important gift of all. A human life. Not just feeding and clothing her and keeping her healthy and safe, but teaching her right from wrong. Teaching her about Jesus.

"I remember sitting with Abigail in my arms in the rocking chair next to the fireplace during a snowstorm a few weeks after she was born. She was so tiny. Her face was all red and scrunched up. She was wailing as usual. I sang to her, and after a while she stopped fussing and stared at me with those big eyes. I knew then she wasn't my adopted bopli. She was mine, my bopli, my dochder.

"Eleven months later, Jane came along. She had the same little fluff of reddish-blonde hair and blue eyes. They could've been twins. People say it all the time, even now. They could've been twins. Sometimes I held them both in my lap, telling them stories and singing to them while Lorene fixed supper. I marveled at Gott's creation, His blessings, His grace."

By that time it seemed as if Freeman had forgotten Owen and Bryan were in the van. He was engulfed in sweet, joyful memories.

"Nothing can take those memories from you," Bryan murmured. "Gott is gut. Gott has a plan. Our job is to believe and have faith."

Freeman nodded, but his gaze remained fixed somewhere in a distant time and place. "You need to seek a fraa whose heart and soul are firmly planted in our faith." The pain in Freeman's voice spoke of what it cost him to admit he didn't believe his daughter was such a person. "Don't risk your own salvation for that of another."

"I know you don't think that woman is Abigail, but I'm not giving up on her."

Freeman swiveled. He drilled Owen with a dark look. "I'm not giving up on her either. She's in Gott's hands. He will work in her life far better than I ever could."

"I know. I understand."

Clouds hid the sun. Splotches of rain dotted the windows. The rushing air outside the van picked up speed. Owen closed his eyes and listened. God was in every raindrop, every gust, every cloud. He carried them along. All they had to do was believe and obey.

That philosophy held true for every aspect of their Plain lives. He couldn't solve the puzzle that was Abigail today. In the meantime he could work on the rest of his life so one day he would have the job, the work, and the life he wanted to offer to her. Starting with sunflowers. "What do you think of sunflower as a cash crop, Freeman?"

"I think a young man such as yourself should look for every chance to preserve our Plain way of life." Freeman wiped at his face with his sleeve. Melancholy lived in the lines around his mouth and eyes. "Farming gets harder and harder. More men are working in factories, stores, and construction businesses. There's nothing wrong with that, but it takes them away from the farm and the family all day long. It changes family life."

"Well said." Bryan nodded. He leaned forward, elbows on his knees, and laced his fingers. "Have you come up with a plan since we last spoke of this, Owen?"

"I have. I'll work at a sunflower farm first, learn the ropes, then ask the Gmay to consider starting a farm co-op. We can work together. Pooling our resources will allow us to farm more total acres. That will allow a bigger profit margin."

"It's a gut plan. After you learn the ropes come back to the Gmay with a proposal." Bryan tugged his journal from his satchel. "I'll take some notes and talk with Delbert and Samuel about it. Have you talked to your daed about this?"

"He's my next stop."

As if on cue the van halted. "Here we are, Freeman," the driver announced. "Do you want me to drop Owen first or you, Bryan?"

"Owen first. He's on fire with all the plans he has." Bryan smiled. "He needs to get home first."

Chapter 33

Sopping wet from the deluge of rain, Owen burst into the kitchen just in time to find his father at the kitchen sink washing his hands. The girls were setting the table for supper. The aroma of fried chicken floated in the air along with a sweetness that might be apple pie. Hairy unfurled his lanky body from the rug in front of the empty fireplace and trotted over to say hello. Owen gave the dog's head a good scratch while he decided how to approach the subject.

It had been easy to imagine his future laid out before him in the van with Bryan and Freeman as his supporters. Now in the sticky, warm confines of his family home, he wasn't so sure his father would be as amenable to the idea.

"There you are." Father grabbed a dish towel and sopped up the water he'd dripped on the counter. "I was surprised when you didn't show up at the job site today."

"I stopped by the office and told Alma I wouldn't be in."

"Just because you're the co-owner's suh doesn't mean you can pick and choose when to work. You should've said something to me. I'm your boss."

"I'm sorry. I didn't think you'd mind." Owen grabbed a second dish towel. He dried his face and hair. He hadn't missed a day's work in over a year, and then it was because of a nasty case of the flu. "I had something important to take care of."

"Running after Abigail Bontrager when she's made it clear she's going back to her Englisch roots?"

Owen dropped the towel on the counter. "Would you have us abandon a member of the Gmay to her fate?"

"That is for Bryan and her eldre to decide."

"We talked to Abigail. She decided to stay in Abilene for now." Owen stepped up to the sink and took his turn washing his hands. It gave him time to corral his emotions, as if that were possible. "It was hard on Freeman. I was glad to be there to share in that burden with him and Bryan."

"I suppose there's merit to that."

"I'm glad you think so." Owen turned to face his father. "I hope you'll see merit in something else we discussed."

His father rubbed his neck. He turned his head side to side and rolled his shoulders. "I also have something to discuss, but I'd like to do it at the supper table so everyone gets the news at the same time. It's been a long day. I'd rather not repeat myself."

"I'll make it quick. I've been saving every cent of my salary. I'd thought to buy a piece of property and build a house when I marry. Now that you're thinking of selling the farm to the McCormacks, I'd like to make you a proposition."

"Suh, I agreed to sell to Bill today."

Owen's stomach dropped like a boulder. "Have you signed the contract?"

"Nee, but I gave my word."

"Can you amend the agreement to sell me the house, outbuildings and ten acres?"

"You want the house?"

"I do. This is our home. I want it to stay in the family. I want to raise my future family here."

The tension drained from Father's face. The stress lines eased. "It's a nice thought. Your mudder would've liked it."

"Then it's possible."

"It's time to eat, you two." Kayla sashayed into the kitchen, all bluster and light. "The food is getting cold."

"We're coming." Father clapped Owen on the shoulder. "We've news to share."

"There's more."

"More?" Father moved toward the door. "What else?"

"I'm going to talk to Dick Silverman about a job."

Father nodded. "Gut."

"What do you mean gut? I thought you needed me to work for you."

"I want willing hands and willing hearts. An obedient suh is a gut suh, but I remember what it was like to spend from dawn to dusk in the fields, to reap and sow, to know that we were putting food on the table for families. It is gut, honest, hard work. Mary's son Tobias is interested in coming to work for me."

The blending of families had begun. Mary's son taking Owen's place in the family business didn't hurt the way it once might have. "That is gut timing. I want to learn the business from the ground up." Owen followed his father into the next room, where his siblings had already gathered. "My long-range plan is to create a co-op for Plain farmers to pool their acreage and product. Bryan's broaching the subject with Delbert and Samuel. Eventually I hope to bring it to the entire Gmay."

"You have been busy." Father eased into his chair. "You have a plan, and you've taken the first step. I don't want to sound proud, but it is gut for a daed to see his suh seek ways to help the whole community while finding his own way."

"I'm glad you see it that way."

"Can we pray so we can eat?" Micah had one hand on the platter of chicken and the other on the basket of biscuits. "I'm so hungry I could eat a cow."

"Patience, Suh." Father's chuckle took the edge from the admonishment. "Let's pray."

Owen's stomach rumbled, but no one could hear it over the noise that immediately erupted at his father's "amen." Micah spilled his water in Claire's lap. Eli tossed a roll to Lee instead of passing the basket, and Kayla proceeded to argue with Claire about whether to have the canning frolic on Tuesday or Wednesday of the following week.

"Enough." Father clapped his hands. Silence ensued. "Could we have a quiet conversation at the table like regular folks? You're giving me a headache."

"Sorry, Daed." Kayla handed him the platter of fried chicken. "Did you finish the horse barn in Parsons?"

"Nee. We had other business to attend to." Father smiled at Owen. "So did your bruder."

"You sold the farm?" Lee paused, a bowl of pickled beets in one hand. "To the McCormacks?"

"I did. We'll plow the money back into the business. Rob wants to open a second office in Wichita. We'll hire another crew." Father waved his hands as he talked, more animated than he'd been in years. "We have more work now than two crews can accomplish."

"How does Onkel Wayne feel about that?" Lee seemed to have forgotten he still held the beets. "He had first option."

"Wayne understands. He and I talked far into the night about the pros and cons. He went with me to the McCormack office in Hutchinson."

"He could've done a lot with that acreage."

"He doesn't have the equipment or the capital to invest in the equipment." The animation died a little. Regret cut in line. "He recognizes that. He'll work the acreage he has, and he's agreed to do some work on Mary's farm. She's prepared to pay him from her proceeds. Plus he has the option of working for the McCormacks. He's covered in work."

"Which brings me to my other news." The words wobbled. Father rolled his shoulders. His Adam's apple bobbed. "I suspect you older kinner know I've been seeing Mary."

How could they not?

Red crept up from his collar and overtook his face. He sipped water. He cleared his throat. "We went to see the deacon last night. Our banns will be published on Sunday." Relief flitted across his face, mixed with a brash dare-to-question-me bravado. "We'll be married in two weeks."

A profound silence descended on the room. No one moved. The *drip, drip* of water from the kitchen faucet sounded from afar.

"Jonas can sleep in me and Eli's room. The baby, too, when he gets old enough." Micah piped up from the other end of the bench. "It'll be fun to have more brieder and schwesdchdre."

His observation burst the dam. Everyone talked at once. Would they move to Mary's house, or would the Wagners move to their house? What about all the animals? And all the furniture and dishes? Wasn't the house too small for six more people? Would they be brieder and schwesdchdre?

"Whoa! Whoa! Everyone stop." Smiling, shaking his head, Father held up both hands. "Actually, we'll be moving into Mary's house. Owen is buying this house and the ten acres of land around it. He's looking ahead to the day when he marries and has kinner of his own. In the meantime the house stays in the family."

"Gut for you, Bruder." Kayla elbowed Lee. "Right, Lee?"

"Right." Grinning, Lee set the bowl of beets aside. "I guess that means you're leaving the family business too."

"Right now we're talking about Daed's news." Owen summoned his best smile. This wasn't about replacing Mother. It was about his father's happiness. Change was hard. Having a bad attitude only made it harder. "Congratulations, Daed."

Father's smile faded into a sober appraisal. "I hope you mean that, Suh."

"Of course I do."

"Gut. That's gut."

"Mudder would be happy for you." Kayla slid from the bench. She did a two-step just short of dancing. "And I'm happy to have help with the cooking, laundry, and cleaning—not that it's about me or us."

"Think how much more there will be with six more people," Claire, ever the practical sister, observed. "That's more laundry than a person can do in a day."

"We'll have lots of helping hands." Kayla skipped—literally—toward the door. "I'm getting the pie. This announcement deserves pie. I wish we had ice cream—"

"Let me finish first." Father caught her hand as she attempted to pass him. "You're always on the run, Dochder."

"I'm just happy." She flew back to the bench, where she proceeded to butter another roll. "And excited."

"There's much to do." Father sniffed and swiped his napkin across his face. "Mary, her schwesdchdre, her *aentis*, and her mudder will take care of the wedding. Your aentis and *groosmammi* will help, but we men will need to spruce up her place and whatnot. After the wedding we can think about moving and all that entails."

It was better to talk about the nuts and bolts, the details, than the flood of feelings with which they were all contending.

Micah slid from his bench and went to lean against Father. "Can the hunde go too?"

"The hunde, *bussis*, the geil—except for Owen's." Father slid his arm around Micah. It would be hard to say who loved animals more. The dog, cats, and horses were part of the family too. "The more the merrier."

"Now can we have pie?"

"Now you can have pie."

A cheer went up. Did Mother hear it? Was she happy? She never seemed to find cheerful obedience a chore when she had lived. She surely wouldn't now.

Chapter 34

The rap on the door at eight on Sunday morning sent Abigail racing down the hallway. The Hansons were still asleep, as usual. At least the visitor hadn't rung the doorbell, which sounded like bells pealing throughout the house. She opened the door, prepared to shush whoever it was.

Rhett let his fist drop. "Howdy, sugar."

"My name is Abigail. Why are you knocking so early?" She pushed open the screen door and stepped onto the porch rather than letting him in. He stood not far from where Owen had stood not so long ago. They were dark and light in looks. Rhett was book smart, while Owen worked with his hands. Both had lost a parent in their youth, but they had little else in common. Owen wanted all of her. Rhett just wanted to dip his toes in the shallow waters of romance. Knowing the difference made life so much easier. "You know Heather and the kids don't get up until time for brunch and an afternoon nap."

"Which is why I knocked instead of ringing the doorbell." He took a step back and let her pass. Instead of his usual cowboy attire, he wore black slacks and a short-sleeved, button-down, cotton shirt. The only nod to his preference for western wear was black cowboy boots. "I came to see you."

"Why?"

"Are you mad at me?"

"Why would I be mad at you for not coming around for two weeks? It's given me plenty of time to think about what you're up to and whether I'm interested."

"What I'm up to? I'm not up to anything. Ah, you mean because I kissed you." A slow smile spread across his face. "I didn't call you because I had a lot of work this week. I'm working on a story I hope will get picked up by the wire—"

"You live next door. You couldn't stop by for five minutes? You obviously know my telephone number. You could've called. You didn't because kissing me doesn't mean the same thing to you as it does to me. It's good that I understand that."

He dropped onto the porch swing and patted the wooden slats. "Have a seat. You could've skipped over to my house or called me. My number is in your contacts."

"Friends don't kiss." She crossed her arms and leaned against the porch railing. "And where I come from, women don't call on men and they don't have phones at all."

"Toto, I don't think we're in Kansas anymore." He smirked. "Sorry, that's a line from *The Wizard of Oz* and obviously we *are* still in Kansas, but I keep forgetting you're from a throwback era before women had rights. I'm sorry I didn't call. I'm sorry I hurt your feelings."

"You didn't hurt my feelings." Maybe at first, but after seeing Owen and comparing the depths of his feelings with what Rhett seemed to be offering, she had no reason to feel hurt. "It was no big deal to you. For Plain people, physical displays of affection are reserved for people we love. You don't love me and I don't love you."

"For us kissing is the first step. It's part of the exploration, the finding out if we can love each other. It's nice." Rhett came to stand beside her. He put both hands on the railing and inhaled deeply. He smelled of spicy aftershave and soap. "I love the sweet scent of honeysuckle and morning dew. I love the first beginnings of a relationship. The getting-to-know-you part. I thought I was going slow, but obviously it wasn't slow enough on the physical part but too slow on the call or visit part. I'll try to do better."

"You don't need to do better. Maybe just try being a friend."

His expression puzzled, Rhett touched her face with one finger. "You can never have too many friends, I suppose. We'll see. But now we have to leave or we'll be late."

Not falling for that again, Abigail backed away. "Late for what?"

"Church, of course. Your chariot awaits."

"You found a church you like better than your grandma's?"

"I did. It's small but mighty." He took her hand and tugged her toward the steps. "Will you do me the honor of attending a service with me?"

An English church. Was it better than no church at all? One of the hardest parts of being in Abilene so far had been the absence of that sense of security that came with knowing she had a community of faith around her. This would not be the same. Her family wouldn't approve, nor would Bryan. But surely it would fill that hole in her heart that had grown since arriving here. Hold her over, so to speak.

Abigail tugged her hand free. "I'll get my bag."

"Text Heather so she'll know where you are when she wakes up."

Or she could write her a note. Abigail found a pencil and paper in the kitchen's junk drawer, wrote the note, and laid it next to the coffee maker, Heather's first stop in the morning.

By the time she returned to the porch, Rhett had his car out front. He stuck his head out the window. "Let's go. We're gonna be late."

Ten minutes later they joined a trickle of folks entering a nondescript one-story metal building on Abilene's north side. It had none of the trappings of the English churches in Hutchinson with their stained-glass windows, steeples, and big parking lots. A man in jeans and a gray T-shirt that read He Is Risen greeted them at the door. "Hello, Rhett, glad to see you decided to visit us again."

"I'm thinking about making it a regular thing." Rhett put his arm around Abigail. Her heart, already clanging against her rib cage, revved. "This is my friend Abigail Bontrager. Abigail, this is Neil Brantley. He's the preacher here."

With his overgrown mop of black hair, he looked more like one of Brody's skateboarding friends, but Neil had a deep voice suited for preaching. "It's nice to meet you."

"And you." Neil had a firm handshake. Hopefully he wouldn't notice how damp Abigail's palm was. "It's an unusual treat to have one of our Plain sisters at a service. I hope it feeds your soul."

"That's k-k-kind of you." The words stumbled from her tongue. Heat burning her cheeks, Abigail ducked her head. "I've never been to an English service."

"I suspected as much. I hope it's not too crazy for you. Try to give us the benefit of the doubt." Neil glanced at his watch. "Whoops, we'd better get in there. It's never good when the preacher keeps the congregation waiting. They start to worry about who'll be first in the buffet line at Pizza Hut when the service runs long."

Rhett and Abigail followed Neil inside, where folding chairs were set up in neat rows of twelve with a narrow aisle down the middle. Most were already occupied. A baby fussed. A little girl sang "Jesus Loves Me" at the top of her lungs. Two boys sat on the floor running Matchbox cars between them. Rhett found two seats near the back. Abigail sank onto one and took a shaky breath. The room didn't seem like anything special. Nothing on the white walls. A cement floor.

In front a woman sat behind a set of drums, a man stood at a keyboard, and two women gathered at a microphone on a stand. They were all dressed in jeans and T-shirts. Neil grabbed a guitar and slung the strap over his shoulder. "Welcome, my friends. Please stand if you're able and join us as we worship the Lord."

The band launched into a song that repeatedly stated, "God's not dead, He's surely alive," as if anyone thought otherwise. The words were projected on a white screen behind the band. People clapped and kids shouted. Someone whooped. A man shouted, "Amen."

No chance anyone would fall asleep. Abigail's foot tapped. Her hands wanted to clap. She clasped them in front of her. Rhett had no such inhibitions. He clapped and sang with that same sweet bass he'd employed at her welcome party. And he smiled.

Two more songs followed. The noise reached a crescendo and then softened for "I Stand Amazed (How Marvelous)." This song was familiar. They'd sung it at a Sunday night singing. Abigail joined in, which made Rhett's smile stretch into a grin.

Finally Neil signaled for the members to sit. Rhett leaned back in his chair. He draped his arm across the back of Abigail's. He scooted close and whispered in her ear. "That's what I'm talking about. I'm wide awake now. How about you?"

What could she say to that? She was already wide awake when she walked in the door with her heart pumping and her palms damp with sweat. That her ears liked what they heard but her heart chastised her for it?

God didn't need a sound system to hear their praises.

"It was very loud. I'm sure God heard it, but He hears soft voices too."

"David leaped and danced for joy in the Bible."

That was true. But the congregation shouldn't be focused on the people playing instruments. Instead their gazes should be lifted to the heavens.

Neil began speaking, saving Abigail from responding.

"Hey, folks, now that everyone is tuned in to worship, do we have any guests who need introduction? You'll notice Rhett Strong is with us again today. We're excited to have you, Rhett. Why don't you introduce your guest?"

"I'm happy to be here." Rhett hopped up, hitched up his pants, and flung his hand out in Abigail's direction. "This is my friend Abigail."

"Hi, Abigail," the congregation chorused. "Welcome."

"She's visiting her mother from Haven this summer. We're hoping she'll stay on in Abilene. Make her feel at home here, and maybe she will."

Applause echoed through the tin building. Abigail's body wanted to burst into flames with the heat of embarrassment. She managed a jerky nod.

"Okay, we've embarrassed Abigail enough. Have a seat, Rhett." Neil plucked a high note on his guitar. "Let's open with prayer, and I'll bore you with the message."

A smattering of laughter greeted that statement. Neil grinned. "Just checking to see who's paying attention."

He prayed for several sheep in his flock, as he called them, who were sick. One man had pancreatic cancer. Another's brother had died. A little boy's dog had run away. Neil prayed for its return. The prayers were deeply personal and asked God to perform miracles of healing. There was no mention of abiding according to His will.

For the message Neil settled onto a stool, his guitar on his lap, and strummed several chords to begin. He read from Philippians 2:1–4. "Therefore if you have any encouragement from being united with Christ, if any comfort from his love, if any common sharing in the Spirit, if any tenderness and compassion, then make my joy complete by being like-minded, having the same love, being one in spirit and of one mind. Do nothing out of selfish ambition or vain conceit. Rather, in humility value others above yourselves, not looking to your own interests but each of you to the interests of the others."

A familiar verse, but it was easier to understand in plain English rather than High German.

He went on to talk about Peter's letter to the church in Corinth, begging them to live in harmony, to be united in mind and body, and most importantly, to follow no one but Christ. "Peter wanted all believers to be unified, not on doctrinal issues, but in the way they treated one another."

Neil strummed a chord as punctuation. "In other words not to huddle up in our cliques like we do in this day and age—with our denominational differences. To treat each other with agape love. Brotherly love. To throw away our pride. To give up our right to be right. To embrace our brothers and sisters in Christ regardless of our differences."

Abigail had no Bible book learning. Her knowledge of the beliefs of other denominations would fit in a thimble. Her district didn't allow Bible study for fear that it would stoke arguments over interpretation of Scripture. No need for commentaries or Bible study books that would lead to dissension. She did know what she believed. She'd learned everything she needed to know from her baptism classes. The bottom line was that Jesus was the "way, the truth and light." No one came to the Lord except through Him. The Holy Bible said so. No one could improve on it. Did that make the Amish a clique or true believers?

Rhett tapped her arm. She frowned at him. He cocked his head toward Neil and mouthed the words, *He's great, isn't he?*

Preachers were men. God was great. Men were simply vessels for God's Word and His work. She nodded and focused on Neil. He was winding down. He ended the sermon with an observation that churches were splitting because factions could not agree on certain doctrines found in their books of discipline, which were based on Scripture. "We're a nondenominational church. We don't have to worry about a split." He strummed another chord. "But that doesn't mean we can't have differences of opinions about the meaning of Scripture and how it should apply to our daily lives and our beliefs. Those differences can tear us apart. Peter begs us not to let that happen. To love each other more than we love being right. Can we do that?"

A prolonged round of applause greeted the question. Neil strummed harder. He burst into song. The lyrics on the screen indicated it was called "There Was Jesus."

More applause and shouts of affirmation. Neil rose. The other band members leaped onto the stage. More music, more songs, more hooting and hollering.

They definitely enjoyed their worship time. Was there anything wrong with that? Abigail rubbed her temples. The noise and the question both gave her a headache.

Collection baskets went around. By the time the one on the left got to the back row, it was full. Rhett tossed a ten dollar bill into it.

"Where does the money go?" Abigail had to raise her voice to be heard.

"It pays for the electricity, the phone, the water, the trash pickup, Neil's salary, and the lady who answers the phone and takes care of the office during the week," Rhett shouted in her ear. "They also pay someone who's part-time to be the finance secretary, to keep track of the money and make sure the bills get paid. It's a small church, so there aren't a lot of bills right now, but the congregation is growing. That's a healthy sign."

None of the costs he listed occurred in a Plain district. Having church in people's homes took care of them. The elders didn't get paid. Growth meant splitting into new districts to keep them small. That way everyone knew everyone. "Like a business."

"In a way. This is what Neil does. He doesn't have another job. He has a wife and a baby. He has to feed them."

"It makes sense."

The music finally faded away. "Cookies, coffee, and sweet lemonade in the fellowship hall," Neil yelled over the din. "You snooze, you lose."

"What he means is the kids help themselves to six or eight cookies at a time if the cookie ladies aren't on their toes and policing the tables." Rhett steered Abigail into the aisle, but instead of blending into the flow that went left, he veered right toward the door. "We're not having cookies. I don't want to spoil your appetite."

Relief washed over Abigail. Her stomach got willies at the thought of making conversation with more strangers. She waited until they were outside to ask the obvious question. "Why would cookies spoil my appetite? It's only nine thirty."

Amazing, a church service that only lasted an hour. The service in Haven would be going strong for another two hours. Abigail's heart twinged. The women would serve more than cookies. Sandwiches, pickled beets, coleslaw, potato salad, barbecue beans, pickles, cookies, pies—an entire spread for lunch after the service. Her mother would be there with her sisters Jane, Hope, Rose, Owen's sisters Kayla and Claire, and all the others. They would chat and make plans for frolics. They would wonder how she was doing and why she didn't come home when her father came for her. Her mother would try to hide her tears. Jane would stay close to give comfort.

Owen would be there. He'd come for her and she'd refused to go. He regretted stepping back. He shouldn't. He'd done the right thing, and she'd taken advantage of his willingness to give her room. How long would he wait?

"Because you're about to meet my sister Kiera. She's meeting us at Grandma's house." Rhett opened the car door for Abigail. He waited until she slid in and then bent over to talk through the open door. "She's going to do a session with you, and then we're having lunch with Grandma. She insisted."

He was still talking when he hopped into the car on his side. "Grandma is a good sport. She was disappointed I didn't decide to go to her church, but she didn't say too much. She thinks Neil's church is a little too far out there for a good Baptist boy."

"It's certainly different from our church."

"Grandma's really just happy I'm going to church. She wants everyone to be with her in heaven. She's gonna love you, with your devout faith."

"Wanting everyone to be with her in heaven is a worthy desire."

"So what did you think? Neil's great, isn't he? And the music. And everyone is friendly."

They'd arrived late and left without mingling, so it was hard to say on that last point. "I'm not sure we would agree with his message. The road to salvation is narrow. The road to damnation for nonbelievers is wide. Leastwise that's what we're taught."

"We? Is that the royal we?" Rhett thumped his fingers on the wheel. "You have to learn to think for yourself. What do you think of the idea that how we worship or with whom we worship isn't as important as worshiping Jesus?"

When he put it that way, it was hard to argue. "It's a nice thought. That we would all get along. We *should* all get along. But that doesn't mean we all believe the same thing. A lot of people worship Jesus but ignore Scripture that tells them what is sin and what's not. Some denominations pick and choose the Scripture they live by. All Scripture is God-breathed, not just the verses we like." According to Bryan, Delbert, and Samuel, who took turns giving the message. They were short on book learning, but they leaned on God's guidance for the words they spoke.

"And the Plain don't? The Bible says win the lost and make disciples. Go and spread the Word throughout the nations and the world. You said yourself the Amish don't evangelize."

"Every district has its own rules. Mine doesn't. Most don't. But some do." Abigail held her hands in front of the AC vent. The air cooled her fingers and her cheeks. "I don't like to argue. That part of the sermon I agree with. Interpreting Scripture leads to people fussing about who's right. We should live together in peace and humility."

"That's a nice thought. The question remains simple. What do you *believe*?" Rhett pulled his car into his grandma's driveway next to a bright purple Volkswagen. He turned off the engine. "I'm warning you now, don't expect much peace *or* humility at the Elliott household."

"Why not?"

"You'll see."

Chapter 35

"It's about time you introduced us to your lady friend." Grandma Grace, so introduced by Rhett, pumped Abigail's hand with a surprising iron grip. "Let me get a gander at you."

She stuck the glasses that had been resting on her flat chest on her nose and let her piercing gaze run from Abigail's kapp to her sneaker-clad feet. "You appear hearty and healthy. Not that a person can tell quick as that. I hear you've got a head on your shoulders. You're not a flighty gadabout like your mother, according to my grandson, but then he's been known to let his heart get in the way of his head."

Grace didn't know her mother. A second later understanding bloomed. Heather. She meant Heather. Even after a month it didn't immediately click. Grace certainly spoke her mind. Tall like her grandson, Grace had dark walnut-brown eyes and a full head of curly brown hair—the color likely came from a hair salon. Despite the June heat she wore a royal-blue skirt, matching jacket, white blouse, and blue pumps. A single strand of pearls graced her neck.

Sunday-go-to-church clothes. A good sign. "It's nice to meet you too."

"She's not my lady friend. Not yet." Grinning, Rhett landed a kiss on Grace's powdered cheek. "She's a friend, and you could've met her sooner. You could've come to the party or just stopped by Heather's, Grandma."

Rhett took Abigail's elbow and propelled her toward a floral-print couch in the living room. Grace favored pastel colors and blond wood furnishes. The white curtains were pulled back from four long windows, filling the room with light. Very different from Heather's western themes. Abigail sank onto the couch.

"You know I don't drink, I don't smoke, I don't dance, and I don't hang around people who do." Grace lowered herself into a wingback chair and crossed her legs at the ankles. "If I were a betting woman—which I'm not—I'd bet your friend Abigail doesn't either."

"Not under normal circumstances, no." Nothing about her life was normal right now. Did agreeing with Grace make Rhett look bad? Or feel bad? And what right did Grace have to pass judgment on Heather? *Gott, I'm in over my head—again.* "Heather is my . . . birth mother. I'm trying to . . . figure out some things."

I didn't get to choose my mother. But my adoptive mother did choose me.

"And I'm trying to help." Rhett sat forward on the couch, elbows on his knees, hands clasped loosely. "So where's Kiera? I saw her Bug in the driveway. It's a wonder a truck doesn't run her over on the highway."

"I'm here."

Abigail swiveled. A woman with the same dark-brown eyes and walnut hair as Rhett pranced—literally—through the doorway into the living room. She was even taller than Rhett, a giant of a woman. An Amazon. She wore no makeup. Her hair was plaited in a long braid that hung down her back. Her leggings and tank top, both a creamy caramel color, showed off a slim, boyish figure and a deep tan.

"You do love to make an entrance." Rhett rose and embraced his sister. "You should have been in theater."

"I dabble." Kiera broke free and held out her hand to Abigail. "I'm so pleased to meet you. Rhett has told me all about you. Grandma, your spinach lasagna is in the oven. The peach pie is cooling. I made the salad. I'd like to work with Abigail until it's time for lunch. I'm told we have some negative self-talk habits she needs to break."

She didn't shake Abigail's hand so much as stroke it tenderly. Her skin was smooth as a baby's bottom, her touch feathery. "When we're done, you'll have a better sense of who you are and what you want out of life. I promise."

"Please. Don't fill the poor woman's head with that foolish self-talk and mindfulness babble." Grace snorted. "Her people won't appreciate it, and it will only make it that much harder for her to live the life she grew up in."

"That's sort of the point." Rhett took a seat in the matching wingback chair across from Grace's. "If she's going to figure out what she wants out of life, she has to learn to think for herself. Her people don't do that."

Once again, everyone talked about Abigail as if she weren't in the room. "I do think for myself. We all do. We happen to think alike."

"You think you're clumsy and awkward and don't fit anywhere." Kiera had a good grasp of Abigail's state of mind, thanks to Rhett. "You've been made to feel that way. We need to work on that."

"How?"

"Let's start with a few questions. Where do you see yourself in six months? Followed by a year, and five years?"

Abigail's answer remained the same regardless of time frame. "I hoped to be married and have children."

"Good girl." Grace beamed her approval. "None of that women's libber stuff for you."

"Grandma, hush, please." Kiera pointed to the massive oak grandfather's clock that took up a chunk of wall space between two sets of shelves filled with books and family photos in ornate silver frames. "I think it's time for you to check on the lasagna."

Grace didn't move. "Rhett, why don't you do it? You're not giving your friend any support. I'm not leaving her when your sister is giving her the third degree."

Rhett didn't move. It was a standoff.

Kiera sighed. She turned back to Abigail. "What do you consider your strengths to be? Your talents?"

Those terms were alien in the Amish world where no one strove to stand out. "I don't have many. I'm good at running, playing volleyball, and hunting. I'm supposed to be good at cooking, baking, and sewing, but I'm not." Abigail English Girl could use a microwave, dishwasher, and washing machine quite well now. "I do my best, but others do it better."

"You can be the best. You are the best. You only have to believe in yourself."

"What happened to being humble, to showing humility?" Her expression pained, Grace stood, her knees cracking, and headed for the door. "I have great respect for your people, Abigail. They don't toot their own horns. They know who they have to thank for their talents and their blessings. If your adoptive parents raised you right, you do too."

"It doesn't pay to be humble in today's world. There's truth to the saying that nice guys—and gals—finish last. Even in today's society women are taught appearances are more important than brains. They work three times as hard as men and get paid less for their efforts." Kiera jabbed her thumb in Rhett's direction. "I bet he gets paid more than the other reporter at the *Reflector-Chronicle*."

"I have a better résumé."

"But no more experience. Probably less."

"I don't care." Grace paused at the doorway. "I'm going to take the foil off the lasagna so the cheese can brown. Then I'll let it rest for a few moments. Then I'm putting it on the table. I expect you to eat some, Kiera. As well as the pie à la mode. You're far too thin. A good wind would blow you away."

"Would not. I work out." Kiera flexed her bicep muscles. "I bet I could wrestle Rhett to the ground in fifteen seconds flat."

"Could not." Rhett, who'd looked half asleep the second before, sat up in his chair. "You're a toothpick."

"I run six to eight miles every day. How many do you run? To Burger King and back?"

"That's enough." Grace's voice floated from the hallway. "You'll both be running laps and doing push-ups if you don't stop."

"It's important for women to know they can take care of themselves." Kiera turned to Abigail. "We don't have to have men in our lives to be complete. We can do anything men do and do it better."

"I don't want to do it better." Abigail finally got a word in edgewise. "And I don't want to be alone. That's the problem."

Kiera frowned. She opened her mouth.

"Don't say it, Sis." Rhett spoke up first. "What we have here is a failure to communicate. She isn't you. She doesn't want to be you. She wants to be her. What kind of personal coach are you?"

"The kind who works with women who need their self-esteem bolstered for purposes of pursuing their career goals. Come on, Abigail. We need to be able to talk uninterrupted."

Kiera led Abigail into a spacious bedroom featuring a queen-size bed covered with half a dozen pillows, a dresser, and a vanity with a large round mirror. "Have a seat."

"In front of the mirror?"

"Yes, my friend. I want you to look at yourself."

"I'd rather not."

"You will never be vain. A few minutes of self-reflection will not change that." Kiera put both hands on Abigail's shoulders and propelled her toward the vanity's bench.

Every day in this world was an exercise in embarrassment. Abigail sat facing the mirror. The woman in the mirror had pink cheeks. Despite everything, she still appeared to be Plain. Did she feel Plain?

Kiera sat on a cedar chest at the foot of the bed. "Okay, who do you see?"

"Myself. And you."

"Don't mind me. Focus on the woman in the prayer covering."

There wasn't much to see. Her prayer cap covered her hair. Her blue eyes were average. Her Sunday-service dress was clean and wrinkle-free. "I see me. Abigail Bontrager."

"Who is Abigail Bontrager?"

"A Plain woman from Haven who's twenty years old. Not married. One of eight kids. A waitress at the Buggies and Bonnets restaurant."

"That's not you. Not anymore. Look harder."

The urge to shut her eyes rushed through Abigail. The pink turned to red blotches on her cheeks and neck. The air conditioner kicked on, its cool air a much-needed reprieve from the heat of the moment.

"I'm Abigail Bontrager. I have two mothers and two fathers. I have seven siblings and five half siblings. I was born in a hospital in Wichita. My mother gave me away twelve hours after I was born."

"That's a good start." Kiera gave Abigail an exaggerated thumbs-up in the mirror. "How does knowing that make you feel?"

"Stuck. I'm stuck."

"Stuck how?"

"Maybe I was never meant to be Plain. Maybe that's why I'm so clumsy. I don't fit." Abigail shut her eyes to block out the view of that woman in the mirror who stared back so perplexed and so hurt.

It didn't work. The images whirred. Falling from the tree. Falling at school. A broken nose. A cut that required six stitches. A concussion. Bread that failed to rise. An inedible piecrust. Crooked hems and sleeves two different lengths. Dumping hot coffee on her father's lap. Iced tea on a customer. A plate of food on the floor. "I'm clumsy, awkward, and a terrible cook. I don't sew very well either."

"Let's start with clumsy and awkward. Who says you're these things?"

"I say." Abigail reeled off example after example, ending with the latest fiasco at the restaurant. "It started when I was little. I've been to the emergency room and had more broken bones and stitches than my seven brothers and sisters combined."

"So you had more growing pains." Kiera sat up tall, regal, her posture perfect. "Have you ever met a woman as tall as I am?"

"Never, but what does that—?"

"I was the tallest kid in my first-grade class. The tallest kid in my fifth-grade class." She stood and executed a graceful pirouette in the space between the bed and the vanity. "The kids called me a giraffe. I made the mistake of wearing green one day and became thereafter known as the Jolly Green Giant. I never got asked on dates in high school. The boys didn't want a date who towered over them.

"My PE teachers thought a tall girl should be good at basketball. I was terrible at sports. I tripped over my own feet. I ran into other players. I couldn't hit a basket to save my soul. Even my grandfather described me as 'freakishly tall' to my face."

"But you're so graceful now."

"I'm not twelve anymore." Kiera stretched her arms over her head and then bowed until her fingertips touched the floor. "And my grandma is a smart lady. She made me take dance classes. She signed me up for yoga. I hated it at first, but my dance instructor had the patience of Job. She taught me to slow down, to think through each move, to breathe. When you dance ballet, you break the move into a series of steps. When you put them all together, you have this lovely move like a pirouette."

She demonstrated a second time. Then she proceeded to break it down into each step: "A relevé or lift to the toes, then place one foot in front, one in back, which puts eighty percent of your weight on the front foot, twenty percent on the back. Then you bring your arms into position and relevé again, pick a spot on the wall to look at when you're turning, and then put it all together."

She pirouetted again and again. Perfectly balanced. Perfectly graceful.

"I'm never going to be a ballet dancer or any kind of dancer, for that matter."

"Okay. Is there a prohibition against yoga?"

"It depends. What is it?"

"A Hindu spiritual discipline, a part of which, including breath control, simple meditation, and the adoption of specific bodily postures, is widely practiced for health and relaxation. That's the textbook definition." Kiera must've seen something in Abigail's face. She shook her head. "Don't worry. I'm not Hindu and I'm not trying to convert you. It's a way of reducing stress and becoming more in touch with your body. Just try to keep an open mind."

Kiera folded her legs and delicately sat on her haunches on the carpet. "For example, this is a beginner asana called child's pose." She stretched out her arms in front of her, fingers spread wide, her bent legs underneath her body, knees spread wide. "Join me. It feels so good to stretch."

Abigail pulled her voluminous skirt up and knelt next to Rhett's sister.

"Spread your palms out like starfish. Take nice, long breaths. Now come up on your hands and knees. Stretch your nice, long beautiful neck. Press into the earth with your hands. Lift up your behind into a half downward-facing dog. Keep your elbows in. Heart to earth. Now all the way up to downward-facing dog. Breathe. Be aware of every muscle in your body. Feel your connection to the earth."

So many commands. So much to remember. How did a person relax and breathe? Abigail flopped back on her knees. "This isn't working."

"Don't worry about doing it right." Kiera came up to a sitting position. "Don't worry about how you look. Just get in touch with your body and soul."

"I don't know what that means."

Kiera patted Abigail's knee. "I'll get you a book that shows all the poses and explains how to do them."

What would her father and mother think of downward-facing dog? Her little brothers and sisters would have giggle fits over it, for sure. "You don't have to do that."

"I told Rhett I would use all the tools in my toolbox to help you."

"I don't see how something called a downward dog will help me be a better waitress."

"It'll help you relax. Let's go back to the steps required to do a pirouette. You can use a similar technique to perform daily tasks. Think about what's required to complete that task, break it down, and see yourself doing those tasks carefully and completely, one step at a time, with no problem."

"I serve food to customers in a restaurant."

"Close your eyes."

Abigail complied.

"Now see yourself carrying that tray of food to the table and serving it. Silverware first, then beverages, carefully, slowly, no haste, no waste, then the plates of food."

It sounded so simple. To imagine it so easy. Abigail shook her head and opened her eyes. "It's one thing to imagine it, another to do it when you have six or seven tables filled with people waiting for their food with different orders or changing their orders after I've put them in or wanting a special order. Everyone is talking. Babies are crying. Couples are arguing. It's pandemonium."

"Have you ever considered that maybe being a waitress simply isn't your gig?"

"What do you mean? It should be perfect. I cook and serve food at home."

"To your family. I know Amish families are big, but not restaurant big. Maybe you should think about what job you would be comfortable doing."

Abigail stared at the woman in the mirror. What would she like to spend her days doing—until she could spend them taking care of her husband and children? "I think I'd like to work in a store where I only have to deal with one customer at a time, like a furniture store. Or I could clean houses. That's something I know how to do. Cleaning the house will be part of my job when I'm married and have children. I'm only working until then. I need to be able to sew and cook, though."

"Has it ever occurred to you that even your so-called shortcomings with cooking and sewing may be caused by how tense you are? You're so sure you're going to make a mistake, spill something, mess something up, that you're always tense. One thing leads to another."

It was possible. Probable. "You're saying if I stop worrying about messing up something, I might actually not mess it up?"

"Yep."

Abigail took a deep breath and let it out. *Stop worrying.* Easier said than done. "How do I do that?"

"It's my job to help you with that." Kiera pantomimed giving Abigail a fist bump. "Repeat after me. 'I'm coordinated. I'm in complete control of my arms and legs.'"

"I'm coordinated," Abigail whispered. "I'm in complete control of my arms and legs."

"Louder. No whispering."

"I'm coordinated. I'm in complete control of my arms and legs."

"Louder. Shout it out."

Abigail put her hands to her warm cheeks. "This is silly."

"It's not. Just do it."

So she did.

"Beautiful, beautiful." Kiera whooped and clapped. "Repeat after me. 'My brain tells them what to do. They listen.'"

Abigail shouted it out. Laughter burbled up. She couldn't contain it. "My brain tells my arms and legs what to do. They listen."

"Good job." Rhett stood in the doorway, clapping. "Way to go, Abigail."

Glowering, Kiera whirled and stalked to the door. "Go away, we're working."

"We can hear you all the way in the kitchen."

"Good." Kiera pushed him out the door and closed it. "Again, Abigail. Loud and proud."

Not proud. Just determined. "I'm coordinated. I'm in complete control of my arms and legs. My brain tells them what to do. They listen."

"Again."

Again and again. Abigail's throat hurt and her mouth went dry. Kiera didn't stop there. She urged Abigail to tell her reflection she was a good cook and a good housekeeper. She would be a good wife and mother.

"Your goals are your goals. Not everyone wants a career." Kiera settled onto the bed. "I'm sorry if I didn't get that at first. There are lots of homeschooling moms who are dedicated to their jobs of raising well-adjusted, well-educated kids."

Abigail slid around on the bench to face Rhett's sister. She'd had enough of talking to herself about herself. "What now?"

"Now I think you need to go home."

"But your grandma made lasagna."

"I'm not talking about Heather's house. I'm talking about your real home."

"What makes you say that?"

"It's as obvious as the kapp on your head, girl. You want to be a Plain wife and mother. That has nothing to do with your religion. It's who you are down to the marrow in your bones." Kiera tossed her braid over her shoulder and sighed. "This won't make Rhett happy, I know. He wants you to think for yourself. He doesn't get that you already do. Your dreams are yours. Rhett's going places. He's only here because of our grandma. She's eighty-six. When my mom gets her act together, she'll come take care of her. Rhett will head for the big city. You two are from different worlds. He wants you because he can't have you. Men are like that."

It didn't take a personal coach to know that. The facts stared Abigail in the face, mirror or no mirror. "Rhett was right. You're smart."

"Smarter than he is, anyway. So are you, by the way. Still, I want you to keep a journal. Write down what we talked about here today." A rap sounded on the door, but Kiera ignored it. "I know you don't have a big mirror to use when you get home, but if you have to, write these mantras down twenty-five times or whatever it takes to engrave them on your brain. Turn them into a needlepoint and make a pillow or, better yet, a wall hanging for your bedroom. You don't change your self-image or your self-esteem overnight. You're used to thinking of yourself like that, but I'm betting the people around you don't."

Owen tried to tell her that. He tried to tell her it didn't matter. She was the one who thought it did. "The ones who count don't."

Kiera pulled a small rectangular card from a notebook lying on the bed. She handed it to Abigail. "My telephone number is on there if you ever need to talk. If talking on the telephone isn't an option, write me a letter. My address is on the back."

The card was a pale lavender with gold sprinkles on it. "Thank you."

The rapping turned to a pounding. "Come on, Kiera, the food's getting cold." Rhett did a good job of yelling himself. "Grandma is about to have a hissy fit."

"We'd better go eat." Kiera grinned. "I've seen Grandma's hissy fits, and they're not pretty."

Lunch was a loud, boisterous affair that lasted more than an hour. Grandma insisted on seconds for everyone. She didn't need to worry about Kiera's appetite. The younger woman finished off her lasagna and ate two breadsticks. She kept up with Rhett just fine. The lasagna, layered with spinach, rich tomato sauce thick with ground beef, and a mixture of ricotta, Parmesan, and mozzarella cheese, was the best Abigail had ever eaten. *Sorry, Mudder.*

"I heard you yelling all the way in the kitchen." Grace waited until she served the warm peach pie with a scoop of vanilla ice cream to broach the topic. "What did you think of my granddaughter's methods?"

Rhett's fork, loaded with pie, paused midway to his mouth.

"It gave me a lot to think about." Abigail applied herself to the peach pie, also sweet with a touch of cinnamon, but no one made a crust as flaky as her mother's. "I don't have to be the best at anything, only good enough to please myself and the people I love. They don't care if I'm clumsy."

With a pleased grin on his face, Rhett ate his pie.

"I could've told you that." Grace sniffed. She took a dainty bite of pie, chewed, and patted her lips with her napkin. "Personal coaches are famous for stating the obvious."

"What would you know about personal coaches, Grandma? You've never been to one." Kiera jabbed her fork in the air. "Everyone's a critic. I have some very satisfied clients."

"Are you satisfied?" Rhett directed the question at Abigail.

"I am." *But I don't think you will be.* Abigail savored the last bite of creamy, cold ice cream and laid down her fork. "Thank you for lunch, Grace. The food was delicious. I'll do the dishes, and then I should get back home. Heather will think I've disappeared."

"Guests don't do the dishes." Her tone horrified, Grace snatched Abigail's saucer and her fork. "I've no doubt Heather saw Rhett's car in the driveway. She's probably spying on us with binoculars right now."

"Grandma!" Rhett and Kiera protested in unison, then laughed. "Jinx."

They hooked pinkies and laughed some more.

"I can't let you do the dishes." Abigail scooted back her chair and began stacking plates. "Where I come from, all the women pitch in. Many hands make for less work. Plus it's fun."

"I have a dishwasher." Grace pointed at Rhett and Kiera. "And grandchildren who will load it if they know what's good for them."

"I'll give Rhett a pass for today." Kiera stuck her tongue out at her brother. "He has company he'll want to see home. Go on, Bro, be a good host and see to your friend. I'm sure you and Abigail have stuff to talk about."

It had been a long day and it was only twelve thirty. The thought of another conversation—especially the one she needed to have with Rhett—was unappealing. "There's no need to walk me home. I'm just going next door."

"Be that as it may." Rhett took the opening. It not only would allow him to talk to Abigail, but he wouldn't have to do dishes. Likely a win-win in his book. "I'll see you home."

The afternoon had turned dog-days-of-summer hot. No breeze stirred. Bees buzzed the yellow roses in Grace's front yard. Crickets chorused. Abigail raised her hand to her forehead and squinted against the sun. A stray cat lazed on Heather's front porch swing. He didn't budge when Abigail approached the sidewalk.

"You're sure quiet now. Did Kiera wear you out?" Rhett matched his strides to her shorter ones. "Or maybe you need a nap after that huge meal."

"Both, I reckon."

"So what did you think of the session, really? You can be truthful."

"She just helped me face what I already knew."

"And what is that?"

"That I need to go home. To *my* home."

Rhett's stride slowed. He shook his head. "No, no, no. Those people make you feel clumsy and awkward."

"No, I make myself feel that way. They love me, pure and simple. They don't care. They never have."

Rhett halted altogether. "When?"

"I don't know yet. I have to talk to Heather. And Eric."

"Just don't go without saying good-bye. Give me one more chance."

"I won't leave without saying good-bye, but we're never going to be more than friends."

Rhett lifted her chin and kissed her lips, an urgent, hard kiss. "We'll see about that."

"Stop doing that." Abigail took a giant step backward, beyond his reach. Her decision wouldn't be made based on those kinds of feelings. Heart had to clasp hands with head in a perfect union. Owen understood that. He hadn't tried to influence her decision to come to Abilene by kissing her. He worried about the consequences of her actions. He also cared for her standing as a Plain member of their community more than he did his own feelings. "Good-bye, Rhett."

The self-satisfied expression on his face slid away. “That sounds awful final.”

“It sure does.”

“But—”

“No buts.”

Filled with a relief so intense her body seemed to float, Abigail left him standing on the steps, staring at her, mouth open.

Chapter 36

HER BODY SAGGING WITH SPENT ADRENALINE, ABIGAIL STAGGERED onto the backyard deck. Heather lay sprawled on a futon-style patio chair. She wore her swimming suit top, short shorts, and black-framed sunglasses that made it hard to tell if she was awake. The scent of coconut sunscreen floated on a tepid breeze. The sun beat down on Abigail with a ferocity that signaled she needed to say what she'd come to say. No beating around the bush. She sank onto a lawn chair. Her entire body thanked her.

"You're going back to Haven, aren't you?" Heather scooted up on the futon. She removed her glasses. Beads of perspiration dotted her bronzed skin. She picked up a longneck bottle of beer and sipped. "That's what you came out here to tell me, isn't it?"

How did mothers do that? One day Abigail would be able to read her children's minds too—God willing. "Yes. I have to go back."

"Did something happen with Rhett? Do I need to sic Eric on him? Or Grace?"

Not exactly. Sort of. "In a way he helped me figure out some things. He and his sister both did."

"Kiera, the personal coach? I always thought she was a little out there, if you know what I mean."

Again, not exactly. "She helped me see things differently. Or put them in perspective."

"It's okay." Heather leaned back on the futon. She settled the sunglasses on her nose. "Not really, but I know you belong with Freeman and Lorene. They've loved you so hard and so long. I'm a stranger. I had all those feelings bottled up for so long. They slopped all over you. It has to be totally overwhelming. I can't expect you to love me, Brody, Scarlett, and Fiona like you love the family you grew up with. I waited too long to come for you. You've been a good sport. Now it's time for you to go home to that beau of yours."

Plain folks didn't throw the *love* word around easily. "I do like you and the kids. I like Eric too. I like it here." All true. "It takes time for feelings to grow. But that doesn't mean I have to stay here. I can't stay here. I am who I am because of where I grew up. I can't change that. I don't want to change that. It's hard for me to explain."

How could Abigail put into words the longing that thrummed in her chest? The sense of loss, of missing out, of missing it all. Her mother and father, her brothers and sisters. "I miss the smell of wet dirt in the garden after a good rain. The feel of the silky bread dough in my hands when I knead it. I miss the sound of the treadle sewing machine and the *chug-a-chug-a-chug* of the wringer wash machine. I miss hanging clothes that smell of soap and bleach on the line in the afternoon sun."

Heather threw her legs over the side of the futon and sat up. "I grew up in Haven. I grew up around farming and gardening and such. The difference is I was bored. I wanted more excitement. I wanted to live. I partied and got pregnant. You're not made for fast boys and fast cars. I should be happy about that. I *am* happy about that. I just wanted you to know you could have more if you want it. I wanted you to know you have options. There's a big, wide world out there. If I hadn't come for you, you never would have known how available it is to you."

The big, wide world didn't call to Abigail. Her small, beautiful world back in Haven did. The picture of what she was missing at this very moment filled her mind's eye. The crow of the rooster in the morning. The creaking sound of the buggy wheels and the *clip-clop* of the horse's hooves on the road. The rumble of the tractor engine. Doolittle's doggy breath and baleful stares when she forgot to feed him. The mama cat who sunned on the chicken coop roof while her brood play-fought and tumbled in the grass.

She missed Kayla. She missed Owen. She missed frolics and church services and the bounteous quiet. "I'm sorry."

"You can't go yet. I haven't had enough time." Heather took her hand and held on. Tears ran down her face. "The girls haven't had enough time with their big sister."

"I can stay a few more days. I want to have time to say good-bye to Eric and the boys. Besides, I'm not running back to Haven to pretend I was never here. I won't pretend they don't exist. That you don't exist." Abigail worked to keep her voice steady. She would miss Scarlett and Fiona, even Brody. "It's only an hour and a half. Now that the ice has been broken, I'm sure my . . . Freeman and Lorene will be happy to have you and the kids visit. We can have family picnics and barbecues."

Abigail had two families. Surely they could be knit into one. Somehow.

"They'll never forgive the way we led you down the path to sin—singing and dancing and photo-taking."

"Our faith requires us to forgive." Abigail tugged her hand free. She removed the paper napkin from under the beer bottle and handed it to her mother. Her birth mother. "My feelings are mixed up, but they're strong. Just give me time. Let me figure out how to live in both worlds. I can do it. I know I can."

"They'll punish you for the stuff you've done here."

"There will be consequences, but that's okay." It was scary to contemplate but not as scary as the thought of never getting her old life back. "I can live with that."

Heather patted her face with the napkin. Then she did the same for Abigail. "You are a sweet girl. You try so hard to please. I'm thankful for that."

She stood and held out her hand again. "Let's go tell the kids. I'll let your dad know too. He'll want to rearrange his schedule to spend more time with you before you go."

The girls were flat on their backs on the living room carpet watching a cartoon. "Hey, Abigail, watch *Zootopia* with us. Jason Bateman is the fox. He's soooooo good." Fiona raised herself up in an impossible back position, then did a flip. "Scarlett is gonna make some popcorn. We flipped a coin. I won."

Heather turned off the TV.

"Hey!"

"Family meeting. Where's your brother?"

"Asleep in his room."

"Go get him, please."

Scarlett did as she was told while Fiona sat up, cross-legged, her smile suddenly gone.

The older girl reappeared a few minutes later, dragging Brody by his T-shirt.

"Ma, what's the deal? I'm sleeping." Brody jerked free of his sister. He ran both hands through his hair, making it that much wilder. "Do we hafta have a family meeting right this minute? Seriously?"

"Abigail has decided to go back to Haven."

No one spoke for several seconds.

"Noooo." Fiona launched herself at Abigail. "You can't go. You have to be here for the Fourth of July fireworks. It's so much fun."

"I can't stay until the Fourth, but I'm not leaving right this minute.

I have some good-byes I need to say. Besides, we'll see each other again." Abigail embraced the girl's skinny body. She was all muscle and sinew, so different from Rose and Hope. She smelled like cotton candy lip gloss and hair product instead of peanut butter cookies and clothes soap. "We'll visit back and forth."

"You promise?"

"I promise. You have to meet my sisters Jane, Rose, and Hope. And my brothers Benny, Nate, Eddie, and Joel. And our dog, Doolittle. He's the do-littlest dog around."

"That's a lot of brothers and sisters." Fiona hiccupped a sob. "I guess you don't really need us. You've got plenty."

"That's not true. You can never have enough brothers and sisters." Abigail summoned a smile to hide her own tears. "That's why Amish families are so big. The more the merrier."

"Fine, so go." Brody crossed his arms. His chin jutted out. "Nobody's stopping you."

"Brody, don't be a jerk. Abigail is part of our family now. We'll plan a going-away dinner with your aunts and Eric and the boys. What's your favorite dish, Abigail?"

"You don't have to do that—"

"We'll have homemade ice cream and brownies for dessert."

"I think my favorite food is pizza. With mushrooms, black olives, green peppers, and tomatoes."

"Yuck," Fiona and Scarlett chorused. "Eww, gross."

"Or pepperoni."

"Or both." Heather wrapped one arm around Fiona and Scarlett, the other around Abigail. "Group hug. Come on, Brody."

"Awww, Ma." Despite the protest Brody trudged forward. He allowed Scarlett to tug him into the circle. After a few seconds he broke free. "That's enough mushy stuff. Now I smell like girl." He wavered. "Having you here wasn't so bad, Abigail."

"Being here wasn't so bad."

"Call me when it's time for supper."

"I want to watch *Zootopia* with you." Abigail flopped on the carpet with her back against the sofa. "Weren't you supposed to make popcorn, Scarlett?"

She wanted to go home. She had to go home, but that didn't mean she couldn't spend a few more days as Abigail English Girl in her half sisters' world.

"I'm up for that." Heather dropped to the floor next to Abigail. "I always liked this movie."

Chapter 37

Owen smothered a laugh. Serving as a witness for a good friend on his wedding day was occasion for joy. That the joy came wrapped in a somber church service was also fitting. Too bad his younger brother thought the wedding party shenanigans should begin earlier rather than later. He probably thought no one saw him making faces like the monkey he was.

Finally Bryan took Emily's hand and put it in Denny's. They were husband and wife. Even Bryan couldn't contain a smile. The two parted ways. Emily, along with her witnesses, squeezed onto the benches next to Carrie, who beamed at her sister with teary-eyed joy. Owen clapped Denny on the back and gave him a thumbs-up. Denny grinned, but his eyes were red. He swiped his face and returned the gesture. Together they returned to the men's side.

Owen signaled to Lee. They slipped quietly through the barn doors. They'd been assigned to help with setting up more tables and chairs in the Beachys' yard. Thanks to the sunny skies, the wedding luncheon had room to spread out. It would be warm, but the Beachys had purchased fifty pounds of ice to chill the tea and lemonade as well as icing down the watermelons in oversized plastic tubs. Several youngsters had been put to work turning cranks for homemade ice cream.

"I thought that would never end." Lee chortled. "I missed breakfast this morning and I'm starving. I'm going to see if I can sneak a hunk of roast beef and a loaf of bread."

"Loretta will smack your fingers with a spatula if she catches you stealing food." Owen stalked ahead of his brother, intent on reaching the pile of tables that had been allocated for outdoor dining. "If you hadn't stayed out late last night, you wouldn't have overslept this morning and missed breakfast."

"You're no fun. Loretta likes me. She'll probably give me a roast beef sandwich and a whole pecan pie." Lee lived his life absolutely certain he was everyone's favorite. "So how did it feel to see your good friend take his vows? A little bittersweet?"

"Nee. Not in the least. I'm happy for him. I pray he and Emily have a gut life and many kinner." A quick search of his heart found no pockets of slimy green jealousy. Only the certainty that Denny had reached a milestone to which every Plain man, including Owen, aspired. "Gott's plan. Gott's timing."

"He says it, but does he feel it? That is the question." Lee helped push open the table's legs and carry it to a spot in the grass. His earlier quest for food apparently had been forgotten. Picking at Owen gave him more pleasure. "You haven't thought about Abigail once today? I don't believe you."

No use in denying it. He'd thought of no one else since returning from Abilene earlier in the week. When he closed his eyes, he saw her dressed in pants and a short-sleeved shirt, the picture of an English schoolgirl. If he concentrated harder, he saw the Abigail he'd known since childhood, the girl who looked beautiful in a soft, worn cotton dress, the lilac bringing out the cornflower blue of her eyes. Having one person with whom he could be honest was nice. "Jah, I've thought of her."

"You're doing a gut job of being obedient and humble. You set a gut example." Lee covered his heart with his hand. "But have you stopped to think maybe this is part of Gott's plan for you to be honed by trials? Maybe you're supposed to keep trying with Abigail. You've got your plan for the house and sunflower farming. Now all you have to do is convince Abigail to marry you."

"That's a big if. You're sixteen years old. What do you know about trials?"

Lee's smile fell away, replaced with a rarely seen scowl. He shoved the table into place and turned his back on Owen.

"Hey, I didn't mean to make you mad."

Lee spun around. "So you've accepted the fact that Daed and Mary will tie the knot in a few days?"

"Who am I to question Gott's plan? Plus, they deserve to be happy. I thought you were happy about it. You said she was a gut cook."

"I try to make the best of everything. I always have. Isn't that what we're supposed to do?" A mask had fallen away, revealing a younger brother Owen had never seen. One who felt deeply and covered it well. "I was ten when Mudder died. I remember how she smelled when she came into my room to quiet my night terrors. I remember how she scolded me for putting a plastic spider in Kayla's lunch box but grinned when Kayla walked away. I remember how she pretended not to see when I sneaked a cookie from the counter before supper—"

"Ach, I'm sorry, Lee. You never talk about her. Kayla and Claire do but not you."

"Nothing to talk about. I got up one morning and they were taking her from the house and putting her into a hearse that had the words RENO COUNTY CORONER'S OFFICE on the side. I didn't get to see her or say good-bye." He jerked his head toward the stack of tables. Owen helped him wrangle another one onto the grassy yard. "It wasn't until Aenti Lovina sat us down on the couch and explained what happened that I realized Mudder wasn't coming back."

All those same memories nipped at Owen. That day he'd stood face to the hot August sun, but nothing could conquer the chills that assailed him. He could do nothing to comfort his father, who trailed after the gurney, his big hands fisting and unfisting, his face so contorted with grief that his features were unrecognizable. The pitying look the man pushing the gurney gave Owen as he slammed the double doors shut and turned to Father. "There's not room for you to ride with her, Mr. Kurtz. I'm sorry. Can I call a driver for you?"

His father's mangled sob registered as a yes.

"Owen, you're in charge until your onkel Wayne and the others get here." Father pressed both hands to his temples. He cleared his throat. "Feed the animals. Have the girls gather the eggs, and pick the ripe tomatoes and vegetables from the garden. The grass needs to be mowed."

Chores as if the universe hadn't closed for business at some point during the middle of the night. How was it possible that Mother ceased to breathe and no one noticed? Not even Father, who had slept next to her.

"Not knowing what caused her to die is still unfathomable." So was the fact that Owen and Lee had never talked about it in six years. "They can develop vaccines for a life-threatening virus in a matter of months, send rocket ships to Mars, and put computers in itty-bitty cell phones, but they can't figure out what killed Mudder?"

The barn doors opened. A flood of guests poured out. Lee's face shuttered. The grief disappeared behind his usual mask carved with a lazy grin. "I'll tell Denny's mudder the hordes are about to descend. You'd better get inside to the *eck*."

Owen leaned on the table for a second, waiting for the whiplash from devastating emotion to wedding high spirits to calm. He wasn't as adept at controlling his emotions as his younger brother.

Get it together. If Lee could do it, so could he.

Owen rolled down his sleeves and grabbed his jacket. Life did go on. *Why* Mother died didn't matter. God knew the number of her days just as He knew the number of hairs on her head. He'd written her name in His book before she was born. Like Lee had said, it was easy to mouth the platitudes, much harder to live them.

Denny and Emily strolled from the barn, heading toward Owen. Denny held her hand, a rare display of public affection allowed on such a day as this. He whooped and pointed at Emily. "Have you met my fraa?"

"I have. Congratulations and blessings." Owen chucked his friend's shoulder. "May you have a long, happy life together."

"From your lips to Gott's ears." Emily laughed, a giddy sound filled with happiness and a dash of disbelief. "Have you met my mann, Denny?"

"It sounds so strange, doesn't it?" Denny's loopy grin matched his wife's. "You wait so long for the day to come, and then when it does it doesn't seem real. I reckon it will feel gut to call you my fraa for the rest of my life."

"And you my mann." Emily couldn't smile any bigger. Her dimples would pop off. "From this day forward."

Such joy. A moment in time filled with the possibilities to come. A future that gleamed shiny and new. Babies, a family, life spent together growing old.

God willing.

"We'd better move inside."

Owen led the way, stopping every few feet so another family member or friend could congratulate the couple. The joy spilled over on Owen. No matter what happened in his life, his closest friend had found happiness. For that he was grateful.

Inside, the Beachys' living and dining rooms had been transformed into a banquet hall. The women had covered the tables with white tablecloths and placed the settings. Every table had a decorated jar of orange and yellow marigolds on it. Silverware had been wrapped in yellow paper napkins. Balloons of all colors floated from the ceiling, their ribbons dangling below them. Ushers helped seat guests. Unmarried men and women were seated at the line of tables that extended from the corner table where the wedding party would sit. The women sat on one side, men on the other.

"You're here." Emily patted a chair two down from Denny's. "Take a seat. Your work is done. It's time to enjoy."

Sitting would mean no more working instead of thinking. "I'll just—"

"Everything is taken care of."

Owen sank into the chair just as Carrie Beachy settled into the one directly across from him. As was tradition Emily had taken the opportunity to do some matchmaking involving her younger sister. Carrie smiled. Owen smiled back.

"You missed the last singing."

"I intended to go, but some things came up that I had to take care of."

Carrie took a sip of water. She had the same dimples and rosebud lips as her sister, along with the blonde hair, sapphire eyes, and tiny figure. What wasn't to like? "In Abilene."

So she'd heard. The grapevine had done its work.

"Jah, but I'm back now."

"The thing you were searching for wasn't there?"

"I don't know. It remains to be seen."

"I'm sorry. It's hard to be in limbo like that." It spoke well of her that she did indeed sound sorry. "I know how it feels to long for something, only to find it's not possible."

Heat burned through Owen. Was he wasting his chance with Carrie, chasing a pipe dream? He cleared his throat. "Do you think there's any truth to that cliché good things come to those who wait?"

"It would be nice to think so." She touched the marigolds that sat on the table between them. "Aren't these flowers pretty?"

"They are." He glanced both directions. Denny and Emily were absorbed in each other. Denny's cousin to Owen's right was deep in conversation with Emily's cousin who sat across from him. Owen put his elbows on the table and leaned in. "So are you. You deserve better than you've received."

From others and from him.

She blushed a deep red. Her hands dropped into her lap. "Danki."

"Gern gschehme."

At that inopportune moment, the servers descended on the corner table. The newlyweds and their wedding party, including the unmarried young folks, would be served first, family style. They took turns serving Denny and Emily and then handed the large bowls to their guests.

Owen dumped food on his plate with abandon. It saved him from watching Denny and Emily swoon over each other or looking up to find Carrie staring at him. Every time he did, her gaze dropped to his plate. With reason. He kept adding food until it was overloaded with chicken, mashed potatoes, noodles, mixed vegetables, a lettuce salad, and a dinner roll.

The laugh lines around her eyes and mouth on full display, Aenti Nelda filled Owen's glass with lemonade. "I reckon you worked up an appetite standing up with Denny. Don't forget to leave room for dessert. There's cake, dirt pudding, cherry, pecan, and peanut butter pie, and every candy bar imaginable."

"He must have a hollow leg." Carrie held up her glass so Aenti Nelda could fill it as well. A chicken thigh looked lonely next to the noodles on Carrie's plate, along with a modest pile of potato salad and one dinner roll. "My breider eat like that after they've been out in the field all day."

"Your daed is still farming?"

"He is. He also builds furniture on the side, and my mudder makes quilts on consignment for the furniture store in Yoder."

Cobbling together enough income to support a large Plain family took creativity and the ability to juggle more than one job. Fortunately they were an industrious lot. "And your daed makes room for his minister duties. He's a busy man."

"But he always sits down at the supper table with us. He never lets those duties interfere with family life. We play our share of checkers or the Life on the Farm game in the evenings. Sometimes he settles into his rocker and reads tidbits from *The Budget* to us. You'd never know he has a care in the world."

Interesting behind-the-scenes view of their minister when he wasn't busy fulfilling his duties. "He is a gut daed and mann."

Carrie ducked her head. "I know *you* will be too."

Had he heard right? Owen inhaled a bite of his roll. The bread wouldn't go down. He coughed, grabbed his lemonade, and gulped down half a glass.

Denny's cousin slapped him on the back. "Are you okay?"

"Gut. Gut." Owen coughed again. He wiped his face with his napkin. "I'm gut."

Her gaze on her plate, Carrie tucked a chunk of chicken in her mouth and chewed vigorously.

"I'm stuffed. I don't think I could eat another bite." Owen pushed back from the table. "I think I need to walk some of this off first."

Carrie laid her fork on her plate. Her napkin followed. "Me too. I think I'll have to wait until later to have dessert."

What was she telling him? *Gott, help me, I have no clue.* He glanced around. Everyone was deep in conversation. The hum filled the room. He cocked his head toward the door. *Meet me outside?* He mouthed the words.

Carrie nodded. At least it might have been a nod.

Owen wove his way through the tables, dodging folks who'd stopped to chat in the middle of the narrow aisles and servers intent on delivering pies and cakes safely.

Through the door, across the porch, and down the steps. The early afternoon sun bore down on him. Someone called his name. Owen kept going.

"Suh, come sit with us." His father waved from a table under the shade of an enormous maple tree. "We have room."

Owen waved back and kept moving. "I already ate."

He finally slowed at the long line of buggies parked on the dirt road that led to the highway. At his buggy he stopped. His horse lifted her head and whinnied. "Jah, it's me. I'm here." He smoothed Cupcake's tangled mane. "You have it easy, you know. You just hang around and eat grass until I tell you what to do."

Cupcake nibbled at the grass and whinnied in agreement.

Had Owen imagined Carrie's nod? Maybe he should simply go home.

"There you are."

He turned.

Carrie strolled toward him. "I wasn't sure where you'd go."

"I wasn't sure you'd come."

"I'm not sure I should have."

"How's your summer going?"

"Did we come out here to make small talk?" Carrie rubbed the horse's forelock. His head bobbed. "My summer is gut. Bonnie Quinlan asked me to work at her day care in town. I'm enjoying it."

Bonnie had been Amish back in the day. When she decided not

to join the church, she'd moved into town and started a day care for English children whose parents worked.

"That sounds like a gut job."

"It's good practice for when . . ." Her voice trailed away. She picked straw from Cupcake's mane and let it fall onto the rocky road. "Not that I need practice. I have five younger brothers and sisters, after all. I'm an expert with diapers, colic, teething, and potty training."

The silence hung between them, awkward and heavy.

"I should go back in. It's my turn to wash dishes. The stacks of dirty plates are so high you can't see the poor girls trying to keep up. They're standing on step stools."

"Let me walk with you." Owen grappled for a topic of conversation not fraught with undertones. "Do you like taking care of kinner all day and then going home to more kinner?"

"It's the perfect job. It lets me mother kinner until I have my own." She skipped a step or two in her enthusiasm. "I hope I have at least six or eight, Gott willing."

"Is it different taking care of Englisch kinner?"

"Nee. Kinner are kinner. They ask a million questions, love to eat, cry over silly stuff, and give the sweetest hugs and kisses." She wrapped her arms around her middle as if hugging herself. "Of course they sometimes watch animated movies in Bonnie's living room like *Zootopia* and *Moana*. They know who Bluey, Arthur, and Daniel Tiger are. So I guess that's different. They wear sneakers that have action figures on them and light up when they walk."

Like Abigail's half siblings. They would know about such worldly things.

Why did all topics lead back to her? No matter how hard he tried, every road led to a woman who'd left her family, her home, her faith—and Owen. "I'd better see if the men need any help with the grills."

He veered toward the barn, where a series of gas grills were situated for grilling ribs, chicken breasts, and sausages.

"Did I say something wrong?"

Owen risked a glance back. Carrie had stopped in the middle of the road. She squinted into the sun, a perplexed frown on her face.

"Nee, it was nothing you said."

Nothing she did. It was all on Owen. The thought chased him all the way to the barn.

Chapter 38

"Heather says you're leaving."

"In a few days." Abigail moved the phone farther from her ear. Eric's gruff voice blared. "Heather wants time to set up a little family get-together with the aunts and uncles and cousins."

"I need more time too."

No one ever had enough time. "I'm sure Heather told you that I don't plan to shut you out of my life. I live nearby. It's not like you can't come to see me." Her real parents would understand. They understood loving their children. They understood the fear of losing them. "My . . . Freeman and Lorene will welcome you."

"It's not a matter of distance. I think you know that. You live in a different universe."

"I grew up in a Plain home. I love my Plain life. I'm sorry if that hurts you, but I know now that I belong back in Haven."

"Look out the living room window. Please."

Abigail scurried from the guest bedroom to the front window where she opened the plantation shutters closed against the morning sun. Eric leaned against a blue car parked on the street in front of the house. "I see you."

"I brought you something. Could you come out here? I'd like to give it to you."

"You didn't need to do that—"

"Just come out here. Please."

He hung up, giving Abigail no choice but to comply. She padded down the sidewalk. She stopped at Heather's miniature red barn mailbox. How did a daughter greet her biological father? "Here I am."

Eric held out a key attached to a key ring with a piece of leather that had her name etched on it. "I repaired the engine, redid the brakes and the struts, and touched up the paint job. I bought it from a guy who got married and needs a family car." He waved at the dark-blue car. "It's got eighty thousand miles on it but no accidents. It's nothing special, but it's solid. It has airbags, and it gets good safety ratings from *Consumer Reports*. It's a 2015 Chevy Impala. Sporty but solid."

Most of that information might as well have been imparted in French. The keys hung in the air. Finally Eric let his hand drop. "It's yours free and clear. I put the title in your name. It's paid for."

"You shouldn't've done that." Finally Abigail found her voice, though it sounded strange and wooden in her ears. "Surely you know I don't drive."

"I can teach you, but first just let me take you for a test drive." Eric opened the passenger door. "The inside is cherry. The upholstery is in perfect condition. I put in new floor mats too."

"I can't accept it."

"Let's take a drive."

"What about Heather? She'll wonder where I am."

"She knows . . . about this. She approves. Your . . . the Bontragers aren't expecting you, are they?"

Of course Heather approved. And no, her parents didn't know when to expect her. But they were sad and hurt that she hadn't returned when she had the chance. Her going home would heal some of that pain. *Gott, what do I do?*

"Please. They've had years with you. I have had a few weeks."

Eric's face held another brand of hurt and sadness. Abigail balanced on a narrow path between two deep chasms. Neither of her making. The sins of the fathers visited on the children? She swallowed the knot in her throat and got in.

The car's engine had a low rumble. The AC cooled her warm cheeks. A fresh pine scent wafted on the air. Eric fumbled with the radio buttons until a soft melody with no voices played. He put the car in Drive and headed east from town on old U.S. Highway 40. "Heather's blessed. She has a boy and girls to raise. My ex and I had two boys."

Did the ex have a name? Did he call her Ex to her face?

Choices were made. Choices had consequences. Abigail kept quiet.

"Over the years I kept track of how old you would be and the milestones I would be missing." He glanced Abigail's direction, then back at the road. "I missed out on your first steps and your first words. I never got to teach you to tie your shoes, tell time, or ride a bike. I didn't give you your first bite of ice cream or see your face when you ate a dill pickle for the first time. The boys came along, and I did all those things with them. I didn't get to take pictures of you with your prom date. With the boys I taught them to throw and bat and how to make a free throw. I'm teaching them to be gentlemen and treat girls right. I'm teaching them what they need to know to be men. Then you come back into my life, and I thought I can still do what dads do with their daughters. I haven't missed the chance to teach you to drive."

"I can't—"

"I'm hoping you'll stay. Then you'd need to know how to drive. You'd need a car to drive to your college classes or your job. There are more job opportunities in Salina than in Abilene, and it's only a thirty-minute drive. Or you could get an apartment in Salina. Me and Heather could help you fix it up. I teach there, so I could stop by now and then. We could have lunch. Do you know how to bowl? I could teach you to bowl."

He had a vivid imagination. He had the dreams of a father. Not like her father but *a* father. "I can't."

"There's a difference between can't and won't."

"This isn't who I am. I know that disappoints you, but I can't change who I am for anyone." Kiera's words reverberated in Abigail's ears. *"It's as obvious as the kapp on your head. You want to be a Plain wife and mother. It's who you are down to the marrow in your bones."* "I can't change who I am. Not for anyone. And I've finally realized I don't want to. Keep the car. Save it for Kenny. Teach him to drive it."

Eric didn't respond. The silence grew, but somehow it didn't seem awkward. Abigail leaned against the seat and watched the open countryside fly by. The song ended. A melodic voice announced another one. They crossed a bridge over the Smoky Hill River. A sign announced their arrival in Enterprise, Kansas, population 885.

On her left stood the Great Plains Manufacturing Plant. It might be abandoned. Small houses—most had seen better days—lined the road. A gas station. A coffee shop.

"What are we doing here?"

"You'll see."

A few turns and they pulled into the parking lot of a long, low, blond-brick building surrounded by shade trees across from open fields of wheat. The sign read ENTERPRISE NURSING CENTER. Two women and a man in wheelchairs sat out front in the sun. A woman in hospital scrubs supervised.

Eric turned off the engine. He reached into the back seat and produced a blue windbreaker. Why did he need a jacket in the middle of June? The temperatures were already in the upper eighties. "Let's go meet your great-grandma."

Abigail's great-grandparents had passed when she was a small child. Plain families didn't put their elders in nursing homes. That's what a dawdy haus was for. "I thought your family farmed out by Haven."

"My parents do. My mom's parents farmed out here. She went to grade school in Enterprise. She met my dad at Emporia State when they were both in college. From there they settled out by Haven." Eric donned the jacket, zipped it up partway, picked up a small brown paper bag, and stuffed it inside. "My grandma refused to leave the family homestead after Grandpa died. After she fell and broke her hip, she ended up here for assisted living and stayed."

Another branch of Abigail's family tree dipped in a gentle breeze driven by Eric's memories. "What's her name? And what's in the bag?"

"Mae. Mae Shirrer. She's eighty-seven but thinks she's thirty-seven." Eric zipped up the jacket the rest of the way. "She keeps the aides and the nurses on their toes in this place, let me tell you. They don't get away with shoddy service on her watch. Don't worry about the bag. It's just a small treat. The nurses frown on it, but she's not a child. At her age she should be able to eat whatever she wants whenever she wants."

Abigail touched her prayer covering. It hadn't moved. She wore her long dress, no makeup, and no jewelry. Outwardly she remained Abigail Bontrager, Plain woman. Yet when each small piece of the puzzle fell into place, she became someone different. No matter what Kiera said, a person equaled the sum total of all those who came before in her family line. She didn't know much science, but she knew about family.

"Come on. You'll like her. She's a hoot." Eric shoved open his door. Abigail did the same. She'd never been in a nursing home before. Why was it called a home? It wasn't like any home she'd ever been in. It smelled like a hospital. Like antiseptic and cleanser. Only one where all the patients were old. A wizened man shuffled along the linoleum floor, pushing a metal walker with yellow tennis balls stuck to the front legs. He smiled at them. He had no teeth.

Somewhere down the hallway a woman screamed, "Help me, help me, someone help me. Where is everyone?"

Eric put his hand on Abigail's back. "Some of them aren't fully in charge of their faculties anymore."

Or maybe they were lonely and afraid they'd been abandoned.

At the front desk Eric signed them in. A nurse going through a pile of folders looked up and smiled. "Mr. Waters. Miss Mae is in fine form this morning. She didn't approve of the scrambled eggs we served in the dining room, so she tossed a handful over her shoulder. It landed in Miss Ruby's hair. She didn't think it was funny. We almost had a food fight on our hands."

"Sorry about that."

"Hey, I don't like cold eggs either." The nurse, a broad-shouldered woman with her share of gray hair, chuckled. "And she cleaned it up herself."

"I'll remind her of her manners."

"Good luck with that." The nurse glanced at the clock over the desks behind the counter. "She'll be watching her soaps in the community room about now."

They turned and headed down the hallway.

"By the way, Mr. Waters, you're not fooling anybody with that jacket."

The nurse's laughter followed them.

The community room turned out to be a large space filled with comfortable chairs, card tables that held half-finished puzzles, overflowing bookshelves, and a big-screen TV. A fierce card game occupied four men in one corner, while another man sat by the window with a sketchbook in his lap. His right hand held a pencil, but it never moved At least a dozen women crowded the seats arranged in front of the TV, which had the volume turned up full blast.

"There she is. The one in the flowered dress."

Eric pointed to a woman seated front and center. She had wrinkles on her wrinkles. Her white hair was cut short so the curls hugged her head. Mae might have been tall once, but now her shoulders were stooped and her head tucked forward. A rollator decorated with a Jesus Loves Me seat cover was parked in front of her, but her knobby-knuckled hand gripped a purple-flowered cane.

"Hey, Mae, it's your favorite grandson come to see you." One of the other ladies shouted over the din. "And he brought a pilgrim with him."

"Hush, Lois," Mae shouted in return. "He *would* come in the middle of my programs."

Eric's gaze swung to the TV. "*The Young and the Restless.* Seriously, Grandma? The actors on that show have to be older than you are by now. Besides, if you don't watch it for six months, you can still pick up right where you left off."

"So? Old people can't be romantic?" Mae whacked his thigh with the cane. "Shows what you know. Until the day your grandpa died, he could—"

"Ouch. That's okay, spare us the details." His face flushed a bright red, Eric rubbed his thigh. "I have someone I want you to meet. Abigail, this is your great-grandmother, Mae Shirrer. Grandma, this is Abigail."

"She's not a pilgrim, Lois, you silly goose. Pilgrims wore black." The old lady craned her neck to stare up at Abigail. "Well, don't just stand there, child. Help me move over to the table in the corner. I can't hear a thing with this TV blaring. These old ladies are hard of hearing."

Between Eric and Abigail, they escorted Mae to the table she'd chosen. Even then they had to keep their voices up. There was no escaping the drama of hopes and dreams of love and life dashed on the TV.

"Don't just stand there. You're giving me a crick in my neck, child. Sit."

Abigail sat.

Mae stuck a pair of purple-rimmed glasses on her skinny nose and gave Abigail the once-over. Her wrinkles-upon-wrinkles parted into a mischievous grin that revealed coffee-stained teeth. "I guess I've been stuck in this hellhole for longer than I realized. It's possible to birth daughters full-grown now. That's handy. No dealing with breastfeeding at three a.m., diapers, and the terrible twos."

"Don't be smart. Abigail is my daughter with Heather Holcomb."

"Ah, the out-of-wedlock baby. Your mother tried so hard to keep me from finding out. She thought I would disown you and her."

"You wouldn't've?"

"I would've taken a switch to your behind. You're never too old for a good lashing. I blamed her and that spineless man she married for not bringing you up right. I wouldn't have let you give up the baby. That's too easy. Why should you get to walk away from your mistake instead of learning from it?"

Let them talk about ancient history. Mae didn't see Abigail as simply a mistake but, even worse, as the product of sin intended to teach a lesson.

Abigail clutched her bag to her chest and studied the geometric patterns in the blue-green carpet marred with brown stains. By tomorrow she would be back in Haven where people knew her for who she was—a faithful Plain woman, daughter of Freeman and Lorene Bontrager.

"Cat got your tongue, child, or are you hard of hearing?"

Startled, Abigail sat up straight. Apparently the conversation had shifted to her. "Neither. It didn't seem that I needed to be here for this conversation."

"So you're Amish."

"I am."

"Good for you."

"I think so."

"Good clean living and a decent fear of the Lord." Mae smacked her cane on the carpet in a dull *thud, thud, thud*. "Can't beat that with a stick. You and I will see each other in the new heaven on earth one day."

She waved the cane toward Eric. "Not like this ne'er-do-well who thinks he has no need of the Good Book."

Plain folks were careful never to suggest they knew what God was thinking or what He would do. They simply did their best to be faithful followers. "He only needs to ask and he will be forgiven."

"Good answer, good answer." Mae tapped her long fingernails, painted a pearly white, on the table. Her veins stood out, stark blue, against fine white skin and brown age spots. "Don't let him talk you into staying with that harlot Heather—"

"Grandma, she's Abigail's mother."

"I'm betting Abigail has a mother who raised her right. Heather didn't want the job. She cut and ran the second she could."

Eric winced. "You don't know what you're talking about."

"It's not our place to judge, is it?" As hard as it was, as human as it was, to want to judge. "Aren't we supposed to forget? Jesus will do the judging. Leastways that's what our bishop says."

"Smart man, that bishop." Mae slid her hand across the table and grasped Abigail's. Her fingers were icy despite the sunlight from several windows that flooded the community room. "You're a good girl, aren't you?"

"I try to be."

"I can see a little of my grandson in your face, in its shape and your chin." Her grip tightened. "He's grown into a good man. He's learned from his mistakes. But that doesn't make him your father."

"Grandma—"

"Hush, let me finish." The glasses magnified her faded blue eyes. She'd seen a lot in her time, no doubt, and she seemed determined to share her wisdom with Abigail. "I'm happy to meet you. Now go on home to those who raised you. You're blessed to have a good family. Never forget that. Give this guy another ten years or so and he might actually grow up."

"You're missing your program, Grandma." Eric put his hand on her arm and helped her up. "I'm sure you want to know who died a year ago and came back to life in this episode."

"Don't rush me. I'm old." She grabbed her cane and whacked him on the ankle. "Did you bring me my treat?"

"Ouch. Of course I did." Eric stopped to rub his leg again. "Stop hitting me, and I'll think about giving them to you."

"I won't beg."

"Sure you will." Eric unzipped his windbreaker, pulled out the paper sack, and produced a bag of spicy jelly beans. "Don't eat them all in one sitting. And share. It's better for your blood sugar."

"Just you never mind. Those ladies can't eat jelly beans. They stick to their dentures, and then the dentures come out. It's comical." She tugged on his arm. "Give an old woman a kiss and get out of here. Spend time with that girl before she goes back where she belongs."

Eric's mournful expression didn't dissipate when they arrived at the car. He started the engine but didn't put the car in gear. "That didn't go the way I'd hoped."

"Your grandma is a wise woman."

"Your great-grandma likes to stir the pot."

Whatever that meant. "Is it really the end of the world if I choose to remain Plain?"

"I have nothing against the Amish." He groaned and shoved the car into Drive. "In principle. I just don't want my daughter to be one."

"You've known for years. You've known since the day Heather gave me up what I would become."

"In theory, yes, but seeing you and knowing you, talking to you, it makes it so real. You're a smart, levelheaded woman who could take on the world."

"We don't do that."

"No, but you could."

"I'm sorry I can't be the daughter you want." Abigail studied her hands in her lap. "No, I'm not. I am who I am. You'll have to accept that if you want to be in my life."

Eric didn't speak for several beats. He stared out at the wheat fields across the road. Finally he turned to face Abigail. "I'll give the car to Kenny. He'll love it."

With that he pulled from the parking lot and took Abigail back to Abilene.

Chapter 39

People didn't seem able to find anything to talk about besides weddings these days. Two weddings in two weeks had everyone pitching in to help. Owen wielded a hammer with more force than necessary, pounding the nails into a new set of steps for Mary's front porch. His father always prescribed hard work for grumpiness. He was right. Helping someone else in need served to take the focus off a person's own problems.

Owen, Lee, Eli, and Mary's son Tobias had repainted the living room and the porch and fixed two bad stretches in the corral fence. Now Lee and Tobias were cleaning the barn while Eli mowed the yard. The scent of fresh-cut grass soothed Owen after a morning of smelling paint and turpentine.

Twelve-year-old Lorie leaned against an elm tree with baby Matthew on her hip while she supervised a gaggle of younger kids. Their giggles and shouts as they played hide-and-seek were sweet music to Owen's ears while he worked. He tried putting lyrics to their melody.

Life goes on. Gott has a plan. Be patient. Wait upon the Lord.

After all, this was what it would be like after Father and Mary wed. A family blended together by their parents' love for each other. The kids would learn to be more than friends. They would become brothers and sisters—family. Children were less set in their ways, more open to change. When had he lost that resilience?

The screen door squeaked. Owen hazarded a glance. Mary stood over him with tall glasses of iced tea in both hands. Perspiration damped her face. Splotches of dirt decorated her apron. She'd replaced her prayer covering with a scarf that wrapped around her head and knotted under her bun. She smiled. "You were so deep in thought I hated to disturb you, but I thought you might need to quench your thirst."

Owen leaned back on his haunches. He set the hammer aside and accepted her offering. "My throat *is* parched."

"It's hot enough to fry a dozen eggs on the sidewalk and it's only June." Instead of going back inside, she sat in one of the lawn chairs. "I finished washing the windows on the inside. It's time to start on the outside. It should be more pleasant. It's probably cooler out here. There's a breeze."

The breeze came and went. Just enough to tease Owen into thinking it might cool off. Leave it to a Plain woman to look forward to washing windows outside. They also loved scrubbing the oven, just to see it shine. Especially if they could chat with friends while they applied elbow grease to the project. "Are Kayla and Claire making themselves useful?"

"They are. They are gut maede." Mary fanned herself with her free hand. "They're changing the sheets on the beds upstairs so the rooms will be ready for my family coming in from Jamesport. They've got the wash machine going to wash all the dirty stuff. They take turns hanging them on the line out back. They make a gut team."

"Gut."

"You and Lee aren't thrilled about this wedding, are you?"

She did like to get to the heart of the matter. She would be a good match for Father.

Taking his time, Owen swiveled so he could lean against the porch post. From that vantage point he had a good view of her face. Mary was one of those women who grew more pleasing to the eye with age. Streaks of silver highlighted her dark-blonde hair. A tan from working in the garden showed off her blue eyes, made even bluer by her lilac dress. Crow's feet around those eyes and laugh lines around her full mouth hinted at her age. Mother had that same dark-blonde hair and blue eyes.

Only Mother never reached the age of silver hair and fine lines.

"I might have had reservations early on, but not now." He cooled his forehead with the cold glass, rolling it back and forth. Lee would come around in time. "Father has experienced a painful loss. So have you. Having a second chance to make a family is a blessing. The district encourages widows and widowers to marry again."

"Agreed. I hope you make that argument with Lee." Mary tilted her head and studied Owen as if he were a strange animal she'd never seen before. "I pray Gott will soften his heart. That all of you will see that this is more than your daed fulfilling a duty and providing a mudder for his younger kinner. We truly care for each other."

"It's none of our business. You shouldn't feel the need to convince any of us."

"I don't, exactly, but I think it's only human to want everyone to be as happy as I am." She swirled the melting ice in her glass, her gaze distant. "You're right. I experienced a terrible loss, one I didn't think I could come back from. I never dreamed I would marry again. My head and my heart were full of memories crowded with my mann. I see him in my kinner's faces. I hear his voice everywhere, but especially when Tobias talks. I'd be in another room and think for just a split second that it was Tom. But it wasn't. Every single time I was disappointed.

"No one can understand what that's like unless they've been through it." Mary's gaze returned to Owen. "Your daed understands. At first that's what we had in common. Then we realized there was so much more. We like to hunt, fish, and camp. We like our tea sweet and our kaffi black. We like to make s'mores on cold winter nights. We like fall better than spring and summer better than winter. You're young. You've never been married. There's more to marriage than . . ." Her cheeks, already red from the heat, darkened. "Especially as you get older. You're happy just knowing that other person is breathing the same air."

"You don't have to be married to understand all that." Owen worked to strip his tangled emotions from the words. "To want that."

"Your daed has told me some of what you're going through."

Thanks, Daed. Owen took off his straw hat, fanned his face, then laid the hat aside. It wasn't the summer sun causing his face to heat up either. "He shouldn't have."

"He meant no disrespect. Me either." She set the glass on the cooler between the lawn chairs. Hands clasped in front of her, she sat forward, her expression intent. "Tom and I started courting when I was sixteen. He was seventeen. I went full-on with my rumspringa. Tom wasn't happy about it. We took plenty of buggy rides, but I wanted to hang out with Englisch friends so we could ride in their cars into Hutchinson to go to the movies. I wanted to wear jeans and make up my face. I even went to my share of keggers. I smoked cigarettes and sipped wine coolers. Tom was horrified. He stopped coming around. I thought it was over."

"What did you do?"

"At first I pretended not to care. It turns out I just needed time. Somehow Tom knew that. He waited me out. One day I woke up with a headache from not enough sleep and too much of what my Englisch friends called 'party hardy' and realized I'd had a gut full."

She shrugged and smiled. "I was afraid I was too late, but I gathered up my courage, went to a singing, and waited for my chance to tell him how sorry I was."

"And he forgave you?"

"He was gun-shy at first. He didn't want to get hurt again. I understood that. He realized we hadn't been in sync. I needed more time to grow up. He gave that to me. We took our time. Eventually we were ready." Her voice quavered. "Now I wish it hadn't taken me so long. My immaturity cost us two years of married life. If I had known how short our time would be, I would've found a way to get there quicker."

"You couldn't've known."

"When you're young, you think there's plenty of time."

Two long swallows of tea didn't banish the sudden lump in Owen's throat. "Unless you lose your mudder when you're sixteen."

"Jah, unless that happens. Or your daed when you're still a toddler." The kids ran past the porch, laughing and shouting, Jonas in the lead, Micah not far behind. Mary shielded her eyes from the sun with one hand. "Eli and Micah were so young; they might not remember your mudder much, but your daed will tell them about her. I'll make sure of it. Just like I'll tell Lucy and Matthew about their daed. We'll keep their memories alive while making new ones."

"That's gut to know." Owen settled his hat on his head. He stood and held out the empty glass. "I should get back to work."

Mary accepted the glass but remained seated. "Your daed also told me about the sunflowers."

"He's coming around to the idea."

"So much is changing right now." She gestured toward the corral and beyond. "Our lives are changing, which is hard but also gut. He realizes that. Happiness is not our goal in life, but if we find a bit of it along the way, we're allowed to let it bloom. Leastways that's what I think."

Humility, obedience, dying to self, those were the bedrock of the Plain existence. They tried to build happiness on that foundation. "I need to make sure I don't leave him in a lurch."

"Tobias is finished with school. He'll jump at the chance to take your place. He'll need to apprentice, but your daed is a gut teacher."

"That's gut to know. My younger brieder will fill that need as well. Everything will work out according to Gott's plan."

Mary rose. "I truly appreciate everything you're doing around here . . . and your attitude."

"We still need to sand and refinish the picnic table and benches in the front yard. Daed is picking up the stain while he's in town getting the part for your tractor."

"My brieder try to do their part to keep up with chores here, but they have so much work to do on their own farms."

"We don't mind. That's what family is for."

"I can't wait to be that family we'll make." A smile spread across her face. The lines around her eyes crinkled. "I pray one day soon you'll make your own family."

"I'm working on it." Owen picked up the hammer and his tool chest. If only he could mend his relationship with Abigail as easily as the steps. "Nothing is simple, it seems."

"When it comes to matters of the heart, it never is." Mary gathered up the tea glasses and headed for the door. "But it's always, always worth it. I promise."

The rumble of a tractor floated in the lackadaisical breeze. Mary paused. "I reckon Chester is back. Gut timing."

Good timing indeed. Dad and Mary were truly in sync.

Owen had work to do here, but his time was coming. It shimmered on the horizon, full of promise. He would follow his dreams—both of them.

Chapter 40

Abigail sat straight up. What woke her? She rubbed her eyes and squinted at the red neon numbers of the clock on the bed stand: 11:53 p.m. Late.

Tap. Tap. Tap. Unease ran its cold, icy fingers down the back of her neck and spine. Someone tapped on her bedroom window in the middle of the night. Abigail burrowed under the sheets. *Just ignore it. The window is locked. No one can get in. Ignore it and it will go away.*

Tap, tap, tap. Harder this time.

Abigail thrust the sheets aside. She hopped from the bed and marched over to the curtains. *Don't look. Don't look.*

She closed her eyes and sucked in a long breath. Blood thrummed through her. It beat in a staccato in her temples. *One, two, three.* She opened her eyes and threw back the curtain. Rhett stared in at her.

"Rhett!"

"Shush!" He put his index finger to his lips. "Meet me out front."

"No . . . I can't." She wore a thin cotton nightgown. Her hair hung loose down to her waist. "We already said good-bye. You can't wake me up in the middle of the night to try to change my mind."

"It's not that. I need to talk to you."

"Call me."

"I did. You didn't answer."

The phone was on the charger. She'd put it on silent when she went to bed—which was hours ago. "Can't it wait until morning?"

"No. At least open the window. If you don't want me to see you in your jammies, put on some clothes. I'll wait."

"Fine."

She closed the curtains. What would Heather think of a midnight rendezvous with their next-door neighbor? Knowing Heather, she would be thrilled at the thought that Rhett might be trying to convince Abigail to stay. All thumbs, Abigail fumbled with her dress. She wrestled it over her head and clawed her way into the arms. The ceiling fan cooled her sweaty face once she managed to stick her head through the neck's opening.

Getting her hair up in a quick bun went faster. Abigail stuck her prayer covering on her head, pinned it in place, and took another breath. Nothing he said would change her mind, but Rhett had been the first person in Abilene to make friendly overtures toward her. Kindness dictated that she honor his feelings. She went to the window.

Her visitor no longer stood outside it. After all that? Abigail spun around and went to the phone. He'd called three times and sent four texts. The last one asked her to meet him on the front porch after she finished dressing.

Quietly, gently, she unlocked the front door and slipped outside. The porch light was off, but the streetlight midway down the block cast enough illumination to see that Rhett sat on the porch swing.

"Finally. I thought you'd gone back to bed." He stuck his boot out and forced the swing to stop moving. He was fully dressed in jeans and a white dress shirt. His cowboy hat lay on the seat next to him. "I was about to rap on the window again, but I didn't want to give you another heart attack."

"I'm here now. What's up?"

"Come sit with me." He picked up his hat and planted it on his head, then dusted the seat with his bare hand. "I promise not to bite."

Abigail sat, but she left a space big enough to park a laundry basket between them. "What couldn't wait until morning?"

"I'm leaving in the morning—early."

So he'd beaten her to the punch—to the leaving. "Where are you going?"

"I had my own little session with my sister after you left on Sunday. She made it clear you need to go home and I need to get on with my life, so I am."

"She's a personal coach, not the boss of you or me."

Rhett's chuckle floated on the humid night air. He took Abigail's hand in his. "That's one of the many things I like about you. No filter, like me. Kiera isn't trying to boss me around. She just calls them like she sees them. I really wanted to get to know you better." He kissed her hand, a soft delicate kiss, his lips warm on her skin. "I thought there might be a chance . . . But she made me see how it wouldn't be good for either of us."

His words tumbled around Abigail, mixed up, uncertain, untamed. She should answer him. And say what? His words said one thing, his actions another. Despite the June heat, a chill ran through her. *Think, think.* "Kiera's right."

"Are you sure?"

"Yes, but that doesn't mean it's easy. You don't make it easy."

"I know. I'm the king of mixed messages." Rhett let go of her hand. "My mom will get here sometime tomorrow. Her lease is up on the apartment she was renting in Hays. She's decided to move in with Grandma."

"Which leaves you free to go after the big-city job you've always wanted."

"Newspaper jobs are hard to come by these days. I talked to the guy who supervised my internship at the *Topeka Journal*. He said they don't have any openings, but he knows of some public relations contract gigs I might be able to get. I have some savings. I have a friend I can stay with. I can freelance, write blogs, shoot photos, do one-man-band gigs. It's all good."

"You're just going to strike out on your own with no sure job?"

"Sounds like fun, doesn't it? Do you want to go with me? It'll be an adventure. I promise."

It did sound like fun. The part of Abigail that belonged to Heather—Abigail English Girl—cheered Rhett's decision. It longed for that kind of footloose and fancy-free life. The part of her that grew up baking pies and pumping the treadle on the sewing machine applauded from afar while cradling her trusty rolling pin under one arm.

Which one was she? Both. She was both. But Kiera was right. Her deepest desires involved marriage and motherhood. Neither marriage nor parenthood interested Rhett, not yet anyway.

He had a strong moral compass, a capacity for great faith, and a loving heart. All those traits were familiar. They also described Owen. But Owen was ready to be a husband and a father. He didn't need the kind of adventure that involved traveling the country. Life with Owen would be an adventure in planting new crops, exploring new ways to make farming profitable, and battling Kansas's unpredictable weather in order to feed a growing family. The kind of adventure a Plain woman could embrace.

"I wish you the very best life full of adventures around the world that make great stories."

"That's what I figured." Rhett kissed her forehead and drew back. "I hoped, prayed even, that you would get past your upbringing. But then you wouldn't be you. I lay awake last night imagining what you would've been like if you never met your Amish family, if Heather never gave you up. You would've been amazing. But not as amazing as you are now, as an Amish woman."

"Thank you." What else could she say? That he'd given so much thought to her life was a gift. He saw her as she might have been, but more importantly, as she truly was—a product of her upbringing by loving parents and a loving community. His kiss, delivered so gently, was that of a friend. The flame that had flared at his touch had been banked. "I'm no one special, but I appreciate your kind words."

"I need to pack. I want to hit the road at dawn. No traffic. Just me and the early birds."

"Safe travels."

"Same for you." He clomped down the steps. At the gate he paused and swiveled. His face glowed in the harsh streetlight. "Tell Owen I meant no harm. No disrespect. He must be a good man if he sees in you the same thing I do."

Abigail leaned on the porch railing. It was damp and cool with dew. "I will—if he's still talking to me."

"No worries there. He'll jump at the chance. If he doesn't, he's a fool."

He touched his cowboy hat's brim and walked away. His boots clicked on the cement, the only sound in the still night.

Owen wasn't a fool, but Abigail might be. Shivering, she wrapped her arms around her middle. Tomorrow she would find out if she'd done irreparable damage to their relationship.

God said all things could—should—be forgiven. Whether Owen could live up to that standard remained to be seen. Abigail's future depended on it.

Chapter 41

Doolittle shot from the porch in a single leap. With a steady stream of barking, he launched himself at Abigail. She staggered back, lost her footing, and sat on her behind in the grass. "I missed you, too, you crazy hund." Laughing, she leaned back, trying to escape slobbery kisses that covered her face and hands. "I love you too."

Her reassurances did nothing to slow the dog's determination to show his undying affection. Abigail struggled to her knees and kept petting him. "Where's everyone? Where's Mudder and Daed?"

On the trip from Abilene to Haven, Abigail had occupied herself by imagining what Mother's and Father's reaction would be at her decision to come home. She hadn't been able to eat the pancakes Heather insisted on making before they left. They stuck in her throat. Her stomach protested when she sipped Heather's coffee doctored with fancy caramel flavoring.

Returning home represented the first hurdle, with many more to follow. "Are they in the house? Surely they hear you barking."

Doolittle raced toward the porch, circled, and came back, twice, three times. His barking got louder.

No one came out to see what the commotion was all about. Abigail raced up the steps and opened the door. "I'm here. Where is everyone?"

Doolittle's panting and the *click-clack* of his nails on the wood floor provided the only sounds. No AC hummed. No ceiling fan creaked. No stereo cranked out hip-hop music. No TV blared. Abigail stood in the middle of the living room in the house where she'd lived her entire life and let the quiet wash over her. She inhaled the lovely scent of family—bacon, coffee, clothes soap, and freshly mopped floors. A card table by the fireplace held a five-hundred-piece puzzle of wildlife in Glacier National Park in Montana. The rocking chair sat nearby, where Father would read the newspaper and his German Bible. The spot where the boys played checkers. Sun spilled into the room through open windows. The breeze nudged the curtains, creating a riot of shadows on the far wall.

Home.

Abigail's heartbeat slowed, then resumed its familiar, everyday rhythm. The muscles in her neck and shoulders relaxed. The knots in her stomach loosened and disappeared.

The only time quiet ruled at the Bontrager house was when everyone was gone. Where were they on a Thursday morning? Her plan to surprise Jane and the rest of her siblings fell away. The apology to her parents she'd prepared in her head folded itself like a letter slipped into an envelope to be sent later. Heather had chosen not to come in with her for reasons that were more likely excuses. She had to get to work. She had forgotten that Scarlett had a haircut appointment. She might have left the coffeepot on.

Abigail couldn't blame her. Facing Mother wasn't at the top of her list either. She left her suitcase at the foot of the stairs and went to Father's hand-hewn oak desk in the far corner of the living room. Here he kept mail, bills, seed and tool catalogs, and Mother's writing utensils for her pen pal writing circles.

It took less than three minutes to find the clue to her family's whereabouts in the neat piles on Father's desk. A save-the-date postcard announced Chester Kurtz and Mary Wagner's wedding on this day at Mary's farm.

Abigail's heart couldn't maintain its newfound rhythm. Owen would be at the wedding. How did he feel about his father remarrying after six years as a widower? Owen was such a good man. He would want his father to be happy.

That didn't mean he couldn't feel an ache in his heart that Mary would slip into his mother's empty sneakers. Or maybe the ache came from the lack of a wife and family of his own.

Abigail could help with that ache. Time to find him and tell him so.

An hour later she pulled into the line of buggies that stretched along the dirt road that led to Mary's homestead. People were pouring from the barn. The service had ended. Abigail tied the reins to a fence post. She ran her hand along Jocko's silky neck while watching members of her beloved community move toward the house and the revelry that would begin as soon as the women began serving the wedding feast.

The group of men clad in black suits and hats swelled in the yard, some of them working to set up more tables and chairs. Owen likely was among them. Coffee sloshed in Abigail's stomach. Her throat burned. Sweat made her hands slick.

"You can do this. You're not a coward." She whispered the words aloud, then repeated them three times. Kiera would be proud of her student. "You're strong, you're fearless."

A white lie. *Sorry, Gott.*

Go now, before your courage runs away and hides.

God's instructions?

A long, quivering breath. And another. And then another. Chewing on her lower lip, Abigail marched up the road to Mary's front yard. The women had swarmed the area to cover the tables with white tablecloths and decorations. Pretty purple and yellow pansies in jelly jars graced each table.

Just as Abigail reached the first table, Owen turned. He carried a folded metal table in one hand and two folding chairs in the other. The chairs slipped to the ground. He stumbled over one of them. Emotion—surely delight—shone on his face for a split second before he smothered it. Saying nothing, he set up the table and then picked up the chairs.

Abigail's heart clanged against her rib cage. Ignoring it, she kept moving. He needed to know how she really felt. Now. No matter who saw or who knew.

Jane, her face split with a startled grin, stepped into her path. "Schweschder, you're back. You're here. My prayers are answered." Abigail's sister jumped up and down. She threw her hands in the air and danced a jig. "Mudder and Daed will be so happy."

Before Abigail could respond, Jane embraced her so hard Abigail stumbled back. They both teetered. They tumbled to the ground. Jane laughed. The sound was so contagious, Abigail joined her. They howled like little kids. "You'd think I'd been gone for years." Abigail managed the words after a few gasping breaths. "I told you I would be back."

A chorus of laughter and shouts of "Welcome back" greeted the scene Jane had created. Abigail's sister hopped up. She curtsied. "Danki, danki. The show's over. Everyone go back to work."

More laughter. Claire and Kayla burst through the screen door. Yelling, they waved wildly. "You're here. You're here."

So much for carving out a quiet moment with Owen. So be it. These girls were her best friends. Seeing their happy faces sent a burst of joy exploding in Abigail. "I don't know why everyone is so surprised."

"Seriously? You didn't come back with Daed. That changed everything." Jane grabbed Abigail's arm and pulled her to her feet. "Come on, I don't want to wait another moment to tell Mudder. She's been in a funk ever since you left."

Abigail allowed Jane to pull her toward the house, but she glanced back. Owen stood motionless next to the stack of tables. He ducked his head, but not before she saw the happiness on his face.

They would have time later. Somehow she would make it happen.

Inside organized chaos reigned. Chester and Mary sat at the corner table, surrounded by family. Since they were older, they'd chosen to have their relatives fill in the rows of seats that made spokes to the left and right of their table. The young singles were seated at a parallel row of tables. Servers scurried from the kitchen with bowls piled high with mashed potatoes, stuffing, gravy, roasted chicken, coleslaw, baked beans, beets, and more. Guests milled around, getting their fill of visiting before eating.

Dozens of hugs and hellos later, Abigail made it to the kitchen. Mother stood at the counter, cutting slices of pecan, peach, and apple pie. Hope and Rose, who were barely tall enough to see over the edge, placed the pie slices on small paper plates.

"Mudder."

She turned. The pie spatula slipped from her hand and clanged on the wood floor. "My maed, is that you?"

"Jah. It's me. I'm home. For gut."

Mother bolted across the room. Her hug was fierce, almost angry. "My maed," she murmured. "My maed."

Screaming with delight, Hope and Rose followed. Their sticky hands and sweet faces burrowed into Abigail's dress. They smelled like vanilla and peaches, like innocence and sheer happiness. Their welcome held no censure, no uncertainty about Abigail's past, present, or future. They lived in this moment.

Unlike Mother, who finally drew back. "Don't you ever do that again."

"I won't. I promise."

Mother wiped her hands on her apron. She stomped back to the counter. "Maede, back to work." Her gaze encompassed the rest of the kitchen. "What is everyone staring at?"

The other women went back to work. The buzz of conversation resumed. A few nodded and smiled at Abigail. The prodigal daughter had returned. Whether she would be required to confess her *fehla* was not their business—not yet anyway. They likely were on pins and needles, wanting to know what Bryan would do about her foray into English activities like karaoke, dancing, and photos on social media, but they knew better than to voice their opinions.

"What was it like? Did you drive? Did you meet your biological father?" Claire shot questions at Abigail in rapid-fire succession even while moving toward the long worktable that held dishes ready to be served. "What about your half schwesdchdre and bruder? What were they like?"

"Give her a chance to breathe, Schweschder." Kayla handed Claire a pitcher of iced tea. "Take this to the eck. Mary loves sweet tea. See what else they want. By now they've cleaned their plates."

Abigail grabbed a knife and sliced a loaf of zucchini bread. "How have you been, Kayla? This is a happy day for your daed."

The unspoken question: *Is it a happy day for you?*

Kayla's grin told the story. Indeed, a cause for celebration. "Daed is so content. So full of plans. He's been so lonely. Who can be lonely with so many kinner? But he was. He needed a fraa for company. He and Mary make a fine couple. Plus she is a better cook than I am. The chores will double, but so will the help."

She sounded so grown-up. She drew her optimism from all the right founts. "I'm happy for him and for you." Abigail glanced around.

The other women had resumed their conversations. Mother swept from the room, carrying an enormous serving bowl of barbecue baked beans. Hope and Rose followed, two small shadows carrying baskets of fluffy yeast rolls. The women were chattering too loudly to overhear. "What have you heard about my time in Abilene?"

Kayla's grin faded. "Everyone has an opinion. That verse about the plank in their eyes seems to have fallen on deaf ears. So much gossip. If anyone brings it up to me, I just rub my eye, hoping they get the message."

"Singing karaoke, dancing, allowing the photos to be published to the world is a much bigger fehla than gossiping." Not to mention wearing English clothes and going on a date alone with an English man. Not to mention the kiss. The once delightful scents of baked goods turned sour. If she made a goodwill confession of all her sins to Bryan she might not have to make a kneeling confession before the entire Gmay. Or he might decide she needed that experience to reinforce lessons learned. She could even face a period of shunning.

"Fehla is fehla." Kayla's gentle reminder did little to soothe the fearful twisting in Abigail's gut. "That's what they need to remember. Bryan's message last Sunday reminded us that all have sinned and fallen short of the glory of Gott."

For some the distance was shorter than others. "Danki for being so kind."

"What are friends for? I also tried to get Dana to hold your spot, but we are so busy in the summer, she just couldn't do it. The new girl is working out great. She used to waitress at a Denny's in Hutchinson. Maybe you can get on the list to sub when girls call in sick."

"I'm so glad she found a good replacement. I wasn't planning to go back to Buggies and Bonnets anyway."

"Why not?"

"One thing I learned in Abilene is that trying to fit into the wrong mold is bound to cause problems. Clumsiness, for instance. Waitressing isn't the right job for me. It's not a weakness to admit I would do better in a less-stressful, hectic setting. I've decided to apply at the furniture store and Hooks and Needles."

Kayla's lower lip stuck out like a three-year-old denied a piece of candy. "Fine, be that way. You really did change in Abilene. In a gut way."

"I learned a lot." About family, about love, and about faith. Too much to get into right now. "What can I do to help?"

Kayla held out a platter of peanut butter, chocolate chip, oatmeal-raisin, and double-fudge cookies. "You might as well hold your head up high and make the rounds."

You are in charge of your arms and legs. They do what you command them to do. Abigail accepted the platter, lifted her chin, and squared her shoulders. *Thank you, Kiera.* "Here goes nothing."

Here goes everything.

Chapter 42

A man didn't run and hide. He met his heart's desires head-on. Owen strode into Mary's living room prepared to meet his future. He hoped. While shaking hands and hugging guests, he did a surreptitious sweep of the room. No Abigail. She was probably in the kitchen. She had many people to greet, but helping hands were needed too.

"Over here." Denny, who served as an usher for the reception, waved and pointed at an empty chair at one of the tables in a row that ran parallel to the table where his father sat with his new wife. He had to shout to be heard above the din of conversations that sprouted at every table in the room. "Your daed wanted you to sit close to the eck."

As a Kurtz Owen was a member of the wedding party. He needed to do his duty. Denny was a happily married man now. He wanted everyone to be equally happy. Owen squeezed past Uncle Wayne, cousins visiting from Jamesport, and a cluster of kids wandering the aisles searching for their parents.

Carrie waved. "I was beginning to think you weren't coming inside to eat."

"We still had a lot of tables to set up. It took longer than we expected." He couldn't tell Carrie he'd taken his time, trying to make sure he could maintain his composure if he ran into Abigail. She'd returned of her own free will. She wanted to be here. She knew who she was. A Plain woman. Or was this wishful thinking on his part? "Besides, the out-of-town guests should be served first."

"Are you going to sit or what?" Denny gave him a not-so-gentle nudge. "You'll give Carrie a crick in her neck."

Owen sat. He grabbed the glass of water sitting next to his empty plate and took a long drink. Conversation could only be postponed so long. He set down the glass and met Carrie's gaze. "The wedding season is really packed this year, isn't it?"

"Is something wrong?" Carrie's forehead wrinkled. "Your face is red too. Do you have a fever?"

Not the kind you're thinking of. "No, it's from the heat. I probably got some sun while I was setting up the tables."

Did the words sound as lame in her ears as they did in his? As if he wasn't already a deep-brown tan from days of working outside. Her expression thoughtful, Carrie nodded. She handed him a casserole dish filled with roast chicken with corn bread stuffing. "This must be a bittersweet day for you. Such happiness at the blessing of a new fraa for your daed but an ache for the loss of your mudder."

She had a good heart. She deserved a man's full, undivided attention. Even without Abigail's return, Owen couldn't give her that. "It is, but mostly happy because my daed has waited a long time to fill the hole in his life. It's the same for Mary."

"Gut for you." Carrie's wistful tone suggested Owen had waited too long to spare her heart. She, too, longed for the love represented by the couple sitting in the corner, holding hands under the table. "Waiting only makes us appreciate the gifts more when they come. Gott's timing. Gott's plan."

More goodness. More wisdom. Carrie was everything a man could want in a fraa. So why wasn't she enough for Owen?

He took the serving dish coming from the right and ladled gravy onto his plate, then green beans, then coleslaw followed by pickled beets. His plate was filled but his appetite waned. Two rolls, as if he could choke down one. The basket was empty. He looked up to hand it to the server who stood behind Carrie, holding a half-full platter of cookies.

Their gazes collided. A blank brain and a knot in his tongue prevented Owen from opening his mouth.

"Anyone ready for cookies, or are you saving room for wedding cake? The bride chose carrot cake with a cream cheese frosting. She made it herself. There's four kinds of pie." Abigail's face turned a becoming pink, but she delivered the words in a brisk, bright tone. "I'll take that basket back to the kitchen, Owen."

Not a wisp of embarrassment or acknowledgment of how awkward this might be. Furthermore, she deftly moved the tray to one arm and grasped the basket with the other hand. No clumsy maneuvering that ended in disaster for this confident woman.

"Danki. I'll p-p-pass on the c-c-c-ookies." On the other hand, Owen couldn't spit out a response. "I'm saving . . . room . . ."

Carrie twisted to see Abigail. "You're back." She sounded suitably delighted. A lost lamb had returned to the fold. That was what was important. She knew it. Owen did too. This was a good day for Abigail and for the Gmay. Carrie was just better at expressing it. "I'm so thankful. Your parents must be so happy. I've been praying for your return. Everyone has."

"Danki. It's gut to be back." Abigail inclined her head and offered Carrie a grateful smile. "I'd love to catch up later. Right now there is food to be served and this is a hungry crowd. I'd better skedaddle."

Off she went, shoulders back, chin up. She'd changed. Owen

shoveled food into his mouth. That didn't keep him from feeling Carrie's forceful stare. Shoulders hunched, she crumbled her roll onto her plate.

"I'm so happy Abigail has returned." To her credit she did sound happy. "I reckon you are too."

"Everyone is. To lose a Gmay member who has taken her vows to a fallen world would be horrible."

The proper words at last.

Carrie sighed. She took up her knife and cut her chicken into dainty pieces. After a few bites she laid down the knife and fork. "You don't have to pretend."

"About what?"

"Stop pretending."

The excited chatter of the single men and women on either side of them didn't rise to the level that they wouldn't hear this conversation. True, they were focused on this singular opportunity to talk in public with a man or woman who might one day become their husband or wife. Owen struggled to keep his voice down. He leaned forward. "I'm sorry."

"I know you are." Carrie shrugged and sighed again, this time more deeply. "I always knew I faced a rocky uphill road with you."

She tossed her napkin over her full plate. "I'm really not hungry. It's almost time for my shift serving anyway. The more hands, the lighter the load."

"You're a gut soul. You deserve someone as gut as you are."

"That's kind of you to say. I don't know if it's true. I hope so."

She slipped from her chair and left him with a full plate and a certainty that he caused a fracture in her sweet heart. *I'm sorry, Carrie. So sorry.*

Is this what a heart attack feels like? Or heartbreak? Abigail settled the cookie platter and bread basket safely onto the prep table in the kitchen. Owen and Carrie. He'd moved on. It couldn't be allowed to matter. Her return to Haven should not hinge on her feelings for Owen. Or his for her. She'd returned to resume her life as a woman of faith in a Plain community. So why was her first inclination to run back to Abilene? Seeing Owen at church and social functions, knowing he courted another, would be hard. But it would be worth it to be back with her family, friends, and church.

"How did it go?" Kayla tore apart rolls fresh from the oven and deposited them in the basket. "Did you see him?"

No point in pretending. "I did."

"Sitting across from Carrie?" Kayla glanced at the other women. She moved closer to Abigail. Her voice softened. "It's okay. He's been straddling the fence with her since he returned from visiting you in Abilene. Lee, the dummkopp, has been encouraging him."

"Lee's no dummkopp. He's got his big bruder's back. It's sweet of him."

"You're too kind." Kayla rolled her eyes. "Owen cares for you. All he's done is set Carrie up for heartache. There's nothing sweet about that."

"Don't worry. I'll be fine."

At the sound of Carrie's voice, Abigail turned. Carrie went to the sink, where she added her dirty dishes to the growing stack. Red spots glowed on her cheeks, but her movements were slow, measured. Kayla tilted her head and raised her eyebrows.

Abigail went to Carrie's side. "We weren't gossiping, I hope you know." Thankful for the clatter of pots, pans, and excited chatter, she leaned closer. "I'm just trying to get my bearings now that I'm back home."

"No worries." Carrie added more soap to the huge tub, followed by hot water from the pot on the stove. "You've been dealing with a hard situation. I don't know if I could've done it."

Abigail grabbed a towel. "I'll dry while you wash."

"Nee." Carrie stopped washing the plate in her hand. She looked directly at Abigail for the first time. "He's out there waiting for you. He's been waiting for two months. That's long enough."

"Are you sure?"

"I saw his face when he realized you were standing behind me. I've never been more sure of anything in my life."

Abigail laid aside the towel and went to find Owen.

She found him picking tomatoes in Mary's garden behind the house. He'd removed his jacket and laid it in the grass. His shirtsleeves rolled up to his elbows, he knelt in his church pants, his back to her, head bent. Abigail studied his broad shoulders and the familiar locks of light-blond hair that peeked from below his hat. "I don't think that's what you're supposed to do at weddings."

Owen swiveled. Surprise came and went in his deeply tanned face, followed by a carefully assumed neutral expression. "She's my stepmother now. I'm just helping her out." He held up two beautiful, sun-kissed tomatoes. "If she doesn't pick them today, they'll be overripe and mushy. I hate mushy tomatoes."

"She can always use the extra-ripe ones in spaghetti or pizza sauce or for canning." How long could they prolong the small talk? How much time did they have before someone noticed them out here? "You've lost weight."

"You're the same, yet you're different." Owen's smartness didn't come from books. He laid aside the tomatoes, stood, and dusted the dirt from his hands and the knees of his pants. His Adam's apple bobbed. He shoved his hat back. "Are you mad at me for telling Bryan about the videos and the photos?"

He'd followed his heart and done what he thought was best. "Nee."

"I feel bad for interfering after I told you I would step back while you figured out where you needed to be. Two of the hardest things I've ever done—stepping back and then telling Bryan."

"Why were they so hard?"

"Because I care for you. I wanted you to come back so badly." He ducked his head and stared at his feet. "Why did you come back?"

His hurt squeezed through a hole in his carefully constructed defenses. It wrapped itself around Abigail's heart. She had so many hurts to mend. "This is where I belong."

His head came up. His gaze met Abigail's. "Are you sure?"

"Jah, I'm sure."

"You won't change your mind and rush off to your other family at the first sign of trouble?"

Life had no guarantees, of that a person could be certain. The desire to assure him beyond all measure hit Abigail full force, a tumultuous whirlwind of emotion. *Be honest. Be true to yourself. Be yourself.* Owen deserved her true self.

"I'll always have one foot in my Plain world and one foot in the Englisch world. That's not my doing." She picked her words with the same care Owen had picked the tomatoes. "But I know now my faith is stronger than any forces out there in that Englisch world. I took vows. I plan to keep them. That doesn't mean I can't love my Englisch family. The kinner are funny, crazy, narrisch, and kind. Just like my brieder and schwesdchdre here. Heather and Eric want to know me. I want to know them, but that doesn't mean I have to be Englisch."

"It sure could've been an Englisch girl in those videos."

"I went there to find out who I am—Plain or Englisch. It turns out I'm both, but more Plain than Englisch." No words existed that could fully explain her quandary or the tightrope she would walk the rest of her life over a chasm that divided a wide-open, splashy, loud, crazy world and a slower, quieter, gentler world filled with rules, hard work, and faith. Both also filled with people she loved. Had a right to love and honor. "I can't deny my roots. I don't want to. But now I know where to draw the line."

"And where is that?"

"I can visit with my Englisch family. I can spend time with them. But I don't have to be like them."

The stiffness in his shoulders eased a fraction. "How do Freeman and Lorene feel about that? And the elders?"

"We haven't talked yet. I'll have to make a freewill confession to Bryan. I'm willing to do whatever is necessary to repair the damage—the hurt—I've caused."

Would Owen understand her meaning?

He stepped from the garden into the grass, so close she could smell the fresh earth on his hands and his man sweat. "What about the man in the video? Will you be visiting with him too? How does he figure into all this?"

Rhett had given Abigail her first kiss, a right that should've been reserved for Owen. How did she explain the spinning top that defined her feelings for the English man? "No. We were friends, nothing more."

"Are you sad about that?"

"Nee. Rhett is a gut man. Kind. Interesting. I'm glad I met him because I learned a lot from him, but he has nothing else to teach me. He's a newspaper reporter who's searching for adventure now."

Telling Owen about the kisses would only hurt him. But the lessons she'd learned through them would serve her well with him. What Heather called chemistry had little to do with love. Physical touch wasn't a necessary ingredient in order to experience that so-called chemistry, that strange pull described as attraction either.

"Your heart isn't out there with him?"

"Nee, my heart is right here."

Right here in your hands, Owen.

"I'm glad." Owen edged closer. Droplets of perspiration clung to his forehead and trickled down his temples, but the sudden shine came from a spark from within. He picked up the tomatoes and held them out as if handing her a gift. "You've grown into your circumstances. So have I. Tomorrow I start work at the Silverman sunflower farm."

"You do? How? I thought—"

"Your world isn't the only one changing." He flung his arms out in an elaborate flourish. "Daed is married now. I bought our family home and ten acres from him so I would have a place to start my own family. And freedom to choose my path. We Plain folks change slowly, carefully, thoughtfully, but we change. I'm blessed that Mr. Silverman had room for another man on his crew. I can catch a ride from an Englischer who lives in Haven. Everything came together . . . almost everything. Now you're here . . ."

The force of his smile nearly knocked the tomatoes from her hands. Abigail clasped them more tightly, careful not to bruise them. Just the right touch was needed—in all things. "I, too, have job hunting to do. If I can't get on at the furniture store or Hooks and Needles, I may try housecleaning. That's something I'm gut at."

"But not waitressing."

"Nee. It's not my *gig*."

Owen chuckled. "Like working on metal buildings for me."

Abigail edged closer. In many ways they were alike. They didn't fit in the molds. "It's not quite the same, but jah."

Owen took the tomatoes from her and laid them on his jacket with slow, deliberate movements. His forehead wrinkled, eyes troubled, he returned to his spot in front of her. He touched her cheek with a soft sigh. "How can I be sure of you? How can I be sure of anything?"

His touch sent a tremor through Abigail. Her body wanted to

capture the sensation, hold on to it, while her brain ran in circles, trying to find words that needed to be said. Touch might not be the be-all and end-all, but Heather's chemistry did count for something. "You can't. Neither can I."

"Do you want to try?"

"I do."

His other hand came up. His warm, earthy fingers caressed her face. Shaking his head, he frowned. "I should run from this, from you, but I can't. My legs refuse. Nee, my heart refuses."

Abigail leaned into his touch. He had to decide for himself if the risk was worth it. She'd given him plenty of reason to walk away—to run away. *Sei so gut, Gott, let him stay with me.*

He took one more step. His hands dropped from her face to her shoulders. His lips brushed hers for a few scant seconds. Abigail closed her eyes and inhaled his scent of hard work, faith, and hope.

She opened her eyes and slid her hands into his so their fingers were entwined. "We'll figure it out. One day at a time, carefully, slowly, thoughtfully. Because that's our way. The Plain way."

Owen didn't say anything. Instead he answered with another kiss, this one longer, surer, and full of promise.

Chapter 43

Three steely sets of eyes bore into Abigail. Bryan, Delbert, and Samuel leveled somber, assessing, and yes, disappointed gazes at her. She stifled the urge to wiggle in her seat. Or worse, launch into an explanation of her actions, to try to justify them, to make excuses. The silence grew. It became so loud it hurt her ears. Bryan had directed her to come to his house for this meeting—without her parents. She was an adult now, capable of making her own case and receiving her punishment on her own. That didn't mean her stomach didn't clench or her heart didn't beat faster with every step from the buggy into Bryan's house. Only the memory of Owen's hand squeezing hers as he promised to stand by her no matter what happened next kept her back straight and her chin lifted.

Finally Bryan sighed. He tapped his index finger on the pine table that separated them. "We're so happy you decided to come home." He didn't seem happy. He seemed deeply troubled. "We've prayed long and hard for you throughout your absence. I know your eldre have too."

"We prayed Gott's will be done." His tone grave, Samuel inclined his grizzled head. "We prayed you would see that you belong here in your community of faith."

How should she respond to these statements? No words swam to the surface. *Don't speak, just listen.* That had been Father's gruff advice delivered when he handed her the buggy reins earlier that morning. "Humility will go a long way, Dochder. Humility and an attitude of repentance."

"I'm thankful for your prayers."

"Tell us why you decided to return." Delbert leaned back in his chair and crossed his arms. "Why are you sitting here now in Bryan's dining room?"

"I came back because I took vows when I was baptized. I meant them." The words picked up speed on their own. Abigail's stomach rocked harder. Her heartbeat soared. "I broke Ordnung rules while in Abilene. I'm repentant. I won't do any of those things again."

The reasons for her transgressions clamored to be released. These men wouldn't understand or they wouldn't see the reasons as enough to excuse her behavior. Her peculiar situation as the daughter of two English people didn't give her an excuse for her sinful behavior.

"Abigail, have no doubt that we have discussed your unique situation." Bryan's expression relaxed into something akin to fatherly. "We can't put ourselves in your shoes. We can only advise you to stand strong in the faith in which you were raised. Freeman and Lorene are your eldre in every sense that counts in this season of your life."

They wanted to understand. They were trying. Sweet relief blew through Abigail. "Danki for your kindness and your understanding. I don't deserve it."

"We're not here to judge you, but to help you regain your footing." Delbert stroked his long, thin beard replete with silver threads embroidered on black. "I can only hope that others would do the same if it were my dochder."

The knot in Abigail's throat grew. She swallowed, but it didn't help. She gripped her hands in her lap. *Don't cry. Don't cry.* "I needed to know if I fit in better in the Englisch life. Trying it out seemed the only way to find out. But everything—the karaoke, the dancing, the Englisch clothes—felt alien. My biological eldre are Englisch. I'm not."

"Now you know."

"Now I know."

"You repent of your fehla?"

"I do. I've asked Gott to forgive me. And my eldre—my real parents. The ones who raised me, cared for me, loved me for the last twenty years and who will go on loving me until they die."

Mother and Father had accepted her apology quickly and without recrimination. Mother cried. Father tromped from the room after a gruff, "Glad you're back, Dochder."

That had been that.

Bryan exchanged glances with the other two men. Samuel nodded. Delbert did the same. The bishop turned back to Abigail. "We accept your freewill confession. This was a strange situation for you and for us too. We will leave it to Gott to judge you. We've decided not to require a kneeling confession before the Gmay. You have been tested in the fire and returned to the fold, your faith made stronger. We're thankful for that. Your eldre have suffered. We'll not give them more pain. Go and sin no more."

Abigail put her hands to her face. Her thoughts refused to order themselves. Her muscles turned to mush. The ache in her throat made it almost impossible to speak. "Danki," she whispered.

"Nee, don't thank us. What you've done can't be undone, but it can be—must be—forgiven. What you did won't be tolerated a second time."

"I understand." Abigail cleared her throat. The ache subsided little by little. Her body regained its strength. *Danki, Gott. Danki.*

Another rush of adrenaline jolted her. She was Plain. She had no doubts about this. But Heather and Eric and the kids were still family. Nothing could change that. Their appearance had rearranged her life. "I won't do the things I did in Abilene again, but I feel an obligation—no, that's not the right word—a *need* to stay in touch with my biological eldre and their families. My other families. It would be cruel not to."

Bryan frowned. He steepled his fingers and studied them as if searching for answers in the calluses. Finally he raised his head and stared at Abigail. "I agree. It wouldn't be right to ignore them. It would cause them pain. We don't want to do that."

"But we also don't believe it serves you well to spend time with them in Abilene." Delbert mimicked Bryan's frown. "It's best if they come here."

Heather wouldn't agree. Nor Eric. He would be as out of place as his 1969 Chevy Chevelle would be parked among dozens of buggies, It would be their choice. Abigail had defied the elders and her adopted parents once. She wouldn't do it again. For her own sake. For Owen's. For the parents who'd chosen to love her when they had no obligation to do so.

"It might be gut for them." She sought words to describe her birth parents' dearth of faith without implying judgment. "Their kinner rarely go to church. They don't know much about Jesus. Heather left her church when I was born. Eric doesn't seem interested."

"We witness by our example." Bryan's flat declaration needed no explanation.

"Then I'll try to set a gut one."

For the first time, he smiled. "You have a gut heart. Go. We all have work to do."

In more ways than one.

Chapter 44

Returning to life in Haven wasn't easy. Abigail hadn't expected it to be. Her parents—the ones who'd chosen to love her—said little, but sometimes Abigail caught her mother staring, a strange look of longing on her face. The stores in town had no openings, so she hired on as a cleaning woman for three English families. She filled her days with work so hard she fell into bed half asleep before her head hit the pillow. She was good at cleaning, and she no longer had to worry about spilling ice water on tourists. Visits from Owen were the highlight of her weeks. They walked and talked far into the night every chance they got. His delight in his new job renewed her determination to find joy in hers.

As for Abigail's birth family, Fiona sent her short, sweet letters full of herself. Abigail responded with letters she filled with stories about farm life, a life Fiona would never know. Heather and Eric took the elders' edict regarding visits to Abilene better than expected. Determined not to lose the tenuous connection with their oldest child, they became regular visitors to the Bontrager house. Often together. So often and so happy it appeared they might be headed for the wedding they never had twenty-some years ago.

One day an envelope arrived with a Topeka postmark. It held a newspaper clipping from the *Abilene Reflector-Chronicle.* The article carried Rhett's name. He'd written his story about her, full of quotes from people who'd met her during her brief stay. They all said the same thing. Getting to know Amish woman Abigail Bontrager had been an interesting addition to their summers. They'd learned something about the Amish from her. Nowhere did it say what she'd learned from them. Rhett didn't include a note telling her how he fared in his search for adventure. Perhaps it was better left to her imagination.

July turned into August, August into September. Autumn, Abigail's favorite season, beckoned. The weather began to change. The air cooled at night. Abigail and Jane slept with the windows open so a breeze could wash over their room. With it came a breathless sense of anticipation. This time of atonement, of waiting, wound down.

Owen arrived at her doorstep at daybreak one Saturday morning in mid-September. Abigail found him leaning on Mr. Whitehair's minivan when she opened the back door to let Doolittle out before starting breakfast. She took in the minivan for a long moment. "Where are you going?"

More importantly, when was he coming back?

He gestured to a white bag in his other hand. "I stopped at the bakery yesterday and bought an assortment of donuts—including the chocolate cake donuts you like. They're not stale, not yet anyway. I also brought a thermos of coffee. Can you come with me?"

"Where are we going?"

"To see a thing of beauty."

Who could resist donuts and a thing of beauty? "I'll be back."

She dashed into the kitchen. Her mother stood at the stove, using a long fork to turn bacon that sizzled and spit grease. The scent of fresh-brewed coffee complemented the aroma. Together they smelled liked family, like home, like happiness. Abigail grabbed her canvas bag from its hook by the door. "I have to go, but I'll be back."

Mother dropped the fork and went to peek out the window over the sink. Her perturbed expression faded. "Your secret is safe with me. Just be back before dark. Your daed will worry."

"I promise."

A few seconds later Abigail climbed into the minivan's middle seat. Owen settled in next to her. So close. His clean scent of soap floated around her. She clasped her hands in her lap and breathed it in.

"Put your seat belt on." Owen leaned over and pulled the strap over her lap. His fingers brushed hers. Calloused yet gentle. He smiled. How did a person fasten a seat belt? The mechanics suddenly escaped Abigail. It clicked into place. "There you go."

The flush that began on her cheeks raced through Abigail's body. Mr. Whitehair's amused gaze met hers in the rearview mirror. She swiveled to peer out the window. "Danki. Tell me again where we're going."

"I want you to see what I've been seeing every day."

"Sunflowers."

"Just wait."

Sunflowers indeed. More than Abigail had ever seen in all her years. Enormous, stunning sunflowers. Their petals were starting to fall. Heads drooped. But still the sight of thousands of huge, brilliantly yellow flowers waving in unison acre after acre held Abigail captive. Like rolling blankets of spun gold. Her breathing slowed. Her muscles, tight with the fatigue of mopping floors and cleaning toilets, relaxed. The sun kissed her face. The breeze cooled her skin.

Her life could and would go on.

Owen took her hand and guided her closer. He rubbed some of the seeds from the flower's center and dumped them in her palm. "The Silvermans plant a thousand acres of sunflowers every year. The harvested seeds are used for oil and birdseed. The seed meal left after the oil is squeezed from the seeds is used to feed livestock."

"They're so beautiful. I can see why sunflowers are Kansas's state flower."

"It's a different kind of sunflower, but they're all beautiful. These are ready to be harvested."

"How can you tell?"

"The heads are turning brown. The combines will be in the field starting Monday." He slid his arm around her shoulders. "That's why I wanted you to see it today. I couldn't wait."

"This is what you spend your days working on then." Abigail contemplated the startling blanket of yellow that stretched acre upon acre. "It goes to show people truly have different callings and must follow them. Your daed likes building structures for people. You like sowing and reaping. Both are gut."

"You'd rather clean people's houses than serve food to strangers in a restaurant." Owen's arm tightened around her. "We can't shove that square peg into the round hole and expect to be content."

"It's a lesson I learned the hard way." Abigail leaned her head on Owen's shoulder. The desire to snuggle against his broad chest tugged at her heart. "Kayla is so happy feeding folks. It makes her feel gut to see them enjoy their food and breaking bread together as family. Even though neither of us plans to spend the rest of our lives in these jobs, the lessons apply to our lives down the road."

Owen slid around so they faced each other. "I'm glad you think so." His hands cupped her face. "You went through a lot. I wonder if you are sure now of your place in this Plain world."

"I am." His touch made it hard to concentrate. Abigail closed her eyes. His fingers caressed her cheeks. How could he doubt her after months spent building on the foundation they'd laid before Heather's sudden appearance in her life?

Abigail opened her eyes and stared into Owen's. "Do you doubt I want nothing more than to be a fraa and mudder? I can't wait for the day. I long for the day."

"Heather and Eric seem to have accepted you as you are."

"They have. They want me to be happy." Like all good parents they wanted what was best for her. Seeing Abigail live her life as a Plain woman with a loving adoptive family no longer bothered them. The kids had even asked a few questions about Jesus, and Abigail had answered them—with the approval of her birth parents. "Heather wants to plant a vegetable garden in the spring. After she came to the canning frolics this summer, she decided she really likes homegrown produce. Eric likes talking horses with Daed. And I think they want me to be happy like they are. I think they may be considering finally getting married—to each other."

"That's wunderbarr. Gott's plan. Gott's timing." Owen's face lit up with a smile that did nothing to smooth the erratic beating of Abigail's heart. "How do they feel about me? Some find my affinity for growing sunflowers odd. An unlikely occupation for a Plain man. Lee calls me the flower gardener."

"They think you're a farmer, which you are. Lee's being narrisch. You know and he knows it's a commercial crop that is gut for the land, grows well in droughts, is gut for the birds and butterflies, and is used for a healthy oil, birdseed, and seeds to eat." Abigail did her best imitation of Owen when he sang the praises of his favorite crop. "It also turns a tidy profit."

"You *have* been listening to endless, boring monologues about what I do all day."

"Of course I have." She swiveled so she could land a small kiss on his chin. "I'm interested in what you're interested in. I love that sunflowers aren't just useful and make a good cash crop. Gott also made them beautiful. Just like He made the sunshine that chases away dark and shadows. The sunflowers thrive in the warmth of the sunshine. So do you and I."

"It's nice to know you truly understand."

Knowing he was drawn to the beauty of the sunflowers made him all the sweeter to Abigail.

His lips nuzzled the hollow of her neck. A tremor ran through Abigail. His breath tickled her. His hands ran up and down her arms. She closed her eyes again. "Why did you bring me here?"

"To ask you something."

"So ask me already."

"How would you feel about spending your life with a flower gardener?"

"Hmmm." She leaned her head on his chest and let feelings wash over her. *You are strong. Gott loves you the way you are. You are you.* "We already covered that."

"So we did." He raised her chin. "Open your eyes. I want to see your face, and I want you to see mine."

She did as he asked.

"Will you marry me?"

"Finally. Jah, I will marry you. We'll have sunflowers in every jar on the tables at our reception."

His laugh startled a butterfly on a nearby sunflower. It flew away in a huff. "I can see it now."

Owen lowered his head toward hers. She raised hers to meet his. With only the sunflowers to witness their declarations of love, they found that place where they could meet as the man and woman they truly were and would become together.

Acknowledgments

I'M DEEPLY INDEBTED TO THE HARPERCOLLINS CHRISTIAN PUBLISHING team for all their hard work throughout the years, but particularly in the last three. My thanks go out to the sales team, the marketing team, and the editorial staff. I especially want to thank Becky Monds for her patience and unerring eye for story. The years 2020 and 2021 were rough for everyone. The toll is still being felt in 2022, but I see tremendous work ethic and dedication to publishing in the HCCP team as they work from home, and deal with pandemic-related sales issues, warehouse issues, bottlenecks, and the ever-changing landscape of publishing as an industry. As writers we often labor in isolation, but with publishing teams like HCCP, we need never feel truly alone.

All the same can be said for my agent Julie Gwinn and the Seymour Literary Agency. I'm so thankful for Julie's constant efforts to keep me and all her clients informed about the state of publishing in these crazy times. Her help with marketing current projects and placing new ones has been extraordinary—especially in the face of her own trials during the pandemic.

I would be remiss if I didn't mention my line editor, Julee Schwarzburg. Her patience is legendary in my mind. Just keeping track of the monumental number of names in the big Amish families in the books in this series is a formidable task—one I consistently fail at. Then there's the Pennsylvania Dutch language. The less said the better about my lack of consistency when it comes to *The Chicago Manual of Style*. Thank you, Julee, for not throwing in the towel.

I'm so grateful for my family, my church family, and my readers. I've spent the majority of recent years in quasi-quarantine because of health issues. The love and support I receive gives me new energy to see each day as a gift. I'm living my dream of being a full-time novelist. For that I'm forever grateful to my God and Savior Jesus Christ. Bless each and every one of you.

Discussion Questions

1. *The Warmth of Sunshine* opens with Abigail discovering she's adopted—a secret kept by her adoptive parents. She is confused, angry, and uncertain about who she is. Do you think her adoptive parents were right to withhold this information from her? Does the fact that they are Amish and her birth mother is English make a difference in whether they should have told her? Why or why not?
2. Abigail has never felt as if she fits in with her Amish community. She's clumsy, awkward, a poor cook, and doesn't sew well. She embraces the idea that all this difficulty stems from "not really being Amish." What do you think? Could these difficulties be the result of something ingrained in her biological makeup? Is it an excuse? Why?
3. At the restaurant Abigail sees a cute, sweet baby sitting on her mother's lap and wonders, *What mother gives away her baby?* How do you feel about Heather's explanation that her parents made her give up Abigail for adoption? Do you think she was right to seek Abigail out so many years later in hopes of establishing a relationship with her? Should she have

honored Abigail's adoptive parents' wishes that she stay away? Why or why not?

4. Abigail decides to visit her biological family and experience the "English life." She has been baptized in the Amish church. Do you see this as a lack of faith or a turning back on her vows? Or do you side with Abigail in thinking she needs to find out who she truly is before embarking on a life of a wife and mother?
5. Owen is torn between his feelings for Abigail and wanting to be supportive of her decision to spend time with her biological family. He's fearful for her eternal salvation. Does he make the right decision when he tells her to go? Why or why not?
6. Owen lost his mother in a sudden, unexplainable death. He can't imagine what it would be like to have two mothers who care for him and want to take that role. What would you say to Owen about God's plan for him as it relates to the part he plays in Abigail's situation?
7. Immediately upon her arrival in Abilene, Abigail is thrust into "worldly" situations that require her to flaunt the Ordnung (rules). She sits with Rhett. She sings karaoke with him. She accepts clothes and a phone from Heather. Does this surprise you? How do you think you would react in a similar situation? Is it even possible for "English" readers to know what they would do under those circumstances?
8. Owen has his own journey of self-discovery to make in Abigail's absence. Keeping in mind the Amish tenet of faith of "dying to self," obedience, and putting faith and family first, is it wrong for him to want to leave his father's engineered-structures business to farm sunflowers? How are

the messages we receive from the mainstream world different in terms of finding happiness and "self-realization"?

9. Kiera tells Abigail her clumsiness and other problems are born from her tenseness that she will fail, that she's so afraid of doing something wrong, she causes these problems for herself. Do you experience similar doubts and fears that become self-fulfilling prophecies? How do you deal with them?
10. Ultimately Abigail returns home to her adoptive family and her faith. Were you surprised by her decision? What roles do you think Owen, Rhett, and Heather played in her decision? Why do you think she stopped short of accepting the car from her father or the possibility of going to college and becoming "whoever she wanted to be"?

From the Publisher

Help other readers find this one:

- Post a review at your favorite online bookseller
- Post a picture on a social media account and share why you enjoyed it
- Send a note to a friend who would also love it—or better yet, give them a copy

Thanks for reading!

Enjoy more stories by Kelly Irvin in the Amish Blessings series

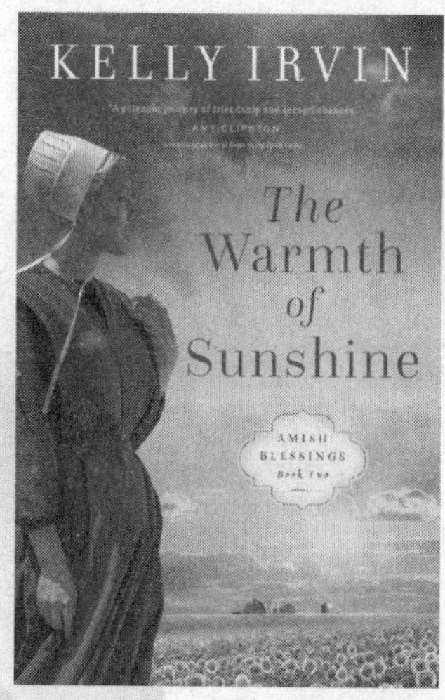

Every Good Gift

Coming February 2023

Available in print, e-book, and audio

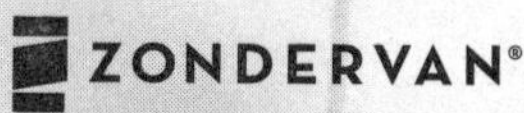

ENJOY NEW STORIES FROM KELLY IRVIN IN THE AMISH OF BIG SKY COUNTRY SERIES!

AVAILABLE IN PRINT, E-BOOK, AND DOWNLOADABLE AUDIO

About the Author

Photo by Tim Irvin

Kelly Irvin is a bestselling, award-winning author of thirty novels and stories. A retired public relations professional, Kelly lives with her husband, Tim, in San Antonio. They have two children, three grandchildren, and two ornery cats.

Visit her online at kellyirvin.com
Instagram: @kelly_irvin
Facebook: @Kelly.Irvin.Author
Twitter: @Kelly_S_Irvin